i will always love you

a gossip girl novel

Gossip Girl novels created by Cecily von Ziegesar:

i will always love you

a gossip girl novel

Created by
**Cecily von Ziegesar**

poppy

LITTLE, BROWN AND COMPANY
New York   Boston

Poppy

Hachette Book Group

237 Park Avenue, New York, NY 10017

For more of your favorite series, visit our website at www.pickapoppy.com

Poppy is an imprint of Little, Brown Books for Young Readers. The Poppy name and logo are trademarks of Hachette Book Group, Inc.

First Edition: November 2009

First International Edition: November 2009

The characters, events, and locations in this book are fictitious. Any similarity to real persons, living or dead, is coincidental and not intended by the author.

Photo on page iii by Andrea C. Uva

Produced by Alloy Entertainment

151 West 26th Street, New York, NY 10001

Special thanks to Pete Holmdel and The New York Palace Hotel.

Jewelry & accessories by Lara Kornbluh of Icon Style

ISBN: 978-0-316-04361-8

10 9 8 7 6 5 4 3 2 1

RRD-C

Printed in the United States of America

*For Anna*

*Love is like war: easy to begin but very hard to stop.*

—H. L. Mencken

I

*Disclaimer: All the real names of places, people, and events have been altered or abbreviated to protect the innocent. Namely, me.*

| topics | sightings | your e-mail | post a question |

# hey people!

**ho, ho, ho!**

*'Tis the season to be jolly. Fa la la la la, la la la la. Don we now our gay apparel* . . . which just so happens to have been made for us by the little elves at Givenchy or YSL or Oscar de la Renta. Who are *we*, you ask? The residents of Manhattan's Golden Mile, of course—that glorious stretch of doorman buildings above Fifty-ninth Street and below Eighty-sixth. It's Christmastime, time to deck our sprawling Upper East Side penthouses with silver and gold baubles, twinkly lights, velvet bows, and chocolates imported from belle Paris. Here the holidays are always a little more sparkly, a little brighter, a little *better*. It's so, so good to be back.

While I'm not about to tell you where I've been for the past few months, I will tell you that there *is* life after high school. Yes, it finally happened: We went to college. During the past semester we encountered people who haven't seen us naked (yet), and who don't know our SAT scores; who don't remember that time we wet our pants in kindergarten, or when we got our ears pierced. We've learned a few new things, made a few new friends, and have even maybe met the loves our lives. We've changed—hopefully for the better. And we're just as fabulous as always.

Take **B**, for instance. She's spending a perfect holiday with her perfect

Yale boyfriend and his perfect family at their idyllic Vermont compound. That girl always had her eye on the prize. Speaking of prizes, what's **S** up to these days? No longer hounded by overeager, fashion-conscious Constance Billard girls, she's now trailed by the paparazzi and a posse of wannabe movie starlets while she cools her Louboutins, waiting for her nomination for the SAG Awards. No matter where she is or what she does, **S** will always be one to watch.

Then there are those who've tried their darnedest to change: **N** has been sailing around the world for the last four months. But as we learned from Kant in our freshman seminars, no man is an island. He'll be back— sooner rather than later, we hope. Then there's **D**, scratching out existential poetry in his black Moleskine notebook in the Pacific Northwest. It may look like a total lifestyle change, but he still insists on Folgers crystals instead of French press in the coffee capital of the U.S. He also spends every waking moment Skyping his shaven-headed, ultra-independent filmmaker girlfriend, **V**, who's at NYU and seems to almost have . . . *hair*. And friends?! And finally there's **C**, last seen with a pack of flannel-wearing, log-lifting, very rugged boys out in Nevada or Montana or someplace with no cities and lots of cattle. Is he into a new type, or has he gone through yet another reinvention? That man puts Madonna to shame.

Mistletoe and New Year's Eve are all about kissing, and something tells me there's going to be lots and lots of kissing this break. Lucky for you, I'll be here to report *everything* worth reporting after the holiday lights are unplugged and the pretty velvet ribbons have been untied. Let the reunion begin!

## your e-mail

**q:** Dear Gossip Girl,

I'm visiting my great aunt in New York City for the holidays, and I heard that Serena van der Woodsen lives here and you know everything about her. Are you her? Oh my God, if you're her, can you please send me an autograph? Or maybe hang out?

—IheartSvW

**a:** Dear Iheart,

While I prefer to live my life outside the spotlight, according to my sources, your heroine's out almost every night. You should be able to find her if you know where to look.

—GG

**q:** Dear Gossip Girl,

My college dining hall only serves, like, deep-fried cheese balls and I may have gained some weight. Should I celebrate NYE with my high school friends, or pretend I have the flu?

—HittingtheBuffet

**a:** Dear HtheB,

While I'm not a dietician or a therapist, I can definitely say you're not alone. My advice: How you look is all about how you pull it off. Go out, wear your little black dress, and show off those curves. No one will even notice those tater tot pounds.

—GG

## sightings

**B** on a train from **New Haven** to **Montpelier, Vermont**, looking very out of place in a sea of multicolored plaid flannel. **S** with three interchangeable anorexic dyed blond girls on the red carpet for a premiere. **V** and some friends from **NYU**, including a very hot hipster teaching assistant, at a film party in **Bushwick**. Is someone trying to get extra credit? **D** and his little sister, **J**, splitting a plate of gooey chocolate-chip pancakes at one of those horribly crowded diners on upper Broadway. **C** and his new horde of cowboy boot–clad dudes ordering Cokes at the lounge at **Tribeca Star**. Should the hotel erect a hitching post?

**still breaking all the rules**

Technically you no longer live under your parents' roof. You've already indulged them with Scrabble and decorating gingerbread men that no one's going to eat. Now it's time to party. You can always reform after January 1st—that's what New Year's resolutions are for. So go out, have fun, and show your former besties and former flames just how much *better* you've become.

Besides, now that you know I'm watching, aren't you just dying to put on a show? Thought so.

You know you love me,

gossip girl

# all b wants for christmas

"You awake, Scout?"

Blair Waldorf awoke from a nap to the sight of her boyfriend, Pete Carlson, gazing down at her. Pete smiled his adorable, lopsided smile. His eyes were ocean blue and framed by strawberry blond lashes, to match his thick, floppy head of hair.

Blair threw the Black Watch–plaid duvet to the foot of the couch and discreetly checked for drool with her index finger. She *loved* being woken up by Pete, especially when he called her by an adorable nickname. Currently, it was Scout, because she'd directed him and his three older brothers to the best Douglas fir Christmas tree, deep in the woods of the Carlsons' expansive Woodstock, Vermont, estate. Early this morning, they'd all opened presents underneath the magnificent tree. Pete had given Blair a pair of navy blue-and-tan North Face hiking boots with the promise that he'd bring her on some of his favorite trails when it got warmer. Blair had never been one for the great wide open, but Pete loved being outdoors, and suddenly the idea of sleeping under the stars with him at her side seemed almost romantic.

"Of course I'm awake," Blair lied, sitting up and yawning. It was only noon, but Pete's adorable-but-hyper nieces and nephews had woken everyone up to open presents at the ungodly hour of 5 a.m.

"Good." Pete settled next to her on the worn navy blue couch, tenderly pushing Blair's long bangs off her foxlike face. Her hair was a little shaggier than she liked, but she simply didn't trust any of the hair salons in dingy New Haven. Besides, what were unkempt bangs when she was with a guy who truly loved her?

"Have any dreams? You were making these little growls in your sleep. It was cute." Pete pulled the woolen blanket off the floor and draped it over their legs.

"Oh." Blair frowned. She was *growling*?

In truth, she'd been having a lot of weird dreams lately. Last night, she'd woken up and thought she was at a sleepover at her old best friend Serena van der Woodsen's house, only to find herself all alone in the dark, regal guest bedroom of the Carlsons' oversize colonial.

Maybe it was just homesickness. After all, she didn't have a home in New York anymore, she hadn't seen Serena since *August*, and no one in her family was even in the U.S. this week. Her father, Harold, was celebrating Christmas in Provence with his boyfriend, Giles, and their adopted twins. Her stepbrother, Aaron, was on a kibbutz in Israel. Her mother, stepfather, brother, Tyler, and baby sister, Yale, had moved to LA back in August, to a gigantic, tacky Pacific Palisades mansion that they were making even bigger and tackier. While the renovations were taking place, the four were traveling in the South Pacific, visiting the islands that Eleanor Rose, in a fit of pregnancy-induced mania last spring, had bought for each member of the family. Blair had been somewhat tempted to tag along, if only to see her baby sister, the least fucked-up member of her tragically absurd family.

That was all before she'd received the holiday card her mother had sent out. CELEBRATE THE WALDORF-ROSE FAMILY'S HOLIDAY MERGER had been written in gold script atop a photograph of her bald stepfather. Cyrus Rose was dressed in a bright red velvet Santa suit, holding an elf-costumed infant Yale in one hand, a menorah in the other. Celebrating the holiday *merger* suddenly seemed a whole lot less appealing. And once she'd been invited to spend Christmas with the picture-perfect Carlsons, she felt it was her duty as a girlfriend to go.

"I was just dreaming about you. Us. I'm just so happy." Blair sighed contentedly as she gazed into the blaze roaring in the quaint brick fireplace across the room. Outside, a thin blanket of snow covered the ground.

"Me too." Pete ruffled her hair and pulled her face into his for a kiss.

"You taste nice," Blair breathed, letting her body relax into Pete's muscular arms. She shrugged off her black Loro Piana cashmere cardigan so she was wearing only her peach Cosabella tank top.

It was funny how things worked out. When she arrived at Yale four months ago, Blair discovered that her incessantly perky roommate, Alana Hoffman, sang a cappella. *All* the time. Blair would wake up to Alana singing "Son of a Preacher Man" to her collection of Gund teddy bears. Avoiding her room, Blair spent a lot of time in the library, where Pete was writing a paper for his magical realism class. Blair hadn't been able to so much as *look* at a guy ever since Nate Archibald, her high school boyfriend and the supposed love of her life, chose not to come to Yale with her, leaving her high and dry at Grand Central Station to head to college alone. But that day, spotting Pete's adorably rugged stubble, the half-smile he always wore, and the intense concentration in his dark blue eyes as he bent over his worn paperback book, Blair felt for the first time that there could be life after Nate. She and Pete had exchanged flirty glances, and finally he invited her for coffee.

They'd been inseparable ever since. In fact, since Thanksgiving, Blair had been practically living with Pete—and his five gin-swilling, athletic roommates—in a comfortably shabby Chapel Street town house. At first, Blair had been nervous about living with so many guys, but she sort of liked having instantaneous brothers, and most of the time being the only girl in the room. Especially when they gave her free rein of the upstairs bathroom and didn't mind helping her with stats homework.

It was amazing how *easy* everything could be with Pete. For the first time in Blair's eighteen years, her life made sense. She loved her pre-law classes, lived in a house of boys who adored her, had a loving, handsome boyfriend, and had even found a surrogate family in the Carlsons.

One that didn't use the word *merger*.

For the past few days, they'd spent every waking hour with the family: Pete's former U.S. senator dad, Chappy; his Boston debutante mom, Jane; his three older brothers, their wives, and assorted cherubic nephews and nieces whom Blair couldn't even try to keep straight. It sounded like a nightmare, but it was actually heavenly. Mr. Carlson was barrel-chested and red-faced and told corny jokes in a way that made everyone crack up, and his mom would randomly recite Anne Sexton poetry at the dinner table without being drunk. The brothers were good-looking, friendly, and smart, their wives were polished and welcoming, and even the kids were polite. So far, it had been a perfect holiday.

And it was about to get even better. To celebrate the New Year, Chappy had booked the entire family at an exclusive five-star resort in Costa Rica. Obviously, Blair could do without the rain forest adventure part, but she'd heard the beaches were pristine, the sun was hot, and the villas had the most incredible mattresses.

Just then, there was a knock at the door. "You kids decent?" Pete's older brother Jason called as he entered. He had the same lanky frame as Pete. Tall, strawberry blond, and handsome, all four of the Carlson brothers—Everett, Randy, Jason, and Pete—looked like they could be quadruplets, even though there was a two-year age difference between each of them. A second-year law student at UPenn, Jason was the second youngest of the Carlson brothers. He was adorable, and Blair would've had a crush on him if she wasn't dating Pete.

At least she has a backup.

"We're playing charades. Carlson Christmas tradition. Your presence has been requested."

"Do we have to?" Blair suppressed a groan. It was cute in theory, but they'd played charades, Pictionary, and Scrabble the last three days. Blair was extremely competitive, and it was exhausting simultaneously trying to win and to not appear like all she cared about was winning.

Maybe they should shake it up with some Truth or Dare.

"And guess who's requested you on his team again?" Jason smirked, flashing Blair the trademark white-toothed Carlson smile. "Our dad loves you!"

"Yay!" Blair replied encouragingly, mustering her enthusiasm. She followed Pete through the wide arching hallway that led to the kitchen. The whole house was a contradiction: The walls were rough wood, but the polished wood floors were covered in antique Turkish carpets. In the kitchen, a large wood stove hunkered in the corner opposite two massive Sub-Zero refrigerators. Several overstuffed yellow chairs sat in front of a large dormer window, each one containing a different member of the family. Chappy, in a cream-colored cable-knit Aran Islands sweater, stood in front of the whole group, calling them to order.

"Scout!" he called gleefully as he spotted Blair and Pete.

"Hi, Mr. Carlson." Blair smiled warmly as Chappy clapped her on the shoulder.

"I already claimed you, so back off, boys," he announced jovially to Pete's brothers, who all smiled politely back at her, even though Everett didn't bother to look up from his iPhone. "I'm telling you, Scout, I don't know how I'm going to manage without you next week," Chappy continued.

"Oh, well, I'm sure we can play on the beach or something," Blair said. She blushed. The phrase sounded totally inappropriate when she said it out loud. "Play charades on the beach," she clarified quickly.

"Yeah, but what'll I do without my favorite teammate?" Chappy shook his head sorrowfully. "No offense, Jane, but you cheat."

"I do cheat, I'll be the first to admit it." Jane Carlson had wheat blond hair cut in a sensible bob and was tall, with an athletic frame. She was wearing the same style sweater as her husband. "I'm glad you're on the straight and narrow." She winked at Blair.

But Blair was still stuck on the part of Chappy's sentence that implied she *wouldn't* be in Costa Rica with them. She'd bought five new Eres bikinis for the occasion. They made the most of the five pounds she'd gained from the gross food she'd been forced to eat on Yale's meal plan. "*Without me?*" Blair blurted stupidly.

"I mean, I'd bring you along, but we've got a saying in the Carlson family . . ." Chappy began, his blue eyes shining, as if he were about to deliver a stump speech. "I believe, when it comes to vacations, in the 'no ring, no bring' rule."

"It's the Carlson curse." Jason sighed, elbowing Blair in the ribs sympathetically. She stepped away. While it was true Blair had never *officially* been invited to Costa Rica, she'd been invited for Christmas, for God's sake. Wasn't that even more exclusive than a beach holiday? And why *not* invite her? After all, she'd brought Nate on her family vacations for years and it wasn't like she'd been married to him.

Except in her dreams.

"Blair, we love you and we want you in our family for years to come, but I need to be a stickler on this," Chappy explained sympathetically, as if she were one of his constituents, arguing over some impossibly arcane rule. "I've raised four boys, and while they've behaved around you, honestly, these gentlemen cause more theatrics when it comes to ladies than the Yale School of Drama," he finished, shaking his head.

"Maybe you could get together with your girlfriends and have a girls' adventure!" Pete's sister-in-law Sarah piped up from the corner of the room, stroking her Lilly Pulitzer–patterned eight-months-pregnant belly. "I remember when I heard the Carlson rule, I had a great time with the Theta girls. We went to Cancún!" A look of happy reminiscence crossed Sarah's lightly tanned, heart-shaped face.

"You did?" Randy asked, shooting a look at Sarah. "I didn't know that."

"Sorry, son!" Chappy clapped Pete on the back. "Sorry, Scout!"

Blair narrowed her eyes at a painting that hung over the fireplace, of a ship in what looked like an exceptionally violent storm. What a boring, random piece of art to hang in a house. Suddenly she hated her stupid nickname. *Scout?*

*Out* would have been more appropriate.

"Blair, I'm sorry," Pete said simply. "I thought you understood. . . ."

"What? I knew I wasn't coming," Blair lied, smiling fakely. Her stomach was churning wildly. For a brief second, she wanted to excuse herself, run to the second-floor bathroom, and puke everything she'd eaten for the past five days.

"Blair, darling, here's your hot chocolate. I made sure to put some extra marshmallows in there." Jane pushed the steaming ceramic mug into Blair's hands. "Won't you sit down?" She gestured to one of the comfortable overstuffed forest green chairs.

"Thanks." Blair nodded. She squared her shoulders and turned to the waiting Carlson clan. No way was she going to let the Brady Bunch see her sweat. "You all ready to play?" She forced herself to smile, a plan already forming.

"Maybe I *will* have a wild girls' weekend," she whispered in Pete's ear. "I haven't been to New York all year, except those two weekends with you, and those don't count, since we never even left the hotel." His face fell as he no doubt pictured all the raucous fun she'd be having without him. Blair raised an eyebrow challengingly. After all, she was a woman. A Yale woman. She had places to go.

And more important games to play.

# *make new friends, but keep the old . . .*

"This came from the man at the other end of the bar," the skinny bartender-slash-model wearing a cheesy Ed Hardy T-shirt said as he proffered a glass of Veuve Clicquot.

"Thanks." Serena van der Woodsen glanced down the long, dark oak bar of Saucebox, the new lounge in the just-opened T Hotel on Thompson Street. Breckin O'Dell, a handsome but boring actor she vaguely remembered meeting a few times, held up his own glass of champagne and saluted her. Serena nodded, brought the flute to her lips, and took a healthy sip, even though she preferred vodka.

"Oh my God, you should totally date him. His agent has ridiculous connections." Amanda Atkins yanked on the sleeve of Serena's black Row scoop-neck jersey dress in excitement. "Can we get some shots down here?" she called to the bartender. Serena smiled sheepishly. Amanda was an eighteen-year-old recent LA transplant best known for her role in a dorky sitcom about a fashionista girl from Paris who moves to a farm in Tennessee to live with her redneck uncle Hank. Recently, though, she'd been cast in an indie film about snowboarders who dropped acid, and was trying to break free from her good-girl reputation.

Another shot and she's almost there.

"Maybe," Serena responded unconvincingly to Amanda's comment about Breckin. She stared at the clear bubbles fizzing to the top of her glass as if they held the secrets to the universe. If she looked around her, she'd see tons of Breckin O'Dell look-alikes with gel in their hair and fitted pressed shirts from Thomas Pink. They buzzed around Serena, Amanda, and her other two actress friends, Alysia and Alison. They called themselves the three A's, even though Alysia's real name was actually Jennifer.

The three A's were admittedly a little too into material things, but they were also goofy and fun and never turned down a party. Usually Serena had a blast hanging out with them, but tonight, she felt a little . . . off. It was two days after Christmas and her parents had just left for their villa in St. Barts, while her brother, Erik, was already back in Melbourne, Australia, where he was spending his sophomore year abroad. It wasn't like Serena wanted to spend New Year's Eve with her family, but she also didn't like waking up in their huge Fifth Avenue apartment alone. She downed her champagne in one gulp, telling herself that she just needed to have fun.

After all, she is the expert.

"Hey, you're that farm chick!" one spiky-haired brunet guy stuttered, not looking Amanda in the eye. He wore a pink and white striped button-down and his teeth were Chiclet white.

"Yes." Amanda sighed. "I am. But I have to stand over here now." She took two steps away as Alysia and Alison snorted in laughter. Serena offered the guy a sympathetic smile. Even though she was beautiful, she was never mean.

An infuriating combination.

"God, you'd think Knowledge would know to not to let guys like that in. Did you see his hair? It was, like, sprayed on." Amanda flipped her long blond extensions over her shoulder as she named the beefy bouncer whose job was to keep Saucebox as exclusive as possible, even though, to Serena, it felt exactly the same as every other bar she'd been to recently.

"Serena?"

Serena whirled around, ready to have another one of those *so what are you working on now?* conversations with someone in the industry she'd probably met once. Instead, she saw a familiar, smiling face that immediately took her back in time, and eighty blocks north.

"Oh my God, Iz!" Serena squealed excitedly. She slid off the smooth oak bar stool and threw her arms around Isabel Coates, a fellow Constance Billard alum who'd gone to Rollins College down in Florida. Her skin was deeply tanned and her thick dark shoulder-length hair had been straightened. Her chest looked suspiciously larger than it did the last time Serena saw her. She automatically looked over Isabel's shoulder, sure she'd see Kati Farkas, Isabel's BFF and constant wingwoman. Isabel and Kati had done everything together since the fourth grade. Kati had even turned down admission to Princeton so she and Isabel wouldn't have to be separated. But instead of Kati, a girl with a ski-jump nose and chin-length straight brown hair stood next to Isabel. She wore a tight black sleeveless satin dress and looked like she could be Kati's slightly older sister. But Kati didn't have sisters.

"This is my girlfriend, Casey," Isabel announced proudly. She readjusted her white Marc Jacobs tote strap on her shoulder.

*Girlfriend* girlfriend? Serena noticed Isabel's hand intertwined with the girl's.

"We met in a women's studies class." Isabel smiled adoringly at Casey.

There's her answer.

"This is Serena van der Woodsen. We went to school together," Isabel explained, her hand now resting lightly on Casey's back.

"Nice to meet you, Casey." Serena smiled, holding out her hand to the tall girl, who took it gingerly.

"Nice to meet you too. I haven't seen any of your movies," Casey announced bluntly.

As if anyone asked.

"Oh, that's okay. How's Kati?" Serena asked Isabel, easing back onto her stool. She couldn't help but wonder if Isabel was really gay, or just going through the fashionable bisexual phase of college she'd heard about.

Isabel sighed and shook her head. "She has this, like, football player boyfriend and is pledging a sorority that wears pink sweat suits to class. It's awful. Casey and I pretty much do our own thing. But what about *you*? I saw the movie. You were pretty good," Isabel allowed.

"Thanks." Serena blushed. She hoped Isabel really meant it and wasn't just being polite. "Things are okay. Just working a lot. We're filming a sequel to *Breakfast at Fred's* that's coming out in the summer, so that's fun. . . ." Serena trailed off. Even though she'd been on the cover of the October issue of *Vanity Fair*, part of her felt stuck. She'd come home from her big premiere, thinking it would be the greatest night of her life, to her same pink childhood bedroom in her parents' sprawling Upper East Side penthouse. If possible, she almost felt *less* grown-up than she had before graduating, especially since she now had an agent and a publicist who told her exactly what to wear, what to say, and who to be seen with. The real world felt a lot different than she'd imagined.

"A sequel sounds great!" Isabel cooed. "Anyway, I was just showing Casey all of our old haunts. Remember hours trying things on at Barneys, and then so much time just eating spaghetti and meatballs upstairs at Fred's? That all feels like so long ago now," she mused, nuzzling her head against Casey's. The guys standing around them were all drooling over the lesbian-chic couple.

"It does," Serena agreed wholeheartedly. Just a matter of months ago, she and Blair and Kati and Isabel would meet before school to smoke Merits on the Met steps and imagine their lives in college. Now, Blair was pre-law at Yale, Isabel was a lesbian, Kati was running around with pink Greek letters on her ass, and Serena was trying to make a go of it in the movies.

"So, have you seen anyone yet?" Isabel asked.

"No." Serena shook her head. For her, only two people really mattered: Blair and Nate. She and Blair had kept in touch since Blair headed up to New Haven, and once Serena had sent Blair a package full of Wolford stockings and black-and-white cookies, in a bow-tied Barneys bag—some of Blair's favorite New York things. Blair had reciprocated with a stuffed bulldog wearing a Yale T-shirt. It was sitting on Serena's dresser, next to a silver-framed picture of the two of them wearing enormous hats at a Kentucky Derby party sophomore year. They'd send e-mails and texts, but never anything long or involved. It was fine, though. Blair and Serena were the type of friends who could go for weeks and even, one time, months without speaking, then pick up right where they left off.

As for Nate . . . Serena hadn't talked to him since he left, to sail the world for a year. He had left her crushed, and she wondered if she'd ever see him again. But she didn't want to think about that right now.

Or ever.

"Are you going to Chuck's New Year's party?" Isabel asked, draining the rest of her Grey Goose and cranberry. "I mean, I know he's, like, such a misogynist, but I figured, you can only protest so much, you know? I prepared Casey."

"Wait, Chuck is back from military school?" Serena asked, suddenly eager to hear *everything*. She hadn't thought about Chuck—with his sketchy history, his trademark monogrammed scarf, or his questionable sexuality—since graduation. But the last she'd heard, after getting rejected from all twelve schools he'd applied to, he'd gone to some tiny underground, remote-country-boot-camp men's college. Of course her parents saw Chuck's parents socially, but they never mentioned what he was doing. It was an unspoken rule on the Upper East Side that parents didn't discuss their unsuccessful children.

"He must be." Isabel shrugged. "The party's on. I saw Laura Salmon at City Bakery this morning and she told me she was hanging out with Rain Hoffstetter at some lame Constance alum tea party that Mrs. M organized. Thank God we missed that. But, anyway, I guess she talked to Chuck. I don't know. It's at his place at the Tribeca Star. But I guess since you're a movie star and all now, you probably have to host some MTV countdown special or something, right?"

"Well . . ." Serena trailed off. In truth, she already had an invite to a New Year's party at Thaddeus Smith's West Village loft. Thaddeus had been her *Breakfast at Fred's* costar and was a true friend. But he wouldn't mind if she stopped by to say hi and then went off to Chuck's party. Maybe seeing old friends was all she needed to pull herself out of her mood.

Alysia tapped Serena urgently on the shoulder. "Let's go someplace else. There's no one fun here," she pronounced as Amanda and Alison nodded their bobbleheads in agreement.

"Please?" Alison whined. She stuck out her Stila-glossed lower lip and whined like a shih tzu.

Serena nodded before turning to Isabel. "I'll see you at Chuck's," she promised. She smiled faintly as she trailed the three A's toward the door. How could she *not* see her old high school crowd? While she might not have been thinking of them all that much recently, it wasn't like she'd forgotten them.

And they certainly haven't forgotten her.

# *a trip can't last forever, even for n*

Nate Archibald's elbow hit a beam, and he woke up with a start. His tanned, athletic frame was wedged in the crow's nest of the *Belinda*, the ship he called home.

Nate was traveling the world with his mentor and friend Chips. Chips had been Nate's father's mentor way back when he was in the navy, and for the past four months they'd followed the wind and the stars and the moon, aided only by Chips's antique silver compass. It was amazing. Nate had always been a sailor, and had even taken his father's boat, the *Charlotte*, up and down the eastern seaboard with his girlfriend, Blair, last June.

Doesn't he mean *ex*-girlfriend?

Nate rubbed the sleep out of his glittering green eyes and yawned. They were somewhere in the Bahamas, but it felt light-years away from the Upper East Side. Maybe it was the tropical air and the nautical living, but everything about his old life seemed far away. Sometimes, he'd try to remember a specific event—the first time he'd bought pot from the pizza dude on Lex by asking for two slices with extra oregano, the time he'd stolen the *Charlotte* and spent a weekend with Anthony and

Charlie, doing bong hits and eating Oreos, cruising toward Bermuda at half a mile an hour—but the scenes were always fuzzy. It was like remembering an old movie, where you could recall random moments, but not the beginning or ending.

Nate leaned back against the rough-hewn beams. There were some memories, though, that he replayed almost every night. In the moments before the subtle rocking of the ocean lulled him to sleep, he pictured Blair, and Serena van der Woodsen, his other best friend and the girl he'd lost his virginity to. Blair cheesily posing in front of the polar-bear exhibit at the zoo; Serena with her blond head tipped back, laughing hysterically at a joke only she found funny; Blair in front of Tiffany, her favorite place on earth, doing her best Audrey Hepburn impression. Serena splashing around in the Venus fountain in his backyard, looking like the goddess she was. He wondered if they ever thought about him.

*If not, there are plenty of girls who* do.

He knew they probably weren't *pining* for him. In fact, they probably hated him. He loved them both, and of course he'd never been able to choose between them. This past summer, he'd even cheated on Blair with Serena. Finally, when he couldn't decide whether to go to Yale with Blair or stay in the city with Serena, he'd chosen to travel the world with Chips. He'd been so confused. So conflicted. So afraid to make a choice, in case he chose wrong. But now, he felt different.

He even *looked* different. Months of sailing had tanned his skin a dark bronze color, and his golden brown hair was now almost platinum-blond in places. His face was angular and hardened and a blondish-brown beard covered his chin. The scruff made his green eyes stand out that much more. He hadn't smoked any pot since they'd left, not by choice, but still, it felt good. His head felt lighter, clearer somehow.

Nate climbed down the crow's nest onto the polished wood deck. It was just after sunrise and the sky was suffused with a pinkish tint. "Hello?" he called out. "Chips?"

"Nathaniel!" Chips called from the boat's stern. He was coiling a mass of rope, a frown etched on his weather-beaten face. With his white linen trousers, navy windbreaker, and shock of white hair, Chips looked like a tall stocky sea captain on the menu of a lobster restaurant. But beneath his stern veneer, he was actually a pretty cool guy, especially after he'd had his evening tumbler of scotch.

"Take a look." Chips passed the binoculars over to Nate. He could just make out land, fuzzy in the distance. "By New Year's Eve, we'll be at the Breakers," Chips declared, almost to himself.

"I'm sorry?" Nate asked. Wasn't the Breakers a resort in Palm Beach? He was ready to stop somewhere, make a couple calls back home, sure. He'd thrown his phone overboard when he'd made the decision to sail with Chips back in August, so he'd only been able to call home occasionally, when they stopped at various islands. He hadn't even been able to wish his parents a Merry Christmas. Still, he'd been hoping their next stop would be somewhere a little more adventurous, like Costa Rica. He'd always wanted to go there.

Join the club.

"So we're stopping in Palm Beach? And where to after that?" Nate asked. Ever since they'd left, he'd trusted Chips to guide them. But he was kind of wondering what Chips's grand plan was.

Instead of answering his question, Chips pulled himself back up into a standing position. He dusted off the thighs of his white linen pants. "When I was your age, I was in the navy. Didn't have the luxury to think about how I wanted to live my life, just had to make sure I got the chance to live it another day. You know what I'm saying, son?" he asked gruffly. His burry Scottish accent reminded Nate of Mel Gibson as William Wallace in the movie *Braveheart,* rallying the clansmen before launching into an epic battle.

"Right." Nate nodded, even though he wasn't really sure what Chips was talking about. "So after Palm Beach . . ."

"After Palm Beach, nothing. It's back to New York for you, sonny. It's time. I've shown you the world. Now you've got to live in it."

Nate felt rooted to the deck of the ship. He'd known he'd have to go back eventually, but this felt very *sudden.*

Just like how two girls might have felt when a certain boy decided to sail off into the sunset—alone?

Nate slid down on the yellow-wood-lacquered floorboards of the boat, trying to wrap his mind around everything. He was going back to New York. Back to his old life. Back to Blair and Serena and his father nagging about what a disappointment he was. *This* was Chips's grand plan?

"Stand up," Chips ordered. He put down the binoculars and began winding a mass of rope around his arm.

Nate hastily got to his feet. "You need help with that?" he asked, noticing Chips struggle as he tried to reduce one of the sails.

"No, I'm fine," his captain responded curtly. Nate nodded, even though he'd noticed that Chips had been dragging his bad leg more than ever. "Listen, Nathaniel," Chips said, more gently than before. "These last few months have been some of the best of my life . . . but I'm getting old. It's Palm Beach season for me. A man needs more than the sea and the sky to survive." He tied the rope into a perfect knot, as if to punctuate his speech. "But for you . . . you can't spend the rest of your life sailing away from everything difficult. It's for your own good."

Nate grimaced. Even though Chips was a philosophical, scotch-drinking old geezer, he always seemed to be able to read Nate's thoughts. And right now, Nate was thinking about the choice that had faced him for too many years.

"You're worried about those two girls of yours, I know it. The ones who keep falling at your feet despite your boneheaded moves? The ones you can't decide between, as if you're facing some life-or-death choice?"

Nate nodded miserably. In two sentences, Chips had pretty much summarized the crisis he'd been struggling with since he was fifteen.

"Well, I'll tell you this. You'll know when you know. And you've got to figure it out on your own. I'm not babysitting your balls anymore." Chips nodded definitively upward at the sails, pleased with his handiwork. "Now, if you'll excuse me, I'm going to have my morning tea. You've got a day to figure it all out." He gave Nate a parting wink, and disappeared down to the galley, leaving him with just the sky and the endless sea for company.

"Thanks," Nate muttered. He gripped the bow of the ancient but sturdy ship, feeling the salty wind on his face. Maybe Chips was right. He'd had some time away. Some time to think and be on his own, to see the world and become a man. He couldn't just sail forever.

It was time to go back and decide what to really do with his life. And when he saw Blair and Serena, he'd be ready to choose. Maybe it was best not to overthink it. When he saw them, he'd just *know*. There was no time like the present. He was ready.

Okay, but are they ready for *him*?

# love and other impossible pursuits

Dan Humphrey poured a cup of black Folgers coffee into a chipped red mug and shuffled toward the living room of his family's sprawling Upper West Side apartment. He sank down on the frayed, overstuffed beige couch, causing Marx, the Humphreys' fat black-with-a-dot-of-white cat, to jump off the cushion in protest.

It was still early, but Dan felt too keyed up to sleep. He'd gotten home from his first semester at Evergreen College in Washington State a week ago, and it was finally beginning to sink in that he wasn't going back.

Ever.

He'd applied to transfer to Columbia for second semester and had received his acceptance letter during reading week before exams. After his philosophy final, he'd packed up his metallic blue '77 Buick Skylark and driven cross-country, arriving in the city just in time to spend Christmas Eve with his dad, Rufus, and his little sister, Jenny.

The holidays had been nice. Jenny had given him a blue Banana Republic sweater, his dad a collection of Charles

Bukowski books, and they'd all eaten dinner at their favorite Chinese restaurant, which served bad boxed white wine with every order. It had been great to see his family, but the whole time, he'd been counting down the hours until he could see his girlfriend—shaven-headed, filmmaker genius, love of his life Vanessa Abrams.

Vanessa had actually been living in Dan's family's apartment for the past semester, while attending Tisch School of the Arts at NYU. Her film equipment sat in one corner of Dan's bedroom, and her black tank tops and bras were in the top drawer of the rickety bureau in the corner. It was sheer torture being surrounded by her stuff, and not *her*—Vanessa was up in Vermont, visiting her parents for the holidays, until Wednesday. She didn't even know that Dan was transferring to Columbia; he wanted to surprise her with the news in person rather than via their evening Skype calls. Now, the anticipation was killing him.

The gallon of Folgers can't help, either.

Dan grabbed his black Moleskine notebook and flipped to a blank page. It wasn't difficult to find one: Practically every page was blank. He'd had writer's block from the moment he stepped on campus in September. When he'd decided to go to Evergreen, it had seemed like a good idea to get out of the city. After all, he'd lived here forever. But in the Pacific Northwest, everything was just. . . . *wrong.* There was too much space, the trees were too tall, and the coffee had names like organic shade-grown mild blend and earth-friendly mellow brew. His dorm fielded its own Ultimate Hacky Sack team, his roommate was a vegan allergic to cigarette smoke, and every single poem his classmates submitted in his creative writing seminar was about pot.

The only thing that got Dan through was the thought of Vanessa. He'd text her all throughout the day, every time something funny or tragic or inane happened, and he always arranged his day around their nightly Skype calls. But Vanessa was so busy with school that she was sometimes rushed or distracted, and seeing her pixilated face just wasn't the same as holding her in his arms.

Dan thoughtfully chewed the end of his Bic pen. Suddenly, for the first time in several months, words began to flow.

*Missed kisses.*
*Missed shreds of carpet.*
*Torn by your Doc Marten feet.*
*I've lost weight.*
*Or maybe it's just you I'm missing.*

Maybe it was the promise of Vanessa or the hiss of the radiator in the corner or the chipped mug he'd drunk millions of cups of coffee out of, but suddenly, he could write. Dan grinned to himself, adrenaline rushing from writing his first almost-poem in months. He was back.

And better than ever?

"Daniel!" Rufus Humphrey boomed as he strode into the living room from his office. He wore a pair of paint-stained blue sweatpants that read BROADWAY BOWLING LEAGUE down the leg and a stretched-out pink T-shirt that said CRUISE TO LOSE below a picture of Richard Simmons. His wiry gray hair was held back with a red velvet bow, left over from Christmas. "It's too quiet around here since Jenny left for Bermuda or Burundi or wherever she went with her fancy Waverly friends. Is it just me, or is Jenny noisier than before?"

"Probably." Dan shrugged. Jenny was currently in the Bahamas with her boarding school friend, the governor of Georgia's daughter. When Dan left in August, Jenny was still his little sister. But she seemed to have matured six years in her four short months at Waverly. Now she was self-assured and confident and didn't cross her arms over her chest all the time.

Rufus leaned down and picked up the notebook from the coffee table. "What is this?" he asked, flipping through pages. "'Doc Marten feet,'" Rufus intoned, as if reciting a monologue. Dan cringed. Rufus was an editor of lesser Beat poets and had always taken special interest and pride in Dan's literary accomplishments. He suddenly felt ashamed that the only thing he'd written in the past three months was a haiku. He'd anonymously posted it on the door of the dorm bathroom, asking his hall mates to please not pee on the floor.

"You know, this isn't bad," Rufus said thoughtfully, holding the book close to his face as he settled on the couch next to Dan. "It's a postmodern interpretation of Sandberg. It's been done before, but it's not horrible."

"Thanks." Dan yanked the notebook away from his dad.

"And this is only the beginning. I just know you'll really let your creative juices flow on our retreat!" Rufus said fondly as he ruffled Dan's hair.

Dan swatted his dad's hand away. Fuck. He'd forgotten that he'd promised to join Rufus and a couple of his Beat poet buddies on an artists' retreat over New Year's. He'd agreed before the Columbia acceptance had come, when anything besides his current reality had sounded like paradise. But he didn't want to leave Manhattan so soon. He had so much to do before the semester started, like look for cheap studio apartments for him and Vanessa.

*That* would definitely surprise her.

"Don't tell me you're not coming!" Rufus pouted, noticing Dan's hesitation. "I haven't seen you since August—the least you can do is spend four days with your old man. I know I won't see you much once Vanessa gets here."

"You'll still see me," Dan mumbled, even though he knew it was true. Once Vanessa was back, Dan never wanted to let her out of his sight again. He sighed. "No, I'll come," Dan said definitively as he headed toward the sink with his coffee mug.

"Great! I'll make sure to stock up on some supplies for you, then. We're going to build a sweat lodge and sweat out our demons. This old man needs a Speedo!"

"Get some bagels while you're out!" Dan called to Rufus's retreating back. He turned on the water and squeezed dish soap into the sink, smiling at the tiny bubbles swishing in the coffee mug. A poem was already forming in his head.

*Avocados in the morning, with cake.*
*Death by chocolate.*
*You kill me, you really do.*
*And I've been alive too long.*

Dan hurriedly set the mug on the dish drainer so he could write down the first few lines. He sank down onto the couch and picked up his notebook. As he started to write, he heard keys scraping in the lock.

"I'm home!" A female voice echoed through the apartment as the door creaked open.

Dan blinked and his breath caught in his throat. So many times he'd imagined her: his perpetually black-garbed muse. But now she was here, framed by the entryway. Her hair had grown into a sleek black pixie cut and she wore a red coat and black jeans. Her cheeks were red from the cold, contrasting beautifully against her alabaster skin.

"Surprise!" Vanessa cried, tossing her army green duffel bag on the floor. It was so familiar, and yet so strange, to see Dan sitting on the couch, frowning down at a notebook. It was as if she'd taken a time machine back four months to last summer.

She threw her arms around Dan and kissed him hungrily. "Mmm, you feel good," Vanessa murmured. She ran her hands all over his thin white Hanes T-shirt. She could feel his heart thumping in his chest.

"How are you here?" Dan croaked. It was hard to believe this was real, and not some post-traumatic stress hallucination left over from Evergreen.

"I missed you." Vanessa shrugged. She'd left Vermont this morning, after she realized that a week with her hippie-parents was more than enough time. Besides, she wanted to surprise Dan. He'd always seemed so down on their Skypes.

"I missed you too." Dan kissed Vanessa again. He didn't like their lips being apart. "I have so much to tell you," he breathed. He'd meant to tell Vanessa about Columbia over a glass of red wine or at least after he'd taken a shower and brushed his teeth. But he couldn't handle the thought of waiting another minute.

"I have so much to tell you too!" Vanessa said eagerly. There was so much he needed to get caught up on in her life. She couldn't wait to bring him to Bushwick and go to one of the all-night parties that her sophomore friends Brianna and Kara held on the first Sunday of every month. She couldn't wait to show him some of the films she'd made. She couldn't wait to spend all day at the International Film Center, making out and watching movies.

Dan stood up. "Follow me." He led the way toward his bedroom.

"Is it a present?" Vanessa asked as she trailed down the hallway after him. She hoped not. They'd decided not to give presents to each other this holiday and instead put the money toward an emergency plane ticket fund so Dan could come visit when the distance was feeling unbearable.

"Nope." Dan grabbed the acceptance letter off his desk and thrust it toward her, buzzing with anticipation. He'd memorized every word.

Vanessa scanned the document while Dan watched. He noticed a sparkly barrette sweeping a lock of hair behind her left ear. Vanessa never used to wear jewelry.

She also never used to have hair.

Finally, Vanessa looked up, a faint smile playing on her full red lips. "Does this mean you're not going back to Evergreen?"

Dan nodded happily as he closed up the space between them and pressed her back against the doorframe. "I hated Evergreen. All I could do was think about you, and about us. I couldn't write without you. I need you," he said. How did long-distance relationships ever work? He could hardly stand to be in a different *room* than Vanessa.

"I know," Vanessa murmured. Dan's breath was hot against her cheek. Had Dan really spent every waking moment at Evergreen just thinking about her and wanting to come home? She knew he hated it there, but hadn't he even *tried* to like his classes? To make friends?

"So, I was thinking we could live here until we find a place. We could get a studio downtown. It wouldn't be that expensive," Dan mused, running his fingers through Vanessa's short hair. It was silky and unfamiliar, but Dan instantly loved it, just like he loved every part of her.

Vanessa nodded, trying to imagine living with Dan. They'd tried a few times last year for short periods of time, but it had never really worked. One of them would always get moody or jealous. But maybe now that they were in college, it would be different?

"And we can arrange our schedules together. There's this one class at Columbia called The Poetry of Film that I was thinking of taking. Maybe you could take it as a visiting student? Or maybe you could transfer." His hand grazed the hem of her black long-sleeve thermal top.

"Transfer?" Vanessa pulled back slightly. "But I *like* NYU." She loved her classes, and most of the people she'd met. The film students tended to stick together, going from screenings to happy hours to late-night onion ring runs at Tick Tock Diner in a herd. In high school, Vanessa would have thought that type of behavior was ridiculously lame. But having a big group of friends was actually fun.

What was she getting so worked up about? Dan was her *boyfriend*, and he was moving back to the city. Of course he just wanted to spend more time with her. And of course that was what she wanted too. "Come here." She smiled and reached toward Dan, pulling him in for a kiss. His lips tasted reassuringly familiar, like Crest and Folgers.

Just then, her cell vibrated from her back pocket. She pulled out the phone and frowned.

"What?" Dan asked impatiently.

Vanessa scanned the display. NEW YEAR'S PARTY AT MY CASA. 210 AVE B. HOPE TO SEE YOU THERE—HOLLIS. Hollis was her TA for her Intro to Film class. He was only twenty-five but he'd already screened a few of his films at the Tribeca Film Festival. One of them had even been picked up by an indie film company. He was intense, but approachable and funny, and would be the first to tell you if your film sucked. In fact, he'd given her first assignment a C+ because he thought it was too perfectly executed. *This has technical precision, but not heart. Do you want to make credit card commercials or films?* he'd asked. It should have been obnoxious, but she respected his honesty.

"My friend is having a New Year's Eve party downtown tomorrow night. . . ." Vanessa tried to picture Dan interacting with some of her new friends, like Matt and Chip, the gay couple who made extremely explicit XX-rated films. Dan could sometimes be a little . . . antisocial.

"My dad wanted me to go on some retreat thing," Dan told her, disappointed. "I just told him I'd come."

"I understand," Vanessa said, pleased that she could go to Hollis's party without worrying about Dan. "I don't want you to disappoint your dad. Besides, we have plenty of time now."

Dan melted all over again. It was so cute that Vanessa was concerned about his dad. He took her hand and interlaced his fingers with hers.

"You're right," he murmured, drawing her close. "I'll be back in a few days." It would mean a lot to his dad to spend some father-son time together. Especially since he and Vanessa would be moving in together soon. He couldn't wait.

Because nothing says forever like a cramped studio apartment.

# *welcome back*

Blair heaved a sigh of relief as she hauled her Louis Vuitton duffel to the curb outside La Guardia on New Year's Eve day. Just a few hours ago, she'd said goodbye to Pete at Logan Airport before hopping a commuter plane to New York.

"Where to?" The cab driver gazed at her through the Plexiglas partition.

"Nine ninety-four Fifth Avenue." Blair rattled off Serena's address as if it were her own and leaned back against the cab's black pleather seats. The past few days at the Carlsons' had been torture. After the "no ring, no bring" announcement, the cozy atmosphere had felt decidedly claustrophobic. Now she was actually looking forward to spending New Year's in the city and seeing Serena again. She rummaged through her thyme green Lanvin weekender bag for her iPhone.

"I'm coming over!" Blair announced as soon as Serena picked up. The cab hit a traffic snarl right before the Queensboro Bridge. Instantly, the cars around them started honking.

"You're in New York?" Serena squealed. "Oh my God, I can't wait to see you!" Her excited, crackly voice filled the cab.

"See you soon!" Blair clicked off. The familiar skyline came into her vision, and a smile curled across Blair's lips. She was *back*.

The cab navigated its way into Manhattan and weaved across the east side. On Fifth Avenue, it stopped in front of a familiar, green-awninged building across from the Met. A familiar blond figure stood outside, two coffees in hand.

Blair rolled down the window of the cab and sucked in her breath. Of course, she'd seen photos of Serena in all the weekly gossip magazines she pretended not to read, but Serena in person took her breath away. She wore a tattered pair of J Brand boyfriend jeans and a fuzzy white cashmere sweater. Her thick blond hair was loose around her shoulders and her makeup-free face was flawless.

Serena yanked the cab door open and tackled Blair in a bear hug. "I've missed you!" She hugged her tightly. Serena had gotten a Cartier watch from her parents for Christmas and a Burberry ski parka from Erik, but this was all she really wanted: her best friend home for the holidays.

"Me too," Blair replied honestly. The cabbie removed her bags from the trunk and set them on the sidewalk. Instantly, Roland, Serena's ancient doorman, took the bags and brought them inside.

Once they were alone, Serena stared dumbly at her friend. She couldn't believe Blair was right in front of her. She looked older, somehow. Her hair was longer than it had been last summer, her small face more angular. But she was grinning widely in a way that reminded Serena of how she'd looked as a little kid.

"I bought you coffee." Serena proffered a white Dean & Deluca cup.

Blair took a sip and smiled as the skim latte with two Splendas slid down her throat. That was the great thing about old friends. They knew you, right down to how you took your coffee.

"Can we sit on the steps for a little bit?" Blair asked almost shyly, gazing at the Corinthian columns of the Met across the street. Back in high school, they spent hours on the steps, gossiping and pouring their hearts out to one another. The steps were the center of their universe. Blair had even had her going-away party inside the famous museum. It felt right that they begin their reunion there, instead of in Serena's apartment.

"I was *hoping* you'd say that." Serena grinned, already crossing the street.

They settled midway down the steps. It was surprisingly warm for December, and the museum entrance was crowded with people. Blair spotted two girls huddled over coffee a few steps below them, and for a moment, thought it might be Kati and Isabel. But when the blonde turned, Blair realized she was only about fourteen. She reminded herself that *everyone* had changed in the past few months.

Some more than others.

Serena rummaged through her oversize See by Chloé bag and pulled out a pack of Gauloises. She handed one to Blair.

"So tell me everything," Serena began, lighting both their cigarettes. "Starting with how and why you're here."

"So . . ." Blair heaved a deep breath. After the horrendous few days she'd had, grinning stupidly as she played board games with Pete's family and pretending everything was okay, she couldn't wait to finally unload the *truth*. "I was at my boyfriend, Pete's, house in Vermont for Christmas." Blair nervously twirled her ruby ring around her finger. "We were staying there just for the holiday, before taking off for Costa Rica. I was so excited and everything was going so well. But then—"

Blair paused as a cute trio of twentysomething guys approached. They stood at a distance of a few feet, shuffling nervously. Guys always approached Blair and Serena whenever they were together, and of course it was flattering. But right now, Blair wasn't really in the mood.

"Are you Serena van der Woodsen?" a lanky blond guy asked in a British accent.

"I am." Serena smiled, displaying her perfect white teeth.

"I knew it was her!" his red-haired friend exclaimed. "Mind if I take a picture?" he pleaded, already removing a tiny Nikon digital camera from his khakis pocket.

"Only if my best friend is in it, too," Serena said sweetly. She threw her arms around Blair's shoulders and stuck out her tongue. Of course she still looked beautiful.

"Thanks, Serena!" the guys chorused as they walked away, crowding around the guy with the camera so they could check out the picture.

"How annoying," Blair grumbled.

"It's not so bad. It happens a lot, ever since *Breakfast at Fred's* opened. It's kind of cute." Serena shrugged. "So, anyway. You were saying. About your boyfriend?"

"He's great," Blair said quickly, taking another sip of coffee. Suddenly, she didn't want to tell Serena about what happened in Vermont. After all, Serena was an internationally worshipped movie star. How could she possibly understand? "It's amazing. A *real* relationship. Nothing like high school," Blair added. "We're thinking of moving in together for spring semester."

"You must really love Yale," Serena said wistfully. She'd chosen not to go to Yale with Blair, and mostly, she was happy with that decision. But it was a little hard to hear about Blair's perfect college life knowing she could have been right there with her.

"I do love it. It's just so nice to be surrounded by interesting people who care about what's going on in the world. It's just so *collegiate*, you know?" Blair said, still thinking about the British guys. Weren't they a little old to be asking for autographs?

An awkward silence fell over them. "Chuck's having his New Year's Eve party tonight," Serena said finally. She wanted to tell Blair how lonely she'd been in New York without her, but it sounded like Blair was having the time of her life at Yale. She probably thought Serena's life was pathetic. "I have to stop by another party first, but maybe we can meet up there later?" she asked hopefully. For all she knew, Blair had dozens of New Year's Eve parties to attend with her Yale friends who lived in the city.

"I guess I could stop by," Blair allowed. It would be fun to see the old crowd. Especially with Serena at her side. Every year at Chuck's party, they'd drink far too much champagne and wind up in the hot tub at ungodly hours of the morning. "Just like old times," she added under her breath. Just then, a cute guy jogging past the steps did a double take when he spotted Serena.

"I'm freezing," Blair announced, standing up and stamping out her cigarette. "Let's go." She quickly crossed the street, and Serena had to run to keep up with her.

The more things change, the more they stay the same.

# hey people!

I was at EAT on Madison getting my usual half-caf double cap when I was asked *the* question. You know the one. I should be used to it by now, but it catches me by surprise every time. And no, I'm not talking about where I get my highlights or who makes my boots or why I look so familiar. I'm talking about the ever popular "What's your New Year's resolution?"

Yes, it's annoying. And yes, it's kind of a personal question. But I for one think you should reveal your resolutions to the world. After all, it's the one time of the year you can publicly declare you'll no longer try to pull off Forever 21 as vintage, you'll no longer run back to a loser ex, you'll no longer head to the gym just for a wheatgrass smoothie. The point is, if you want to change your life, you've got to let people know so they can hold you accountable. And the best place to announce your intentions? The most fabulous New Year's Eve party you can find!

**live it up**

It's all the debauchery of a costume party minus the awkward outfits, the anything-can-happen fun of Fourth of July without the sunburn, and the revelry of St. Patrick's Day without the green beer. It's the night to wear your pink Vena Cava zip-up dress and flirt with your friend's older brother. It's time to grab someone and kiss them, hard, until everyone stops blowing those annoying party horns. And, if a certain bad boy from the past is hosting a party in his parents' exclusive downtown hotel suite, it's the perfect setting for whatever you want to happen—decadent *or* demure.

### sightings

**S** and three A-named (if not A-listed) actresses at **The Standard**. And **Waverly Inn**. And **Rose Bar**. Do those girls ever get tired? **D** climbing into an ancient brown van double-parked on Broadway and Ninety-ninth, followed by his dad, **V** waving them both off from the curb. **C** heading to the **Tribeca Star** with four or five cowboys and several handles of vodka. And this in from Palm Beach: a glittering-green eyed boy who looks mysteriously like the long-lost **N**, getting on a plane bound for JFK. Hellooooooo, sailor!

### the great reunion

I admit it: I thought a certain Ivy League brunette might have forsaken her hometown for warmer climes. But after a change in vacation plans left her temporarily stranded on the East Coast, **B** is *back*. She was last seen smoking Gauloises on the steps of the Met with a certain blond beauty who could *only* be **S**. And my sources say they were making New Year's Eve plans. Just like old times! Now the big question is: Who will **S** and **B** be kissing at midnight?

### your e-mail

Hey G,
An idea: You, me, and a bottle of Dom. We can watch the ball drop and create our own fireworks. Thoughts?
—mackdaddy

**a:** Dear Mack,

Unfortunately, I already have some more heavily populated parties to attend. But, hey, look on the bright side: More Dom for you!

—GG

**q:** Dear Gossip Girl,

It's the first time I'm going to see my ex since we both left for college. I have a new boyfriend now, but he's not in town, and I'm worried what will happen when it's just me, my ex, and the countdown to New Year's. What should I do?

—kissme

**a:** Dear K,

While I don't condone cheating, as they say, *should auld acquaintance be forgot*. Which I interpret to mean that special pardons exist for that New Year's Eve kiss. Good luck.

—GG

### the final countdown

It's already late afternoon and I still have to take a nap before slipping into my don't-you-wish-you-knew-where-it-was-from frock. And while I have my beauty sleep, I suggest you do the same. After all, who knows where and when (and with *whom*) you'll find yourself in bed tonight.

You know you love me,

gossip girl

# double-booking NYE is never a good idea

Serena crowded into the elevator of Thaddeus Smith's loft behind Amanda, Alysia, and Alison. She'd invited Blair, but Blair had declined, saying she'd just meet her at Chuck's later. Serena hoped Blair didn't think she was lame for stopping by an industry party, but she'd promised Thad she would.

"Oh my God, Serena, you should date Thaddeus! His building is soooo pretty!" Alysia enthused in between hiccups. Thaddeus lived in a top-floor triplex in an all-pink eight-unit Julian Schnabel building that overlooked the Hudson River.

"I don't think we'd be good together." Serena giggled. *Because he's totally gay,* she wanted to add. Serena had found this out the hard way last summer, when Thad was her costar in *Breakfast at Fred's.* She'd thought he liked her—until she'd met his boyfriend, Serge, and realized Thad had been flirting with her to cover up his *real* relationship. It was disappointing, but she'd gotten over it quickly. Now, she wasn't about to out Thad. He'd come out when he was ready.

Even though the news would make so many boys' dreams come true.

"Oh my God, I heard Brad and Angelina are going to be here, and that Brett Ratner will be too and is looking for a lead for his next film. Do you think I look too skanky?" Alysia asked, examining her red marabou feather dress in the elevator mirror. She looked like an aging Vegas showgirl.

"No, you look great," Serena lied. The theme of the party was Heaven and Hell. Serena hadn't really planned on dressing up, but at the last moment, and at Blair's urging, she'd decided to wear a short white Calypso sundress that was technically a bikini cover-up, a black garter on her perfectly toned leg, and a headband that had little Swarovski crystal devil horns. The entire look was fun-sexy, unlike Amanda's custom-made angel wings or Alysia's feathered dress.

"You want?" Alysia asked tipsily, passing Serena a silver Tiffany flask. She hiccupped again.

"Alysia, I swear to God, if you embarrass me in front of *any* agents, I'm going to tell everyone you starred in a fat camp commercial when you were twelve," Amanda said haughtily, elbowing Alison in the ribs.

Serena laughed, remembering all the mini fights she and Blair had had in elevators on the way to parties over the years. It all seemed so long ago.

Does that mean it's time for a rematch?

The elevator doors slid open to reveal the living room of Thaddeus's apartment. It was an enormous, loftlike space, with floor-to-ceiling windows that looked out onto the inky black Hudson River below. The space was already crowded with scantily clad girls in red and white, and guys in jeans and white button-downs or red T-shirts. The air felt twenty degrees hotter than in the elevator.

"Serena, baby!" Ira Green, the producer of *Coffee at the Palace,* greeted her, slapping his fleshy palm against her bare back. "I noticed your boyfriend was here. Great career move." Ira nodded importantly.

"My boyfriend?" Serena asked in confusion, glancing around the crowded room.

"Breckin O'Dell? Says in Page Six you've been canoodling." Ira grabbed a glass of champagne off the tray of a passing server clad in a white bikini and red stilettos. "Look, I'm all for it, but I don't want you to get exclusive. Not good for pre-film buzz. In fact, I'd love for you to really spend the evening mingling. I've got a couple of my own friends who'd love to meet you."

"I'd like to meet them," Amanda piped up, sticking her hand out for Ira to shake. Serena took that moment to gracefully duck away, weaving between party guests toward the bar set up in the corner. She usually loved parties, but right now, all she wanted to do was say hi to Thaddeus and then hop a cab to the Tribeca Star and spend the night partying with Blair. Tomorrow, they could have a lazy brunch, nursing their hangovers with glasses of fresh-squeezed orange juice. Then they'd watch *Breakfast at Tiffany's* and all the other old movies Blair loved.

"Serena!" someone shouted from behind her. Breckin O'Dell was lumbering over to her from the bar, looking extremely pleased with himself. His reddish hair was artfully spiked into peaks, and he wore a skinny purple tie and a black vest.

Hell is other people's . . . outfits?

Serena made a beeline for the bathroom. She really didn't feel like getting into another conversation with Breckin. He was definitely attractive and had appeared in a couple spy thriller movies, but his conversation topics ranged from his abs to his agent.

She swung open the bathroom door. A bare-assed girl was straddling a half-naked guy on the edge of the onyx sink.

Definitely occupied.

"Sorry!" Serena squealed, slamming the door shut. Gross.

"Serena!" Breckin sidled up to her. "May I say you look lovely." He snaked his arm around her shoulders, drawing her closer to him. "My agent thinks we should date. What do your people say?"

Serena stifled a giggle. *Her people?* The phrase made her think of little green aliens landing their UFO on Earth. "Do you always do what your agent tells you, or do you have a mind of your own?"

"Oh, I have a mind of my own," Breckin said slimily. He plucked two flutes of champagne from a passing waiter and offered one to her. "And there's a *lot* going on in there." He winked.

"Cheers!" Serena clinked glasses with him while sneaking a glance at her gold Cartier tank watch. Eleven fifteen. She'd planned to *leave* the party by eleven, and she still hadn't said hi to Thad or talked to any of Ira's producer friends.

It's a tough job, but somebody's gotta do it.

"So . . . ?" Breckin asked, clearly waiting for her opinion on their dating future.

"My people will be in touch," Serena lied as she backed away. She pulled her iPhone from her silver Chanel clutch, sending a text to Blair that she was on her way.

"Serena van der Woodsen, you are beautiful!"

Serena whirled around, relaxing when she saw Thad. He wore a tight white cashmere muscle tank and a pair of white linen pants. A six-foot-tall girl with straw-colored, ass-skimming hair held his hand. She wore a red cleavage-baring dress with an amoeba-shaped cutout at the middle. Serena recognized her as an up-and-coming singer who'd won some reality show competition.

"This is Carilee Roberts. Our agent introduced us," Thaddeus said tightly, brushing his blond curls from his forehead as if he had a headache. "Carilee, this is Serena van der Woodsen."

"Hey there, sugar. Why, don't you look like just the sweetest thing? I could just eat you up! Of course, I don't mean that literally. I only like boys!" Carilee said enthusiastically, yanking Serena's shoulders toward her and kissing her aggressively on both cheeks.

"Nice to meet you." Serena said as she backed away.

Thaddeus's light blue eyes flicked down to Serena's almost empty champagne glass. "We need to get you a drink. And we need to get me ten. Can you hang out with us for a bit? Serge couldn't make it. He decided to go to a Boys' Night Out party instead," Thaddeus whispered. Serena could detect a hint of desperation in his voice. Thad obviously wished he was at a Boys' Night Out party, rather than the Hollywood-heavy party Ira had insisted he host.

"Of course." Serena smiled as she trailed after Carilee and Thaddeus to the bar. It was the least she could do. Blair would understand.

Of course she would.

*What the fuck*, Blair murmured as she listened to Serena's voice-mail message click on for the tenth time tonight. She was sitting on the edge of the bathtub in Chuck Bass's Tribeca Star suite. Serena had promised that she'd only stay at her Hollywood is Hell party for an hour, but it was now almost eleven thirty. Of course, Serena had invited Blair along, offering to "add her to the guest list." Like Blair was so pathetic she needed her movie star best friend to get her in places. She'd demurred and opted to meet Serena here instead.

Blair sighed in frustration as she tossed her phone back in her clutch and sauntered out of the bathroom. She couldn't believe Serena would just ditch her like this. They'd *always* spent New Year's Eve together. Blair remembered so many parties in this very suite, splashing around in the raised hot tub in their skimpiest Calypso bikinis, trying to find the cutest guy in the room to make out with when the clock struck midnight.

Of course, they always wound up kissing each other.

"I heard Blair and her Yale boyfriend had this secret wedding in Mexico, but then they had to have it annulled," Laura Salmon whispered to Rain Hoffstetter over by the makeshift bar in the kitchen annex. She wore a glittery sheath dress, and a matching Swarovski-studded headband was perched on her dark roots.

"Really? I heard Blair found out she was pregnant with Nate's baby and now she's trying to make it seem like the Yale guy is the father. Luckily, she's not really showing," Rain Hoffstetter whispered back. A diamond stud glittered in her left nostril, drawing attention to her pug nose.

Blair strode over to her former Constance classmates, aware their eyes were on her.

"Hey," she said to the group. She grabbed a bottle of Ketel One and liberally poured it into a tumbler, then added a splash of tonic. The suite was pretty empty. In the corner, a group of flannel-clad guys were playing Xbox, entranced by the flat screen against one wall. The hot tub, constructed in an anteroom between the bedroom and the main suite, was filled with flat-chested girls Blair vaguely recognized as members of the freshman peer group she'd led last year at Constance. Blair squinted to take a closer look. Through the steam, she noticed two topless girls making out with each other. Obviously slutty L'École girls, trying to get attention. Blair wrinkled her nose. Was this *seriously* how she was spending her New Year's? This party was lame even by high school standards.

"Where's Chuck?" she asked Rain, trying not to stare at the infected boil that erupted from her nose piercing. She'd heard Chuck was in military school or monkey training school or something.

You know, either one.

"I don't know." Rain shrugged. "More importantly, did you see Isabel?"

Blair shook her head blankly. Why the hell would she care about Isabel Coates?

"Look." Laura Salmon pointed a pearly manicured finger toward the two girls in the hot tub. "Isabel's dating a girl named Casey. Except she's just doing that to show off," Laura said in disapproval. Blair squinted through the fog, recognizing Isabel's profile. *Interesting.* She wished she could deconstruct the whole ridiculous scenario with Serena. Where the fuck *was* she?

"Are you dating anyone?" Rain asked nosily as she chugged her vodka soda from a Riedel glass.

"I'm dating a comp lit major. He's a junior and I was just with his family for the holidays. He's in Costa Rica right now . . . working on a . . . project," Blair fibbed, getting more and more annoyed by the second. In the movie of her life, tonight was supposed to play like the scene in *My Fair Lady*, when Eliza makes a grand entrance at the ball and everyone wonders who that stunning, gorgeous girl is. Instead, she was busy trying to impress the wannabes she'd never even cared about in high school.

How the mighty have fallen.

"Serena's dating a movie star," Laura offered, taking a seat on one of the bar stools next to Blair. "I read about it in the *Post*."

Blair pretended she hadn't heard. She did *not* want to get into a conversation about Serena's fabulous, star-studded life. *Was* she dating a movie star? Was she with him right now? And why hadn't any of the flannel-clad guys in the corner even noticed her? Blair unhappily drained the rest of her drink. She pulled out her iPhone and frowned at it. WHERE THE FUCK ARE YOU? she texted, then quickly pressed send with a nude-polished fingernail.

"I'm going out to smoke," she announced, turning on her knee-high Sigerson Morrison boot and stomping toward the terrace.

If you can't make a grand entrance, make a grand exit.

## fancy meeting you here

Nate shivered and stuffed his hands deep into the pockets of his blue toggle coat. He and Chips had docked in Palm Beach in the morning, and Nate had hopped an afternoon flight back to New York, arriving at his Upper East Side town house in the early evening. He'd taken a long shower, then spent hours seated on the floor of his room, unsure what to do. Aboard the *Belinda* he always had tasks. But back in the city, he had nothing to do and nowhere to go. No one even knew he was here. His parents were in St. Barts for New Year's, like always, and Regina, the Archibalds' housekeeper, had the week off. It would be cool to have the house to himself, if he didn't feel so lonely. Everything in his room, from the lacrosse sticks propped in the closet to the framed photos on his desk, reminded him of his old life.

Eventually, Nate had gotten dressed in a dark blue Ralph Lauren sweater and a pair of Diesel jeans and left the house. He'd wandered aimlessly downtown for about an hour, until he remembered that Chuck always threw a New Year's Eve party at the Tribeca Star. As if his feet had a mind of their own, he found himself headed there.

Nate glanced left and right across East Houston and crossed the street toward the ultramodern Philippe Starck–designed hotel that loomed above lower Manhattan. He paused at the corner, gazing up like a tourist. His neatly ironed clothes felt scratchy after months of wearing frayed cargo shorts and T-shirts. What the fuck was he doing? Maybe it was a dumb idea. Maybe Chuck wasn't even having a party this year. Or maybe he *was*, and by some crazy coincidence, Serena and Blair would be there.

But Blair didn't even have a home in the city anymore. She was probably out in LA for the holidays, meeting smooth-talking California surfer dudes who'd take her on moonlit walks on the beach. Serena was probably off filming a movie somewhere, guys falling at her feet. Neither of them would give a second thought to the kid who almost didn't get his diploma and fucked up everything with both of them.

"Nathaniel?"

Nate whirled around and found himself facing a dark-haired guy in jeans and a blue sweater, his arms laden down with two large bags of ice.

"Chuck?" Nate asked incredulously. It was definitely Chuck Bass, but he looked . . . *different*. His features hadn't changed: same sleek dark hair, same espresso-brown eyes. But the mischievous twinkle seemed gone from Chuck's eyes, and he wasn't carrying the bad-tempered, snow white monkey he used to bring everywhere senior year. Gone was his trademark navy blue cashmere monogrammed scarf; his jeans looked like they'd seen better days. It was like those spot-the-difference puzzles Nate's kindergarten tutor had given him as a kid.

"Good to see you, buddy!" Chuck placed one of the bags

of ice on the ground and enthusiastically pumped Nate's hand. Chuck's fingers felt callused, as if he'd spent the past couple of months doing manual labor.

"Should I send your packages up, sir?" The black overcoat–clad doorman immediately bent down to pick up the bag.

"Nah, that's cool," Chuck waved him away. "I'll bring it up myself."

Nate blinked. Chuck Bass *never* did anything for himself.

"Glad you made it. Let's head inside," Chuck suggested, gesturing toward the door. Nate nodded dumbly as they whooshed through the revolving door and into the vaulted-ceilinged, marble-floored lobby. Instead of turning left toward the elevator bank, Chuck perched on one of the low-slung black leather couches in the dimly lit lobby. "Sorry. It was fucking freezing out there. I'm used to California." Chuck smiled. "But I'm not quite ready to head back upstairs. Want to chill here for a sec?"

Nate gingerly sat on an ottoman. "California? What were you doing out there?"

"Deep Springs, my man." Chuck nodded, his eyes glazed over as if in happy reminiscence.

"Deep what?" Nate parroted. Was that some sort of Playboy resort?

Or a gay spa?

"Deep Springs," Chuck repeated. "The all-male college. It's a two-year program on a working alfalfa farm in California. We all run the farm and the school in between humanities classes," he explained patiently, settling back into the couch. Nate glanced down and noticed he was no longer wearing the gold pinky ring he'd worn since sophomore year, after he'd starred in a European cologne campaign.

"Oh." Nate was still confused.

"Look, I didn't get into any schools and I didn't know what to do. My dad's cousin is married to a board member there so they allowed me to do a late interview. It was either that or go to military school, and I just couldn't leave Sweetie." Chuck named his snow monkey. "I was fucking terrified when I got there. They made me give away my Armani sheets to use as tablecloths in the boardinghouse. I had to get rid of all my clothes and find new clothes in the bone pile, which is all the clothing left from guys who have moved on. I mean, I was wearing other people's shit." Chuck shuddered, as if reliving the experience. "But it turned out to be what I needed. I was a mess in high school. I mean, you saw me. I was a dick, and I'm sorry about that," Chuck said, opening his hands as if to ask for forgiveness.

"Thanks." Nate shrugged. He thought of a playdate at Chuck's when they were four. While Chuck's nanny was watching a soap opera, Chuck had bit Nate's arm, laughing the whole time. He'd *always* been a dick.

Just part of his charm.

"I'm a changed man, Nathaniel," Chuck continued, crossing one ankle over his knee. He wore a pair of worn-out-looking cowboy boots. "That's why I needed to take a breather before I headed back upstairs."

"I understand." Nate nodded. He did understand. He needed a breather and he hadn't even gone up there yet. "So what else happened at Deep Springs?"

"So, I get there, I'm wearing some guy's flannel shirt and jeans, we're on this alfalfa farm in the middle of the desert, and I swear to God, I was ready to call my father, our lawyers, everyone, but there was no service. I was in the middle of the fucking desert. Our first night, Sweetie got bit by a rattlesnake. Poor girl."

"Did she die?" Nate asked.

"Yeah, but not because of snakes. She sort of starved herself to death. She just couldn't adapt." Chuck shrugged sadly.

"How did you do it?" Nate asked, awed. "I mean, how did you make it through?" Chuck was nothing like the Mercedes-S-class-driving, pink-shirt-wearing douche Nate remembered.

"I mean, the first month sucked, but then they changed my job from farm team to dairy boy and everything just changed. I'd be up at dawn with these cows, and I realized that there's more to life than just acquiring things and people. You know, hooking up with someone's easy. Castrating a bull is fucking hard, man."

"I guess so," Nate grunted. In a way, he and Chuck had been through similar experiences. They'd both separated themselves from society, they'd both thought about their lives while doing manual labor. But why did Chuck seem so grounded and happy and normal while Nate felt more fucked-up than ever?

"So, what's going on with you?" Chuck asked companionably, steepling his fingers against his chin. "You and Blair still together? Or what about Serena? Dude, some guys at Deep Springs watch *Breakfast at Fred's* over and over again in the rumpus room. During the next calving season, we're going to name the firstborn Holly." Chuck shook his head fondly, his eye resting on the bags of ice melting at his feet. "Shit, I've gotta get back upstairs. Are you coming?" Chuck's brown eyes bored into him.

"I'm coming." Nate stood up and grabbed one of the bags of ice. As they made their way into the elevator, Chuck went on about all the Deep Springs buddies he'd invited to New York, but Nate was only half listening. Chuck really had changed. And if college could change someone like Chuck Bass, Nate couldn't begin to imagine what it could do for him.

It was freezing on the terrace and Blair had already smoked two Merits, but she didn't want to head back inside. She didn't want to pretend to care what Laura and Rain were doing with their lives. She didn't want to watch Isabel slobber all over her girlfriend. She didn't want to watch the cowboy guys try to beat each other in Grand Theft Auto as if they'd never played a video game before in their lives. No wonder *Chuck* hadn't even bothered to show up at his own party. Nothing was happening, no one interesting was here, and she was going to fucking kill Serena as soon as she saw her. But first, she was going to have to beg the concierge to get her a suite in the hotel—it was New Year's Eve and they were probably all booked. She couldn't wait to take off her dress, order room service, and drink vodka sodas from the minibar while watching AMC.

Sounds like a rockin' New Year's Eve.

Blair yanked open the sliding door into the suite just as someone else was stepping out onto the terrace. She caught her breath. Broad shoulders. Tanned skin. Light brown hair streaked blond from the sun. Hollowed-out cheekbones and a scruffy beard. Glittering green eyes that were staring right at her. Adorable smile.

"Hi," Blair finally managed. She twisted her ruby red ring around and around her little finger. The last time she'd even heard from Nate was when he'd sent her a text message telling her he'd decided to sail the world instead of coming to Yale with her. She wasn't sure if she wanted to kick him, or . . . kiss him.

"Blair," Nate croaked. He couldn't believe it. Blair was

standing before him like an angel. A sexy, dark-haired, slightly pissed-off angel.

"What are you doing here?" Blair spat. She wanted to tell him how devastating it had been to go to Yale by herself, after she'd spent the whole summer imagining their life together. She wanted to tell him how she dreamed about him every night the first month of college, or how her roommate, Alana, offered Blair a teddy bear from her prized collection because she seemed so lonely.

"I didn't think you'd be here," Nate breathed. Blair's small face looked more angular, her skin paler. She wore a ladylike black dress that hugged every curve of her body. Her chest seemed bigger, but her waist somehow smaller. Nate wanted to wrap his arms around it.

"Well, I am." Blair felt rooted to the ground.

Nate wanted to hug Blair and bury his nose in her hair, to smell the delicious shampoo she always used. He wanted to press his lips against hers. He wanted to run his fingers along the curve of her back. Chips's words rang through his head. *You'll know when you know.*

He knew.

"I'm back," he said finally.

"I can see that," Blair hedged. She didn't want to make this easy for him. He'd broken her heart, and she'd sworn she'd never forgive him.

"Blair, I know I messed up. I was scared and didn't know what to do. You know I love you. I always have."

"That's what you texted. To me *and* Serena." Blair put her hands on her hips. The fact that he'd sent the exact same *I love you, goodbye* message to her and Serena had always been the most difficult thing.

"I know. I was so confused. I've known you both forever. Serena's a friend, but I love you, Blair. I understand if you can't forgive me, but I hope we can at least be friends." Nate's eyes were pleading.

Blair studied Nate's face and softened a bit. His green eyes were dull and his face was ashen. He looked like a guy who'd just realized he'd made the biggest mistake of his life. "So much has happened," she began, but then trailed off. Where to even begin?

Blair glanced around. Rain and Laura and a whole bunch of slutty L'École freshmen were peering toward the terrace, watching them. She didn't know what she wanted to say to Nate, but she knew she didn't want an audience.

"We could talk about it somewhere else," he suggested, as if reading her mind.

Blair gazed at Nate, holding eye contact. Every night before she went to sleep at Yale, she'd revisited the same fantasy, like a movie playing itself on loop in her head: Nate opening the door to her tiny dorm room and sitting down on the edge of her regulation-size bed. Telling her that he'd gone out to sea to forget her, but that he couldn't stay away. That he couldn't live without her. That he loved her, always and forever.

It wasn't happening exactly as she'd imagined it. But it was still happening.

"Can we go back to your house?" Blair asked boldly, surprising herself. She knew what would happen when she was alone with Nate. But she also knew, *finally*, that Nate loved her. And he deserved a second chance.

Or a third, or a fourth . . .

# *the last moment is the one that counts*

Vanessa ran up the steps of the First Avenue L train station at eleven thirty on New Year's Eve, eager to get to Hollis's party before midnight. The stairwell smelled like pee and was crowded with scantily clad revelers getting a late start on party hopping.

She spontaneously pulled out her camera from her bright orange Brooklyn Industries bag. Last year, she'd captured footage from a midnight run in Central Park. She loved the idea of having an archive of footage of anonymous New Yorkers, celebrating the start of a new year. She began filming the packs of people swarming out of the subway station and onto the sidewalk. Avenue B had been a sketchy avenue in the eighties and nineties, but it was now dotted with gourmet coffee shops and wine bars. The entire street had the atmosphere of an enormous party, and Vanessa felt a shiver of anticipation run up her spine.

She made her way to the address from Hollis's text. The black door to the four-story-tall building was propped open with a broom, and strains of the Clash emanated from the top floor.

The apartment was sticky and humid from so many bodies in such close proximity. Vanessa pulled off her puffer coat and draped it over her arm. She was wearing black jeans and a black hoodie emblazoned with the logo of her sister's band, Sugar-Daddy. She felt plain and underdressed compared to the guys in skinny jeans and ironic T-shirts and the girls in vintage silk dresses, toasting each other with plastic cups.

Vanessa felt a tug on the hood of her sweatshirt and turned around.

"You came!" A slow smile spread across Hollis Lyons's face, reaching his slate gray, thickly lashed eyes. He was tall and lean, and wore jeans and a purple-and-black-striped vest over a white button-down. A black newsboy cap sat jauntily on his head, his messy black hair sticking out from underneath. On anyone else, the outfit would've looked ridiculous, but on Hollis, it somehow worked. Vanessa randomly thought of a young Christian Bale in *Newsies*, a movie Jenny loved for no apparent reason.

Hollis draped his arm over Vanessa's shoulder and led her into the kitchen.

"As you can see, we're extremely well stocked." He gestured to the makeshift bar like a game show host. The cracked laminate counter was littered with empty bottles and cans. "What can I get you?"

"Whatever you're having."

"PBR?" Hollis opened the refrigerator and held out a can toward her. "Seems to be all that's left. I thought we'd just have a couple of people, but we're at capacity." He passed the beer to Vanessa. "Just so you know, I don't make a habit of drinking with my students."

"I'm not your student anymore!" Vanessa had to yell above the music. Le Tigre was pounding so hard through the stereo that the hardwood floor seemed to be shaking.

"I know!" Hollis grinned and clinked his glass against hers. "Let's go upstairs!"

He opened the door of the apartment and Vanessa followed. He swung his leg onto a rickety fire escape ladder installed four feet above the floor, holding his beer precariously with one hand the whole time. Vanessa clambered after him, her hands gripping the freezing fire escape, and stepped onto a narrow landing. They faced a large black metal door with a note tacked on: DO NOT OPEN, ALARM WILL SOUND.

Hollis pushed open the door. They were greeted by silence instead of a loud siren. "That's been there for years," he explained, walking out onto the unfinished tar-covered roof. Around them, other people were on their own rooftops, setting off rogue fireworks, toasting each other, and laughing.

"I love it up here," Hollis said. "It's like a party in the sky. LA was nothing like this. In LA, you always have to get in your car to do just about anything. Here, everyone's so connected." He shrugged as he sipped his beer and surveyed the surrounding rooftops. "I kind of wish I had my camera."

"I have mine." Vanessa pulled her camera out of her messenger bag and offered it to him. She crossed her arms over her chest and clamped her teeth together so they wouldn't chatter. She didn't want Hollis to know how cold she was, because she didn't want him to suggest they head back downstairs.

Is that so?

Hollis took the camera carefully from her hands and pointed it in her direction. "I'm glad we came up here," he said, slowly panning the camera so it took in the other rooftops. He stopped once he came to Vanessa. "So, tell me the story of your life.

Maybe I can make it into a movie that'll get me out of my five-hundred-square-foot apartment."

"Do you use all your students for story ideas?" Vanessa took a sip of PBR to stop herself from saying anything else stupid. Why was she suddenly so nervous? She'd spent plenty of time alone with Hollis, debating the merits of Cassavetes after class. But for some reason, being alone with him right now felt scary and thrilling at the same time.

"As you pointed out: You're not my student anymore. Now, sit on the picnic table over there and tell me more about yourself. That's an order," he added, a playful smile snaking across his lips.

"What do you want to know?" Vanessa perched on a rickety picnic table surrounded by rusted lawn chairs, the cold seeping through her jeans. No guy had ever asked to film her before. She used to film Dan a lot. But she didn't want to think about Dan right now.

Wonder why?

"Right now, you're doing this little snarl thing with your upper lip, but you're smiling the whole time. It's cute. Has anyone ever told you you do that?" Hollis asked.

"No." Vanessa shook her head. She smiled while *snarling*? And Hollis thought it was cute?

We all have our special talents.

Below them, people from the bar across the street were spilling onto the sidewalk, blowing noisemakers. "It's almost New Year's!" someone yelled into the night air.

"Should we go back downstairs?" Vanessa asked nervously. Hollis put the camera down on the bench and sat down next to her.

Just then, the group clustered on the sidewalk began counting down: "Five, four, three, two, one . . .

"Happy New Year!" The phrase rose like a collective chorus, from the streets below and the roofs around them.

Hollis brushed his hand against Vanessa's cheek, then cupped her chin and pulled her mouth toward his. "In case you thought you missed your opportunity for a New Year's kiss," he murmured as his lips brushed hers.

Vanessa hesitated for a fraction of a second, as an image of Dan's sallow face flashed across her mind. Dan, her Dan, who was back and wanted to move in together, go to school together, start a life together. But it was this thought exactly that made her kiss Hollis right back. His mouth tasted clean and cinnamony and not at all like Folgers. She knew it was wrong and that she'd have a lot of thinking to do in the morning. But up here, on the roof, so close to the winter stars, it felt so right.

In film-speak, this is called a central conflict.

# missed connections

**From:** svw@vanderWoodsen.com
**To:** bcw@yaleuniversity.edu
**Time:** Friday, December 31, 11:58 p.m.
**Subject:** Re: Here!

. . . with 2 mins to go before New Year's! A million sorries and a thousand ridiculous reasons why I'm late but I'll make it up to you, I promise! Just let me know where you are because this party needs fun and you and I are the only ones who can supply it. Xoxoxoxoxoxox Serena

**From:** bcw@yaleuniversity.edu
**To:** svw@vanderWoodsen.com
**Time:** Saturday, January 1, 12:18 a.m.
**Subject:** Re: re: Here!

Left party early and found another place to stay. Will call you tomorrow. Happy New Year.
Xo,
Blair

## the honest truth and other rewards

All of the lights in Nate's Eighty-second Street town house were off. Nate didn't bother to turn them on as he led Blair up the stairs to his room. They hadn't talked at all in the cab uptown. Talking—even if only the cabdriver could hear them—felt unnecessary. Besides, it was impossible for either of them to know where to begin. Instead, they'd both stared out at the city as it passed, their hands intertwined.

Blair followed Nate up the familiar creaky stairs toward the three rooms that made up his private third-floor space. Nate paused in the doorway.

"Blair," he said urgently. He planted his lips on hers. She tasted familiar, like peppermint gum and vanilla lip gloss. He'd never, ever leave Blair again. He was so thankful she'd given him another chance. He wouldn't fuck it up this time.

We've heard that one before.

Blair pulled away, her hands resting lightly on Nate's strong back. The moon cast a wide shaft of light on his Italian cotton duvet and part of her was eager to lie down and have Nate ravish her. But part of her—the grown-up part—needed to know that what had happened four months ago wouldn't happen again; that Nate really *was* hers forever. She sat on the bed, knitting her perfectly manicured fingers together in her lap.

"You really hurt me this summer," she said quietly.

It was funny. In the past, when Blair was pissed, she'd scream or throw a Manolo. Her hesitant manner was almost worse. "I know I did. I feel so guilty about that." Nate hoped his words conveyed how sorry he was. He'd never meant to hurt her. She needed to know that. "I just had to figure out some stuff. But I know what I want, now. You," he said huskily. He couldn't believe the words he was saying. They seemed so cheesy, like lines from one of those black-and-white movies Blair used to force him to watch.

A single tear fell on the hem of Blair's dress. Normally, she never let anyone see her cry. "You left me. You *left* me, Nate," she whimpered, finally letting go of all the anger and frustrations and dashed hopes she'd carried with her for the past four months.

Nate felt his heart breaking in two as proud tears rolled down Blair's beautiful cheeks. He wanted to kiss her again and again until everything was better. Instead, he sat beside her and placed his hand tentatively over hers.

"I'll never leave you again. Blair. I love you." Nate's stomach knotted, willing her to echo his feelings.

"I love you too," Blair said finally, another tear trickling down her cheek. She wasn't sure why she was still crying. She was just so relieved and happy and homesick and excited, all at once. Nate gently wiped the tear away with his index finger.

Blair leaned in and kissed him, hard. "I love you," she said again.

Together, they lay down so they were facing each other. The strap of Blair's dress was falling down her shoulder. He reached out and eased it down, so Blair's skin was exposed. They didn't need to talk anymore. All they needed was each other.

Just then, a loud buzz emanated from Blair's Chloé clutch where it had been hastily tossed on the wood floor.

"Let's ignore that," Blair said, reaching toward the waistband of Nate's khakis. She wasn't mad at him anymore. What he'd done last summer didn't even matter anymore. All that mattered was this—them, together.

# breakfast of champions

*Please answer the phone,* Serena whispered as she dialed Blair's number on New Year's morning. It was 10 a.m. and she'd been up since seven, feeling guilty about abandoning Blair last night. She wasn't sure how to interpret Blair's e-mail. It wasn't bitchy, exactly.

Not *exactly.*

But what could she have done? It wasn't like she could leave Thaddeus alone with his homophobic ditz of a date. She'd only been able to leave after Carilee passed out on Thaddeus's bed after one too many amaretto sours. It had proved impossible to get a cab, so she'd gone back up to the party and begged Ira to let her use his town car. Finally, she'd gotten to Chuck's party. It was crawling with L'École and Seaton Arms underclassmen she'd never met before, all eager to hang out with her. But no sign of Blair.

Knowing Blair, she'd probably gotten a suite and was watching an Audrey Hepburn marathon and hating her life—and maybe even Serena. She felt guiltier each time she thought about it.

*Hi, you've reached Blair Waldorf. . . .* Serena threw the phone on her bed in frustration.

Just then, the intercom buzzer to the apartment rang. Serena sprang up and buzzed Blair in.

She raced back to her bedroom, plucked a pair of black Stella McCartney for Adidas yoga pants off the floor, and yanked them over her Cosabella boy shorts, padding to the door on her size nine bare feet.

"Hey Booger Braids!" Serena called the kindergarten-age endearment down the hall, not caring what her neighbors might think about her inappropriate greeting. "Sorry I missed you last night."

Blair rounded the corner of the elevator bank into the hallway. But she wasn't alone.

"Look who I found!" Blair announced, feeling a slight thrill of pleasure at the look of shocked surprise on Serena's face.

"Natie?" Serena said weakly, letting her arms fall slack against her body as she leaned against the doorframe for support. How was Nate here? How were he *and* Blair here, together? Blair's hair was damp and tousled around her small, pretty face. Nate's expression was dazed and happy, like he was in a dream he didn't want to wake up from.

Suddenly, everything came horribly together. Blair and Nate were here with each other because they'd been *with* each other. Blair had spent the night at *Nate's*. No wonder she was in such a good mood.

Serena sighed, trying to will her bad feelings away. This fall she'd tagged along to a yoga class with Alysia, where the instructor told them to think of their minds as an endless blue sky, and any negative thoughts as little rain clouds that would eventually go away. She would *not* let her rain clouds ruin her reunion with her two best friends. "Blair, I am so sorry about last night!"

"Oh, it doesn't matter." Blair shrugged, as if she hadn't been cursing out Serena for the entire night prior to meeting Nate.

Nate licked his lips nervously as he glanced between Serena and Blair. Serena had that sexy, just-rolled-out-of-bed look. Blair wore jeans and an old navy blue Ralph Lauren sweater of his. He loved the way his sweater hung off Blair's frame, reminding him of how small she was compared to him. They were both beautiful. But Blair was *his* girl.

For now, at least.

"It's great to see you, Serena," Nate said awkwardly, offering his adorable, lopsided smile. Serena felt her stomach twist in jealousy. *Let it go.* She imagined her angry storm cloud thoughts disappearing to reveal a blue sky.

"I don't know about you guys, but I'm *starving.* Let's go out!" she announced brightly, sounding like an overcaffeinated camp counselor.

Or a jealous best friend?

The cab pulled up to Serendipity on Sixtieth and Third, which was equally famous for its retro-kitschy Tiffany glass lampshade decor as it was for its high-calorie desserts. Once they were seated, Serena glanced down at the cracked hexagonal floor tiles so she wouldn't have to watch Blair and Nate gazing adoringly at each other. She didn't get it. Didn't Blair have a boyfriend? And wasn't Nate supposed to be off sailing the world still?

"So, Nate, where the hell have you been?" she asked. She poked the ice cubes in her water glass down with her straw as if she were trying to drown them.

"All over." Nate shrugged uncomfortably. He'd been everywhere, from sailing around Latin America to exploring the Pacific Northwest, but he didn't know where to start. Besides, no matter where he was, he'd been thinking about both of them. But he couldn't say that to Serena in front of Blair. Serena's navy blue eyes gleamed, and she looked like she wanted him to talk for hours. But he didn't know what else to say. "We sailed without a navigation system. It was really cool," he added vaguely.

The waiter, a chipper man who had way too much energy for New Year's Day morning, approached the table. "Happy New Year!" he practically shouted, causing droplets of spit to rain on the table. "Now, where are you folks from?"

"I'll have the eggs Benedict and coffee and he'll have scrambled eggs and bacon that's just a little crispy," Blair said, ignoring the waiter's inane question. How embarrassing to be taken as tourists. Then again, this *was* a tourist trap. Sure, they used to come here all the time when they were little and split a frozen hot chocolate while their nannies gossiped over coffee. But that was years ago. Didn't Serena realize they weren't kids anymore?

Serena smiled tightly. "I'll have coffee. And toast," she said, brushing away the menu. She didn't have much of an appetite.

"You're not eating? That's no fun!" Blair wrinkled her nose. "She'll have chocolate chip pancakes. With extra whipped cream," she announced.

"Sure thing, captain!" The waiter dorkily saluted her. Blair rolled her eyes.

"So are you back for good?" Serena asked, turning to Nate. He looked gaunt and more careworn than she remembered. She wanted to call the waiter back and order extra pancakes and sausages and eggs for Nate, then feed them to him until he regained his strength.

Nate shrugged. "Maybe I'll borrow the *Charlotte* and do some sailing," he said. The boat was docked in Newport, Rhode Island, for the winter. He hadn't really thought about what he was going to do with the rest of his life. Chips was still in Florida, and Nate doubted he was going to set sail again anytime soon. And now that he knew Blair didn't hate him, he didn't really want to go anywhere. "I could train for the America's Cup," he added. That would be pretty cool. He could sail up and down the East Coast during the week, see Blair on the weekends, and maybe catch up with Serena for coffee on Monday mornings. It would be perfect.

Blair's eyes lit up as if she'd just had the best idea in the world. It was a look Serena recognized all too well.

Uh-oh.

"Come to Yale!" Blair cried. "They have a sailing team."

"Could I do that?" Nate wondered. For the past four months, he'd barely read a book. Hell, he'd barely even *spoken* to anyone except Chips. Even here, it had felt too overwhelming to order breakfast; he was thankful Blair had stepped in. There were too many choices, too many decisions in the real world. He felt like he needed a remedial course in life before he started at an Ivy League university.

"Of course." Blair patted him on the knee. "You only just deferred. You could start spring semester. I can e-mail my advisor and ask him to help you pick classes. He's the best," Blair said, busily creating a mental list of all the things she had to do. First, she'd have to head to New Haven to find an adorable town house she and Nate could rent. Then, they'd go shopping at ABC Carpet & Home to decorate. She'd have to help him pick the right classes and she'd have to talk to Petra, a nice but way-too-sporty girl from her econ class, to see if she knew any of the sailing guys. . . .

"How's the movie biz?" Nate asked Serena, interrupting Blair's reverie. Blair felt a wave of annoyance ripple through her. Who cared? After all, they were talking about Nate's *future*.

"It's fine. It's a lot of sitting around and waiting for something to happen or running from place to place, meeting people you're never going to see again. I kind of wish I could just lie in the grass somewhere and read books," Serena mused.

"College isn't really about lying around and reading books," Blair scoffed, placing her hand territorially on Nate's thigh.

"I know." Serena sighed. "I just miss the way it used to be, sometimes."

"I don't," Blair said as the waiter set their plates of food in front of them. "I feel like our *real* lives have started. Don't you agree?" She turned sharply toward Nate and snatched a slice of bacon from his plate.

Suddenly, Serena couldn't stand it anymore. If she had to watch them be couply with each other, she at least needed a drink.

She cocked her head and gestured to the waiter. "A round of mimosas? We're celebrating!" she announced. All she had to do was pretend she was in a movie, and she'd be able to make it through the rest of breakfast.

And would that movie be called *The Flat Tire on the Perpetual Third Wheel*?

# *who says you can't go home?*

"Daniel-*san*!" Can you get more rocks for the fire pit?" Rufus asked, poking his head out of a lopsided canvas-and-log structure that served as a sweat lodge. Dan had spent the last few days in an upstate New York campsite with Rufus and his motley group of friends: Mika, Herbert, and Ron. Ron preferred to be called Running Rainbow, and when he wasn't serving as a barista at Starbucks, he taught tai chi for free in Central Park. Mika and Herbert were tall, skinny, bald members of a folk-rock band that played open-mic nights around the city. Rufus had met all three of them at a seminar at the Ninety-second Street Y called *Bringing the Age of Aquarius into the Age of the Internet.*

Rufus emerged from the sweat lodge wearing a blue-and-yellow striped towel around his waist and white Crocs. He didn't seem the least bit cold, despite the fact that the temperature hovered near freezing. Dan was shivering in a Patagonia parka he'd inadvertently stolen from his Evergreen roommate.

"Okay," Dan mumbled. They'd only been in the woods for

two nights, but it felt like a lifetime, especially since he didn't even get cell service. He'd wanted to call Vanessa at midnight on New Year's Eve, but no matter how far away he walked from the campsite, he couldn't get reception.

Dan sighed and grabbed a large moss-covered rock, groaning as he picked it up.

"Here." He dropped the rock next to Rufus's Crocs. Inside, Herbert and Mika were banging on bongo drums.

"Thanks," Herbert called. "I think we're ready to begin the ceremony." He poked his head out of the structure like a puppy in an extra-large doghouse. "And Dan, since you're the youngest, you can be the dog soldier," he announced.

"Excuse me?" *Dog soldier?*

"You need to protect the door while we chant away our demons," Herbert explained. "We have extra animal skins if you get cold."

Dan did a double take. Was this guy serious? *Protect the door?* Not only was it broad daylight, but the wooded area they were staying in was right next to a farmhouse. What he'd thought had been a rushing river when they'd gotten to the site after dark on New Year's had actually been the whooshing of cars across a highway. But it was no use arguing. Herbert had already retreated back into the sweat lodge with his bongo drum.

Dan sighed and sat on a log outside the lodge. Fuck, he was cold. He wondered what Vanessa was doing. Knowing she was in New York while he was here was almost too much to bear.

Sounds like *he's* the negative spirit.

He pulled a pen and a crumpled receipt from the pocket of his jacket. Maybe he should focus on writing. Maybe suffering would be good for him—he wasn't going to suffer at all once he and Vanessa were living together. Smoothing out the paper on his thigh, he began to write.

*Sweat, skin heat, cold, wet sweet.*

It was no use. The poem sounded like the beginning of an erotic version of *The Cat in the Hat.* There was no way he could do this for two more days. Besides, sitting outside and guarding against evil spirits didn't really equate to bonding time with his dad. That was it. He was going home.

"Dad?" Dan whispered hesitantly through the canvas-flapped door of the lean-to.

"What?" Rufus's wiry hair was slick with sweat and his face was bright red as he swayed back and forth in front of the central fire.

"I don't think this is working for me," Dan said carefully. "I need to see Vanessa."

Rufus shook his grizzly head sadly and stood up. Dan cringed. His dad was only wearing a tiny purple Speedo that sagged in the ass. "Are you sure?" he asked, clapping Dan on the shoulder. "Because if you want me to take over dog soldier duty so you can sweat it out, that'd be fine with me. You know, I never believed this New Age crap, but it's good stuff."

Dan shook his head. "I think my spirit guides are telling me to go home," he said seriously.

The bongo playing stopped. "Door to the farmhouse is open if you need to call Al's taxi service," Running Rainbow yelled, then resumed drumming.

Rufus shrugged. "You'll be okay?"

"Yes. Have fun, Dad!" Dan yelled as he practically sprinted away from the campsite and toward the highway. He didn't want to wait for Al's taxi service. He just wanted to go home. Stamping his feet on the asphalt, he put his thumb up.

A truck slowed down.

"What do we have here?" The driver leaned out his window. He was missing three front teeth and was probably around sixty. His long bushy hair reminded Dan of pictures of Jerry Garcia in his later years. Was this where all the sixties stoners came to die?

"I'm heading to the city. New York?" Dan said, trying to play it cool, as if he hitchhiked all the time.

Jerry Two nodded thoughtfully. "Hop in!" he announced grandly. Dan nodded and took a breath. The cab of the truck smelled like patchouli and jasmine.

"Bringing my candles to sell in the big city. You ever been to the Union Square greenmarket? I have a booth!" Jerry Two said proudly as he floored the accelerator.

"Oh?" Dan said politely. At least the cab of the truck was warm. And he really doubted a candle-selling hippie would be a serial killer.

"Yep. Me and my wife make 'em. You got a wife?" the driver asked companionably.

"No." Dan shook his head. He tried to imagine himself and Vanessa in their sixties. Would they still be making poetry and films? "I have a girlfriend, though. I'm going back to the city to see her," Dan said, surprised at how much information he was volunteering.

Jerry Two nodded thoughtfully. "When I was your age, I was already married. My wife's name is Joan, and she's just as pretty and smart as the first time I laid eyes on her. When you find a lady like that, you don't let her go, you know what I mean?"

"Yes," Dan mumbled, already antsy to get back to the city. The stretch of highway was practically empty and surrounded on both sides with fields of cows. He wanted to crawl next to Vanessa and feel her body next to his. A poem was forming in his head, and Dan's fingers were itching to write it down. He pulled his notebook from his duffel and grabbed an ancient Sharpie rolling on the rubber floor mat of the truck. Uncapping the marker, he quickly wrote.

*Dreaming in Technicolor black and white.*
*I'm no Technicolor prince, no black-and-white tragedy*
*What you see*
*Will be us, you me.*

Dan grinned. It was so obvious. He didn't need a retreat, what he needed was Vanessa. And he couldn't wait to have a sex-and-poetry fest as soon as he got home. He leaned back. The vinyl seat squeaked, making a farting noise.

"You let one rip? Good! I will too!" Jerry Two said. A loud noise emanated from the driver's seat. Dan wrinkled his nose. It was going to be a longer drive than he thought.

What some people will do for love!

# nothing can ever go wrong at tiffany . . . right?

Blair leaned back against the Frette pillowcases of Serena's canopy bed. She'd always felt like Serena's house was her second home—or third home, once she and Nate started dating sophomore year—and had been more than happy to spend the day relaxing and watching endless hours of crappy MTV while Serena was at a shoot for *Tea at the Palace* or *Snacks at the Strand* or whatever her movie was called. Now it was almost four o'clock, and she felt kind of gross and bloated from spending the entire day lying in bed and eating Godiva chocolates from one of Serena's discarded gift baskets. She needed to get out.

She hadn't seen Serena since brunch the day before. It was sort of for the best, though. After all, she and Nate couldn't keep their hands off each other. They'd spent all of yesterday cuddled in Nate's bed, whispering remember-whens in between kisses and feeding each other eel rolls from Blue Ribbon sushi. She only left Nate's house because his parents were due home from St. Barts today. It would be enough of a surprise for them to see Nate. She didn't want them to think the first thing Nate did when he came back was take advantage of the empty house with his girlfriend.

Wait, girlfriend?

She sighed and turned off the TV. Ever since she was fifteen and had seen *Breakfast at Tiffany's*, she'd played a game with herself called What Would Audrey Do? If Audrey found herself alone at dusk on a cold January day, she'd probably sit near the window of some cozy café like Le Refuge on Eighty-Second Street and people-watch, the whole while blissfully unaware that from behind their menus, everyone was whispering about the charmingly gamine girl. Besides, she'd been back in New York—her city—for almost three days and had barely seen anything besides Nate's bedroom.

And it wasn't like she'd been admiring the décor.

Blair pulled her Burberry coat from the Eames chair in the corner, exited the building, and automatically turned left, exactly as she had a million times before. She wasn't sure where she was going, but she'd know when she got there.

She paused at Seventy-second and Fifth and looked up at the row of limestone buildings standing at attention across the park. The building on the corner was her building, the one she'd lived in for eighteen years of her life. Her gaze traveled upward to the top floor, where a dim light emanated from the room that used to be hers. Suddenly it hit her that she didn't live here anymore.

She knew a new family lived there now, one with triplets a few years younger than her. Did they have boyfriends and best friends within walking distance? Did they sit for hours on the steps of the Met, smoking Merits and talking about nothing? Blair had always wanted to grow up, but for the first time, she suddenly felt old.

As Blair walked east toward Madison, her iPhone rang the

familiar strains of the opening bars of "Moon River."

She pulled it out of her Lanvin hobo, surprised to see an unfamiliar 212 number flash across the display. She pressed talk, her mind bubbling with possibilities. Was it Nate, ditching his parents to meet her for a Per Se dinner?

"This is Blair," she answered curiously.

"Blair Waldorf?" a surprisingly high man's voice repeated on the other end of the phone.

"Yes," Blair said cautiously.

"Miss Waldorf, this is Freddie from Tiffany and Company. We have your order here. We close in an hour," he finished.

Blair racked her brain. "I don't think I ordered anything," Blair began. Unless her father had ordered something for her as a late Christmas present. But he'd already sent her a pair of limited edition snakeskin Christian Louboutins. Besides, she and Harold bonded over shoes or purses, *not* jewelry. Which could only mean that it was a surprise from *Nate*.

"I'll be by in a few minutes," she said eagerly, her hand shooting up in the air to hail a taxi.

"Okay, miss. We're located at—"

"I know where you are," Blair said quickly as she stepped into the first cab that pulled up, stealing it from a harried-looking woman in a chinchilla coat. Blair felt guilty for a moment, but this was an emergency.

"Fifty-seventh and Fifth," she said quickly as the cab peeled away from the curb. Maybe Nate had just *said* his parents were coming home so he could stage an elaborate surprise for her, to show her how truly sorry he was for running away last summer. And a surprise was so sweet—she *loved* surprises, especially when she knew about them.

Naturally.

Blair's heart thudded in anticipation as the cab turned onto Fifth. Outside, the stately doorman buildings of the Upper East Side gradually gave way to the brightly colored window displays of high-end shops. Garlands of greenery were wrapped around streetlamps and light displays were lit up across the avenue. Blair felt like it was Christmas and her birthday and the Barneys warehouse sale rolled into one.

"Here's fine," Blair said as the cab idled in traffic on Fifty-ninth Street. She could walk a few blocks. She handed the driver a ten from her Prada wallet and slipped out the door.

She paused in front of the limestone corner building that housed Tiffany & Co.

A dapper doorman in a three-piece suit pushed the revolving door, and she entered, enjoying the feeling of her Sigerson Morrison boots sinking into the plush carpet. The iconic store was filled with tourists eagerly gawking at the merchandise under thick glass counters. Ordinarily, the bustle would have annoyed her, but she didn't mind today. She liked how everything in the store felt so alive and exciting, as if anything could happen. She marched over to a customer service desk in the left corner of the room.

"Hello, I'm Blair Waldorf," she announced to the tiny man behind the counter. He wore a pink striped French cuffed shirt and a red tie. His robin's egg blue name tag read FREDDIE. "I believe you called me."

"Of course, Miss Waldorf!" he shrieked. He glanced meaningfully over at the beige couches in the corner. Blair followed his gaze, expecting to see Nate. An overweight guy wearing a pink baseball cap on his bald head stood beside two women arguing with each other in French, and a handsome guy in shorts sat with his back to them.

Blair knew only one guy who wore cargo shorts in the winter, as if he simply wasn't affected by the cold. And she'd sort of forgotten that he existed.

"Scout!" Pete looked up and grinned devilishly as he sauntered toward her. It was as if he'd just spotted her across the dining hall.

"Hi," Blair said weakly. It wasn't like she'd *forgotten* about Pete, exactly, but he certainly hadn't been front and center on her radar.

"But what about Costa Rica?" Blair asked, confused. Pete was supposed to be there for another week.

He shrugged and smiled. "I couldn't do it. I needed to be with you. So I got to thinking . . ." Pete smiled as he reached into the pocket of his cargo shorts, removed a blue box, and held it out to her.

"What?" Blair asked, a wave of dizziness hitting her.

"Open it." Pete pushed the box into her hands. Fingers trembling, she opened the Tiffany blue cardboard box to find a small black velvet jewelry box. Blair's heart careened through her chest to the floor.

Was he *proposing*? At Tiffany? She'd imagined this was how she'd get engaged a million times. But in all her fantasies, it wasn't Pete asking her. It was Nate.

She pried open the hinged lid of the box. There, sitting on a bed of blue satin, was a white gold ring. It was circled by tiny pink sapphires that captured the light.

"Is this . . ." Blair began, her fingers trembling.

"It's not an engagement ring," Pete explained hurriedly, reading the shocked expression on Blair's face. "At least not yet.

But I do want you to come on Carlson vacations. I feel like this sort of answers my dad's 'no ring, no bring' rule, don't you?" he asked with an adorably lopsided smile.

Around them, tourists craned their necks to see what was going on. One paunchy man had even pulled out his camera phone and was filming the whole incident. Blair wanted to yell at everyone to go away. She gazed into Pete's ocean blue eyes, unsure of what to do. She knew she didn't want to touch the ring. She couldn't.

"Thanks," she began weakly, forcing a smile at the customers surrounding her. Four years ago, Nate had bought her an ugly gold heart on a plain black cord. She'd hated the necklace. She loved this ring. But somehow, it wasn't to be.

She shut the jewelry box with a deliberate snap. "I can't." Her voice broke on the last word. "I just can't." Then she turned and walked out the revolving door, not looking back to see the heartbroken look on his face.

Breakup at Tiffany's?

# it's not acting if it's the truth

"Cut, cut, cut!" Ken Mogul yelled, his bloodshot blue eyes bugging from his head. He threw his bullhorn down, where it clattered on the soundstage.

It was the last week of filming *Coffee at the Palace*, the much-anticipated sequel to *Breakfast at Fred's*. They were on a set in Queens designed to look like a large New York City hotel penthouse that opened onto a rooftop garden. Thaddeus placed his hands on Serena's tanned shoulders protectively. They'd worked long enough with Ken as a director to know that once he started throwing things, he rarely stopped with one object.

As long as he doesn't move on to the talent, they'll be fine.

"Serena, for fuck's sake, you're supposed to be Holly. Goddamn Holly who's in love with her goddamn husband but is tormented by the memory of her goddamn ex-lover, whom she's supposed to be fucking seeing in five minutes for coffee. Where the holy fucking hell is the *passion*?" Ken screamed, his freckled face turning as red as his curly shoulder-length hair.

"Sorry," Serena sighed, pulling anxiously on the sleeve of her vintage black and white wool Givenchy dress. It had been a long morning. Really, it had been a long *week*. Nate had hardly said two words to Serena at brunch the other day. And the only words Blair had said to her since then were about Nate.

"Okay. Let's start all over again. Take!" Ken screamed loudly, his voice cracking up an octave.

"I *love* you." Serena concentrated on Thad's large, wide-set, *I'm completely gay* eyes. "There's never been anyone else. My dreams didn't lie. Even when I sleep next to you, I dream about you."

"CUT!" Ken shrieked angrily. "You sound like you're talking to your goddamn guinea pig. Who the fuck cares if you love him? I don't. Anyone? Anyone on set?" One timid, owlish-looking assistant raised her hand. Ken held up his clipboard as if he were going to throw it. "Great. Fucking Mousy Girl over there will net our film ten dollars. Off my set!" he yelled theatrically as the terrified-looking assistant scampered away. Ken cradled his head in his hands and sighed.

"You okay?" Thad whispered. Serena nodded, but she could feel beads of anxious sweat creep down her spine. She took a seat on a peach jacquard–covered wingback chair in the corner. A makeup assistant immediately scurried up and dabbed powder on her forehead.

"Okay," Thaddeus whispered. "I think you know me too well. Forget about me and just pretend you're talking to the love of your life. Listen, this is how I would say it if I were talking to Serge." Thad turned toward Serena and closed his eyes.

"There's never been anyone else," Thad began dramatically, opening his eyes once more and gazing at Serena, as if he wasn't sure if she were real or a figment of his imagination. "My dreams didn't lie. Even when I sleep next to you, I dream about you."

Serena pulled her hair into a tight ponytail at the crown of her head. It was sweet of him to try to help, but it was useless. "I don't love anyone that way," she cut him off. In this scene, Holly was supposed to recognize that the only person she really loved was her husband. That, no matter what, and no matter how many stupid things he did, he was the only person who could ever make her feel happy and complete.

She sighed and leaned back into the wingback chair. She wished she, and not her alter ego, Holly, was face-to-face with the man of her dreams. She wished the wind was blowing through her hair and that she was holding a real drink instead of a seltzer mixed with food coloring. She wished she was out on a sailboat, in the middle of the deep navy ocean, under the wide blue sky, with him.

She wished she was with Nate.

Serena felt a sob rise in her throat.

"Don't worry about the scene for right now. Is everything okay?" Thaddeus asked in concern as he perched on the arm of her chair.

"Okay, princesses, teatime's over. Let's work. My sanity's at stake." Ken rolled his eyes.

Serena stood up, crossed toward the camera, and blinked at what was supposed to be the Hudson River in front of her. She imagined Nate, far away, on a sailboat, a tiny dot in the middle of the ocean. She turned her head, her chin grazing her tanned, bare shoulder. "I love you. I always have." She brushed a lock of hair out of Thaddeus's eyes, the way she used to after she'd hugged a sweaty and disheveled Nate when he'd just won a St. Jude's lacrosse game. "I'd never leave you. Sometimes I wake up and I think I must be dreaming. I love you so much. Just—

make me the happiest girl ever and love me back." A single tear trickled down her cheek. "Please?"

"And, cut!" Ken stood up, waving his stubby hands wildly in excitement. "Fucking brilliant, Serena. Love the way you went off script there. You put me through the fucking wringer so you can show that shit off? That's my girl!" He grabbed Serena's waist and awkwardly spun her around. "We've got a fucking hit on our hands if you keep it up. Now, let's get back into the next scene. Coast on this moment of brilliance."

Serena shook her head definitively. She needed to say those words to the one person who mattered. She needed to find Nate. Maybe he was in love with Blair. But she couldn't *ever* be happy unless he knew how she felt.

"I can't!" Serena told him. She didn't care if she got fired. Who *cared* about Holly? Serena's life was real. And it was time she stopped pretending.

"'Bye!" She called, nearly tripping as she ran outside into the cold January afternoon.

Who doesn't love a Hollywood ending?

# *b's surprise, take two*

*"I have to leave you now. I'm going to that corner there and turn. You must stay in the car and drive away. Promise me not to watch me go beyond the corner. Just drive away and leave me as I leave you."* On-screen, Audrey Hepburn, as Princess Anne in *Roman Holiday*, turned away from Gregory Peck. The camera zoomed to Gregory, who was eyeing her with a mix of sorrow and awe and sadness on his face. Blair pressed rewind and watched as Gregory's face built itself back up.

She sighed. It was so romantic and clean the way Princess Anne broke up with him. She felt bad for Gregory—and Pete—but, like Audrey, she'd known it was the right thing to do. There was no way she and Pete could be together when she and Nate had always been destined for each other. Pete had been a charming distraction, but he wasn't her leading man.

Blair turned off the TV and glanced down at her Rolex. It was almost eight. Nate should be back from Le Cirque, where he'd been forced to attend dinner with his parents before they went off to the opera. And Serena probably wouldn't be back from rehearsal for hours.

She dialed Nate's number. "Are you home yet?" she demanded.

"Yeah, my parents actually—"

"Great. I'll be over in ten minutes," Blair said. She was having a serious Nate craving, especially now that there was *nothing* to keep them apart.

She rummaged through Serena's closet and found a long Dries van Noten black tunic that looked like it had never been worn. Knowing Serena, it probably hadn't. She pulled it on over a pair of gray Wolford stockings, then eased her feet into her slouchy black Frye boots. She pulled on a gray beret, slung her large Lanvin hobo bag over her shoulder, and ran out.

Snow was beginning to fall, and Blair wished she'd worn a coat as she walked the familiar path from Serena's limestone building on Eighty-third and Fifth to Nate's stately town house on Eighty-second and Park. Blair gingerly picked her way up the icy steps and pressed the button for Nate's room, relieved that he had his own private doorbell.

The buzzer rang to allow her in, and Blair gingerly pushed the door open, inhaling the entryway's familiar scent of floor polish and lilacs. Everything—the Van Gogh above the mantle, the austere chandelier in the main dining room, the white marble kitchen—looked exactly like it had since she'd first started coming to Nate's house when she was five. She took the stairs two at a time and burst into Nate's bedroom.

"Hey!" Nate was seated at his desk in front of his Mac Air. He wore the moss green sweater Blair had given him in high school. Back then, she'd secretly sewn a gold heart pendant into the inside—the same gold heart he'd given her from Tiffany—so Nate would always be wearing her heart on his sleeve. "I have a surprise for you," Nate said, swiveling in his Eames chair to face her.

"Really?" Blair asked uncertainly, tugging her hat off and shaking her hair out around her shoulders. She'd had enough surprises for the day.

Nate grinned. He couldn't wait to tell Blair what he'd decided. He hooked his fingers underneath the sweater and pulled it up.

"*That's* the surprise?" Blair rolled her eyes, even though she got a little excited at the sight of Nate's taut, tanned abs.

"No, look!" Nate yanked the sweater over his head to reveal a white T-shirt with a navy blue Yale insignia.

Blair gasped. He was coming back to school with her? This was *way* better than any ring. "Oh, Nate!" she exclaimed, throwing her arms around his neck.

Nate smiled happily. He couldn't believe it had taken him so long to realize that he and Blair were meant to be together. Sure, she could be a pain in the ass, but she was *his* pain in the ass. And after his conversation with Chuck the other night, college suddenly seemed like a good option. He couldn't sail around the world forever.

"I don't want to say goodbye to you again. Maybe I can even get placed in your dorm." He grinned. He still couldn't believe how easy the decision had been.

"I'll arrange everything," Blair said matter-of-factly. She couldn't believe how, after her shitstorm of a year, her life had *finally* settled down. Everything was perfectly in place. "We'll get an apartment together. Then we can have a huge party and I'll introduce you to everyone!"

Blair ran her hands over the Yale insignia across his strong chest. "I love you, Nate," she whispered.

Looks like someone got a Bulldog for Christmas.

# les liaisons dangereuses: upper west side edition

Vanessa slammed down the top of her MacBook Pro in frustration. It was now totally dark outside, and she'd spent the past two hours sitting at the laminate counter in the Humphreys' kitchen, Googling Hollis. She'd found out he ran track in high school, that his mom was a sociology and gender studies professor at UCLA, his dad was a pioneer in philanthropic microlending to developing countries, and that he'd won several film contests as an undergrad. He'd also showed up in a couple Tribeca Film Festival party photos, above the caption "The Sexy Side of Celluloid."

She couldn't stop thinking about him. She wondered what his bedroom looked like and if he had a girlfriend and what he was doing now. And, of course, what he thought of the kiss.

*The kiss.*

It shouldn't have happened. Vanessa knew that. She'd immediately broken it off and run all the way down the four flights of stairs and hailed a cab. It wasn't until she was halfway home that she'd realized she'd left her video camera at his apartment. She'd sent him a quick e-mail asking him to drop it off at the

Cantor Film Center, where she'd pick it up next semester, but hadn't heard anything back. Which was a good thing. Maybe Hollis regretted the kiss just as much as she did. After all, Dan would be back in a few days—back for good. They were about to start a new life together. Entertaining a crush on her former TA was *not* a promising start.

The loud screech of the buzzer yanked Vanessa out of her reverie. She slid off the steel stool and ran over to the ancient intercom system.

"Hello?" she asked curiously. Maybe it was one of Rufus's Beat poet friends. They sometimes stopped by without warning.

"Vanessa?" a gravelly voice asked. *Hollis.* Fuck. Why had he come here? Was he stalking her?

Asks the girl who's spent the entire afternoon on a Googlefest.

"Hey," Vanessa said. She tried to sound casual, but it came out more like a bark.

"I have your camera. Buzz me up?" Hollis yelled into the intercom. Vanessa looked around in panic. The general level of cleanliness of the Humphrey apartment always hovered somewhere between dusty and disastrous, and it was closer to the disastrous end of the spectrum today. With Rufus and Dan away, Vanessa had gotten lazy. There were half-empty mugs of tea everywhere, her clothes created a messy trail from the living room to the bedroom, and she was in her pj's, a cut-up black sweatshirt and boy shorts.

She quickly ran into the bathroom and combed her fingers through her short black hair. Right now, the back was misbehaving, turning up in a little ducktail no matter how many times she smoothed it down. She frowned as she noticed a deodorant stain on the outside edge of her sweatshirt. She hurriedly threw the sweatshirt on the floor and ran into her bedroom. She rifled through the dresser drawer and picked out a gray long-sleeve thermal T-shirt and an old Marc by Marc Jacobs jean skirt she'd co-opted from Blair Waldorf during the few weeks they'd been roommates the year before. She just finished buttoning the skirt when she heard a knock on the door.

She swung open the door and stood in the entrance. Hollis wore a messenger cap and square Prada glasses. His gray eyes looked slightly tired, like he hadn't gotten a good night's sleep in a few days.

Vanessa grinned firmly, but kept her body wedged in the doorframe. It probably wasn't a good idea to let him inside.

"Ever heard of e-mail?" she challenged, crossing her arms over her chest. In her haste to get ready, she hadn't put on a bra, and hoped it wasn't obvious.

Hollis grinned. Vanessa tore her eyes away from his broad, easy smile. "Hey yourself, Cinderella."

"Sorry about that," Vanessa apologized. It must have seemed pretty weird when she'd run away at the stroke of midnight.

Hollis gently brushed past her and into the apartment, surveying the surroundings. A large abstract charcoal portrait Jenny had done of Dan and Rufus hung above the lumpy, mustard-yellow couch. "So, this is your place." The way Hollis said it, she couldn't tell if he was making fun of her.

"Sort of," Vanessa said defensively. "I mean, I live with my friend's family."

Doesn't she mean *boy*friend's family?

"For some reason I always thought you were a Williamsburg girl." Hollis shrugged off his coat and hung it over the back of one of the rickety wooden chairs in the kitchen. He walked over to the floor-to-ceiling bookshelf in the corner and squinted at the book spines.

"Um, I used to live in Brooklyn," Vanessa said nervously. What was her *problem*? Even Jenny at her most awkward would have had more poise. "Anyway, do you want something to eat?" she asked lamely. She needed something to do besides stare at Hollis.

She opened the fridge. There was a half-eaten tub of hummus that had turned an odd green color, a coagulation of some sort of stew, three cans of a strange red Bavarian beer Rufus liked, and a mysterious protein shake. "Scratch that!" Vanessa hastily slammed the door shut. "Do you want to go out and get a drink? Or a snack? The diner on the corner has really good cheese fries," she babbled.

"I hope you don't mind, but I watched the footage on your camera," Hollis said, ignoring her nervous chatter. "It's really fucking good, Abrams."

Vanessa blinked in confusion. Hollis sounded like her TA again. Had the kiss even *happened*?

"Can we watch it together? I'd love to talk to you about it," he prodded.

"Sure. Sorry it's a mess." Vanessa pushed open the door to Dan's room and kicked a pile of dirty laundry away. She awkwardly stuck her hands in the pockets of her skirt. Dan's bags from Evergreen were stacked against the wall, and the bed hadn't been made. She knew she should feel weird about having Hollis in the apartment, but it was really hard to think about Dan when she could sense Hollis's eyes on her, watching her every move.

"I like it here. You saw my apartment, and that was before complete party carnage. I'm twenty-five and I live in a shithole." Hollis busied himself with attaching the camera cables to the computer, then sat on the edge of the bed expectantly. He took off his hat and ran a hand through his thick jet-black hair.

"Okay," Vanessa muttered, pressing play. She took a seat on the floor, as far away from Hollis as possible. The screen sprang to life, panning out from a MetroCard stuck to the floor of the subway car to a homeless man on the plastic orange seats, surrounded by all of his belongings, peacefully reading a book.

Next, the camera zoomed wildly, capturing the faces of people as they were rushing to the subway. Hollis sat up. "This is my favorite part."

"Really?" Vanessa asked, flattered. He'd critiqued her work before, but this felt so much more *personal*.

The bedroom setting can have that effect.

"Yeah. But sometimes you're so removed. I just want to know more about your subjects. Why you chose them. Who they are," Hollis mused as the camera jump-cut from an old lady feeding pigeons in Union Square to a group of revelers spilling out from the subway.

Vanessa continued to watch as the camera shakily followed two girls wearing matching silver sequined dresses trip up the First Avenue L station stairs. From their backs, you couldn't tell how old they were. They looked like they were searching for danger.

Hollis tenderly cupped Vanessa's chin and pulled her into him. "This is what I've been wanting to do since the party," he whispered. She felt his stubble against her cheek. They weren't kissing, but their lips were millimeters apart. Vanessa leaned in, and her lips touched his.

Cut!

"We've had a great day together, haven't we, sonny?" The truck driver, whose real name was Hank, asked as he rested his beefy arm on Dan's shoulder. The truck pulled onto the West Side Highway.

*Yeah, right,* Dan thought. The whole time, Hank had given Dan life lessons on women. "You can just drop me off at Ninety-sixth Street," Dan said hurriedly. "Actually, here's fine." Close enough.

"Okay," Hank said, looking disappointed as he reached over Dan to open the door of the truck.

"Thanks!" Dan yelled as he slung his duffel bag over his shoulder and began making his way to his apartment three blocks up. New York was freezing, but the air felt redemptive. He felt like he could run up a mountain.

He bounded up the stairs two at a time. Maybe it *had* been the outdoor air, but he barely felt winded as he reached the fifth-floor landing outside the apartment. Or maybe it was the fact that, unlike his roommate at Evergreen, who'd hooked up with almost every girl in the Victoria Woodhull Vegan Womyn's Co-Op, Dan would never have to go through his life uncertain that he was loved and in love. He dug into his khakis and found his keys, held on a simple lanyard key chain that Jenny had made one summer at craft camp.

He opened the door and heard the muted sound of a film playing in Vanessa's room. He couldn't *wait* to see her face when he surprised her.

"Honey, I'm hooooome!" Dan called eagerly. He cracked a grin at how simple and lovely the phrase sounded. He swung the door to his bedroom open.

"Dan!" Vanessa was lying on his bed, naked save for her red boy shorts with black X's all over them. But she wasn't alone. She was with a guy. An equally naked guy.

Dan gaped, unsure of what was going on. Was this a bad joke or a dream or some weird sweat lodge vision?

Vanessa scrambled out of bed and stood up, holding the blue flannel duvet around her body. "I can explain," she stuttered helplessly. Her face was flushed, her lips looked red and bee-stung, and her dark eyes were wide and confused.

"Who the fuck is that?" Dan heard himself asking. He felt like he was a character in one of those lame romantic comedies that Jenny loved. In just a second he'd find out that this wasn't Vanessa, but her long-lost twin, who'd sneaked into the Humphreys' house to hide her boyfriend from the Feds.

Right.

"I'll leave you guys alone," Hollis said bluntly. He shrugged his shoulders and pulled on his T-shirt. He shot Vanessa one last, long look, and then stalked out of the bedroom and out the front door.

Vanessa felt rooted to the spot. She wanted to run after Hollis, and she wanted to comfort Dan, all at once. This was very bad.

The understatement of the year.

Dan could feel the tears beginning to well up in his hazel eyes. He felt his heart clench. Was this what having a heart attack felt like?

He looked around for something to throw. He needed to hear

something shattering, because that was what his heart was doing right now. He picked up Vanessa's video camera and hurled it, as hard as he could, against the opposite wall. Instead of breaking, it bounced onto the floor, then rolled under the bed.

Art *is* indestructible.

"Fuck you," Dan shouted. "And by the way, you can't live here anymore!"

He stormed out of the room and through the front door of his apartment, slamming the door behind him, and hurtled down the fire stairs. His hands were shaking. He was *home*, but he felt further away from anything he'd ever known.

Sometimes home is where the heart breaks.

# that's what makes *b* a fighter

"Here's good!" Serena announced to her driver as the Lincoln Town Car sailed past Nate's limestone town house on Eighty-second. Normally, Serena was embarrassed that her agent demanded she be provided a town car for transportation to and from *Coffee at the Palace* shoots, but today, she was thankful that she could easily slip away from the soundstage.

"Sure thing," the driver said easily.

Serena slipped out of the car and bounded up the snowy steps of Nate's town house. As she ran, she didn't notice the fresh set of footprints on the snow leading up to the door.

She yanked off her ugly red Hermès goatskin driving gloves, a gift from her chain-smoking LA publicist, and stuffed them in the terra-cotta planter sitting to the left of the entrance. She pressed Nate's buzzer with her red polished fingernails. It was dark outside, and the freshly falling snow made Serena feel nostalgic. Always on the first snowfall of the year, she, Blair, and Nate would meet for hot chocolate, then sit on the steps of the Met, not caring how cold it was. Maybe she and Nate could go there tonight.

"Hello?" Nate's voice sounded sleepy. Had she woken him up? Not really.

"Natie!" she yelled into the intercom, trying to calm herself. She didn't want to just burst in his room and profess her love. "It's me and it's freezing!"

"Serena?" His crackly voice sounded incredulous through the intercom.

"No, silly, it's your mom. Of course it's me!" she said impatiently.

"Oh." Nate paused and Serena held her breath. She didn't have another script to follow. Nate *had* to let her in. "Come in," he said finally, pressing the buzzer long and loud.

Serena pulled open the door, ran up the stairs, and burst into Nate's bedroom. One of the best things about Nate's house was the fact that the third floor was entirely his. When they were younger, they used to pretend his bedroom, den, and bathroom were their own private apartment.

Some people *still* like playing house.

"Hello?" Serena called again, hearing her voice bounce off the dark oak ceiling.

Nate walked out of the bathroom, wearing a wrinkled green T-shirt and green plaid boxers. Serena looked gorgeous and healthy and happy, all in one spectacular package. He was suddenly very aware of the fact that Blair was still showering. "What are you doing here?" Nate asked. Blair had said Serena was at rehearsal all day.

"I was just in the neighborhood!" Serena wandered over to his dresser and picked up a model sailboat. She passed it gently from hand to hand as if playing a game of catch with herself. "So, what have you been up to today? It's freezing."

"Not much," Nate mumbled. How long had Blair been in the shower? Ten minutes, fifteen minutes? She usually took forever, but he wasn't sure how much time he had.

To do what, exactly?

Nate felt confused. Just as he'd always felt whenever he was with Serena and Blair at the same time. Why did they have to be so confusing? He loved Blair. He was following Blair to school, for God's sake. So then why did Serena, with her deep blue eyes that reminded him of the Pacific Ocean and her long limbs, tight and taut like the strings of a tennis racket, make him feel . . . well, make him feel the way he felt right now.

Serena put down the tiny sailboat model and picked up another, larger ship with three tiny canvas sails. Ever since she could remember, Nate had been obsessed with sailboats. She knew she was avoiding what she really wanted to say, but now that she was here, there were so many emotions bubbling inside her, she wasn't sure where to begin.

"You know, we're supposed to wrap *Coffee at the Palace* next week. After that, I don't have any projects. My parents were hoping I'd start at Yale in the spring, but I think I need an adventure." She felt her heart hammering in her chest. "Are you going sailing again? Maybe I could come," she offered, her face breaking into a sunny smile.

"It's not that much of an adventure. A lot of knot tying," Nate said nonsensically. He knew he should explain that he and Blair were together now, and that he was going to Yale with her, but he couldn't. Instead, he imagined what it would be like on the ocean with Serena.

"I like tying knots. I showed you how to tie your shoes when we were kids, remember? Take me along. I can be first mate!

Aye, aye, Captain!" Serena goofily did a mock salute, her dark eyes looking straight into Nate's glittering green ones. *Please say yes*, she willed.

"Like that would ever happen." Blair strode out of the bathroom, wearing just a towel wrapped around her body, her chestnut hair damp around her shoulders. "Nate and I are going to Yale, *together*," she added, narrowing her eyes. Why the fuck was Serena here? And had she really just asked Nate what Blair thought she had? Was she inviting herself to sail the world with him?

Serena felt like she'd been punched in the gut. Of course Blair had been eavesdropping from the bathroom this whole time. Of course she was here, watching over Nate's every move, not letting him out of her sight. Of course they were riding off into the sunset together. "How does your boyfriend feel about that?" she muttered under her breath.

Blair narrowed her icy blue eyes. "*What* did you say?"

Serena crossed her arms over her chest and glared at Blair. If Blair wanted a fight, fine, she'd give it to her. She wasn't going to let Blair get away with stealing Nate.

Again.

"I said," Serena repeated coolly, making sure to enunciate each word, "What. Does. Your. *Boyfriend*. Think. About. That?"

"Boyfriend?" Nate asked moronically, looking between the two girls as if he were watching a tennis match. Blair had a *boyfriend*?

"I don't have a boyfriend. How would Serena know, anyway?" Blair challenged.

"I don't know, because you wouldn't stop talking about him the other day? You know, after you spent Christmas with him and all?" Serena said sarcastically.

Nate glanced between the two of them in disbelief. Out on the ocean with Chips, they could always tell a storm was coming by the change in the air. It was the same with Serena and Blair. He could feel a change in the room, as if a palpable electric charge was emanating from the girls' skin.

"Serena, just get your own fucking life," Blair snapped. "You know nothing about me." Her white Egyptian cotton towel was askew, and blotches of pink appeared on her pale neck. She looked like she was ready to claw Serena's eyes out.

Uh-oh.

"Oh, please. You think you can just have whatever you want, whenever you want." Serena's voice had taken on a slightly hysterical edge.

Instead of speaking, Blair hurled a Mason Pearson hairbrush at Serena. Because Blair had terrible aim, she missed, creating a dent in the wall. The brush clattered onto Nate's dresser and hit one of the sailboat models, splintering it into pieces.

"I can't do this," Nate yelled, surprising himself. His voice echoed in his head. "You two always fight. I never should have come back. I'm leaving. Don't look for me." He grabbed a few pairs of clean boxers from his dresser, tossed them in the duffel he hadn't bothered unpacking since the *Belinda*, and stalked down the hallway.

"Nate, wait!" Serena yelled, running behind him.

"Nate!" Blair called at the same time, racing after Serena.

The door slammed, leaving Blair and Serena alone.

Blair glared at Serena. "We're no longer friends," she spat. Then she turned on her heel and followed Nate down the hall and out the door to the stairs that led to the street.

"Good!" Serena retorted. She knew she sounded like an

angry four-year-old whose best friend has stolen her favorite toy.

Familiar story.

Serena collapsed on Nate's bed and stared up at the ceiling. The skylight window up above was covered with pure white snow. She wanted to cry, but no tears fell. Instead, she seethed. Everything that had ever gone wrong in her life was Blair's fault.

Happy fucking New Year!

# II

Disclaimer: *All the real names of places, people, and events have been altered or abbreviated to protect the innocent. Namely, me.*

| topics | sightings | your e-mail | post a question |

# hey people!

As we've all learned by now, the etymology of the word *sophomore* comes from the Greek words *sophos*, meaning "wise," and *moros*, meaning "foolish." It's a contradictory term for a contradictory year: We've learned that pizza and PBR don't mix with our favorite skinny jeans, that a TA can be extremely hot if we look past his dorky collection of PBS tote bags, and that placing a kegerator in the common area of your dorm does not constitute a design decision. But we still have a lot to figure out.

Take, for example, **N**, who's displaying a lot of sophomoric tendencies despite his official class year. Last year, he may have toyed with the idea of attending Yale, but as a tussle between **B** and **S** became his own personal crash course in conflict, he realized that he might be better off with just boys—at least for now. He's now a first year at Deep Springs College, an all-male two-year academy on a working alfalfa farm in California. To each his own. . . .

For many, the key to figuring out your future is determining whom you want to spend it with. Case in point: **B**. She and her boyfriend, **P**, patched things up quickly after their Tiffany fallout last year, and are now happily ensconced in their Chapel Street town house. But what will happen to their cozy domesticity once **P** graduates in the spring? Or consider **V**. Her boyfriend, **H**, may have wowed the critics at Cannes, but Hollywood hasn't gone to his head—he's often spotted picking up **V**'s favorite

Hummus Place order while she studies late in Bobst Library. How sweet. Or, um, salty.

On the other hand, you could do some soul-searching and find that the only person you want to spend time with is *you*. Take **S**, who's often curled up with a cappuccino and Kant at Doma Cafe around the corner from her Perry Street apartment. Or our favorite shaggy-haired poet, **D**, surrounded by plenty of girls in his Columbia poetry seminars, but always leaving campus solo. After all, the most important thing you learn about in college might just be yourself.

### sightings

**B**, with her boyfriend, **P**, at **LAX**. After a sunny West Coast holiday, is the happy couple headed back our way? **D** shuffling from his apartment up to the **Columbia** campus, muttering to himself and chain-smoking Camels. Still playing the tortured artist, or has he really lost it? **V** and **H** at a Miramax holiday party, talking to a *New York* reporter about **V**'s decorating plans for **H**'s brand-new **Williamsburg** loft. And the biggest transformation award goes to? **S** at **Doma** (again!), reading *Civilization and Its Discontents* and looking pretty discontent herself. Research for a role, or is someone having a little slump of her own? **D**'s little sister, **J**, at **JFK**, boarding a flight to **Paris**—Bonne Année! **N** in flannel, hitching a ride to Eastern Sierra Regional Airport, his green eyes glinting with tears. Why so sad, **N**?

### your e-mail

q: Dear Gossip Girl,
I'm a sophomore womyn who's always dated other womyn. I had a sense my last girlfriend was more of a BUG—you know, a bisexual until graduation, which is one of those acronyms I hate, but it's become so accepted in popular society that at least

people are talking about it. Anyway, this BUG not only broke up with me, but she's dating this dumb football player who I know for a fact always defaces our womyn's center posters. Should I stage an intervention?

—stilllove

a: Dear Still Love,

I'm sorry to hear about your romantic woes, but if your ex is just a bug to you, then maybe she wasn't worth it to begin with. Instead of postering for the womyn's center, post a personal ad. Who knows what will happen!

—GG

q: Dear Gossip Girl,

There's a guy in my poetry class who's that tortured, soulful type—the kind of guy who's too busy being an artist to even think about things like food. I've only seen him ingest instant coffee and cigarettes, which I think is cute, but my suitemates find creepy. What do you think?

—hotforsoulful

a: Dear HFS,

Sounds like this particular soul may be in mourning for a muse. My advice: Tortured artists rarely make stable partners. Instead, find a happy-go-lucky communications major and *read* poetry to each other.

—GG

**ready, set, go . . . again**

One of the best things about being in school is the opportunity to have two fresh starts a year. There's September, with the new housing assignments, new books, and new professors; it's the start of the academic year. But January 1 is a golden do-over opportunity. And some of us just might need a do-over. Here's to second chances.

You know you love me,

gossip girl

# *you never can say goodbye*

"You okay, son?" Captain Archibald placed a firm hand on Nate's shoulder outside All Souls Church on Lexington Avenue. Around them, patrons were spilling out of the church onto the cold stone steps. White lilies were set up around the entrance of the church as if for a celebration, not a funeral.

"I'm fine," Nate muttered, though he was anything but fine. His Brooks Brothers blazer was too tight across his shoulders, and his sky-blue Hermès tie felt like it was choking him. It didn't feel right to be dressed like this, it didn't feel right to be back in New York, and it definitely didn't feel right to be at Chips's funeral. He couldn't believe Chips was *dead*. He'd had cancer and hadn't even bothered to tell Nate he'd been sick. He'd been slowly dying for months now in Lenox Hill Hospital and hadn't bothered to call, or e-mail, or even send a letter.

Nate hadn't planned to come back to New York for the holidays. He'd been at Deep Springs College for the past eight months, trying to sort his mind out. He'd thought he'd done that with Chips on the *Belinda*. That he had a handle on who he was and what he wanted from life. That Serena and Blair wouldn't confuse him as much as they had before.

But nothing could have been further than the truth. After he saw them fighting, it was all too apparent that he could never be around them anymore. There were too many feelings, too much history, too many swirling emotions. It practically killed him that he was the one who'd caused all the problems in their friendship.

He'd immediately run to his parents' vacation home on Mt. Desert Island, Maine, and it was there, sitting on the beach and watching the waves roll in, that he thought of Chuck and his transformation from a monkey-toting metrosexual to a decent-seeming dude. Immediately, he'd called Deep Springs and interviewed for a spot for spring semester. Because all the students of Deep Springs sat on the admissions committee, and all had a tremendous amount of respect for Chuck—and because Nate was consistently lucky—he'd gotten in.

Since then, he'd done a total one-eighty. Deep Springs was intense and unlike anything he'd ever experienced. Thirty guys living in one house, studying and working the farm together. No girls. No pot. No drinking. No drama.

Sounds, um, fun!

Maybe it was because the schedule sort of reminded him of his life aboard the *Belinda* with Chips, but he liked waking up at 5 a.m. to milk the cows, then heading to the old-fashioned one-room schoolhouse to discuss Plato. He'd always half-assed it in high school, so this was the first time he'd ever really *tried* to study and learn. It was surprisingly satisfying. It was sort of like what Chips had taught him: that you have to own the work before you can own yourself. Chips had given him a ton of good advice. And now he was gone.

Nate sighed in frustration. It turned out he'd known he had cancer the whole time they were aboard the *Belinda*. Nate thought of the days they spent exploring the world, docking on islands that seemed almost untouched by man. Days spent at sea so far out you couldn't see land, methodically fishing. Of their quiet dinners on board, where they ate their daily catch and contemplated the multicolored sunset. He'd had all the time, all the opportunities in the world—why hadn't Chips said anything? His father squeezed his shoulder in a gesture of solidarity. Chips had been the Captain's mentor as well.

"Thanks for coming," Captain Archibald said, shaking hands with Chuck, who had been standing at a respectful distance. Nate and Chuck had become close this year, and when he heard the news about Chips, Chuck had insisted that he come with Nate, for moral support.

"Well . . ." The Captain trailed off uncomfortably, shifting from one tan leather Gucci loafer to another. "I'll be off now. You'll be all right?" he asked, as if unsure whether it was okay to leave.

"I'll be fine," Nate said stiffly. He looked down and realized his knuckles were white from gripping the iron railing. He loosened his grip and held out his hand. The Archibald men weren't huggers. His dad took his hand, but instead of shaking it, gave it a gentle squeeze before turning crisply on his heel, heading down the stairs and up the avenue. There was hardly any traffic today, as if out of respect for the dead.

"You okay, man?" Chuck asked, clasping Nate's shoulder. Nate nodded, glad that Chuck had insisted on coming with him. In a crisp charcoal Turnbull and Asser suit with a white handkerchief in his breast pocket, Chuck looked like he had back in high school, but he still acted like the guy Nate had come to think of as his best friend at Deep Springs.

Nate squeezed his green eyes shut, hoping when he opened them he'd discover he'd been dreaming during one of his daily naps in the cow barn. But when he opened his eyes, he saw the dark, overcast sky, hovering above the Upper East Side rooftops. The clouds looked ominous, ready to unleash a torrent of hail that would destroy the white lilies outside the church.

A tear begin to trickle down the side of Nate's nose. He squinted to try to stop the flow, but it was no use.

"Fuck it." He roughly wiped his eyes with the back of his hand.

"Dude, you okay?" Chuck pulled his gold Gucci aviators out of his pocket and handed them to Nate. "You're crying," he remarked, unnecessarily but not unkindly.

"Thanks, man. It's just a lot. . . ." Nate's voice cracked. Chuck had been surprisingly thoughtful this trip, but he hadn't known Chips, and Nate felt like this was something he needed to handle on his own.

"Are you Nathaniel?" A tiny, elderly woman wearing a pink tweed St. John's suit wobbled from the church entrance toward him on a pair of black Prada pumps.

Nate nodded. Did he know this lady?

"Well, aren't you handsome," she mused, smiling broadly as if they'd met at a charity event and not outside a funeral.

"Thanks," Nate grunted. He was used to women of all ages commenting on his looks. It was just a fact of his life, like the fact he liked to sail and was naturally good at lacrosse.

Hey, it's not bragging if it's true.

"You know, Charles never had a son. I see why he took a

shine to you. I'm his sister, Nan. He and I had our differences, but I won't speak ill of the dead," she clucked as she reached into her ivory-colored Chanel purse. "This is for you," she said, thrusting a thick, ivory-colored envelope in his hand. "And, of course, you're invited to the small luncheon I'm having for friends. It's at my apartment. Shall I give you the address?" she asked expectantly.

"I'm afraid—I can't attend," Nate said haltingly, hoping he wasn't being rude. All he wanted to do was go home, curl up in his bed, and shut the world out. He wondered if he had any pot knotted in a black dress sock stuffed in the back of his top drawer. He hadn't wanted to smoke in ages, but right now he wanted to enter a deep pot-induced haze and never come out.

Nan gazed at Nate quizzically. Deep crinkles appeared around the edges of her blue eyes, eyes that if he looked at from a certain angle, reminded him of Chips's. "Of course. Good luck, son," she added as she tottered away on her high heels.

"Thanks." Nate regarded the wrinkled cream-colored envelope quizzically. A wet snowflake landed on the envelope, smearing the *N* in his name. Now it looked more like *Fate*.

"Ready to get out of here?" he asked Chuck as he marched down the wide stone steps. He wondered if he could get a flight back to California tonight. "I think I'm going back to the airport. See if I can get back to Deep Springs," Nate explained as they waited for the light to cross Lexington.

Chuck looked at him skeptically. There was a glimmer of how he used to look back in high school, whenever someone suggested leaving a party. "Are you sure about that?"

Nate stiffened, balling his hands in his jacket pockets. "Yes," he said firmly. There was no one in New York he wanted to see. New York was bad for him—full of past mistakes and regrets.

In little black dresses.

The light changed and they crossed the street. "It's New Year's Eve. No way will you be able to get out of here. Just stay a couple days." Chuck pointed out, trailing behind him across Eightieth Street. Snow was beginning to stick to the street, blanketing the city in a thin layer of white. "Besides, I'm having a party."

Nate stopped in the middle of the sidewalk and turned to Chuck. Didn't he get it? He'd just been at the funeral of someone who'd meant a lot to him, and all Chuck could talk about was a party? "I don't party anymore," Nate said flatly.

"Too busy feeling sorry for yourself?" Chuck asked, briefly losing his patience.

Nate narrowed his green eyes. Chuck sounded like Chips. Nate could almost conjure the salt-sea air, standing on the deck of the *Belinda*, Chips angrily waving his tumbler of scotch out to an uncaring ocean. "Come on!" Chuck said, slapping Nate on the back as if to force him to buck up.

Chuck put hailed a cab. "You're coming with me," he commanded, pushing Nate into the backseat.

Aye, aye, Captain!

# bohemian like them

"Is that it? Or was that just your winter-into-spring wardrobe? At least summer into fall might be slightly lighter." Hollis wiped his brow theatrically and plopped down on the red hemp-fiber sewn couch. He sighed in exhaustion, as if he'd nearly broken his back. Really, all he'd done was help Vanessa carry her two suitcases of worldly possessions into the new Williamsburg apartment.

The new apartment, on the *right* side of the sugar factory this time. In a brand-new luxury building with a *concierge*. "Shut up!" Vanessa teased, perching on the overstuffed taupe ottoman across from him.

After Dan had kicked her out of the Humphreys' last year, Vanessa had felt lost and heartbroken. Not to mention very, very guilty. Everything with Hollis had happened so quickly, she didn't really have time to think about it; they had kissed once, and then they had kissed again, and then suddenly there was Dan, watching it all happen. After he told Vanessa that he never wanted to see her again, a tiny part of her had died. But there was nothing she could do to change what had happened. She had to look forward, not back. With nowhere else to turn, she'd called Hollis. They'd slowly gotten to know each other over long nights of falafel, cheap red wine, and Vanessa with no place to crash except Hollis's bed.

For the last year, she'd spent most nights at Hollis's Alphabet City apartment. But technically she resided in a curtained-off corner of the living room of a Bushwick apartment with Mackenzie and Rhiannon, two girls from NYU. It was a far cry from what she now called home: an eighteen-hundred-square-foot glass and exposed-brick apartment with its own elevator, black-stained wood floors, and a winding staircase that connected a sleeping loft to the sprawling main living area. It was incredible. She and Hollis had been planning to move in together after her lease was up on December 31, but she hadn't expected an apartment so . . .

"It's so *big* here," Vanessa said, her voice echoing off the still-bare walls. Hollis had hired a decorator to furnish the apartment with the basics, but neither of them had put up any artwork yet. She couldn't wait to find cool prints and stills together to put on the walls, and really make it their own. For now, she just wanted to run around the loft in her socks. Because she could.

That's one way to dial down the maturity level.

It was all like a fairy tale, with Hollis as her indie prince. He hadn't even told her how expensive it was, assuring Vanessa that her tiny contribution to the rent from her student job working in the digital film archives at school would more than cover her share.

At first, Vanessa had protested. It felt so terribly cliché. She was practically a kept woman! Although it wasn't her fault Hollis's film *Between the B and the A,* a coming-of-age story about a twenty-one-year-old's spiritual journey, had been the darling at Sundance and a surprise indie hit the summer before. It was pretty obvious he wasn't exactly living off a TA salary anymore. And Hollis had countered Vanessa's protests by explaining that his success was her success and vice versa. They were a team. Even though it was sort of corny, she couldn't help but swoon a little.

She wandered over to the large arching windows, where she could just make out the East River rushing by in the distance. She could hear Williamsburg denizens on the sidewalk below, just getting started on their New Year's Eve festivities. Vanessa was happy she and Hollis weren't going out.

There are plenty of ways to have fun staying *in*.

Hollis hoisted himself up from the couch and wrapped his strong, lean arms around her. Vanessa smiled and leaned back into him, feeling safe and protected. Before Hollis, she'd always been a teenager dating other teenagers. Even when she and Dan were serious, it had always felt to her like they were still so young, still so unformed. But now, Vanessa felt like an adult. And she was surprised by how much she liked that feeling.

"What are you thinking?" Hollis murmured in her ear.

"That I'm happy." Vanessa tilted her chin up to kiss him, enjoying the way his slight stubble scratched her chin.

"I'm happy too," Hollis said, pulling her in closer.

"And I'm hungry." Vanessa pulled away, breaking the mood. She was in love, but Vanessa Abrams was never going to be sappy about it.

And we love her for it.

Vanessa skidded on her socked feet toward the kitchen and pulled open the Sub-Zero refrigerator, which was stocked with osetra caviar, Cristal champagne, and other presents from talent agents, producers, and A-list directors.

"Champagne?" Vanessa handed one of the bottles to Hollis. "And then can we order from Sea? I'm in the mood for Thai." She watched him expertly open the bottle and suddenly laughed. "You know, the first time I had champagne was for my eighteenth birthday. The Raves played." That was when Ruby was touring Prague with her band, SugarDaddy, and Blair Waldorf had moved in as a temporary roommate. Things were so different now. Ruby was married and five months pregnant. But back then, they *all* seemed so young.

A smile crossed Vanessa's face at the memory of Blair living in the tiny, ramshackle one-bedroom apartment. She'd tried to class it up by having her mom's interior decorator redo the living room in shades of lilac and celery, but eventually, Blair had realized that she'd never be a Brooklynite. They'd had fun, though, and Vanessa would always remember that time fondly.

Hollis opened the glass-fronted cabinets and poured two glasses of champagne. "To us."

"To us," Vanessa repeated absently. Her mind was far away, trying to piece together the events of her eighteenth birthday party. The night had begun as just a few friends coming over, but had morphed into an all-night rager, the one and only she'd ever thrown. She plunked down on one of the metal stools surrounding the granite kitchen island and furrowed her brow. "The Raves were obsessed with Serena van der Woodsen. And Dan was writing their lyrics and serving as front man. Or he *was*, until he threw up all over himself onstage." Vanessa giggled at the memory. It had gone down in history as an anecdote she or Jenny would *always* bring up to annoy Dan.

"Wait, the Raves were at your party to hook up with that actress from *Coffee at the Palace*?" Hollis asked, ignoring Vanessa's reference to her ex.

Hollis sat down across from her at the counter and ran a hand through his jet-black hair. His gray eyes were smiling. "You, Ms. Abrams, are full of surprises. You told me you were the girl with a shaved head and no friends in high school. Now, I hear you were partying with Serena van der Woodsen, getting the Raves to perform at your birthday . . . and you say *I'm* the one who sold out by working with a distribution company?" He laughed.

"No." Vanessa shook her head and polished off the rest of her champagne. The tiny bubbles tickled her throat. Saying it out loud made everything sound so fun and carefree, but it had never really been like that. She'd been completely out of place at school; all the prim and proper Constance Billard girls had made fun of her Doc Martens and shaved head. Now, her straight, shiny black hair fell in a curtain to her shoulders, she occasionally wore black mascara and a smudge of lip gloss, and she had a wardrobe of skinny jeans, form-fitting sweaters, and colorful tops to offset her black skirts, pants, and hoodies. She would've had a much easier time of it at Constance if she looked then the way she did now. But even if she could go back in time and change things, she wouldn't. Her experience as an outsider had made her who she was. It had given her the sharp point of view that led her to become a filmmaker.

"Most of the time, it was really hard. I mean, I was fifteen when I moved here to live with my sister. Ruby was out a lot with the band, but she had a bird named Tofu and seriously, sometimes he was the only living thing I spoke to all day." She sighed. "One time we had this weird roommate, Tiphany, who moved in with a ferret named Tooter . . . and then there was the time that I got kicked out by Piotr, my sister's husband," Vanessa babbled. Once she started talking about some of the crazier things that happened during her high school career, it was hard to stop, especially since Hollis was staring at her with such intensity.

"Wait." He grabbed her hand and stared deep in her eyes. "How come I've never heard any of these stories?"

Vanessa shrugged. "It's not that interesting." She'd never really talked about her past before. Not because she thought Hollis wouldn't care, but because so much of her past involved Dan. It was kind of awkward.

You think?

"No, it's great. Girl moves to Brooklyn and everything goes so wrong, it's right. The ferret's name was *Tooter*? You can't make that shit up," Hollis laughed. "It'd be a great movie. It's gritty and raw and funny as hell. It makes me want to know more. I want to see it! I want to see it all!" Hollis began pacing back and forth in the kitchen, the way he always did when he was trying to work out the logistics of an idea.

"Are you going to make a movie about my life?" Vanessa teased, refilling both of their champagne glasses.

"No." Hollis took the glass and cocked it toward Vanessa. "We are."

Vanessa shook her head. Her life wasn't a movie! It was just . . . her life. *Tragic and absurd*, she thought randomly. Dan had probably said that. But maybe that was the point. Her life—her high school life, anyway—had been tragic and absurd, but she'd gotten past it and was now happy and in love. She thought of her high school self. Shaven-headed, self-righteous Vanessa would have scoffed at a film about a naïve Vermont girl who learns to tell people to go fuck themselves. No. Actually she would have loved it.

"Let's do it." Vanessa drained her champagne glass, slipped off her stool, and hugged Hollis hard.

"We can start tonight," Hollis murmured into her now-shoulder-length black hair.

Vanessa grinned and kissed him softly on the lips. "I have another idea for tonight," she said boldly, looking him straight in the eye.

This particular film will go unrated.

## everyone loves a reunion

"Serena van der Woodsen's here," Laura Salmon whispered to Rain Hoffstetter. Isabel Coates nodded. They were perched on one of the low-slung black leather couches in the Bass suite at the Tribeca Star. The expansive space was decked with plain white Christmas lights, and large plate glass windows led to the terrace overlooking the shining lights of the city below. Laura had gained ten pounds for each semester at Wellesley and was now squeezed into a stretchy black Narciso Rodriguez dress. She looked exactly like her mother.

"I heard she got married to Breckin O'Dell. It's still super secret, though," Rain whispered back, taking a long swig of her vodka tonic. Her hair was pulled into a messy chignon, revealing a slightly off-center infinity symbol tattooed on the back of her neck. It looked like she'd drawn it on herself with an eyeliner pencil.

"I heard she's pregnant. She's due in June. Her agent wanted her to have an abortion," Isabel Coates chimed in, straightening the hem of her black satin Marc by Marc Jacobs dress.

"Guys!" Serena called, pleased to recognize some of her old

classmates huddled on the black low-slung couch in the corner. She'd been close to staying in tonight, tempted by the idea of ordering an extra-large pepperoni pizza and watching movies in her one-bedroom apartment on Perry Street. But she'd surprised herself by coming to Chuck's party at the last minute.

It was already after eleven, and the suite was filled with guys in khakis and wrinkled button-downs and girls in tight dresses or bikinis. Everyone looked like they were trying to look fifteen years old.

You never can go back.

"How are you?" Serena exclaimed eagerly as she plopped on the couch next to Isabel. "How's Casey?" she asked, remembering the name of Isabel's lesbian lover from last year.

"Oh." Isabel turned bright red. "I have no idea. I'm actually dating this guy named Chad," she announced as she pretended not to stare jealously at Serena's legs. Serena was wearing a denim miniskirt she'd fashioned out of a pair of ancient Sevens and an extra-large Marc by Marc Jacobs sweater. On anyone else, the outfit would have looked sloppy. On Serena, it looked stunning.

Of course.

"How are *you*?" Laura cooed, as if she hadn't been gossiping about her just moments before. She grabbed Serena's long blond hair and combed her manicured fingernails through it enviously. "Are these extensions?"

"No. Love your hair though. It's such a pretty shade of red," Serena lied. Laura's normally brown hair had been dyed an unnatural Hawaiian Punch color. "I haven't been to a salon in *forever*."

"Are you working on a movie?" Rain asked, wrinkling her

ski-jump nose, which now had a small scar from where her nose piercing had been.

"No. I'm not sure I really want to do movies anymore." Serena shrugged. She hadn't acted since *Coffee at the Palace*, and had decided to take a break for the foreseeable future. The only problem was, she wasn't sure what she wanted to do now. Part of her was thinking about going back to school—she had only deferred from Yale and could still go if she wanted to—but the idea of sitting in a classroom seemed so confining. She'd taken a couple of acting classes at a downtown studio that Thad had raved about, but they'd mostly consisted of pantomiming dreams from the night before. No, thank you.

Especially not when most of her dreams involve a certain someone.

"Is it because of the reviews?" Laura took a swig of her cranberry vodka.

Serena stiffened and suddenly wished she'd made herself a drink before she sat down with her old friends. The reviews for *Coffee at the Palace* had been less than stellar, though the *New York Times* had called Serena a breath of fresh air. But it was conversations like this that made Serena hate acting. She loved being in front of the camera, but she hated all the drama that went on when the cameras weren't rolling. She never set foot in anywhere trendy, because she hated getting followed by paparazzi and having her picture taken with camera phones. It was so silly to get that kind of attention when she wasn't *doing* anything.

"I've been reading a lot of Thomas Mann lately," Serena said, changing the subject. "I just finished *The Magic Mountain*. With everyone else in school, I don't want to fall behind," she added. She was greeted by silence.

"Well, what classes do you guys take?" Serena prodded. It had never been hard for her to make conversation, but now, among the girls she'd known since kindergarten, she had no idea what to say. She awkwardly crossed one leg over the other.

"I don't even know," Isabel giggled. "I spend all my time with my boyfriend. I do his Influential Movies of the '80s homework sometimes. His football schedule is really demanding," she explained, brushing her long dark hair off her shoulder self-importantly.

"Oh." Serena didn't know what else to say. Since when did Isabel do someone else's homework? Serena used to always beg to borrow Isabel's calc problem sets.

"I take golf," Rain yelled over the awful Madonna/Britney remix that boomed through the room, courtesy of the giggling L'École sophomores huddled around the Bose sound dock near the bar. "I'm pretty good."

Serena nodded. Were they serious? Was that what college was about? At Constance, they'd all taken Latin and physics and AP French. Sure, they'd complained about it, but deep down, they all knew it was important to do well in high school so they'd get into a good college and succeed in life. But the classes they were taking now sounded like a joke.

"Okay," Serena trailed off uncertainly. She was used to being the life of the party, but now she felt like that awkward guest who people only talked to out of a sense of obligation. "Does anyone else need a drink?" she asked, not bothering to wait for an answer.

Serena hugged her arms against her chest as she walked over to the bar. Didn't they say that people grew apart after high school? Maybe it was natural to not have anything in common once you no longer shared terrible teachers and lunchtime gossip. She'd fallen out of touch with her actress friends—Alysia was engaged to some B-list actor, Alison was pregnant, and Amanda was in rehab. Besides, she kind of hated going to Hollywood parties. The people there only cared about themselves and their careers. Right now, she'd give anything just to talk to someone who actually *knew* her. But the only people who did were her brother Erik, Blair, and Nate. Erik was spending the holidays in Australia with his girlfriend; Blair hated her; and who even knew if she'd ever see Nate again? The last she'd heard, Nate was at that same crazy farm school as Chuck. She'd tried to write him e-mails, but always deleted them before she hit send. She wanted to tell him she understood why he freaked out last year, but could never find the words. She wanted to let him know that she was sorry, that she never meant to hurt him, and that it was fine if he never wanted to be together. But she needed to be friends with him—somehow. She couldn't imagine her life without Nate in it.

"Serena!" Kati Farkas cried from the other end of the bar. "Did you break up with Breckin O'Dell?"

Serena tried to smile. It was going to be a long evening.

The best ones always are.

Serena took the bottle of Ketel on the bar counter, splashed it liberally in a Riedel glass, then topped it with a thin layer of cranberry juice. Maybe a drink would help her feel better. She took an unhappy sip and scanned the room.

Which was when she saw him—all five feet, ten inches of tall, honey gold hair, glittering green-eyed goodness. He wore a dark blue overcoat and looked out of place in the overheated suite.

Serena held on to the granite bar for support. Around her

L'École girls were passing around a joint and laughing. She felt like she was going to faint. She had to talk to him, but what if he didn't want to talk to her? Or worse, what if he was just polite? What if he talked to her like she'd been his high school lab partner?

She drained the rest of her drink and spontaneously threw her arms around his back. "Happy New Year, Natie!" she yelled into his shoulder blades as if it were the old days, and she'd just seen him a couple hours ago, rather than a whole year. His body felt stronger than she'd remembered, and she could feel his taut muscles through his shirt.

"Serena," Nate said dumbly, turning so his face was inches from hers. He could smell her familiar patchouli-infused essential oil scent, and at first he wondered if this was some very weird reaction to the pot he'd smoked earlier. Somebody at the party had had a bag of incredible Thai stick and had generously shared it with him.

"How are you?" he finally asked. It was a dumb and obvious question and not at all what he wanted to say. He wanted to tell her he was sorry, that he still loved her, that Chips had died and he was high and didn't even know what to do about it. He wanted to hold her and never let go.

Serena shrugged and smiled. Her navy blue eyes looked far away. "I'm okay. How are you?"

"I'm . . . okay," he said, shifting from one Stan Smith sneaker to the other. Talk about the understatement of the year. He wasn't, not at all. He was a fucking mess. But right now, with Serena near him, he felt better than he had in a long time.

"Nathaniel fucking Archibald!"

Nate whirled around. Towering above him was a guy with a

familiar shock of reddish-blond hair. It was Jeremy Scott Tompkinson, one of his old St. Jude's classmates. Jeremy had always been excessively skinny and only about five foot two, but he'd obviously had a late-adolescent growth spurt in college. He was huge, massive! Jeremy was trailed by Charlie Dern and Anthony Avuldsen, who were wearing matching Hamilton College visors perched on the sides of their heads to complement their matching beer guts.

Nate held out a hand and Jeremy, Charlie, and Anthony all slapped it in turn, their customary salute. Charlie's eyes bugged beneath his floppy bangs as he took in his old friend. "I thought you were in, like, the army."

Close enough.

"Nah, I was in school," Nate said. While he was excited to see his old St. Jude's buddies, he didn't really feel like playing catch-up. How could he explain about sailing the world, about Chips, about what he was up to now? They probably had no clue what Deep Springs was or what it was really about. But he knew Serena would get it. He suddenly wanted to be with Serena, *alone*.

"Where have you guys been? Beer Pong State?" Serena easily teased the guys.

Nate cracked a grin, glad that Serena was acting so chill. She hadn't grabbed his wrist, dragged him to a corner, and yelled at him for being an asshole. That was nice.

Nate realized that everyone was looking at him curiously and snapped out of his reverie. "I know how to milk a cow," he said randomly.

Congratulations.

"Man, really?" Jeremy asked, his eyes wide. "So, like, you just squeeze?"

"Well, sort of." Nate thought back to Juliet, his favorite cow in the barn. He'd sometimes find himself whispering to her, telling her stories about the day or asking her questions. He'd always feel reassured when she'd moo back, as if she understood what he meant. In a way, it was the same way he felt when he was with Serena. Not like Serena reminded him of a cow, but he didn't feel nervous or scared or judged when he was with her. It was nice.

"Really?" Serena asked, grinning as if it was the most amusing thing she'd heard all day. Nate felt a surge of pride to realize he could still make her smile. Did that mean she forgave him?

Maybe he should ask his cow what she thinks.

"Yeah. Her name's Juliet," Nate said. He didn't really want to talk about cows anymore, but if he wasn't talking about that, he didn't know what he'd start babbling about. Cows seemed like a pretty safe choice. "She has really long eyelashes and likes to be touched behind the ears."

Don't we all?

"Should I be worried?" Serena giggled. She couldn't believe she'd been so nervous about talking to Nate.

"Dude, you either got really fucking weird or you have some fucking amazing weed I need to sample immediately." Anthony wiggled his eyebrows crazily.

"Nah," Nate replied simply.

"I'm getting some brews." Anthony turned on his heel, trailed by Charlie and Jeremy.

Nate shook his head dreamily, as if he hadn't noticed they'd already left. "I can't believe you're here," he said to Serena. A stray eyelash sat on her cheekbone. He gently brushed it away with his index finger before he realized he should have saved it.

When they were little, Serena had taught him to make a wish on an eyelash and then blow it away.

"Did you steal my wish?" Serena asked, tilting her face up toward him.

"I hope not," Nate whispered huskily as he leaned down to kiss her.

Wish granted.

## for auld lang syne

"Are you *ready*?" Blair fidgeted with the clasp on her Prada clutch while Pete sipped his cappuccino. It was already eleven o'clock. They were at Da Silvano on West Fourth for a romantic New Year's dinner before they headed to the party in the Bass suite. She couldn't wait to show off Pete to all her bitchy former Constance classmates—including Serena. Blair figured she'd be there and planned to act cordial. After all, it must be hard to be a boyfriendless, confused, washed-up ex–movie star at the tender age of nineteen.

How generous of her.

Blair wore a tight black and silver DVF dress, and Pete's blond hair flopped adorably into his blue eyes. In his bright blue Thomas Pink button-down, he made the perfect accessory.

She smiled in satisfaction, trying to stifle a yawn. She didn't want to be tired, but it had been a long day. They'd spent Christmas in LA with her family, and had just gotten to the city this afternoon. Pete had always wanted to celebrate New Year's in New York, and Blair was excited to show him where she grew up, especially after spending a week in her family's tacky Pacific Palisades McMansion. She couldn't wait to reexperience all the cheesy romantic things New York had to offer with her boyfriend. She wanted to go skating at Wollman Rink, take a horse-drawn carriage ride through Central Park while sipping mulled wine out of a thermos, and have drinks at Top of the Rock. Even though Blair *hated* cheesiness, she didn't mind it when she was with Pete.

Aw.

"Ready." Pete put down his cup and signaled to the waiter for the check. "So, remind me who I'm going to meet tonight?" He took his AmEx from his worn leather wallet and slipped it in the folder.

"Well, Chuck is hosting the party. He's . . . complicated," Blair began. Complicated was an understatement. Senior year, Chuck had practically molested every member of the Constance Billard student body, then had become what could only be described as gay, wearing socks with monkey appliqués on them. Now he went to Deep Springs, some queer-sounding all-guys college in California. Deep Springs was a working farm where students cultivated alfalfa and read Proust. Which was all random, but sort of fit Chuck's try-anything-once personality. The most bizarre thing was that Nate was apparently there as well. When he'd run out on her and Serena last winter, Blair had half expected him to come to Yale anyway. But when the first week of classes came and went without him, and when she called his cell and found it was disconnected, she'd known he was gone for good. Which was probably for the best.

A few weeks after the start of the semester, on a snowy Wednesday, she'd spotted Pete walking into the student center. She'd spontaneously gone to the coffee bar, bought a medium coffee, skim milk, no sugar, walked up to the table where he was reading *The Love Poems of Pablo Neruda*, and offered it to him. It was a gesture that surprised him—almost as much as she surprised herself. They'd ended up cutting their afternoon classes, cuddling underneath his duvet, and ordering a greasy pizza from Yorkside. And ever since then, it had been her and Pete. They'd lived in New Haven together over the summer— Blair had worked on the campaign for a Connecticut senator while Pete did research for his history professor. At night, they'd wear as little clothing as possible to keep cool in the un-air-conditioned house. She'd make brunch every weekend and they'd spend Sundays in bed reading the *Times*. Being with Pete made her feel like a grown-up. Pete was a real man, and Nate was just a sad little adolescent who had no idea what he wanted.

Is that so?

"Well, it's Chuck's party, and then there'll probably be Kati Farkas and Isabel Coates and Laura Salmon. Just these girls from school," Blair said hurriedly, trying to get the conversation back on track.

"What about Serena?" Pete cocked his head expectantly. Blair shrugged. Normally, she *loved* how Pete remembered every little thing she'd told him—like how the only Audrey Hepburn movie she didn't like was *Wait Until Dark* and how she'd accidentally *kissed* her first Yale interviewer. But he *didn't* know how complicated her best friendship with Serena was, and Blair wanted to keep it that way.

Wonder why?

"I don't know." Blair shrugged and scraped her chair away from the table. They'd barely spoken at all since last winter.

Serena had sent her tickets to the premiere of *Coffee at the Palace*, but of course Blair hadn't gone.

She hovered over Pete as he signed his messy boy signature on the check. Briefly, she wondered if Nate could possibly be at the party, then shook off the idea. Once, in high school, when she and Serena were smoking Merits on the steps of the Met, they came up with the theory that you had an almost psychic connection to anyone you'd ever kissed. If you really concentrated, you could almost sense where they were in geographic relation to you. And right now, Nate felt very far away.

Time to rethink that hypothesis.

Besides, why did it matter? She was *happy*. Sure, she didn't go out all night and dance until dawn, but there was something to be said for the simple life: arguing with Pete about what movies to put on their Netflix queue or whether to order Chinese or sushi on a Friday night. It all seemed so . . . normal.

If you're into that sort of thing.

They exited the restaurant and walked out to the curb. Pete tentatively held up his hand to hail a cab.

"Not like that, like this!" Blair stepped forcefully out onto the street and threw her hand in the air. "You have to be aggressive. Rule number one of living in New York!" Blair smiled happily. She looked uptown and saw the Empire State Building, still decorated in red, green, and white lights for Christmas. Around them, pedestrians were traveling in merry packs, wearing Happy New Year headbands and blowing those totally annoying noisemakers, even though there was still an hour to go until the ball dropped. "Happy New Year!" She squeezed Pete impulsively as a taxi roared to the curb.

The cab easily navigated the short distance from the tangled streets of the West Village to the wide streets of Tribeca and dropped them off in front of the purple awning of the Tribeca Star hotel, where they had checked in earlier in the day.

Blair confidently led Pete to the elevator bank, where two girls were also waiting, looking miserable and cold in matching backless dresses and five-inch heels. Blair smiled benevolently at the younger girls, feeling infinitely superior and happy that she was so beyond the stage of dressing for shock value at parties. It had never been her thing—Serena had always been the one to goad her into dressing scandalously, like the time they showed up at a Valentine's party without underwear.

That's one tradition not worth revisiting.

"After you, ladies," Pete said as the elevator door slid open. Once they reached the ninth floor, Blair and Pete followed the younger girls into the Bass suite. Blair's eyes adjusted to the dim light. It looked just like all the dozens of other parties she'd been to at the suite: The hot tub was overcrowded with half-dressed girls, couples were making out on the leather couches, and the lonely, dateless girls were all clustered around the makeshift bar, desperately trying to make eye contact with any guy who passed their way.

"So, who is everyone?" Pete asked affably, smiling at the room in general.

Blair frowned, trying to spot any familiar faces in the crowd.

"Let's see . . ." she began, before trailing off in disbelief. Framed perfectly by the floor-to-ceiling window that overlooked downtown New York, she saw Serena—kissing someone. She could only see the guy's back, and Serena's blond hair obscured her face. Her white halter top was blindingly bright against the sea of black outside the window and her long, tanned limbs were clenched against the guy's back. She looked like she was trying to devour him.

For a split second, Blair was transfixed. Then, as if stepping closer and closer to an Impressionist painting, Blair noticed the messy golden hair, the easy posture, the Stan Smith canvas sneakers.

"Blair?"

She heard Pete say her name, but she didn't respond. She couldn't blink. Serena's chin was tilted upward, and her eyes were half closed. She looked totally blissful. Just then, the pair pulled apart and Blair saw Nate's face. He was smiling happily and staring at Serena like the party didn't exist, like the lame Justin Timberlake song wasn't playing on the sound dock, like the L'École girls in the hot tub weren't shrieking. It was like Nate and Serena were in their own little world.

Blair felt like she was going to throw up. How the *fuck* had this happened? Were they dating? And how could they just stand there, making out like that, oblivious to the entire world?

"We have to go." She dug her fingernails tightly into Pete's wrist.

"Ow!" Pete yanked his hand out of Blair's grip. "What are you doing?"

"Leaving," Blair announced. "I don't feel well." She would throw up if she stayed an extra minute. She needed to get out. She pushed her way past a gaggle of high school girls standing in a tight circle, not even noticing when she knocked one of the girl's drinks out of her hand and onto the bodice of her ugly pink dress.

And that's what she does to people who *aren't* making out with her exes.

Blair and Pete wordlessly rode the elevator up to the eleventh floor. Blair ran down the carpeted hallway and into their suite, where they'd gotten dressed only a couple of hours before. She stalked over to the minibar and pulled out a tiny bottle of Absolut, unscrewed the cap, and drank it, not caring that she looked like an unstable alcoholic.

"What would you like to drink?" she asked, trying to stop her voice from shaking.

"Blair," Pete said firmly.

"What? The party was lame anyway. I think we should just celebrate here. And I have stomach cramps," she lied. "Anyway, do you want vodka? Or Jack Daniel's?"

"Blair." Pete wrapped his strong arms around her waist and dragged her away from the minibar. "Look at me."

He pulled her onto the edge of the bed and cupped Blair's chin. It was a tender, sweet gesture he did dozens of times a day, but now, his touch made her recoil. The tears that were threatening to fall sprang from her eyes.

"I'm fine," Blair squeaked.

"No, you're not," Pete said gently. "Last year, it was Tiffany, this year it's New Year's. I don't understand," he said, a note of suspicion evident in his otherwise concerned voice.

"It's . . ." Blair sighed. "I'm just so tired," she said finally. She wanted to tell Pete how much seeing Serena and Nate had shaken her. Being back in New York was like pulling a gigantic Band-Aid off her whole fucking life, exposing the raw, oozing parts of her past that hadn't healed.

Pete kept his gaze on Blair. "Help me understand," he said slowly.

Blair looked from the flat-screen television mounted against the wall to the black and granite wet bar in the next room. She usually loved hotels, but now everything seemed too sterile, too anonymous. She wished they were back in their cluttered New Haven rental.

Blair kicked off one Sigerson Morrison pump, then the other, and folded her legs under her on the bed. She had to tell him. He'd met her weird mom and her gross, fat stepfather. He'd spent hours taking pictures of Blair and her toddler sister, Yale, playing in the pool in the backyard of her family's Pacific Palisades home. He *knew* her.

Blair took a deep breath. "I saw my ex. Making out with my best friend. And we're not together anymore, *obviously*." Blair mustered a weak laugh that came out like a bark. "But it was still weird . . . hard, I guess," she added.

A cloud had passed over Pete's usually open face.

"Do I know who this ex is?" Pete asked, taking his hand off hers.

"It's Nate. It was Nate and Serena." Blair said simply. She'd talked about Nate only in vague terms, usually in reference to a story from when they were kids. Before things got so complicated.

"Nate," Pete repeated. "The one you used to go to the zoo with."

Blair nodded, trying to figure out what she should say next, but all she could do was think about meandering lazily through the Central Park Zoo with Nate. He'd liked the penguins, she'd liked the polar bears. That is, until Serena decided she liked the polar bears more. Serena used to stand in front of the habitat talking to them, as if she knew some sort of secret language only they could understand. Blair laughed bitterly. Why did Serena have to pop up in all her memories?

Maybe because she was there?

"We were all friends, and then in tenth grade, Nate and I started dating. And then that summer, when I was in Scotland for a wedding, Nate and Serena slept together, and I didn't find out until senior year." A fresh sob escaped Blair's throat. She suddenly recalled how she'd first found out. It was when she and Nate were just about to sleep together for the first time.

"Do you still have feelings for him?" Pete asked. Blair cleared her throat a little haughtily. What was with the third degree? His ex-girlfriend, an anthropology bitch named Lindsey, glared at Blair whenever they crossed paths on campus and Blair never complained.

Blair stood up and wavered over to the minibar. She was determined not to let the image of Serena and Nate fuck up her night. And what better way than to have another drink?

"Are you still in love with him?" Pete pressed, trailing behind her.

Blair whirled around, a mini bottle of vodka in her hand. Why couldn't he just let it go? "No," she said flatly. She wasn't in love with Nate. She'd moved on. She had Pete now. Duh.

"Okay," Pete said slowly. His blue eyes still looked slightly wary, but he wearily ran a hand through his thick blond hair.

"I'm in love with *you*," Blair clarified. It was true. But she was surrounded by all these feelings from her high school past and it was hard to let them go just like that.

"I just need you to be honest with me. . . ." Pete pushed away the tumbler of vodka impatiently. "Just tell me that nothing has happened between you since high school."

Blair looked at her reflection in the mirror above the bar. Her chestnut brown hair was limp around her face and her black La

Perla bra strap had inched down her shoulder. Her small, lean face was blotchy and red. And still, Pete loved her. Real couples loved each other no matter what. He needed to know everything. And then it really would be over.

She ran her hands through her hair and turned around, waiting until Pete's eyes connected with hers. "Last winter break, Nate and I hooked up on New Year's," Blair said quickly. "I didn't even know he would be in New York, I thought he was sailing around the world, but then we ended up at the same party, and we were both by ourselves and you were in Costa Rica and 'no ring, no bring,' and it just happened. But that was last year, it only happened once, and now it seems he and Serena are together, so good for them," Blair finished. There. That didn't sound too bad. She'd acknowledged it for what it was: a dumb mistake that would never happen again.

Never say never. . . .

Blair picked up her glass and took a long, relieved sip. She felt like a weight had been lifted from her chest. "I'm really glad I told you," Blair confessed, reaching out to grab Pete's hand.

Pete yanked his arm away as if he'd been burned. His face looked ashen. "You mean, you slept with him," he finally choked out.

"But it didn't mean anything!" Blair said quickly. She hadn't really thought through what her confession would mean to Pete. "It was just a dumb, onetime mistake that happened because a lot of old feelings got stirred up."

"You cheated." Pete shook his head in disbelief. "Jesus Christ, I'm a fucking idiot! You cheated and you never told me. I gave you a ring!"

"No!" Blair said desperately. She had to make him understand that it hadn't meant anything. "I haven't thought about him since," Blair added, her voice rising hysterically.

"Bullshit." Pete stood up and paced the room. "You cheated and then you kept it a secret. How do I know this . . . this love triangle isn't always going to come back to haunt you—to haunt me?" Pete shook his head sadly. He looked awful, like a kid who'd just seen his golden retriever puppy get run over by a car. "I'm going to take a train to Philly and stay with my brother for a bit. I'll call you."

"Wait," Blair screeched, gripping a handful of the dark green duvet. She couldn't believe she was so close to *losing* Pete. "Are you breaking up with me?"

Pete grabbed his small wheeled Tumi suitcase from the floor and paused to look at Blair. "I just need some time to think," he said, a little bit more gently. With one final look, he headed for the door. As it closed behind him with a thud, Blair collapsed into the goosedown pillow, her body racked with sobs.

They do say the holidays can cause depression.

# d on deadline

*Turtles sleep under the mud, while our hearts break . . .*
 *Two zebras together, so separate.*

Dan crumpled the piece of paper and threw it onto the coffee-stained tan rug. The room smelled like cigarettes and incense, which Dan had first started burning a year ago to erase the smell of Vanessa, but hadn't broken the habit. The alarm clock he'd had since seventh grade read eleven thirty-four in luminous green letters. For everyone else, it was twenty-six minutes until New Year's, but for Dan, it was less than half an hour until he failed his poetry class and botched his writing career.

Of course, he'd been an idiot to even sign up for a writing seminar called Poetry and Passion when there was so little passion in his life. But Colm Doyle, the legendary Irish writer, was the instructor. Colm wrote angry, honest poems about love. After his fourth divorce, he'd written a poem called "Hand on the Frying Pan," and Dan had memorized every line. Besides, he'd hoped he could benefit from taking a class on passion when he wasn't in love. After all, back in high school, he'd written his best poem, "Sluts," after he'd broken up with Vanessa the first time. That had been published in *The New Yorker*.

It was also submitted not by the writer but by its unjealous subject.

But now, he couldn't write anything. It wasn't like he hadn't tried, over and over, for the last year. It was just always the same: He'd loved Vanessa, Vanessa had cheated on him, he hated his life, and he wanted to move on but for some reason couldn't. He was angry at her and missed her and hated the fact that he'd seen a photo of her and that Hollis guy on one of the party pages in *New York* magazine, looking so happy together. He wished that he'd never met Vanessa, so he wouldn't have to feel this way.

Sounds like someone skipped the *better to have loved and lost* lesson.

Dan lay down on his bed and pulled the flannel sheets over his head. All he wanted to do was fall asleep so he didn't have to think, but unfortunately he'd had fourteen cups of black coffee today and his hands were vibrating. He just couldn't fucking write the poem. And he'd tried. So far, pages and pages were scattered across the room and on his bed. The zebra and turtle poem had actually been one of his better efforts. At one point, he'd thought he was onto something, but then realized he was just transcribing an Indigo Girls song playing on the radio his father had left on in the kitchen.

"Daniel?" Rufus appeared in the doorway. His wiry salt-and-pepper hair was tucked into a pink beret that was obviously Jenny's. Jenny had spent Christmas with them, but was spending New Year's on a Waverly field trip to Paris. Dan wished he could have gone with her. He wished he could be anywhere but here.

"I was just going to call for some Chinese food. What do you say?" Rufus asked almost tenderly. "I find I work better with a little MSG in my system."

"I'm not hungry," Dan mumbled. He swung his legs out of bed and picked up the half-empty cup of coffee from his night table. It was cold but he gulped it down anyway, enjoying the bitter, acrid taste as it traveled down his throat. That was how he felt.

*My love is like stale coffee. . . .*

Dan sighed. It was official. He sucked.

"Should I be worried about you?" Rufus asked sternly as he sat down on Dan's bed. Rufus was one of those dads who believed in a less-is-more approach to parenting, but was always attuned to the lives of his two children. Dan felt bad dragging him into his den of despair. It wasn't his fault Dan had peaked at seventeen.

"I'm trying to write a poem, and I can't do it," Dan admitted.

"What do you mean?" Rufus roared. He stood up, placed his hands on his hips, and looked down at Dan in exasperation. It was the same gesture Jenny would make when she wanted to prove that Dan was being ridiculous. "You're brilliant, boy!"

"Thanks," Dan mumbled, glancing away. "I'm going to fail this class unless I write a love poem, and I just . . . can't," he said miserably. "I was supposed to finish last week but the professor gave me an extension until midnight tonight. After that . . ." He trailed off.

"Ah, the poet under pressure." Rufus shook his head. "I

remember one time upstate. Summer of '67. But instead of Woodstock, we were creating art. We were free-versing around the campfire, and I didn't know what the hell to say. So then I used some of my old stuff knocking around my noggin. Toast of the evening," Rufus said proudly.

Dan smiled tightly. His dad's hippie free-versing wasn't exactly the same as a poem he had to turn in for a *grade* at a class at *Columbia*.

"I'm off to order. I'll get you the chicken fried rice and let you know when the grub's here." Rufus stood up and wandered out, leaving Dan alone.

Thankfully.

Still, maybe there was something to what his dad was saying. After all, Colm hadn't said specifically to *write* a poem. He'd said to *turn in* a poem. And Dan had just been musing that he'd peaked in high school. He stood up from the bed and padded across the stained carpet to his makeshift desk, made from milk crates and an old door. Maybe he could find a poem from the past. It wasn't like he had much of a choice.

He picked up one folded loose piece of paper on top of a pile of Moleskine notebooks and spiral-bound pads, unfolded it, and began to read. *Blonde coming out of the store/Whatever you buy, I want you more.* It was one of the first poems he'd ever written, after he'd seen a picture of Serena online, coming out of Barneys. It was terrible.

He shuffled through more of the papers. Each poem reminded him of another piece of his past. He'd been in love with Vanessa, dated Serena, had had a torrid affair with a kinky, yellow-toothed poet named Mystery Craze. He'd even had a fling with a sensitive gay guy named Greg—if you called Greg trying to kiss him one night after drinking way too much absinthe a fling. He'd had experiences with almost every type of love there was. But now, he just felt empty.

Maybe *that* was his problem. He'd forgotten what it was like to love and lose and love again. After all, the poems about Serena were about untapped desire, about ideal love, about a love that could not be consummated. They were sad and desperate and longing. They were real *poems*.

He pulled out one, from when he and Serena had just broken up in the fall of senior year.

*Perfect blond celluloid teen queen*
*Heart of glass, Wyeth-stark Kansas landscape.*

Dan grinned. That wasn't bad. He turned on his MacBook, jiggling his leg as it powered up. The clock read eleven fifty-one.

Quickly, he typed with two fingers, pulling the best lines from different poems to create an impassioned, pleading poem to love. Outside, he could hear neighbors on the street. For as long as he could remember, everyone on his block had gathered outside to count down to the New Year. But Dan didn't have time for that. Instead, he logged into his Columbia account and quickly composed an e-mail to his professor. At eleven fifty-eight, he pressed send.

Well, at least he didn't wait until the last minute.

# the morning after is never as magical as the night before

Serena stretched her arms over her head, surprised when her elbow hit something hard. She opened her navy blue eyes and realized her elbow hadn't connected with something, but some-*one:* Nate.

Scenes from last night came floating back to her. She'd only had one drink, but everything seemed cloaked in a golden, glowy haze. As soon as she and Nate had kissed, it was as if the whole party had faded away and the only thing that was left was the two of them. It was only the countdown to midnight that had broken the spell. They'd found a cab and gone back to Serena's apartment.

"Morning!" Serena whispered, even though she wanted to scream for joy. She'd never been so happy on a New Year's Day. It was the perfect start to the rest of their lives.

Doesn't she mean year?

"Uh," Nate grunted sleepily and turned over, throwing his arm across Serena's golden, naked body. "I've got farm duty," Nate murmured. "The cows are hungry."

"Wake *up,* silly!" Serena gently pushed his blond-streaked

brown hair from his eyes. Nate was probably still high. All night, he'd said cute things he never would've said sober, like how he'd be out in the alfalfa fields at school, look up at the sun, and think of her, and how he stole a copy of *Breakfast at Fred's* from the school's rumpus room so he'd always have her picture.

"Serena." Nate smiled a slow smile and pulled her closer to him, then blinked, just in case this was a dream. But Serena looked very real. "Hi," he added incredulously. Seeing Serena naked reminded him of the first time he'd seen her naked, back when they were fifteen-year-old virgins. But even then, it had never been awkward between them. They'd laughed about the clumsiness of it all, and it was the same this time. It was as if no time had passed, and their bodies had just *melded* into each other. He kissed her smooth, bare shoulder.

"Hi, you," Serena murmured. Finally, her one-bedroom apartment felt like home. She'd lived here for almost a year, but it was unfurnished save for her childhood bed, a gauzy lilac curtain tacked carelessly over the window, a cactus she'd bought at the bodega downstairs, and a few childhood photos. She'd always meant to decorate, but there just hadn't seemed to be a point. It had sort of felt like a hotel room—nice to stay in, but nowhere you *yearned* for. But now, she never wanted to leave. She and Nate could just stay here forever, calling in for take-out and taking turns going downstairs to pick up new Netflix movies from the mailbox.

"Do you want anything?" Serena swung her long legs onto the floor. She was naked but didn't feel embarrassed. "I think I have water," she continued as she walked toward the short hallway to the small eat-in kitchen. The ancient radiator hissed. Despite having been renovated before she moved in, the apartment still had an old-time feel, with marble floor tiles in the kitchen, worn wood floorboards, and crown molding.

Serena flung open the fridge door. Inside were a few cans of Diet Coke, a box of clementines, a few containers of yogurt, and a bottle of champagne left over from a gift basket. The only packages Serena ever received these days were gift baskets; the only mail, invitations to parties and events; the only phone calls, from her agent or publicist. Mostly, she ignored all of it.

She pulled out a bottled water and brought it back to the bedroom. Nate was sitting up, her Frette Egyptian cotton sheets strewn across his torso. His chest was muscular and tan. Serena climbed back into bed and wrapped her arms around him.

"You feel nice," Serena murmured, nuzzling her head against his shoulder.

"How long have you lived here?" Nate asked, taking in the gauzy white curtains and Serena's familiar old canopy bed. It was warm and inviting, and all hers. Just thinking about the fact that they had the whole place to themselves made him horny.

"A year. I don't spend too much time here." Serena shrugged. "I get lonely, so a lot of times I head up to my parents' place."

"Are you lonely now?" Nate gently bit her shoulder.

Serena squealed and fell back against the pillows. For the first time in the year that she'd been living in the apartment, she appreciated all its possibilities. She could do whatever she wanted.

With *whomever* she wanted.

Nate grabbed the bottle of water from the nightstand and unscrewed the cap. His eyes landed on a silver Tiffany frame. Inside was a picture of him, Blair, and Serena. It was a photo from Blair's party at the Met the summer after senior year, the night before he left with Chips on the *Belinda*. Nate was standing in the center, looking straight at the camera. Serena and Blair were both laughing, their faces turned toward him.

Nate picked up the frame and held his index finger over Blair, so he could only see him and Serena, his arm draped over her shoulder. They both looked so happy. Then, he experimentally moved his thumb so it covered Serena. In the photo, Blair's face gazed adoringly at Nate. Nate sighed in frustration.

"How is she?" he asked. He couldn't help himself. He'd tried to forget about Blair, and sometimes, he could almost convince himself he had. But seeing the photograph of her grinning so easily at him stirred up all the feelings he'd tried so hard to get rid of.

"I don't know." Serena and Blair hadn't talked all year, and Serena didn't really feel like talking about her now either. Especially not with Nate. She pulled her dusky rose duvet cover around her and leaned back against the carved-oak headboard. "She was in LA visiting her family," she offered, remembering the strained e-mail she'd received from Blair after Thanksgiving. "She and her boyfriend were there together."

"She's still with him?" Nate dropped the photo. It bounced once on the bed, then clattered to the hardwood floor. He wasn't sure why he was so surprised. Blair was at Yale, not a nunnery. For all he knew, she'd had hundreds of boyfriends since last year.

"I think so. I don't know," Serena said softly, feeling a tingling in her fingertips that always preceded tears. She turned away from Nate so she faced the window. Outside, the treetops were barren. Icicles hung from the building's eaves, slowly melting in the morning sun. She didn't want to turn around until Nate spoke. To say that he was in love with *her*, to say that Blair didn't mean anything to him, to say he was glad Blair had a boyfriend because all he wanted was Serena.

Serena breathed in and out slowly, trying to even out her breath so each inhale and exhale lasted exactly three seconds. It was a trick she'd learned from one of her acting teachers, a way to remain in control if you felt like your emotions might overtake you in a scene.

Too late.

Angry tears pricked her navy blue eyes. Was he still in love with Blair? Would she always be his backup?

"Serena?" Nate tentatively touched her shoulder, as if she were a stranger.

"You know, I have a lot of stuff to do today," she announced, swinging her feet onto the hardwood floor. She yanked a rose-colored sheet off the bed and primly wrapped it around her body like a bathrobe. No way was Nate allowed to see her naked now.

"Serena, wait," Nate said helplessly. He wanted to hold her and kiss her and make it better. After all, he loved her, too.

Serena whirled around. "What?"

"I just . . ." Nate's glittering green eyes clouded and he looked at his hands.

"Happy New Year, Nate," she said, and closed the bathroom door behind her, not wanting to let him see her cry.

(Happy) New Year, indeed.

# d earns his poetic license

**From:** colmdoyle@columbia.edu
**To:** dhumphrey3@columbia.edu
**Subject:** Re: poetry submission

Danny Boy!
I thought you were going to submit shite, but this is
the real thing, boyo. Sent it to Jaymi Matteo at *The
New Yorker.* She wants it. They're going to crash it
into their next issue, printing tonight! What's it
called?
CD

**From:** dhumphrey3@columbia.edu
**To:** colmdoyle@columbia.edu
**Subject:** Re: re: poetry submission

Dear Professor Doyle,
Thank you, sir. I'm honored. You can call the poem
*Serena.*
Sincerely,
Dan Humphrey

## *true confessions*

"Are you all right, miss?" a black-vested waiter asked as he rolled the room service cart into Blair's Tribeca Star suite Wednesday morning. "Your usual," he added, lifting the silver cover from the plate. It was the same waiter who'd brought her dinner last night. And dinner the night before. Blair glared mutinously at him. Didn't he have a life?

Doesn't she?

"I'm fine," Blair growled, causing the waiter to scurry out of the room, leaving her alone with her leek and goat cheese omelet and bacon. Blair took the tray from the side table and brought it back to the bed, balancing it on her knees. Her boyfriend had deserted her. She didn't have to worry about calories.

It had been four days since Pete had gone to stay with his brother Jason in Philadelphia. Since then, Blair had barely left the Tribeca Star. She'd been ordering room service, but room service was never fun when you had no one to share it with, and she'd caught up on all of her favorite gossip blogs and online shopping sites until she felt like she'd reached the end of the Internet. She'd meant for this break to be relaxing, a reward for surviving an academically challenging semester. Instead, it was more stressful than an early morning final exam.

The hotel room looked like it had just been cleaned by the maid service, even though she'd placed a DO NOT DISTURB sign on the doorknob Saturday morning. She'd kept the room clean just so it would be ready for Pete whenever he came back. It was only now that she realized he probably wasn't coming back. All of her phone calls had gone directly to voice mail. All of her texts had been unanswered.

Last semester, she'd taken a psychology class in which they learned about the five stages of loss. Right now, Blair had just passed stage one—denial—and was in stage two: anger. How could Pete do this to her? At least she'd been *honest* with him.

Blair pushed her anemic-looking omelet around on her plate, suddenly losing her appetite. It was cold and she was tempted to call the downstairs restaurant and complain, just to have the satisfaction of hearing someone apologize to her.

Or the chance to speak to another human being?

She unearthed her iPhone from the depths of her white down comforter, but dialed her mother instead.

"Hello, Blair darling," Eleanor Waldorf answered the phone breathily. "I'm just in the middle of my private doga session. Mookie loves it! I may not let Aaron bring him back to Boston," she trilled, naming Blair's stepbrother and his mangy mutt.

"Hi, Mom," Blair sighed. She was immediately reminded why she didn't often call her mother. Eleanor Waldorf had always been slightly batty, but living in LA had pushed her over the edge. Now, in addition to a maid and a chef on the payroll, she also had a reflexologist, an astrologist, and a crystal-arts healer. And apparently, a dog-yoga teacher, too.

It takes a village.

"So, how is New York?" Eleanor asked, doga forgotten.

Blair shrugged, even though her mom couldn't see her. She flipped the channels on the muted TV, setting down the remote when she got to an old black-and-white film. "It's sort of weird to not have a home here anymore."

"That must be hard," Eleanor's voice softened a bit. "But you must be having fun showing Pete around. Has he met Serena and Nate yet?"

No, but he knows *all* about them.

"Yeah," Blair said dismissively. "But I don't think I'll be back here for a while." She took a bite of crispy bacon and wiped her fingers on the duvet.

"Blair, don't be ridiculous. It's your city no matter where we live. Now, do me a favor, go to Barneys and buy yourself something fabulous," her mother urged. Mookie barked in the background. "Oops. I think Mookie's losing his focus. Gotta jet—love you, sweetie!" Eleanor trilled before hanging up.

Blair sighed and lay back on the bed. If only her life could be sorted out by a pair of Manolos. But Eleanor did have a point. It wasn't healthy to be by herself in the room, watching endless ancient movies and episodes of year-in-review shows. Maybe a little shopping trip *was* what she needed. Audrey had said that nothing bad could ever happen at Tiffany, but surely that rule applied to Barneys, too.

After her shower, Blair pulled on a pair of new J Brand skinny jeans she'd ordered, pleased that they felt a little loose around her hips, and pulled on a thin eggplant-colored Theory cashmere sweater. She belted her Burberry coat, pausing for a moment at the door. What if Pete came back and she wasn't here? She shook her head, dismissing the notion, and let the door close with a definitive click.

She rode the elevator downstairs and tromped noisily through the parquet floor lobby in her dusty pink Chanel pointy-toed boots. She passed through the revolving door and took a deep breath. The air felt cold but fresh. She looked hopefully at the bright blue sky. This was a new day.

Blair stepped into one of the yellow cabs idling at the entrance of the hotel. "Sixtieth and Madison," she commanded, feeling better than she had in almost a week.

It is called retail *therapy* for a reason.

She entered Barneys, invigorated by the multicolored purses, the scent of Creed Fleurissimo in the air, the upbeat chatter of excited shoppers surrounding her. In her hotel room, time had felt suspended. Here, people were moving, buying, laughing in a way that was reassuring.

Blair followed a thirtysomething Gucci-clad woman toward the elevator bank. She had honey blond hair, an Hermès scarf tied around her neck, and a huge five-carat diamond ring on her left hand. She'd probably never been left by her boyfriend, Blair thought jealously.

Upstairs, she idly strolled through the expansive loftlike space, not looking for anything, but shopping purely on instinct. She'd know what she needed when she saw it. She picked out a black and white dress by Alexander Wang that was hanging by itself on a silver rack in the center of the sparsely filled floor. It looked like something Edie Sedgwick might have worn to a fabulous Factory party.

"May I help you, miss?" A saleswoman came up to her eagerly, her Prada pumps clacking against the floor. Her name tag read DANIELLE.

"Thanks." Blair offered a small smile as she plucked the dress from the rack. The tag sewn into the thick wool said eight, far too large for Blair's size-two frame. "I need this in a two."

Danielle's friendly smile turned into a frown. "I'm sorry, it's the only size we have left. It does run small though. Would you like to try it?"

Blair narrowed her eyes. Was Danielle calling her fat?

"No," Blair snapped angrily. Suddenly her eye caught sight of the same dress, hanging next to a corner dressing area. "There it is!" Blair announced gleefully, charging toward the dress.

Danielle followed on her heels. "Someone else is trying that on. I'll be sure to find you if she doesn't take it."

"But she's obviously done with it," Blair protested, already pulling the size-two dress off the hanger. "Now, where can I try this on?" She used the same voice she had last semester when protesting the B she'd received on a paper in Persuasion in Politics. Professor Balmer had changed it to an A-, simply because of the passionate way she'd argued her point.

Danielle wrung her hands nervously. "Miss, I'd be happy to call in the dress, but—"

"Blair?" came a voice from behind the heavy black dressing room curtain. Out stepped Serena van der Woodsen, clad in a flesh-colored scoop back Catherine Malandrino knit dress that made her look naked. What the fuck? Blair narrowed her eyes, praying that in just a moment she'd wake up with a Veuve Clicquot hangover and the promise of room service just a phone call away.

No such luck.

"Oh my God!" Serena squealed when she saw Blair. She'd been feeling lonely ever since she'd kicked Nate out on New

Year's Day. She'd thought of calling Blair but had always stopped short. She'd spent a lot of time at Doma, reading *Anna Karenina* and trying to make eye contact with the weirdos at her communal table. In the book, Anna was forced into bad choice after bad choice, until she eventually threw herself under a train. Serena wouldn't do *that*, but there were only so many times she could pick herself up, dust herself off, and pretend everything was fine.

No matter how much she tried to pretend otherwise, the Nate thing had taken a lot out of her. The love of her life was in love with someone else.

Sounds familiar.

"How are you? It's good to see you!" Serena enveloped her old friend in a huge hug. Now that Blair was here, maybe things would be different. After all, it wasn't Blair's fault Nate was still in love with her.

Blair stood stiffly, her arms at her sides. It was *good* for Serena to see her? Well, it was terrible for Blair to see Serena. Serena was the *reason* she had just spent four days locked in a hotel room. If Serena hadn't been at the party, making out with Nate, Blair would still be with Pete. Serena had fucked up Blair's current relationship, her past relationship, and if she gave her the chance, she'd probably fuck up her future relationships too.

"Are you okay?" Serena stepped back and frowned. Blair's cheeks looked flushed.

"Well, I'll just hold on to this, and when one of you ladies would like it, just find me." Danielle grabbed the dress and quickly speed-walked away, as if at any moment one or both of them might tackle her.

"How was your New Year's?" Blair asked icily.

"It was good," Serena said lightly. "I saw Nate. . . ." She trailed off uncertainly, noticing an ominous flicker in Blair's blue eyes. "Where's your boyfriend?" Serena changed the subject. Maybe giving Blair the chance to talk about her perfect relationship would warm her up a little bit.

Blair shook her head. There was no way she was going to tell Serena what had happened between her and Pete. She hugged her arms across her chest. "You *saw* Nate?" she repeated sarcastically.

Serena's blue eyes widened as she caught on to the meaning behind Blair's tone. Could Blair have heard what happened? Or worse, *seen* her and Nate together at the party?

But it wasn't like Serena had done anything wrong. After all, she and Nate were both single. *Blair* was the one with the boyfriend.

"You're not with Nate anymore," Serena reminded her. *Even though he wishes you were.* Serena suddenly remembered fighting with Blair over the battered polar bear they'd gotten on their first-grade field trip to the Central Park Zoo. Serena had snatched it from Blair in an uncharacteristically aggressive move, and Blair had broken into tears. "It didn't mean anything. It was just a dumb New Year's Eve hookup," Serena said softly, searching her friend's face.

Blair narrowed her icy blue eyes. What the fuck was Serena's problem, practically screaming that she and Nate had hooked up? Serena had probably *followed* her into Barneys, just to have the chance to gloat and humiliate her. Blair knew it didn't make sense, really, but she also knew that there was no room in her life anymore for Serena. Maybe when they were younger, they could laugh and make up, but they were adults now. And it was time for Serena to start taking responsibility for her actions.

"Maybe we can go get lunch?" Serena smiled encouragingly. "At Fred's?"

Blair glared at Serena. Was she totally dense? Did she actually have to spell it out for her? "I don't think so." She shook her head. "We're not friends anymore." She turned on her heel and angrily stomped off to the elevators.

Bitchfest at Barneys?

Disclaimer: All the real names of places, people, and events have been altered or abbreviated to protect the innocent. Namely, me.

# hey people!

### everything old is new again

Maybe you dusted off your white Oscar de la Renta commencement dress and repurposed it for your angel costume this Halloween. Maybe you stole a few of your mom's vintage Pucci dresses from her closet over Thanksgiving and now wear them to cocktail parties. Or maybe you just keep bringing up that story about how you used to be friends with Hollywood's latest It Girl.

The point is, things that seemed same-old in high school take on a shiny newness in college. That rule applies to the people in our lives, too. Which is why I, for one, can't say I'm surprised that **S** and **N** were spotted getting hot and heavy in a darkened corner of the Bass suite at the Tribeca Star on New Year's Eve. So why was **N** seen leaving **S**'s Perry Street abode at the ungodly hour of 9 a.m. on New Year's Day?

### the walk of shame

**N**'s walk home reminds me: It's time for a refresher course on graceful exits from overnight arrangements. While it may not be on the official college syllabus, the walk of shame is a test everyone must complete at least once. You're practically guaranteed to run into someone you know.

So hold your head up high, and remind yourself that *they're* strolling the campus at 8 a.m. on a Sunday, too.

**sightings**

**V** and her boyfriend **H** having brunch at **Egg**, the inexplicably popular breakfast joint in **Williamsburg**, throwing around phrases like *development exec* and *gross points.* Could **V** be making the move to the big time? And will any of *us* be invited to make cameo appearances? Better get ready for your close-up! **S** at **Doma**, the coffee shop near her apartment, reading *The New Yorker* and looking forlorn—until she flipped a page, and her face lit up. Maybe poetry *is* good for the soul. A very drunk **D** and a ruddy-faced older Irish man at a pub on Upper Broadway, noisily reciting Joyce. Poetry may be good for their souls too, but can they keep it down?

**your e-mail**

Dear Gossip Girl,
Hello. I'm a sous chef at the restaurant of an exclusive downtown hotel, and we've been getting quite a few room service requests from the same patron. I was curious, so yesterday I delivered the order myself. She's very beautiful, but looks very sad. How do I let her know that I would be happy to hang out while she eats her omelet without seeming creepy?
—topchef

Dear Top Chef,
I hate to disappoint you, but if you're talking about the same tragic brunette beauty I know, I think what she needs right now is some time to herself. If you'd like to do something for her, I suggest a complementary order of cheese fries, onion rings, or any other too-bad-to-order foods *all* girls secretly love.
—GG

**q:** Dear Gossip Girl,

I can't *wait* to get to college. Or at least get a college boyfriend. Should I graduate early? Show up at my sister's campus, even though she never invites me? Advice please!

—mature

**a:** Dear Mature,

While it's always admirable to aspire to a position greater than the one you currently occupy, why the rush? High school may seem tedious, and your uniforms may seem tacky. But trust me, you'll miss it when it's over.

—GG

**q:** Dear Gossip Girl,

My girlfriend and I are visiting her hometown, and she's been acting kind of strange. She hasn't introduced me to any of her old friends from high school. It's like she's trying to hide something. What do you think?

—New Boy

**a:** Dear NB,

There are a few possible explanations: Maybe she's shy. Maybe she's hiding some skeletons in her closet. Maybe she just wants to keep you all to herself. Or maybe she just doesn't want to introduce a paranoid weirdo to her friends.

—GG

**theory in action**

In literary theory, a liminal space is somewhere in between—a place that's neither here nor there. I think it's safe to say we're at a liminal space in our lives: We're not teenagers, but we're not quite adults. At times we're being chastised by our parents for not calling; at others, we're starting internships at companies we might want to work for someday, in our real, adult lives. My advice: Instead of worrying about who you were or what you'll become, try to just enjoy the moment.

You know you love me,

gossip girl

# *boys should always ask for directions*

Nate lumbered into the kitchen of his town house Friday morning, in search of food. His raging booze and pot hangover had finally dissipated enough for him to roll out of bed. He felt disgusting, like one of the frogs that lived at the bottom of the pond at Deep Springs.

How far our golden boy has fallen. . . .

He opened the door to the Sub-Zero refrigerator and pulled out a Jell-O chocolate pudding snack pack. Not bothering to get a spoon, he tore open the foil wrapper and licked the top of the pudding. It was good. And simple. Just the way life should be. Life only got complicated once you started interacting with people. But who needed that when he had food, shelter, and plenty of pudding and Pop-Tarts?

Nate reached into the pocket of his cords and pulled out the roach that had been stuck in the folds of his pocket. He'd slept in them last night because it had seemed like too much effort to change. This was the last of his supply. He'd definitely have to call Jeremy or Anthony for a hookup, which was unfortunate, because he didn't want any human contact. He wasn't very good company right now. Chips was dead. He'd hurt Serena. Blair had a boyfriend. The three people he cared about most in the world, and he couldn't reach out to any of them.

The past few days had gone by in a blur. He liked the way the hours bled into each other in front of the television, especially after he fired up his bong. *Oprah* had featured teen entrepreneurs the other day. There was one kid who made jellyfish tanks instead of going to college. Maybe he could drop out of school and do something like that.

Nate inhaled deeply from the joint. He sat at the large marble island in the center of his family's French country-style kitchen, feeling contented. Maybe this was happiness.

And maybe someone needs to change his pants and climb out of his pot haze?

Just then, the doorbell rang a pleasant three-tone chime. *Fuck.* Nate ignored it and took another hit. Then he felt his iPhone buzzing in his pocket. He slipped it out and glanced at the display. Chuck.

"Hello?" Nate croaked.

"Open the door," Chuck said.

"No," Nate said lamely. He didn't want Chuck to see him in this state. "I'm in the shower," he added nonsensically.

"No, you're not," Chuck responded matter-of-factly as the chime filled the house again. It didn't sound pleasant at all anymore. It made Nate feel like his brain was going to explode.

He sulkily pulled open the large oak door and crossed his arms. Chuck pulled off his Gucci aviators and coolly appraised Nate. "You're a mess," he said finally.

Thank you, Mr. Observant.

Chuck brushed past him through the entryway and into the

kitchen. Nate trailed behind. It wasn't like he had a choice. Chuck wrinkled his nose at the disarray. A joint lay on the counter, a pizza box and some random takeout containers were shoved in the sink, and a pile of dirty shirts formed a messy trail from the kitchen to the winding staircase that led to Nate's room. This was what happened when he was left to his own devices. His parents had gone on their annual vacation to St. Barts a few days ago—they'd postponed their trip because of Chips's funeral—and their maid, Regina, was on vacation until tomorrow.

"What are you doing here?" Nate asked lamely as he kicked one of the T-shirts out of the way.

"Inviting myself over for a cocktail?" Chuck said sarcastically. He shook his head in annoyed frustration, as if he were disappointed in Nate. *Join the club*. Nate was disappointed in himself.

Chuck walked to the stainless steel Sub-Zero refrigerator, pulled out a Corona, and pried the cap off with his teeth, a trick all Deep Springs students learned their first week on campus. "This will do," he said, taking a small sip and holding it out to Nate in a mock toast.

"Can I offer you something?" he asked politely, as if Nate had just randomly shown up in Chuck's kitchen.

"No." Nate shook his head. "Listen, Chuck, I'm kind of busy. Why are you here?"

Chuck raised an eyebrow. "You know, Nathaniel, I've been thinking a lot about you," he began, as if he were ready to barrel into a speech on philosophy, like he usually did after a few ginger beers back at Deep Springs. "You won't answer my calls. I saw you partying pretty hard on New Year's. And you look like you haven't stopped," Chuck said, taking note of the empty cans on the granite counter. "What the fuck is up?" He perched on one of the stools and raised a dark eyebrow.

Nate sighed. Chuck obviously wasn't going to leave until he'd heard his life story. "I hooked up with Serena the other night," he finally admitted.

Chuck raised a hand up for a high five, impressed. Nate kept his arms firmly at his sides. Chuck shrugged, lowering his hand. "I fail to see why that's a bad thing. After all, you've known her forever, you lost your virginity to her, she's always been there for you. . . . I mean, what's the problem?"

"I know." Nate sighed heavily and sat at the table, his forehead cradled in his hands. He was just so fucking confused. Serena was great. Blair was great. Blair had a boyfriend. Both of them hated him.

"Technical difficulties?" Chuck asked.

Nate shook his head. "The next morning, I brought up Blair, and Serena just totally closed off and kicked me out. She probably thinks I still have feelings for Blair." Nate paused. "And I guess I do, even though Blair has a boyfriend."

"You have a hard life, Nathaniel," Chuck scoffed.

"I know I'm being a pussy. But every time I come home, I make a mess. Maybe I'm better off not coming home. Just leaving New York totally," Nate said bluntly. Only a year ago, it would have felt extremely gay to talk about his emotions with another guy. But now, after all his time at Deep Springs, he was okay with it. Maybe he needed to get back there—and never leave.

"What would El Capitan say?" Chuck prodded.

Nate sat up, suddenly remembering the letter Chips's sister had given him. He hadn't felt ready to open it before. He'd needed more time to process things.

And by "process" he means smoke and drink himself into oblivion.

"The letter," Nate said simply. Maybe Chips *did* have something to say. For the first time since the funeral, he felt optimistic.

"Good idea. I'll let you be alone," Chuck said, finishing off his beer and sliding off the stool. "Look, I'm heading to Aspen tomorrow. You should come. Or at least promise you're not going to freak out again. Okay?" Chuck locked eyes with Nate.

"Thanks, man." Nate walked him to the door. "I'll think about Aspen," he lied to Chuck's retreating back. Then he ran upstairs and yanked open the top drawer of his Chippendale desk. He pulled out the wrinkled cream envelope. It felt weighted and heavy. Instantly, Nate knew what it was.

He slid his index finger under the envelope flap, ripped it open, and allowed Chips's antique silver compass to drop into his palm. It looked tarnished and worn and felt reassuringly heavy. Chips only trusted his compass, believing computer navigational systems made people lazy and made them forget what it was like to trust their own minds. Nate had been freaked out at first to head out onto the ocean with no computer system, but soon realized that Chips was right: When you had nothing else to trust, you had to trust yourself.

He pulled out the ivory card stock that accompanied the compass, written in Chips's spiky-scrawly handwriting.

*Nathaniel—*

*Thanks for coming on the journey, and I'm glad you learned something from this old man. Remember: Read the compass, and stay the course.*

Nate sighed, disappointed. All of Chips's lessons were summed up in two sentences. He wasn't sure what he'd been expecting.

A self-help manual?

He knew what Chips meant: that the compass only gave you directions—it was up to you to *interpret* the directions. He wished charting his life was as easy as following a map. He glanced down at the compass, which had led Chips in the right direction for years. Maybe it *did* have some sort of power. Maybe he could use it to help him figure things out.

He held the compass in his hand and squeezed his eyes shut. If it pointed to *W*, it would mean Waldorf. If it pointed toward *S*, it would mean Serena.

And if it points to N, would that mean *Not a Good Idea*?

The thin red needle swung back and forth, first wavering on N, then slowly falling down. It wavered uncertainly before settling right on the letter W.

Nate smiled. Everything seemed absurdly simple for the first time in a while. He needed to find Blair.

Let's hope he finds the shower first.

# *you've got mail*

**From:** svw@vanderWoodsen.com
**To:** dhumphrey3@columbia.edu
**Subject:** Your Poem

Hi Dan,
I'm hoping this is the same Dan Humphrey who went
to Riverside Prep, and who wrote *Serena* in *The New
Yorker*? It's Serena van der Woodsen, from high
school. How are you? I just read your poem and loved
it. Would you want to meet me for coffee sometime?
SvD

**From:** dhumphrey3@columbia.edu
**To:** svw@vanderWoodsen.com
**Subject:** Re: Your Poem

Serena,
Hey! It's really great to hear from you. How've you
been? I'd love to meet up for coffee, where and
whenever.
—Dan
P.S. Glad you liked the poem. Sorry for stealing your
name for the title.


**From:** svw@vanderWoodsen.com
**To:** dhumphrey3@columbia.edu
**Subject:** Re: re: Your Poem

Great! Four o'clock at Doma on Perry Street on Fri?
I remember you love coffee. Hope that hasn't changed!
Xx S

# *the curse of the creative power couple*

"This is it?" Vanessa asked Hollis dubiously on Friday morning. They were standing outside one of the tall, glass-box, personality-less skyscrapers near Grand Central for their meeting with the executives of Streetscape, a small indie studio. Hollis was taken by the idea of making a movie out of Vanessa's life, and had immediately set up a meeting with some people he knew. Vanessa was excited, but suddenly a little nervous. She'd imagined the Streetscape offices would be in Dumbo or SoHo or some other artsy neighborhood, not a random Midtown office building.

Hollis nodded as he gestured for her to go first through the varnished chrome revolving door. The lobby floor and walls were black marble, and men and women in crisp business suits were hurrying back and forth like worker ants. If Vanessa had known she was visiting a corporation, she'd have worn something other than jeans, a black, vaguely Western button-down shirt she'd found at Beacon's Closet, and a pair of Chloé flats that Blair had left behind in high school.

Hollis squeezed her hand reassuringly and pulled her into

the elevator. It whooshed up to the nineteenth floor. "We'll have fun," Hollis promised, readjusting his fedora, which had now become his trademark.

Hollis pushed open the glass door that led to the reception area. A petite blond girl in a black dress glanced up. She looked like a banker. Vanessa smiled, reminding herself not to be so judgmental.

"Andra, great to see you!" Hollis said warmly. The banker got up from behind the desk and hugged him.

"It's been too long!" She smiled, her eyes flicking up his tall, lean form. "You look good."

"Hi." Vanessa said pointedly to the girl. Was she flirting with her boyfriend? While Vanessa was right there?

Aw, can't we all just get along?

"Oh, hi! You must be Vanessa," Andra said warmly. "Hollis told me so much about you, I feel like I know you!" she cooed. Vanessa smiled despite herself. It was nice that Hollis was talking about her when she wasn't around.

"Anyway, I'll let everyone know you're here," Andra said, sitting back down at the desk and picking up a receiver. "Stacy, they're here!" she yelled into the phone. When no one answered she padded down the carpeted hallway to tell them.

"You'll be great, champ," Hollis said, squeezing Vanessa's shoulder as he led her to one of the low-slung couches set up along one cream wall.

"Thanks," she whispered. She usually prided herself on being ultraindependent, but right now, she was glad Hollis was right by her side. He did this kind of thing all the time, but of course Vanessa was nervous. This was her chance. And so what if it was a little more corporate than she expected? After all, this wasn't some student film produced by a purple-haired, multipierced grad student. This was Streetscape, an actual production company.

Just then, a skinny guy with an asymmetrical haircut emerged from a labyrinthine hallway.

"Hollis!" He hug-patted her boyfriend.

"Zach, what's up, man?" Hollis said enthusiastically. "This is my girlfriend, Vanessa. She's an amazing filmmaker. I can't wait to see what happens when she and Stacy get together in one room. Vanessa, this is Zach, Stacy's assistant."

"Hi Vanessa." Zach smiled. Vanessa grinned back. *This* was more like it. Zach looked like the guys in her film class: smart, a little pretentious, and fiercely devoted to making movies. Vanessa understood these people. They were her people. "So, you guys ready to come on back?" Zach asked rhetorically as he walked at breakneck speed through the hallways and toward an empty glass-walled conference room. Vanessa glanced at the large production stills framed on the walls and recognized one from *Between the B and the A*. It was a scene where Blake, the main character, stands forlornly on the roof of his East Village apartment complex, looking out at the buildings surrounding him and feeling so small and insecure and unsure of himself. Vanessa squeezed Hollis's hand. She wanted to scream to everyone that that was her *boyfriend's* brilliance, immortalized on the walls.

"Hollis, darling, where have you been all my life?" A six-foot-tall woman wearing towering five-inch purple Manolos and a gauzy blue Diane von Furstenberg wrap dress strode in. Her body was skeletal, but her chest was huge, and her hair fell almost down to her butt. She looked like a transvestite.

Stacy Brower was the creative exec known for championing

the weird, the obscure, or the ignored. Stacy had discovered *Between the B and the A* after she'd met Hollis at an NYU film student thesis screening event and had wholeheartedly championed it straight to Sundance. She was the perfect creative exec to hear Vanessa's pitch.

"Hi, I'm Vanessa Abrams," Vanessa began, hastily standing up and sticking out her hand. But instead of taking it, Stacy breezed past her and sat down in one of the large Eames chairs in the corner, folding up her legs underneath her so she looked like a praying mantis. Vanessa sat back down.

"I'm really interested in this pitch. Sounds amazing. So, let's hear more about it," Stacy said, sounding bored. Next to her, Zach pulled out a thin Mac Air and gazed at Hollis and Vanessa, his hands poised above the keyboard.

Hollis squeezed Vanessa's hand underneath the glass table. Vanessa smiled at Stacy and took a deep breath before launching into the pitch she'd rehearsed so many times. "Well, it's about a girl who moves from a Vermont farm to Brooklyn to go to an all-girl private school. She lives with her tattooed, musician sister and has some friends who are obscenely wealthy, whom she uses as subjects for film projects. But, mostly, it's about growing up and finding yourself in the weirdest, most wonderful city in the world," Vanessa finished bravely, sneaking a glance at Stacy. Stacy's gaze was fixed out the window. "That city being New York," Vanessa added, her voice scratchy.

Stacy still didn't say anything. Vanessa followed her gaze and saw a suited man in one of the offices in the building across the street, tossing his stapler up and down in the air and catching it. "I could watch that all day. So Zen. He thinks no one can see him because his office door is closed. The fucker," Stacy cackled. She turned her chair back to the table and steepled her violet-colored fingernails together.

"Girl growing up, finding herself," Stacy said, almost to herself. "I like it. But what if it was a boy?" Stacy mused. "You know, I'm going to call Geoff in. He's doing a lot of work on projects with the eighteen-to-thirty-five male demo in mind. I think he'd like to discuss this." Stacy smiled as Zach scurried up and out the door.

"I'm sorry, but you want the main character to be a boy?" Vanessa asked, trying not to sound horrified.

"Excuse me?" Stacy asked, arching one blond eyebrow at Vanessa in curiosity. Just then, Zach returned, trailed by a five-foot-tall man wearing a lilac button-down, tight black jeans, and cowboy boots.

"Hello!" the man said in a high-pitched voice. "Hollis, baby, you look amazing. So, let's talk. Stacy said you needed some insight into the male mind?" he asked, winking showily and not bothering to introduce himself to Vanessa before he plopped down next to her.

Vanessa gazed at Geoff in horror. She didn't care about pleasing a *demo*. She wanted to make a film.

"So, here's my pitch," Geoff said, flapping his arms in excitement. "Eighteen-year-old boy. He lives in Australia or, you know, that country with the hobbits . . . New Zealand? And he has to move to a city?" Stacy nodded enthusiastically.

"No!" Vanessa broke in. Suddenly, all eyes turned to her.

"Of course, you're right," Stacy locked eyes with Vanessa and smiled. It was the first time Stacy had directly interacted with her. Vanessa smiled back, relieved. So Stacy was a little eccentric, but she got it.

"Of course it can't be set Down Under," Stacy said definitively, as if she were the one rejecting the idea. "Ever since *Australia* hit the shitter, the antipodes are fucking career suicide." Stacy shuddered. "But I like your thinking, Geoff. I love the idea of doing location, a different culture. People like that. Good date movie, good press. So what if the Maori boy moves to Iceland and *that's* how we open the film. It's perfect. It's diverse, it's *Slumdog Millionaire* meets *Kids*. Hollis, you're a genius." Stacy clapped her hands in excitement.

Vanessa squeezed Hollis's hand tightly. She expected him to roll his stormy gray eyes and tell them to fuck themselves. But instead, he was nodding as if he was agreeing. What the *fuck*? Vanessa yanked her hand away, aware that her palms were clammy.

"Here's my pitch," Hollis said, his deep voice commanding the room. "Love the Maori boy, love Iceland. So what if we double the fun and add some twins? That way, we can really explore identity and selfhood and what makes a family." Hollis nodded, leaning forward on his elbows as if he couldn't wait to see what *else* Stacy would add to the idea. Vanessa felt like she was going to throw up. He was *agreeing* with them?

"What makes a family," Geoff piped up, his voice going up an octave in excitement. "That could be a great title."

"Only if we're a fucking television network for women." Stacy rolled her eyes in his direction. "Remember, we need to get the guys. Are you having trouble in that department?" she asked sarcastically. "No, what if it's something like *The Tribe Goes Down*? See, that's sexy."

Vanessa couldn't take this anymore. If Hollis wasn't going to say anything because he was afraid of offending Stacy, well then, she was. She knew you had to make some compromises to get financing, but this was absurd. "No," Vanessa said loudly, her voice seeming to ricochet off the glass walls.

"Alyssa?" Stacy asked curiously.

"It's *Vanessa*," Vanessa snapped. "I'm sorry, but the pitch was about a teenage *girl* who moves to *Brooklyn*. I'm not making a movie about twin Maori *boys* who move to *Iceland*," she said firmly, hoping Stacy would understand. "I don't know anything about Iceland. Or Maoris."

"Right." Stacy nodded. "But this is a Hollis Lyons film. If Streetscape is producing it, Hollis is directing it," she said, as if she were a kindergarten teacher explaining to a five-year-old why she couldn't have two snacks. "It'll really be great, Hollis." Stacy smiled. "Now, let's keep going. So, we get them to Reykjavík, and then . . ." She trailed off, glancing around the room for the next pitch.

"Then I guess I'm not needed here." Vanessa stood up. Tears were dangerously close to flowing, and she *would not* cry in front of them. She walked toward the door. Hollis was still sitting on the edge of his chair, leaning his elbows on the table as if he couldn't wait to hear Stacy's latest absurd idea.

"Hollis?" Vanessa asked, her voice shaking.

"See you later," Hollis called distractedly. He turned back to the table. "I think it might be cool if one of them got involved with a Dutch girl from Amsterdam," he mused.

At this, Vanessa froze. Her hand was on the doorknob, but she felt paralyzed. What was Hollis doing? How could he *betray* her like that?

"Zach, can you walk Alyssa out, while we hash out the Amsterdam plot twist," Stacy asked, mistaking Vanessa's pent-up rage for confusion over where the exit was located.

Vanessa swallowed her anger. She was going to head back to the apartment, pack her stuff, and then go straight to Ruby's. If Hollis thought she would continue to live with him, he was dead wrong. "Hollis is great at plot twists," Vanessa managed icily before she closed the door.

The best endings are the ones you don't see coming.

## the marriage of two minds works better over beers

Dan lit up a Camel as he stood outside Doma, the busy café on Perry Street. It was already almost dark, even though it was just four in the afternoon. The café looked warm and inviting, with people reading tattered paperbacks and couples leaning over their lattes. But Dan didn't go in. He never knew the protocol for meeting someone for coffee. Did he go in and scout out a table and order? Did he wait outside?

Someone's really taking this seriously.

He pulled out his phone. Four-oh-eight. She probably wouldn't even show. This was the last time he was meeting up with a model-slash-actress or whatever Serena was. He stuffed his hands in the pockets of his corduroys, ready to walk off.

"Dan!" He whirled around and saw Serena. Dan sucked in his breath. She was even more stunning than he remembered. She was wearing a long gray coat, her cheeks flushed from the cold and her long hair loose and golden around her shoulders. She looked beautiful, otherworldly, like a Hans Christian Andersen princess who'd taken a wrong turn and wound up in the city instead of a forest in Norway.

"Oh my God!" Serena exclaimed, hugging Dan. She kissed him on the cheek, leaving a sticky lip gloss mark and a tingling sensation.

"Hey," Dan said casually, trying not to squeak.

"So sorry to keep you waiting!" Serena shook her head apologetically. "Should we go in?"

"It's sort of crowded," Dan pointed out. Suddenly, he didn't want to share Serena with the nosy coffee drinkers inside.

A shadow of a frown crossed Serena's face. "Then let's go somewhere else!" she decided, grabbing Dan's hand. Dan felt himself blush. "We could go for a walk or something," she said easily.

Walk? No. Dan did not want to walk. In fact, all he wanted to do was stare at Serena's silken hair and ocean blue eyes and . . . "There has to be a bar around here somewhere," he croaked.

Liquid courage always helps.

They crossed Seventh Avenue, and as they did, a flash went off. Serena turned her head away from the photographer, clearly used to this kind of thing. "How about there?" She nodded toward an oak door to a bar with dark windows and no discernable sign.

Dan nodded. It seemed like a good bet, the sort of place where a New York writer would take his muse. "Let's go," he decided, pulling Serena inside.

The bar was grimy and dark and smelled like Lysol and Bud Lite. They were the only people there besides two red-faced old men frowning over crossword puzzles.

"I love it!" Serena pronounced, sliding onto one of the cracked vinyl booths in the front. She shrugged off her coat, then took off her gloves. "Aren't you hot?" she asked, looking expectantly up at Dan, who was still clad in his black puffer coat.

"Yeah," Dan admitted, feeling slightly nauseous. He shrugged off his coat and slid it on the bench opposite her. "I'll get drinks." He strode up to the pockmarked bar, wondering what the hell he should order for Serena. She probably drank hundred-dollar glasses of champagne.

"We've got five-dollar pitchers of Bud Lite until five. Manager's special," the ancient bartender growled, not looking up from his sudoku puzzle.

"Sure, fine," Dan said distractedly, slapping the money on the table. He carried back the pitcher, along with two plastic cups, and carefully poured drinks for both of them.

"Cheers!" Serena held up her cup toward Dan. "Thanks for meeting me. I know it's random, but when I opened up that *New Yorker*, I can't even tell you how badly I needed to hear something nice. And then I saw my name . . . and then I saw *your name*. . . . Anyway, I really liked it," Serena trailed off uncertainly. Did she sound like a total stalker? Maybe the poem wasn't about her at all—maybe it was about his dog or his mom or maybe he just randomly chose the name from a name book. Maybe her whole problem was she was just too much of a romantic, seeing love when it wasn't there. She took a long swig of beer.

"Oh." Dan blushed. He'd been trying to figure out how to explain the poem to Serena without sounding like a stalker or a loser, but so far, he had nothing. He figured the words would come to him. He took a big gulp of beer, even though he hated the taste of it. He much preferred scotch or whiskey. "I actually wrote that in high school. Right after we dated." Maybe the truth was the best way to go.

"Really?" Serena gazed up at Dan's sweet and sincere face. She and Dan had dated for a little bit their senior year, but had quickly realized they were just too different. He'd been nice, but way too intense with his poetry, and looking back, she could hardly remember what they'd done or spoken about when they'd been together.

"I hope you don't mind," Dan mumbled. He couldn't believe he and Serena van der Woodsen, his high school crush, his former muse, were just chatting over Bud Lights at four o'clock in the afternoon. It was so bizarre, it almost felt normal.

Serena broke into a smile. "I loved it. Except I had to look up a few of the Ovid references. If you weren't such a good writer, I'd think you were trying to make people feel dumb." She smiled, then ducked under the table, pulling out a dog-eared copy of Ovid from her large white purse. "It's from that myth, right? About the two lovers who are turned into birds because one can't live without the other? I cried when I read it," Serena confessed. It was so nice to actually *talk* about everything she'd been reading.

Dan blinked. Serena had actually looked up the Greek mythology allusion in the poem? He didn't think Serena van der Woodsen read literature.

Or *The New Yorker*?

"So, how's Columbia?" Serena asked after a pause. She hadn't been sure what they'd talk about when they met, and right now, Dan wasn't doing much talking at all. Maybe it was an artist thing. Maybe she was distracting him from an afternoon of poetry writing. What was he thinking? His eyes looked so large and brown and kept flicking toward her, then away. He was mysterious. He had substance. And, especially recently, Serena hadn't hung out with many guys who had substance.

"It's great!" Dan said enthusiastically, glad they'd landed on a less awkward topic. He could talk about college. "I get to spend my time reading great books and talking to people who actually care about them, not just people who are trying to get good grades," Dan said, hoping Serena didn't think he was hopelessly dorky. "In high school I felt like I was just wasting my life doing what other people wanted me to do. I'm reading *The Fountainhead*. Have you read it?" Dan asked hopefully.

Serena shook her head slowly. She'd forgotten how *intense* Dan Humphrey was. She leaned in close. "Tell me about it."

"Oh, well, it's about this architect who decides to accept obscurity and ridicule instead of compromising his ideals in his designs. It's about choosing good art above all else," Dan said seriously. "And that's what I feel like college is all about. Figuring out what's important to you in life, the thing you'll follow to the end of the earth. Figuring out what you care about most." Dan blushed and looked down into his mug. If she didn't think he was a giant dork before, she definitely would now.

Serena nodded. That made sense. "I could see that," she offered. "I've been taking a break from acting to figure out what I want, but I still don't know." She grabbed the pitcher and refilled their plastic cups. "I'm not really passionate about anything like you are."

"I think you're passionate," Dan said. "I mean, I think you must have a passion." He blushed and gulped his beer. What was his problem? The more he tried not to sound like a creepy stalker, the more stalkerish he sounded. "Would you ever think about college?" he asked, hoping he didn't sound like a pushy parent.

"I'm actually deferred from Yale right now." Serena sighed. Instantly, her blue eyes seemed clouded by sadness. "It's sort of a long story."

"You should go," Dan said seriously. Instantly, he felt like an idiot. Why was he telling his dream girl to move hours way?

"Really?" Serena stared into her cup of watery beer. She had been thinking a lot about going back to school, recently. . . . And besides, it wasn't like Blair was in charge of Yale. If Serena wanted to go to Yale, she should go to Yale. "Are you trying to get rid of me?" she asked, raising a playful eyebrow at Dan, who instantly reddened.

"No!" Dan protested. "But there's more to college than beer pong and a T-shirt. I think you might like it." Why had he been so nervous about meeting Serena? Sure, she was beautiful, but she was also goofy and fun and smart and sweet.

Serena smiled across the table. She couldn't remember the last time someone had listened to her—really listened. "Well, if I do go to Yale, I'll still come back and visit. New Haven's not far from the city, you know."

"No, it's not far at all." Dan smiled back, sloshing his beer so a tiny dribble fell onto his blue Gap sweater. But he didn't care. Serena was still beaming at him, and in her deep blue eyes was the promise of the future. "I'd like that," he said finally.

See what I mean about history coming back to haunt you?

# if you don't know who you're sleeping with, who does?

"Shut up!" Blair screamed, hitting the wall by her headboard on her way from the minibar toward her bed. She was on her fourth vodka soda refill and the couple in the room next door seemed to be on their fourth round of noisy, athletic sex. Blair had had enough. Even if they were on their honeymoon, didn't they get tired? And hadn't the Tribeca Star heard of soundproofing?

And doesn't she have anything better to do than sit in her room and listen to them?

The noises in the next room subsided slightly. There. That was better. It was only ten o'clock, but Blair was exhausted. For the past twenty-four hours, she'd been holed up in her room. Nothing bad ever happened in the hotel room.

There's a first time for everything.

Besides, what was the point of even trying anymore, Blair thought as she took a gulp of her drink, then hiccupped. She knew drinking away her sorrows wasn't exactly ideal, but she didn't want to face her gigantic shitstorm of a life right now. Her relationship was ruined. She hated Serena. Nate was just a dumb, horny *boy*, and the thing that sucked about *that* was that she'd known it for years. And she had no idea where the fuck she'd even live when she got back to Yale. Would she be homeless?

Maybe she should just move to another country and start all over again.

She drained the rest of her drink and switched out the light. Maybe if she lay still and focused on breathing in and out, she could at least fall asleep for a few hours. Then tomorrow would be a new day. She'd make herself leave the hotel, buy a pretty orange leather Hermès notebook, sit in Amaranth, order a vodka gimlet, and write a to-do list. She always used to make to-do lists for class, and they helped keep her on track. Maybe she'd also buy herself a bag from Hermès, just as a congratulatory present for making it through what was probably the worst winter vacation anyone had ever had.

Just as she was falling asleep, she was aware of the sound of the door clicking open. It was either Pete or a serial killer. And really, what did she have to lose either way?

Blair quickly adjusted the straps of her Cosabella tank top and folded her hands by her head, as if she'd just moved in her sleep. If it was Pete, she wanted him to see her sleeping sweetly. He'd soften and profess his love, thinking that she couldn't hear. Then, he'd kiss her awake, like the prince waking Sleeping Beauty, and they'd live happily ever after.

And if it's a serial killer?

Blair felt a warm hand on her hip, just above her La Perla boy-cut panties. She murmured slightly, nestling into the warm body settling in next to her. She smelled the scent of L'Occitane soap and a little bit of pot. As soon as she inhaled, a tingly feeling shot through her. It smelled like Nate. Nate had somehow sensed her distress, and come for her. Maybe this was all a dream, but at this point, she'd take dream Nate. She squeezed her eyes shut, not wanting to wake up and break the spell.

"You're my East, my West, my North, my South. Blair, you're my girl," the voice said hoarsely.

Blair bolted upright and reached for the lamp. Bright light filled the room. There, wearing a pair of rumpled khakis and a misbuttoned dark blue Ralph Lauren shirt, was Nate. Real Nate. Not Dream Nate.

"What the fuck?" Blair's heart was hammering in her chest. She yanked the duvet cover around her body and covered herself.

Not like he hasn't seen it all before.

"You're beautiful," Nate said slowly. His large green eyes were hazy and his hair was sticking up on one side.

"You're drunk and high and you need to get out of here," Blair said shortly.

"I love you," Nate said simply. He propped his head up on his hand and continued to gaze at Blair. "I needed to see you."

"Oh," Blair considered, still blinking in the bright light. What was she supposed to say to that? She felt like she was watching a foreign film whose subtitles had suddenly stopped running. "How did you know I was here?" she finally asked. Nate was obviously hammered, but he looked so sincere and innocent lying on his side, as if they were back in high school. It made her want to punch him, then hug him, then push his hair back and tell him everything would be all right. She appraised him again. Maybe after he took a shower.

The door clicked open, shedding amber light from the hallway onto the off-white rug.

"Blair?"

Blair whirled around to see Pete standing in the doorframe, holding a bouquet of red roses. His face drained of color as his blue eyes flicked between Blair and Nate. He opened and closed his mouth, like a goldfish.

"Pete!" Blair squeaked.

He exhaled loudly, the sound of his breath filling the room and morphing into a strangled cry. He hurled the flowers to the ground and an explosion of red petals scattered on the thick blue carpet.

"I can explain," Blair said in horror. She knew how bad this looked. She knew there really wasn't a logical explanation. But she needed Pete to know this was a total misunderstanding. "Please listen," Blair choked out, diving toward Pete.

"You're in bed with that asshole?" Pete asked. And then he laughed, one short, angry bark. "Of course you are." He shook his head.

"No," she protested. She felt like she was going to throw up. This could not be happening. Please believe me, she silently begged. "He's drunk and he just found me. He just came in like two seconds ago. I thought he was you."

Pete shook his head sadly, as if Blair's explanation was so ridiculous he felt embarrassed even to be hearing it.

"Dude, sorry," Nate said, trying to stand up. He understood this was bad. He didn't want Blair to go back to that other guy, but he also didn't want to hurt her. And now he was, and it was all so fucking confusing. His foot got caught in a tangle of sheets and he face-planted on the floor.

Karma's a bitch.

"You deserve each other," Pete said, turning on his heel and slamming the door. Blair could hear his footsteps tromping down the hall. The elevator whooshed open and he was gone. She turned and gazed down at Nate, pathetically collapsed in a pile.

"Fuck you," she whispered, her eyes finally filling with all the tears she'd held in for the past day. Every time. Every time. Every time she was almost happy, Nate managed to fuck it up. Even worse, every time she managed to fall for it.

"But Blair . . ." Nate struggled to his feet.

Suddenly, she felt the vodka sodas from earlier swirling in her stomach and knew she was going to throw up. Just like always. She felt like a confused and lonely fifteen-year-old. And it was all Nate's fault.

She ran into the bathroom, kneeled down, and retched into the toilet bowl again and again. When she was finished, she leaned her forehead against the cool whiteness of the toilet seat, knowing she looked as pathetic as she felt.

"You okay?" she heard from the other side of the door. Nate's voice sounded whiny, the way it sometimes did when he was really, really baked. That was what gave her the motivation to stand up, splash her face with water, vigorously brush her teeth with her imported Marvis toothpaste, and emerge from the bathroom. Nate was standing at the door, his hands at his sides, shifting from foot to foot.

"Blair—" he began.

"Get out!" Blair yelled with every force of her being. "You're bad for me. I never want to see you again." She opened the door, her whole body shaking, but Nate just stood there.

"Fine," she said. "If you won't leave, I will." And with that she was gone.

Sometimes misery doesn't love company.

## *puppy love*

Vanessa banged around the kitchen of the loft, feeling like an angry housewife. It was almost ten o'clock and she hadn't heard from Hollis since she stormed out of their pitch meeting. No, scratch that. Since she stormed out of *his* pitch meeting. She pulled out a mug from the cabinet and boiled water to make tea. She wasn't one of those people who drank when she was upset, so organic chai would have to do.

The worst thing about it was that she'd done this to herself. She used to be a shaven-headed, black-garbed, kick-ass filmmaker who always wore steel-toe boots and didn't put up with shit from anyone. Now she was this needy girlfriend type without any projects of her own, without an apartment of her own, and with no one she could even talk to. Last year, Vanessa had spent practically every Friday night with the other NYU film majors at Bushwick Country Club, a Williamsburg bar with mini golf. But ever since she and Hollis had become serious, it had become harder and harder to carve out time to meet with her old friends. She considered calling her sister, Ruby, but all she and Piotr could talk about was whether the fetus was the size of a gerbil or an avocado.

She heard the whir of the elevator and felt her stomach twist in contempt. What the fuck was the point of living in Brooklyn if you had an *elevator* leading straight to your apartment?

"Hey." Hollis sheepishly walked into the apartment, holding a box of Franzia wine out like a peace offering. In his other hand was a leash—attached to a brown and white puppy. The wine was an inside joke, since one of their first dates had been at a tiny Chinese restaurant that served free boxed wine.

And the puppy?

"Celebrating your new deal?" Vanessa refused to take the wine from his hands or even ask about the dog. She grabbed her mug of tea and walked into their newly set-up corner office. One side was hers, the other his. She opened her MacBook Pro and clicked onto the apartment listings on Craigslist. She didn't *really* want to move or break up with Hollis, but she didn't know what else to do.

"Don't be mad." Hollis put his hands on Vanessa's shoulders and whirled her Aeron chair around so she faced him. His gray eyes were wide with concern, and his chin had a tiny bit of the five o'clock stubble that Vanessa had always found so sexy. "I have someone for you to meet. This is Norma Desmond. She sort of has this diva-ish personality, but I think there's a lot going on beneath the surface. She's certainly a charmer." He scooped up the tiny puppy and waved its paw at her.

"You decided to get a dog. Any other decisions you made today that you didn't tell me about?" Vanessa asked crisply. She gazed down at Norma, who was shaking her tiny butt uncontrollably. The name was from *Sunset Boulevard*, a film Vanessa and Hollis both loved.

"Look, Vanessa, I know you're mad. I'm really, really sorry about the way everything went down. I should never have had you pitch the film to Streetscape." Hollis's eyes looked so sweet and sincere that Vanessa wanted to believe him.

"So then why were you going along with them? Why didn't you leave with me?" Vanessa asked sharply. She glanced down at her beat-up Doc Martens so she wouldn't have to look at his face when he lied. She willed her boots not to kick him.

"Because Streetscape has changed. I realized that when I saw it was Stacy handling the meeting. Stacy is under a lot of pressure to make movies that will sell. Before, no one knew who she was, so she could afford to take risks. Now, she's known in Hollywood and she's scared shitless. That's why she called that other exec in. I know the demo talk is bullshit, but it's the formula that works. I mean, I'm still building my career and they're the best and I trust them, but I know they're not the best for you," Hollis explained. "And I just got Norma because I felt so guilty and she's so cute. She's part chow and part poodle. She's a choodle," Hollis explained proudly. "And I wanted to see you smile."

The puppy was adorable, and Vanessa fought a smile. She didn't want to be won over so easily. "Why did you even set up the meeting?"

"I got excited. I love your story," Hollis said earnestly. "But what they want to do isn't your movie. Once I saw how off-track they were getting, I pushed them away from your idea on purpose. I didn't want you to wind up making a movie that would compromise your vision."

"Really?" Vanessa grinned shyly. Now that she thought about it, Hollis hadn't really spoken up at the meeting until after the story had gotten so off-track—and *after* Stacy had made it clear she wasn't going to have it any other way.

"Of course. So they want me to direct the film. It's on location—in Iceland. And I'll have to go to Australia too, to cast the Maoris. The twin kids evolved into a whole family, like *Cheaper by the Dozen* but with Maoris, in Iceland. But I told them I needed to think about it. I'll drop it in a second if you want me to." Hollis gazed down at Vanessa.

Vanessa glanced around the apartment—the brand-new eco-chic furniture, the clean, bare walls they hadn't decorated, the expansive living room they planned to throw so many dinner parties in. If Hollis went to Iceland, it would be a long time before they really lived in this apartment together. But dropping a Streetscape project was equivalent to career suicide.

Just then, Norma whined plaintively. "Well, I'm going to take Norma's protest as a no," Hollis shrugged, scooping up the puppy.

"No." Vanessa shook her head definitively. They had plenty of time to build a life together. After all, she was only a sophomore. "You need to do it. I *want* you to do it—we both do." Vanessa reached for the puppy and buried her nose in its soft and fluffy fur. "How long will you be gone?" she asked.

"A few months. But you can come to Reykjavík whenever you want. I mean, you need to. I don't know what I'll do without you."

"You're not gone yet," Vanessa murmured. It was a lot to process. She was sad, but not upset. Yes, Hollis was leaving, but somehow, their relationship seemed stronger than ever—strong enough to stand the distance. And maybe a few months apart would be good for her, too. She could concentrate on her own work.

"Thanks for bringing me a friend," she added, still cuddling with the puppy.

"I'll miss you guys," Hollis said huskily. He kissed Vanessa's forehead, then the puppy's. "Take care of each other. You two are my family now."

Vanessa smiled. "Absence makes the heart grow fonder, right? And a few months isn't too long," she insisted.

Right. And Iceland isn't very far away at all.

# on some nights, frenemies beat strangers

"Vodka tonic," Blair said brusquely to the Tribeca Star bartender, a pretty platinum blonde who looked like she'd never had her heart broken before. Unlike Blair, who'd had her heart broken—five? Seven? Nine times?—by the exact same guy.

"Another one?" The bartender arched one penciled-in eyebrow.

"Yes," Blair said icily. It was her right to get as drunk as she wanted after the night she'd had. She pulled out her cell and dialed Pete's number again. Of course it went to voice mail. Tears pricked her eyes. It was really over.

Blair felt a tap on her shoulder. She whirled around, ready to tell whoever thought it was a good idea to talk to her to fuck off.

"You okay?"

Blair looked up and into the eyes of . . . Chuck Bass? What the hell? Where was his pinky ring? Or pet monkey? Blair had heard that Chuck had transformed, but seeing it in person was so shocking she almost forgot her tragedy of a life. His dark brown hair was cut close to his head, and his dark eyes looked serious and friendly at the same time. He wore a blue cashmere sweater, khaki pants, and loafers. He looked surprisingly good.

"Hi," Blair said finally.

"Good to see you," Chuck said enthusiastically. He slid onto the metal bar stool next to her. "Jameson on the rocks," he ordered. "And we'll also have a grilled cheese. And the hummus plate," he added.

"I'm not hungry," Blair said shortly, hoping Chuck would get the hint and leave. After all, she hadn't come down to the bar to socialize—she'd come down because her drunk ex-boyfriend was in her bedroom and she had nowhere else to go.

"Well, in case you change your mind. You want to talk?" Chuck asked.

Blair considered. She and Chuck had never really gotten along, but they'd known each other forever, and someone was better than no one. "Have you seen Nate this break?"

"I have. He's been a little . . . bent out of shape. Have you?"

Blair nodded. "He thought it would be a brilliant idea to come here. To find me. And then *crawl into bed with me*. Which was fucking perfect, because five minutes later, my boyfriend came into the hotel room and got the wrong idea. So let's just say I've had a shitty night," Blair said tightly. She grabbed a cocktail napkin and began shredding it. Tiny pieces of paper rained down on the oak bar like snowflakes.

"That's rough," Chuck exhaled. He stared into his drink contemplatively.

"I just don't know why he always does that. He always fucks up my life. He always has," Blair said in a small voice. The tears started again. Chuck took another cocktail napkin from behind the bar and offered it to her.

"You're probably the only person he can trust," Chuck said gently as the bartender placed the grilled cheese and hummus plate in front of them. Blair eyed it hungrily. She'd never been one of those girls who lost an appetite in a crisis. "Here." Chuck grabbed half of the sandwich and held it toward her. For a second, Blair thought he was going to try to feed it to her, but he didn't. She took the sandwich from him and Chuck pushed away her half-finished drink.

"What you need is a bubble bath, some candles, and some chocolate," Chuck said. Blair rolled her eyes. Of course. *This* was what the whole conversation was leading up to. Chuck just wanted to take advantage of her.

"And I suppose I need company in that bubble bath," Blair replied sarcastically, draining the rest of her drink and standing up. She grabbed the bar counter for support, feeling shaky.

"Look, you can stay upstairs in my suite, and I'll sleep in my apartment." Chuck gently put his arm on her shoulder to steady her. "And tomorrow, we can go to brunch."

Blair wanted to shake him off, but she was too tired. Instead, she gratefully leaned into him.

Upstairs, Chuck led Blair down the hallway to the Bass suite. "Good night, Blair," he said, kissing her on the forehead. "I'll pick you up tomorrow morning."

She may be down and out, but that doesn't stop the boys from falling for her.

## *if all else fails, move across the ocean*

Serena sat at a banquette of the Star Bar at the Tribeca Star hotel on Saturday afternoon, nervously chewing on a pink star-shaped cocktail stirrer. She wore a clingy blue Alice+Olivia dress and Christian Louboutin over-the-knee boots, her hair pulled into a high bun. She was utterly oblivious to the admiring glances shot her way, lost in her own little world.

The Star Lounge had never carded, so she'd been coming here since she was fifteen, when she used to meet Blair for a drink before going up to Chuck's suite. The lounge looked the same as always: black leather ottomans and couches surrounded the perimeter, and the walls were covered with shelves of flickering candles. It was only Serena who'd changed.

Cue the Joni Mitchell sound track. . . .

She'd sat on her bed in her empty apartment last night, leafing through scripts her agent had sent along. She could be a young woman looking for love in the city; she could be the beautiful former golden girl who gets sucked into a downward spiral of coke and vodka; she could be the love interest, a beautiful but vacuous blonde who was only the end goal; or, for a real change of pace, she could be the bitchy villain in a superhero movie, wearing a leather catsuit and a dark wig.

Serena didn't want to be in any of those movies. She didn't want to be in any movies, period. Sure, the press junkets, the swag, the glitz and glamour had been fun at first, but they'd quickly lost their appeal. Instead, she'd thought a lot about what Dan Humphrey had said, about Columbia giving him the chance to think and learn and explore. The more and more she thought about it, the more appealing college seemed. Where else could she spend her time reading and growing up and figuring out what she wanted to do with the rest of her life?

Just this morning, she'd summoned her courage and made a call to the Yale admissions office, to let them know her deferral period was over. Now she was officially in, ready to matriculate next fall. She'd told her parents and brother at brunch. There was only one other person who needed to know.

*I'm sure that person will be thrilled.*

"Your friend coming?" the server asked dubiously, picking up Serena's now-empty vodka soda.

"Who knows?" Serena sighed. She knew Blair was staying at the Tribeca Star, and was counting on her coming in or out at some point in the evening. But she'd already been waiting for an hour, and so far, no sign of her. "I'll have another one."

Serena glanced up at the entrance again. If she didn't come in five minutes, she was leaving.

*That won't be necessary.*

Sweeping into the bar, not bothering to take off her over-size Louis Vuitton sunglasses, was Blair. She wore a dark pair of skinny jeans and an oversize black sweater, looking like a more glamorous version of Katie Holmes.

"Blair!" Serena called, standing up and waving wildly. Blair flicked her eyes to Serena's corner, as if she were completely uninterested or unimpressed to see her there.

Blair put her hands on her hips and glared at her former friend. What the *fuck* was Serena doing here? First Nate, now this? That was it, she was *never* coming back to New York after this trip. She'd have bagels FedExed to her in New Haven and deal with the Barneys at The Grove when she visited her mom in LA. She could probably go through the rest of her life never coming to the city again.

"What are you doing here?" Blair finally asked. She felt like hell. She'd barely slept last night. Chuck had been true to his word and had picked her up for brunch. It might have been fun— Chuck had ridiculous stories about life at Deep Springs, and had done his best to avoid the topic of Nate—but Blair had been hungover and shaky and tired. She'd been napping on and off all afternoon. She probably looked like hell, too. She was still wearing the same jeans-and-sweater combination she'd been wearing last night, but no way did she want to go back to her own hotel room and take the chance of running into Nate or Pete. She was sure they were both gone by now—long gone. But just in case.

"I wanted to see you. Please sit down?" Serena begged. Blair paused, but then reluctantly slid onto a leather ottoman opposite Serena.

"What is it?" Blair snapped.

Serena took a deep breath. At first she wanted to tell Blair everything: that she'd been burned by Nate, that she hadn't been able to stop thinking about Dan Humphrey for two days, and that, most important, she was going to Yale. But she didn't know where to begin.

"Vodka soda?" the server said, plunking a tumbler on top of a pink star-shaped coaster. "And what would your friend like?"

"Nothing." Blair impatiently waved the server away with her hand. "You came to tell me something?" Blair asked pointedly, as if she were conducting a job interview with someone who had absolutely no shot in hell of getting the position.

"Look, I know you're mad at me. I'm sorry. I hate how we fight. It's so pointless. And I wanted you to know—I'm coming to Yale next fall," Serena blurted. "We'll be at the same school again—without Mrs. McLean watching us!" she joked, hoping Blair would laugh, remembering their Talbots pantsuit–loving former headmistress. Blair just raised her eyebrow and sighed.

The sound track at the bar suddenly changed to a cheesy pop song, reminding Serena of how much fun the two of them used to have, back when they would dance around her bedroom until they collapsed in a tired heap on top of each other. Back before Nate came between them. Serena managed a watery smile. "Can't we be friends?" she asked finally.

Blair stared into Serena's large blue eyes, which looked so innocent and pleading. They'd had so many fights, followed by so many teary makeup sessions. For a moment, Blair wanted to throw her arms around Serena and tell her everything would be okay, that they would always be friends. But that wasn't exactly true. Everything *wasn't* okay. Serena had stolen Nate, had cost her Pete, and now wanted to come to Yale—and who knew what she would do once she got there?

Blair stood up. Maybe forgiveness had worked in the past, but she had to move forward. And her future had no place for Serena. Serena had taken Nate from her and now that she'd already lost him, she wanted to take Yale. She could have it. Blair wasn't going to be around to watch.

"Actually, I'm going abroad next year, so we won't really see each other." She slung her Chloé hobo bag over her shoulder. "'Bye!" she called, not bothering to look back.

*Au revoir . . .*

III

Disclaimer: All the real names of places, people, and events have been altered or abbreviated to protect the innocent. Namely, me.

| topics | sightings | your e-mail | post a question |

# hey people!

**a note to all you study abroaders**

We know who you are. We can hear and smell you from a mile away. You're the guys and girls who pronounce everything with a slightly clipped British accent, like Madonna, or roll your *r*'s even when you're speaking English. You're the ones talking about how the *siesta* really suits you, or how a glass of wine with lunch really calms the nerves. You're the ones who won't shut up about how much *better* your adopted country is—even though you've spent most of your first semester getting drunk with fellow study abroaders and you can only say one sentence in the language of your host country: "Where's the bathroom?" or "toilet," as they say in the U.K.

Don't get me wrong—I understand the appeal of your international environs. Take a look at **B**. Even though a bevy of well-bred British boys have been following her through the medieval streets of Oxford, she's been spotted drinking pints and sharing snogs with a fellow American . . . a very familiar one. Is it just me, or are American boys that much sexier when they go abroad?

## on the home front

I haven't forgotten about all of you who stayed stateside. My first subject: **S**, current cause célèbre at Yale. Sadly for the Yale drama club and all the other school societies eager to claim her as a member, she's practically a part-time student, hopping on the Metro North every Thursday afternoon after Moral Philosophy class. Her destination? The Upper West Side, where she spends most of her time holed up with **D**. Those two only venture out occasionally, blissfully disheveled, for pancakes and coffee on Sunday mornings. Boring couple alert!

Meanwhile, **V** has been keeping a low profile at her Williamsburg loft, occasionally emerging to walk her adorable dog. Whatever happened to that filmmaker boyfriend of hers? It's an awfully big apartment for just one person. **N** has been spotted out at Deep Springs, his eyes glittering for one girl only . . . a newborn albino calf named Gertie. Or perhaps I should refer to her as Baby G? Finally, little **J** is back in the city for the holidays, last seen lunching at Balthazar and poring over college catalogs with her dark-haired, violet-eyed boarding school friend. Is our little **J** all grown up? All I can say is, boarding school has been *very* good to her.

## your e-mail

Dear Gossip Girl,
So, I'm a freshman and when I got my housing assignment last August, I was thrilled to find out I was rooming with **S**. As in, the famous **S**. But she's never around, and when she *is*, all she does is read philosophy and have sappy convos on her cell with her boyfriend. Isn't she supposed to be the dancing-on-tables life-of-the-party? What happened?
—roomie

**a:**

Dear Roomie,

It's called acting far beyond her years, because she's all boring and married. Hopefully she'll grow out of it soon and will start having fun with the rest of us. Or at least attempting to entertain us again.

—GG

## sightings

**J** piled in a car with **S** and **D**. Destination: **Providence, Rhode Island.** Can't believe she's ready to tour colleges! . . . **B** being picked up at **Logan Airport** in **Boston** by her gay dad, **H**, his new husband, and her adopted stepbrother and sister. What a beautiful, accepting family! . . . **N** at **Grand Central**, drinking a large coffee and glancing wistfully at the clock in the center of the station. Headed somewhere, or just remembering the road not taken? . . . **V** walking her chow-poodle mix around **Williamsburg**, watching all the hipster couples holding hands. Lonely much?

## college confidential

For most of us, the exhausting process of choosing a college is in our distant past. But for those of you using the holiday break to plan your future, here's a helpful hint: College tours never give an accurate representation of what your experience will be like. You may never even set foot in that fabulous science library or use the multimillion-dollar athletic complex. But you *do* have to make friends. My advice: Go on a tour of your own and see what—or who—you come across.

You know you love me,

gossip girl

# *an almost missed connection*

"This is the John Hay Library," Naomi, Nate's tour guide at Brown, explained, stopping in front of a large Gothic building in the chilly late-December afternoon. The aged brick buildings of the Brown campus looked stately in the crisp winter air and there was a light dusting of snow on the campus green. "It houses our collection of rare books. Most students prefer to study at the John D. Rockefeller library, which we call the Rock," Naomi continued with a smile. She was a pixieish junior with spiky short brown hair who majored in feminist dance, and had proudly explained that Brown allowed its undergrads to design their own major. Back in high school, Nate had thought designing a major seemed cool, but now it seemed sort of dumb. What *was* feminist dance, anyway?

I'm sure he could get a private lesson.

"They say rubbing the nose of the John Hay statue brings good luck." Naomi rolled her eyes as if to show how ridiculous she thought the tradition was. It didn't stop several students from dipping away from the group to forcefully rub the sculpture, determined to increase their chances of admission.

Nate sighed. He'd been at Deep Springs for the last year, but the college was only a two-year program. Afterward, students transferred to schools like Harvard, Dartmouth, Yale, or Brown, which Nate had always heard was the most flexible and mellow of all the Ivies. But no matter how laid-back Brown was, after living on a farm with thirty dudes, going to an actual university was going to be a giant jolt to the system.

"Let's keep going! I can't wait to show you the science library!" Naomi trilled, walking backward. Nate tried not to groan. The more he heard, the less he felt like he belonged *anywhere*.

He jammed his hands in the pockets of his khakis. It was just a few days after Christmas, and the Brown campus was practically deserted. Nate looked around dazedly, trying to place himself here, but he couldn't.

As he approached the campus gates, he noticed a pretty girl in a bright red coat, squinting at the campus map. She was obviously lost. Something about her made Nate want to go over and help her, and he found himself stepping away from the group.

As he got closer, he took in the girl's long, curly brown hair and milky white skin. It was Jennifer Humphrey, the sweet, big-chested freshman he'd hooked up with senior year!

Jenny squinted up at the map of the Brown campus. She'd come to Providence to tour RISD, where she'd applied back in November, but Brown was right next door, and she figured she might as well look around. *If* she could ever find anything. It looked a lot like Waverly—the snow-covered green, the over-size brick buildings, the occasional preppie-boho student who crossed her path—except bigger. She felt a tap on her shoulder and turned to find herself looking up into a familiar pair of glittering green eyes.

"Nate?" she squeaked, her voice going up an octave. "I mean, Nate," she repeated, trying to sound like the mature and collected eighteen-year-old she was. Or would be, if she hadn't just been confronted by her high school crush.

"Jennifer, right?" Nate smiled easily, his whole face lighting up.

Jenny nodded mutely, trying to ignore the sweat beads forming along her hairline and her heart hammering in her chest. She was glad her belted red Searle coat was buttoned up all the way, so Nate couldn't see the red hives that sprang up on her chest when she was embarrassed.

"Long time no see." Nate smiled. "Do you go here?" His green eyes searched Jenny's dark brown ones.

Jenny shook her head, her brunette curls bouncing around her head like vines. "I just went on a tour of RISD. I applied there, and Pratt, but I can't decide between them. I'm a senior this year," she explained nervously, feeling like she'd traveled back in time to her awkward high school years. She might as well be wearing her seersucker Constance Billard uniform, worrying about whether Mrs. M was going to bust her for talking to a boy on campus. "Do you go here?"

"Nah." Nate shuffled from side to side. "Just looking. Where are you headed now?"

"My brother's supposed to pick me up on Thayer Street. Think you can help me find it?" Jenny asked coyly.

Who can resist a damsel in distress?

"I think it's that way." Nate pointed to a set of tall wrought-iron gates on the other side of the snowy campus. "I'll walk over there with you," he offered, and led the way down a path that ran along a squat, ivy-covered building.

"Thanks!" Jenny practically had to run in her distressed Frye cowboy boots to keep up with Nate's long strides.

Nate slowed down. He'd gotten used to a faster clip, keeping up with Gertie and the other girls on the farm. "So, do you go to Constance?" he asked.

"No, I go to Waverly. It's a boarding school upstate. But what about you? Didn't you go to Yale?" She remembered hearing about Nate getting into all the schools he'd applied to, despite being a well-known stoner and slacker. She hoped she didn't sound like a stalker.

"I go to Deep Springs. It's a working ranch in California. We spend the morning reading and in classes and then the afternoon doing manual labor on the ranch."

"Oh." Jenny wrinkled her nose. Poor Nate! "Did your parents make you go there?"

Nate shook his head, his green eyes suddenly far-off. Jenny wondered what he was thinking about. He seemed so much older than the guys at Waverly, who bragged about sneaking booze to the Crater, Waverly's best outdoor party spot, or how many times they'd fallen asleep in Ms. Hummerton's Texts of the Twentieth Century class. She loved Waverly, but she was more than ready for her next adventure.

And it might just be more imminent than she thinks.

They were nearing the center of campus and Jenny felt her heart flutter in anticipation. She could imagine everyone passing them thinking they were a couple back early from break, deep in conversation about what to do for New Year's.

"So, why did you go to Deep Springs?" Jenny pressed.

"I just needed to get away from everything. But the program only lasts two years, and then you transfer. Next year, I'm thinking Brown." Nate nodded definitively. The tour guide had been annoying, but the campus was pretty and Yale was out of the question now that both Blair *and* Serena were there. Or so he'd heard.

Jenny scanned the parked cars for Dan's beat-up Buick Skylark when they reached Thayer Street. The redbrick sidewalk was confettied with coarse salt. "I'm seriously considering RISD. . . ." She trailed off, hoping Nate would make the connection.

Nate smiled. Jennifer looked really cute in her red coat, with her hair pulled back from her round, cherubic face. "Well, if you're at RISD and I'm here, I guess we may be seeing each other a lot next year."

Jenny smiled right back. She'd make *sure* of it!

Just the sort of determination every college admissions officer wants in a college candidate.

## watching him watching her watching him

It was a Saturday night and Vanessa was curled up on the black leather couch, eating takeout straight from the carton and watching *Flesh*, the 1968 Paul Morrissey movie about a hustler in New York who has a whole lot of sex. When she'd first watched it in high school, she'd thought she'd missed something. Now, she realized that there really wasn't much else going on in the film. It was practically a porno.

In a way, everything—the movie, the takeout, the fact that it wasn't even ten o'clock on a Saturday night and she was curled up on the couch wearing an oversize purple NYU sweatshirt and a pair of Hollis's boxer shorts—was the same as her life had been five years ago, when she was fifteen and friendless.

Except she wasn't fifteen anymore, and she was far from friendless—she was dating Hollis Lyons, even if he had been away in Iceland for the last ten months. She was living in a spacious loft with its own elevator and a gorgeous view of the Williamsburg Bridge. She was a junior at the Tisch School of the Arts. She had a so-ugly-it's-cute reddish-brown choodle, currently snoring gently on the floor. She had everything she wanted. So why did she feel so lame?

The intercom buzzed, which was odd, since she wasn't expecting anyone. She didn't hang out with her friends much anymore, preferring to be home in case Hollis called from Reykjavík. The movie shoot had raged on for months and months longer than originally planned, and now he was still there, editing on location until the end of January. She'd visited once, during her spring break in April. It had been amazing to see him, but devastating to leave after only five days. They e-mailed as much as they could, but between the time difference and his insane work schedule, they'd barely even spoken save for a crackly ten-minute call on Christmas. It had been so long since they'd seen each other that Vanessa sometimes wondered if Hollis had been a figment of her imagination.

Filmmakers *are* creative people.

Vanessa quickly threw the empty aluminum container into the plastic takeout bag and skidded on her stockinged feet over to the door, pressing the video intercom buzzer. A grainy image of Ruby and her baby, Moxie, sprang onto the screen.

"It's your sister and your favorite niece!" Ruby trilled, unaware that Vanessa could see them. "And it's fucking freezing down here," she added.

"Come on up!" Vanessa yelled happily. Ruby and Piotr had moved to a two-bedroom apartment in Prospect Heights right after they'd had Moxie. It was two subway rides away, and Vanessa missed having them right around the corner. She hurriedly picked up a pair of jeans from the floor and pulled them on over the boxers.

The elevator door slid open. Ruby was bundled up in a black

Brooklyn Industries puffer coat and a red hat, and eight-month-old Moxie wore a white fur hood. She looked like the monkey Chuck Bass used to tote around in high school.

Vanessa immediately plucked the baby from her sister's hands.

"Don't say hi to me. I'm just the mom," Ruby joked as she walked into the large loft. "So, Piotr's family is here through New Year's and I seriously need a break." She pulled out a bottle of wine from her voluminous bag and set it on the counter. She paused and glanced around the room suspiciously. "God, it's always so neat in here."

"I like it this way," Vanessa explained. She naturally had slob-like tendencies, but in the last year that had all changed. She liked scrubbing the tiles in the shower and Swiffering under the Sub-Zero. It gave her something to do besides miss Hollis.

If it makes you happy . . .

Vanessa pulled Moxie's hood off her tiny head. "Still no hair," she observed, checking the baby's bald head.

"You didn't have any hair for four years," Ruby observed blithely, settling in on the leather couch. Now, Vanessa's silky jet-black hair fell inches past her shoulders. "Hand her over, she needs to feed." Ruby pulled the neck of her gray Hanes T-shirt down to expose her boob, and cradled Moxie in the crook of her arm. Vanessa looked away politely.

Ruby's head fell back against the couch. "You know, you should really throw a New Year's party. I mean, with an apartment like this, it's practically your duty. Do you ever have people over?"

"Sometimes," Vanessa said evasively. In truth, she'd never invited anyone except Ruby up to the loft. She felt it would somehow be disloyal to Hollis, having people over in his apartment while he slaved away in Iceland. She checked the fridge to see if there was anything she could offer her sister. A forgotten carton of lo mein from last week, a container of orange juice, and a plastic tub of almonds sat on the center shelf. "Nuts?" Vanessa pulled out the container and threw a couple in her mouth.

"Thanks." Ruby took a couple, crunched them loudly, and threw one over to Norma. It bounced off the dog's nose and onto the floor. She just stared at it. "Seriously, Vanessa, you've become weird."

"*I* have? Look at your shoes," Vanessa shot back. Ruby wore a pair of burnt sienna–colored Dansko clogs, cutoff sweatpants, and the same red woolly cardigan that she'd worn on Christmas.

"They're not weird, they're *comfortable*. You're the one wasting your youth. I already had mine." She sniffed, tucked her boob back inside her shirt, and passed the baby to Vanessa.

"Hi, Bunny!" Vanessa cooed, inhaling the sweet scent of Johnson's baby shampoo, which Ruby used despite the fact that Moxie had approximately three strands of hair. Moxie felt reassuringly heavy in Vanessa's lap.

"Listen, you're acting like you're in mourning or something. Live a little! I've been given the night off from Piotr's family and I intend to use it for good." Ruby grinned. "Let's buy some slice and bake cookies and listen to Christmas music. I'm not ready for the holidays to be over yet. What do you say?"

"I'm in!" Vanessa smiled and then headed up the winding staircase to the sleeping loft. Their California king-size bed was immaculately made, with a white duvet cover contrasting with the black bed frame. Vanessa wasn't sure when she'd slept there last. It felt too big by herself, so she often curled up with Norma on the couch. She pulled a scarf from her closet and wrapped it around her neck. Her sister was right. Maybe she *had* gone a little bit overboard with the reclusive-widow thing, acting like Hollis was a ship captain lost at sea instead of a film director caught up with editing. It would be good to get out for a little bit.

"Ready!" Vanessa yelled down the stairs as she ran her fingers through her long hair. Her index finger caught on a large snarl. "And FYI, I didn't take a shower today so sorry if I smell," she called as she ran down the steps. She reached the bottom and gasped.

There, standing by the elevator, his hands in his pockets and a smirk on his face, was Hollis.

"Okay, we've already got our first date planned. Shower, here we come!" Hollis grinned. He had slight bags under his gray eyes, as if he hadn't slept in months. He wore a black leather jacket and his trademark fedora over his thick dark hair. He stood there casually, like he'd only been gone a matter of minutes—not months.

Vanessa didn't say anything. She felt like she was going to cry. Even though it was practically a scene from a terrible chick movie, she couldn't resist running to him and wrapping her arms around him tightly. She lifted her face up until her mouth met his.

"Remember, there's a kid watching!" Ruby called from the couch. Moxie gazed, entranced, at Hollis.

"Hi," Vanessa said dumbly, staring up at him as if he were a vision.

Courtesy of too many Scrubbing Bubbles fumes?

"I couldn't wait a month. I don't want to be in Iceland. I want to be with you," Hollis said simply.

"You're back?" Vanessa asked. "For good?"

Hollis nodded. "Unless you're hiding a boyfriend somewhere."

"Just Paul Morrissey." She gestured to the DVD case on the coffee table.

"We'll leave you alone," Ruby said, bundling Moxie back into her snowsuit. "Maybe there's a movie about talking penguins we can see."

Vanessa didn't even notice her adorable niece and sister as they made their way into the elevator. She was too busy kissing her boyfriend.

Beats mopping the floor.

# survivor

"Do you think Jenny will choose RISD or Pratt?" Serena asked, taking a thoughtful sip of her organic chai. She and Dan were seated at a small table in Blue State Coffee, one of the cute coffee shops on Thayer Street in downtown Providence.

"Pratt," Dan said confidently. His hair was sort of shaggy—Serena hadn't been able to drag him to John Barrett's—and he wore a rumpled blue cotton oxford shirt and jeans. He looked slightly homeless, but to her, he was absolutely adorable. "Jenny's wanted to go there since she learned how to draw," he said proudly.

"I didn't have a clue when I was her age." Serena wrinkled her nose. "But I guess it just depends on the person. Blair always knew she wanted to go to Yale. . . ." She trailed off.

"Have you spoken to her? Is she in New York for the holidays?" Dan asked before emptying the last of his double espresso from his mini porcelain cup. It made him feel like a character in *Alice in Wonderland*. The espresso was his second, and they'd been in the shop for less than an hour, hanging out while Jenny took her RISD tour. She was due back any minute.

"I don't know." Serena shrugged, thinking of her and Blair's huge fight last winter. A blowup between them wasn't anything new—they'd been fighting since before they could properly form sentences. But their arguments usually blew over quickly. *This* one hadn't. Blair had gone to study abroad at Oxford while Serena had gone to Yale, and they hadn't spoken since last January. "It doesn't matter. I just hope she's had as good a year as I have," Serena added, smiling at Dan.

She and Dan had gotten together the previous winter break, and the relationship had quickly turned serious. By April, Serena was spending most of her weekends at Dan's Upper West Side apartment. They'd sit at the tiny kitchen table, studying together, or go to the coffee shop on his corner and read. Dan was a junior at Columbia and Serena wasn't quite sure what she was at Yale. She'd just started in September, but she'd carried over a few credits from courses she'd taken at the New School earlier that year.

Being at Yale was more complicated than she'd thought it would be. It was strange living in a dorm when she was used to having her own apartment. She felt years older than her fellow freshmen, and it wasn't easy to get back into studying mode, especially since she'd only taken fun classes at the New School, like screenwriting and New York in Literature. She liked reading books, but she'd never been one for taking tests and writing papers. And even if she did go back to the city every weekend, it was hard to be separated from Dan from Monday to Thursday.

She did miss acting, but she didn't miss having an agent and a publicist and getting followed around and pointed at everywhere she went. Her first few weeks on campus, she'd get the occasional second look or stare, but she'd quickly found a degree of anonymity she relished. Yale students were so busy with their own lives that for the most part they couldn't get worked up over a girl who was an actress once.

"Another cup?" Serena teased, noticing Dan's jittery hands.

"Nah, I'm good," Dan said, missing her sarcasm. Sometimes, like right now, Dan still couldn't believe Serena van der Woodsen was his girlfriend.

She laced her fingers in his as she gazed absentmindedly out the window. It was starting to snow, and the flakes swirling around the Gothic buildings of the Brown campus were very romantic. It reminded her of playing in the snow with Nate back in high school. It made her want to start a snowball fight, but Dan wasn't really the roughhousing type.

Dan's cell buzzed in his pocket. "It's Jenny. She's meeting us at the car."

"Let's go." Serena stood and made her way out of the coffee shop. Together, they headed to the parking lot and settled into Dan's blue Buick Skylark.

Dan rested his hands on the steering wheel and leaned back into the bucket seat as they waited for Jenny. He was suddenly glad he'd had the two espressos. He loved Jenny, and he loved Serena, but the two girls together had made for an exhausting ride up. They'd bothered him every fifteen minutes to stop for coffee, snacks, and bathroom breaks, making what should have been a three-hour trip more like five. Dan didn't want a repeat performance on the way back, especially since the snow was starting to stick to the ground.

Jenny bounded in the back door of the Buick, looking red-cheeked and radiant.

Wonder why?

"You'll never guess who I ran into—Nate Archibald! Isn't that crazy? He was going to take the train back to the city, but I figured we could just give him a ride," Jenny said without taking a breath. Her gaze landed on Serena. Oops. In her excitement, Jenny had almost forgotten about Nate and Serena's complicated history. To her, Serena was simply Dan's girlfriend. Would this be weird?

Of course it will!

Dan narrowed his eyes at the dark blond, green-eyed figure outside his car. Nate Archibald was the asshole who'd broken Jenny's heart three years ago, and had broken *Serena's* heart just the year before. Dan had only heard the vaguest details about what had happened, but he knew Nate was bad news. What the fuck was he doing here? "Actually, I think we're pretty full—" Dan began. He racked his brain, trying to think of some lie to prevent Nate from driving home with them. A weight limit?

A no-assholes rule?

"Natie!" Serena squealed, peering out the window at Nate. "What are you doing here?!" Serena couldn't believe Nate was right in front of her. She'd hardly thought about him this past year. She knew she should still be mad at Nate after what happened last winter, but it all seemed so far in the past. Besides, she could afford to be generous. If Nate hadn't made her so miserable last year, she'd never have reached out to Dan. So in a way, she owed her current happiness to him.

"We totally have room!" Serena announced, getting out of the car. Nate looked so cute and helpless, with snowflakes sitting in his dirty blond hair. She threw her arms around Nate in an affectionate old-friends hug. "Hop in," she told him, getting in the backseat with Jenny.

Dan sputtered, his blue fleece–gloved hands gripping the steering wheel. He didn't love the idea of Jenny talking to this douche, and he really didn't like the familiar way Serena had hugged him. And now he had to give the guy a ride?

"Hey, I really appreciate the ride, especially with this snow. I'll take middle," Nate offered, climbing over Serena and wedging his lanky frame into the middle of the seat between her and Jenny.

Serena squeezed his shoulder. "Let's go," she said.

Dan glared mutinously toward the backseat. Why didn't Serena offer to sit up front with him? What was he? Their fucking chauffeur?

"Great. Let's go," Dan growled, navigating out of his spot and slowly driving down Thayer Street toward I-95.

"Dan, aren't you going to ask me about RISD?" Jenny needled in her little-sister voice.

"How was it?" Serena asked curiously.

"So good," Jenny gushed. "And guess what? Nate's going to Brown!"

"You are, Natie? Oh my God, that's awesome!" Serena cried. "Wait, we need something to celebrate. Dan, can you stop for snacks?"

Dan grunted. The last thing he wanted was for them to eat a fucking cake in the backseat of his car while he drove them around like a fucking soccer team. "I think we should just try to get home as quickly as possible. The snow's really coming down," he pointed out.

"Whatever you say." Nate shrugged. "I'm still not used to being back on the East Coast. We don't get snow at Deep Springs."

"Did you know that Nate knows how to birth cows?" Serena said proudly as Dan merged into the bumper-to-bumper traffic of I-95 South. The cars were jockeying for road space, and the steadily falling snowflakes made for poor visibility. Dan sucked in his breath. He hated driving. Part of the reason he loved living in New York was that he never had to drive.

"I need to concentrate," he muttered, turning on the windshield wipers.

Nate tapped Dan's shoulder. "You want me to drive? I'm pretty good at dealing with the dust storms in California."

"No," Dan said shortly. He looked in the rearview mirror. Jenny was leaning toward the middle section of the seat, practically on top of Nate. She was a smart girl, but when it came to boys, she could be sort of a ditz. Dan knew his sister, and right now Jenny was in full-on flirt mode.

God help us.

"I got stuck in the snow once," she offered. "With my friend Tinsley. Our car broke down in the middle of the highway, and we had to spend the night in it. We thought we were in, like, the middle of nowhere, but when we woke up the next morning we realized we were right in front of a hotel. The owners felt sorry for us and gave us a free breakfast."

Nate chuckled. "That's funny. I always wondered what went down at boarding school. Serena would never give up any stories about Hanover."

"What do you want to know?" Serena stuck out her tongue at Nate. "That was a million years ago, anyway."

Dan pulled forward into an empty lane and accelerated angrily.

Suddenly, the car swerved toward the shoulder. Dan whipped

the wheel in the opposite direction, the back of the car swinging like the tail of a snake. Behind them a car horn blared. Jenny shrieked, and Serena braced herself against the back of Dan's seat.

Dan pressed on the brake and pulled over, his breath short and heart pounding. Everyone was silent. They could've been *killed*. He peered out the window. Fat flakes were falling, and the stormy clouds meant it was only going to get worse. Fuck. Stuck in a fucking blizzard, hours from home. "It's too dangerous to try to get all the way back to the city in this. I don't have snow tires, and this car isn't exactly in the best of shape." Dan said flatly, hating the truth of the statement.

They all peered out at the swirling snow. "Damn, dude," Nate swore sympathetically. Dan just glared at him in the rearview mirror. Helpful. Really helpful.

"We could stay at a hotel!" Jenny offered happily. She *loved* hotels. They could get two rooms: one for Dan and Serena and one for her and Nate.

"I have an idea. . ." Serena offered. "Blair's Newport house isn't far from here. It's empty. Her mom's in California and her dad's in France. And I still remember the security code."

Dan shook his head. That was the thing about Serena. Everything always worked out for her, so it never occurred to her that breaking into someone's house could be a bad idea. "I don't think—" he began.

"Perfect," Nate enthused. "Man, I used to love that house. Remember how we always used to play croquet on the lawn and talk in British accents?"

"Oh my God, yes! And Blair would always get so competitive?" Serena rolled her eyes. "I'm going to drive. I know where it is," she announced, already unbuckling her seat belt and climbing up front.

Wordlessly, Dan slid out of the driver's seat and walked through the falling snow to the passenger door.

Buckle up! The road ahead sounds seriously bumpy.

# the more the merrier

"More wine, Blair-Bear? After all, you've been legal in England for months!" Harold Waldorf held up a bottle of his vineyard's Côtes du Rhone. Blair sighed in contentment. It was the perfect winter break: no drama, no one protesting her movie choices, and plenty of cozy time with her family and her fabulous boyfriend.

And who might that be?

"Thanks, Daddy," she cooed, holding out her glass. Harold wore a red cashmere sweater and tight jeans that, really, no man should ever wear, but he looked surprisingly good. It was hard to remember a time when her dad was a straitlaced partner of a Park Avenue law firm and not a French vineyard–owning gay man with a partner named Giles and adopted twins from Cambodia named Pierre and Pauline. As infants the twins had been named Ping and Pong, because of their cute round hairless heads, but as soon as Harold and Giles began applying to nursery school programs, they realized their son and daughter might be teased.

You think?

"'For auld lang syne' . . ." Harold warbled as he stepped between the pieces of the elaborate train set the twins had gotten for Christmas spread out on the floor. In the corner, Giles was having a tea party with the twins.

Blair contemplatively swirled the wine in her glass. It was nice to be in Newport, where she'd spent so many of her childhood holidays. Christmas had been perfect: They'd spent the morning opening presents underneath the gigantic Douglas fir, then taken turns helping Pauline and Pierre build their train set. She'd gotten a pair of limited edition Chanel booties from her father, and she'd spent the afternoon curled up by the fire reading and drinking wine. There'd been no unexpected surprises, and she liked it that way.

She was even looking forward to a quiet New Year's. No drama, no hangovers, and the only brushes with the past would be in the form of pleasant memories. The house smelled like oranges and cinnamon, and if she closed her eyes she could imagine herself as a teenager, annoyed to leave New York—and Serena and Nate—for boring, lonely Newport.

"It's good to have you back, Bear," Harold told her.

It felt like she'd been gone forever. Blair was spending her junior year at St. Peter's College in Oxford. She'd pictured herself living in one of the Gothic buildings near campus, surrounded by posh classmates who kept flats in Sloane Square, attending thought-provoking lectures given by aged professors who drank scotch throughout their insightful monologues. But as had so often happened in Blair's life, things hadn't quite turned out as she planned. She'd been assigned to live in the basement of a dorm, where her hall mates were shrill girls from Mount Holyoke. Blair hated the weather, hated the snooty

Oxford students who considered her a second-class citizen because she was American, and hated the fact that most of the pubs in Oxford closed at 11 p.m.

It was almost like fate intervening one cold and rainy afternoon in mid-October. She'd been riding a bike to the library, the idea of which she'd thought seemed cute and quaint. What she hadn't anticipated was how difficult it was to bike on cobblestone. She wound up falling in the center of town. She was sitting there miserably, soaked from the rain, knees skinned, when like a knight in shining armor, he appeared; just as he always had, she'd just never noticed him before. . . .

"These cookies are just delicious, Harold." Chuck Bass ambled in from the kitchen, nibbling on one of the snowman-shaped sugar cookies Harold had baked with the twins. He eased down onto the sofa next to Blair.

Blair smiled and squeezed Chuck's hand. It was Chuck who had rescued her that day, except instead of shining armor he wore Thomas Pink, and instead of a knight, he was an Oxford University scholar. He'd transferred there after completing two years at Deep Springs, and ever since their paths crossed that fateful day, they'd been practically inseparable.

"I'll give you the recipe," Harold offered, smiling at the compliment. "As if you can really cook in those horrible dorms Blair's complained to me about. Many times," he added with a teasing wink at his daughter.

Blair rolled her eyes. "I was thinking about moving to a flat in town when we get back. We could probably find something on College Street." Right now, Chuck lived with a bunch of his rowing buddies in a house on the mortifyingly named Titmarsh Lane. It would be nice to have a little more privacy, and a bigger bed.

And a better mailing address?

"If that's okay with you, Daddy," Blair added.

"Wonderful," Harold said. He'd always trusted Blair completely.

Blair sighed happily and nuzzled closer to Chuck. She couldn't believe this was the same Chuck Bass she'd known growing up. He was sweet and sensitive and got along well with everyone. Blair imagined them settling down in Sloane Square. She'd be a barrister, he'd work as a banker in Canary Wharf, and they'd have three children with adorable accents and picnic in Kensington Gardens on weekends.

"Moving in already. Sounds serious!" Harold said with a twinkle in his eye.

"I apologize for your meddling dad," Giles piped up from his tea party in the corner. "That's why I prefer hanging out with the knee-high set." Giles ruffled Pierre's dark hair.

Suddenly, the sound of the doorbell filled the house.

"Did we order something?" Giles asked.

Blair threw the plaid blanket from her knees, ran to the entryway, and flung open the door, half expecting to find a singing messenger or some over-the-top surprise that Chuck or her generous father had planned for her as a post-Christmas surprise. A car? A pony? A private plane to sweep them all off to St. Barts for New Year's?

Instead, her eyes fell on Serena van der Woodsen, Nate Archibald, that younger girl who'd been kicked out of Constance for extreme sluttiness, and her shaggy-haired older brother, who she'd heard Serena was actually seeing. It was like a band of carolers gone wrong.

*What. The. Fuck?* Was this some sort of joke? A hallucination from too many glasses of red wine and not enough exercise?

Or a late visit from the Ghosts of Christmas Past?

"What the hell are you doing here?" Blair asked rudely. The shaggy-haired guy awkwardly shifted his weight from foot to foot, as if he had to pee.

"We'll leave. Sorry for the confusion," he said quickly, turning on the sole of his ugly loafer.

Serena finally managed to clear her throat. Of course she'd suggested staying at Blair's house, but the thought that Blair might actually *be here* hadn't even occurred to her. "Yeah, we'll find a hotel in town." Serena glanced nervously at Blair, whose veins were throbbing at her temples. This was *not* how she wanted to see her former best friend for the first time after a year apart. Blair had gone to Oxford to get away from Serena, and now here she was, standing on her doorstep like a stalker.

"Hey guys!" Chuck said, sidling up next to Blair. Serena tried to stop the gasp that formed in her throat. What was *Chuck Bass* doing here? Chuck's hand rested protectively on Blair's petite shoulder. Was he . . . *with Blair*? "Dan Humphrey, long time no see," he said enthusiastically, reaching out a hand.

"Hi Chuck," Dan muttered, limply shaking Chuck's hand. He hadn't thought it was possible for the night to get any weirder, but apparently, it could. What the fuck was his Riverside Prep nemesis doing here, in a pair of cashmere pajamas?

"Who do we have here?" Harold boomed as he strode down the entryway. "Serena van der Woodsen and Nate Archibald! Why didn't you tell me they were coming, Bear?" Harold cried, kissing Serena on both cheeks and leaning in to clap Nate on the back. "Come in, come in!" Harold escorted everyone inside, pumping hands enthusiastically as if he were an ambassador.

To a very hostile country?

"Thanks, sir!" Serena said weakly as she shuffled into the house. She didn't really have a choice.

"So, what brings you this way?" Harold asked, throwing more logs onto the crackling fire and settling back into his leather wingback chair as if preparing for an all-night chat. Jenny, Nate, and Dan all clustered around Serena, delegating explanation responsibilities to her.

"Mr. Waldorf, I'm *really* sorry to intrude. This is my boyfriend, Dan Humphrey." Serena emphasized the word *boyfriend.* Maybe if Blair knew she wasn't with Nate, she'd soften a little. "And his sister, Jenny. Jenny was visiting colleges and ran into Nate on a tour of Brown. And we were all driving back to the city and got stuck in the snow." She shrugged, as if that explained everything.

Blair narrowed her eyes. Of course Serena would play the Miss Innocent card, as if they'd just *happened* to be driving right past the Newport house. Newport wasn't exactly in Brown's backyard.

"So you just ran into each other?" Blair asked icily.

"Yeah." Nate tried to catch Blair's eye. In his time at Deep Springs, he'd almost forgotten how pretty she was. Her hair framed her small, fine-featured face, her eyes were bright, and she wore a black sweater that hugged her petite frame. Nate forced himself to glance away. She looked happy now. The last thing he wanted to do was get in the way. "We can leave. Blair, we'll leave," he repeated quietly, trying to let Blair know that he wasn't here to fuck up her life.

Again.

"In this weather? Nonsense! We're thrilled to have you. I see Pierre and Pauline have already made a friend!" Harold nodded to the corner, where Jenny was kneeling on the Oriental-carpeted floor, patiently asking the twins about their train set. "It's almost their bedtime. Almost my bedtime, too," Harold chuckled, draining the last of his wine. "But we have plenty of food, and we all know Blair has plenty of clothes to share with the girls. Our house is your house, so please, make yourselves at home. It'll be like a big pajama party!"

Hooray!

"We'll set Serena and Dan up in the downstairs guest room. Jennifer, you can have the upstairs, and Nate gets the attic. Will that work?"

Blair shrugged. "Fine. Chuck and I are going to bed," she announced, grabbing Chuck's elbow and yanking him up the stairs. Hopefully by tomorrow morning the snow would have stopped and they could all go back to wherever the fuck they came from. Better yet, she'd wake up and discover this was all just a big, terrible nightmare.

Sleep tight!

# nice day for an imaginary white wedding

Jenny woke up to sunlight streaming onto her face. She stretched lazily, reveling in the softness of the goose-down pillows surrounding her. The delicate hands of the silver clock on the nightstand pointed to 7 a.m. She was momentarily disoriented, then remembered that she was at Blair Waldorf's Newport house.

It had been awkward when they'd first arrived. Everyone had guiltily headed to the rooms Harold assigned them, but Jenny had lain awake in bed, thinking about Nate in the attic above her.

She swung her feet onto the walnut floor and looked out one of the east-facing bay windows. Frost covered the windowpanes, and in the distance she could see the ocean, waves slowly rolling toward the shore. The expansive land surrounding the house was covered with a thick blanket of snow, and icicles hung on the branches of the fir trees that edged the slate walkway. Snow was still falling heavily. Jenny felt a shiver of anticipation run up her spine. How could she *possibly* sleep when she was in such a beautiful place?

She carefully pushed the door open and padded down the

lengthy hallway, bringing her sketchbook and a pencil from her bag. She'd head to the attic and sketch the snowstorm, and if she just happened to run into a boxer-clad Nate, she wouldn't complain.

She slowly tiptoed up the creaky stairs that led to the attic and gasped. She'd been imagining a creepy, cobwebby crawl space. Instead, Oriental rugs covered the dark oak floors. Louis Vuitton steamer trunks and abandoned antique furniture vied for space. Clothes were hanging on coatracks, and bookshelves were overflowing with first editions. The old sleigh bed in the corner looked slept in, but Nate wasn't in it. She couldn't be disappointed, though—there was so much else to look at.

Jenny timidly pulled open one of the doors of an antique-looking wardrobe.

"Oh!" she breathed in surprise. Packed in the small space were dresses of all different colors and styles, hundreds of thousands of dollars' worth of couture. It was even better than shopping at Next to New, the vintage store in Rhinecliff that all the Waverly girls visited when they needed a one-of-a-kind party outfit. Jenny found herself pulling out a short Nina Ricci sparkly halter dress. It probably hadn't been worn or even looked at in years. It was practically her *duty* to try it on.

She wedged herself behind the wardrobe, pulled off the baby pink Senior Spa Weekend T-shirt she'd found in the guest room, and shimmied into the dress.

She scampered over to a freestanding mirror and gazed at herself. Her chest didn't look as ginormous as usual, and her petite frame was lengthened by the halter straps. She shook her curls around her face. She felt like she was headed to a party at Studio 54.

Jenny continued to paw through the dresses in the wardrobe until she came to an oversize garment bag. It was taller than she was and could fit a person inside.

We may need that body bag soon. . . .

She wrestled the hanger off the rack and pulled the heavy garment to the bed. Then she unzipped the bag, revealing a white wedding dress with a heavily beaded bodice and a long train. It probably cost more than a year at RISD, but she *had* to try it on. She yanked the Nina Ricci dress over her head and dropped it on the floor in a sequined puddle. Next, she stepped into the wedding gown feetfirst and pulled the heavy bodice up her torso. She struggled with the zipper at the back, finally giving up when it was halfway done. Her boobs easily held it up anyway.

Jenny eagerly scampered over to the mirror and sucked in her breath. She looked *beautiful*.

If she does say so herself.

Jenny smiled at her reflection and a pretty, rosy-cheeked bride smiled back. Would she ever get married? And to whom? She'd spent the past four years of her life falling in and out of love with various boys. How could you *possibly* only kiss and love one person for the rest of your life?

Jenny twirled again, then paused. Were those footsteps on the other side of the door? She looked around for a place to hide. A steamer trunk? The wardrobe?

The body bag?

Too late. A door on the other side of the attic opened, and Nate wandered out. He wore a pair of blue boxers with sailboats printed on them and his hair was sticking up in every direction.

"Hi!" Jenny squeaked, her hands flying to her chest.

"Jennifer?" Nate blinked. Was this some weird dream? He

opened his eyes again. She was standing there all right. Dressed in a wedding dress that created amazing cleavage and made her look innocent and sexy as hell all at once.

"I was just exploring. Sorry! I'm just going to take the dress off. I mean, I'm going to change!" Jenny said quickly, even though she kind of liked the way Nate was looking at her. "I didn't think you were here."

"I was in the bathroom."

Nate grinned, causing cute crinkles to emerge around his sleepy green eyes. "The dress looks nice. You look nice," Nate clarified, his eyes flicking from her chest up to her large dark brown eyes, and then, without meaning to, to the old antique sleigh bed behind her.

"You look nice too," Jenny said, hooking her dark curls behind her small ears. She grinned.

"Thanks." Nate willed his bare feet to remain planted on the cold beams of the floor. Girls made him crazy, an unproductive, pot-smoking mess. The past year at Deep Springs he'd worked harder than he had in his life and had finally lived up to his potential in school. And it was all because he'd given up chicks. *They're bad for you,* he told himself now. But Jenny seemed so simple and pure, and Nate couldn't imagine her being bad for anyone. He took a tentative step toward her.

"So, I guess this is Blair's mom's dress, right?" Jenny asked, shrugging her milky white shoulders.

He reached up and brushed an errant curl off Jenny's shoulders, then quickly yanked his hand back to his side.

So much for staying strong.

Jenny giggled and tilted her face toward his. He pressed his lips against hers, slowly at first, then more urgently.

"Nate," Jenny murmured. She felt his hand on her bare upper back, right above where the zipper had stopped on the dress. She wondered if he could feel how quickly her heart was beating in her chest. The stubble from his chin tickled her face. Her fingers fluttered up behind his head, to pull him closer.

Suddenly, Nate pulled away. "Do you hear that?" He cocked his hand in a way that reminded Jenny of a golden retriever. Jenny listened. She could hear the twins' wavering toddler voices singing an off-key rendition of "Frère Jacques" from downstairs.

"Sounds like the twins are up. We should . . ." Nate trailed off, shrugging.

"Yeah," Jenny agreed, disappointed. "I should change," she added sheepishly. She reached behind her, fumbling for the zipper.

"Can I help?" Nate reached for the zipper and eased it down, gently allowing his fingers to brush against the soft skin of her bare back. He'd forgotten how soft girls' skin was.

"Thanks." Jenny crossed her arms tightly over her chest to make sure the dress didn't fall down. She suddenly felt shy.

"I'll give you some privacy," he offered, and stepped back into the bathroom. He closed the door and she quickly stepped out of the dress. She made her way over to the wardrobe, but before she could set the heavy dress inside, her foot caught on the leg of the mirror. It toppled to the ground with a crash. *Fuck.*

"You okay?" Nate called, popping his head around the door.

"Everything's fine!" She yelped. The mirror hadn't broken, but it was lying on its side. She hastily set it upright, threw the dress back on the bed, then sprinted down the attic stairs and back to the tiny guest room, her heart pounding from adrenaline.

Not to mention infatuation.

## crushes cover for each other

Blair heard a loud crash from the attic and woke up with a start. Sun was streaming through the east-facing windows of the guest bedroom and Chuck was breathing easily beside her, oblivious to the noise.

Blair cocked her head and heard the sound of loud footsteps right above her. Immediately, she remembered how many houseguests were under the roof. How Serena and Nate had crashed what was supposed to be a normal, sane holiday vacation.

Doesn't she know by now that doesn't exist?

She threw on a silky peach Cosabella robe, double-knotted it over her cami and boy shorts, and stomped toward the attic stairs.

"Hello?" she called, an edge to her voice as she stomped up the rickety attic stairs. If Nate was up here with Serena . . . well, Blair didn't even know what the fuck she'd do if she found them together. And if Serena and her gross pseudo-intellectual boyfriend were doing anything up here, she'd still be annoyed. Just the fact that Serena was in the house pissed her off. What part of her speech last winter had made Serena think it was a good idea to follow her to Newport?

Blair swung open the door, ready to tell whoever was up there to get the fuck out. But it was just Nate, standing near the large antique wardrobe in the corner, holding what looked like her mom's wedding dress out in front of him.

"Oh, hey," Nate said, turning around to face Blair.

"What the hell?" Blair demanded angrily. This was one scenario she hadn't anticipated. Had Nate been *trying on her mom's dress*?

"Sorry, I was just looking around. Remember how we used to play hide-and-seek up here?" Nate asked innocently.

Blair softened slightly. Nate might be insensitive and have idiotic lapses of judgment, but he definitely wasn't a cross-dresser. "I thought I heard a noise." She folded her arms over her chest.

"I accidentally bumped into the mirror. It's fine, though." He gestured toward her great-grandmother Cornelia's gold mirror in the corner.

"What are you doing with my mom's wedding dress?" Blair asked pointedly.

"Sorry." Nate racked his brain, trying to come up with an excuse that didn't sound *too* idiotic. He'd wanted to clean up after Jenny. Blair would rip Jenny's sweet little curls from her head if she knew she'd been up here, snooping and trying on Blair's mom's old stuff.

And kissing him?

"I was just . . . reminiscing," Nate said finally. "This house brings up a lot of memories."

"It does for me, too," Blair admitted. She sat down on one

of the large steamer trunks, hugged her legs to her chest, and stared at the dress, which Nate had placed over his rumpled sheets. She used to play dress-up with her mom's clothes until well into high school. She'd even worn this very dress and imagined walking down the aisle at St. Patrick's, with Nate waiting for her at the altar.

"You would look beautiful in it," Nate mused. In the picture in his mind, he substituted Jenny's sloping curves for Blair's sharp collarbones.

Blair smiled despite herself. "I always thought I'd marry you wearing this," she said honestly. "We'd get married in St. Patrick's. . . ."

"And honeymoon in Capri," Nate finished.

Blair laughed. It was genuine, and the sound surprised her. "We were so young."

"I'm glad you and Chuck are happy," Nate said softly. He remembered the awful, wild look in Blair's eyes last year at that hotel room, when he'd accidentally ruined her relationship with her Yale boyfriend. She deserved to be with a good guy.

"I hope you're happy too," she offered. She knew Deep Springs had done a lot for both Nate and Chuck, but something in Nate's green eyes still looked lost. It made her want to smooth his hair and hold his hand and climb back under the sheets on the sleigh bed and—

"I should go find Chuck, actually," Blair said, standing up abruptly.

"Good," Nate said quickly. "I mean, I have to take a shower."

Blair padded downstairs, wondering why her brain had to be such a dangerous place. What was she doing fantasizing about

Nate when she had Chuck—Chuck, who made her feel like a princess, and never, ever fucked with her—just down the hall? It was infuriating.

Blair paused at the top of the stairs as she heard Serena's voice mingling with the twins' high-pitched, French-accented lisps. What the fuck? She descended into the kitchen. Serena sat with the twins at the large round wooden kitchen table. A jar of peanut butter, a jar of jelly, and a red box of graham crackers sat in front of them.

"Blair!" Serena called joyfully.

"Bear!" Both twins yelled, their faces sticky with peanut butter.

"Hi," Blair said stiffly.

"Did you sleep well?" Serena asked hopefully. She hadn't slept well herself, and had spent most of the night listening to Dan's even breath and feeling guilty about intruding on Blair. Finally, she'd gotten up early and had been playing with the twins for hours.

Blair stalked over to the coffeemaker on the counter, ignoring Serena's inane question. The stainless steel carafe was empty and cold. "No coffee?"

"The twins wanted tea this morning." Serena shrugged playfully.

"Ha," Blair replied sarcastically, and pulled a bag of espresso beans from the freezer. She poured the bag into a coffee grinder and noisily ground the coffee, not caring if anyone was still asleep. It was time to wake up and get the fuck out.

Good morning, sunshine!

Blair finished grinding the coffee and the electronic whir gave way to Serena's patient voice.

"Okay, Pauline, now crumble the graham crackers really

hard," Serena told the little girl. Pauline's face was scrunched in concentration as she squeezed a Ziploc bag filled with graham cracker squares.

"What can I do?" Pierre piped up, his expression full of naked adoration.

Blair turned, softening. She knew exactly what had to be done next. She and Serena had invented peanut butter pie—peanut butter and jelly mixed together on top of crushed graham crackers—when they were in first grade. Sometimes, they'd add marshmallows, which their nannies hated because it made their hands impossibly sticky.

"You can take the peanut butter and jelly and mix them," Blair said, searching the cabinets for a mixing bowl and setting it in front of Pierre. "I can't believe we used to eat this," she said to Serena, shaking her head.

"Do you have marshmallows?" Serena asked hopefully, reading her mind.

"Probably." Blair rummaged through the cupboards, finally finding a bag. She tossed it over to Serena and leaned against the counter, appraising her. Serena's golden blond hair had grown even longer in the last year, and was badly in need of a cut, but somehow managed to still look glamorous. Her navy blue eyes had slight laugh lines around the edges. She looked just a little bit older than she had a year ago, or maybe just more grown-up. "So, you're dating Dan Humphrey," Blair said finally.

Serena nodded. "Pretty weird, right?"

"Yeah," Blair laughed. It *was* sort of weird. But Serena had always been unpredictable. It was one of the things about her that Blair loved most. It was also one of the things that had driven her crazy.

"You're dating Chuck," Serena countered.

"I know!" Blair laughed. The blue teapot on the stove whistled and Blair poured the steamy water into a French press. "Do you want any coffee?" she asked. It was the Blair Waldorf version of a peace offering.

"Is it ready?" Pierre and Pauline interrupted, slapping their sticky hands against the counter.

"Sure." Serena gazed dubiously at the gooey mess in the pie pan. "I don't know how they should eat this."

"Spoons?" Blair shrugged. "As long as they stay in the kitchen, my dad won't care."

Doesn't she mean dads?

Serena carefully set up the twins at the toddler-size table in the corner, remembering herself and Blair as children sitting at that very table, doing that very thing. Blair was watching them too, cupping her coffee mug between her hands.

"I was just thinking . . ." Serena began. She wanted to apologize to Blair, to say she didn't even remember why they'd gotten so mad at each other the previous winter, that she just wanted to go back to being friends again. But she couldn't find the words.

She didn't need to. "I know," Blair said. "Me too."

It was still snowing heavily outside, but inside, it seemed the ice had finally thawed.

# dinner for eight

"I thought Giles and I should show off our Provençal cooking skills," Harold announced as he set a heavy red Le Creuset casserole on the long, rough-hewn table in the comfortable sunken dining room. It had been snowing heavily all day with no signs of stopping, and Harold had insisted that Dan, Jenny, Serena, and Nate call their parents and stay at the Newport house until the storm let up.

Blair hadn't minded—in fact, it had actually been kind of fun. They'd all watched *Gone With the Wind*, played Boggle and Monopoly, and drunk way too much of Harold's special mulled wine. Dan kept excusing himself and Serena, either to make out or read in the library. Nate and Chuck had kept them entertained with crazy stories about Deep Springs, while Jenny quietly looked on and giggled. Now, even though it was only eight o'clock, everyone was exhausted and drunk.

"Lamb daube with red wine and olives," Harold explained from the head of the table. "I bet this is a far cry from dorm food."

"Blair survives on jelly babies." Chuck named the weird

British candy that had been the only thing Blair liked about England before she and Chuck started dating.

"Shut up," she said good-naturedly. She'd spent the whole first month surviving on whatever she could find at the newsagent's near her dorm before it closed at 6 p.m.—potato chips and candy mostly—but the whole table didn't need to know about it.

"Well, enjoy. I'm telling you, kids, it's great for us that you're here." Harold held up his glass of champagne as he slid into the chair at the head of the table. "To youth," he announced solemnly.

"And wisdom!" Chuck cried, clinking his own glass with Harold's.

"I've always liked you." Harold winked showily at Blair.

Nate stiffened as he cut into his lamb. Chuck had e-mailed him this year to tell him that he and Blair were dating, but it was one thing to *know* they were together and another to *see* it. He stared down at his plate. The olives looked like little beady eyes, challenging him. Just then, he felt something touch his foot. Jenny was smiling at him mischievously. Footsies? Really? That was kind of . . . hot. Nate smiled back at her.

"I saw you girls making peanut-butter-and-jelly pies this morning," Harold said, waving his flute at Blair and Serena. "I wish you'd stuck to doing that, instead of raiding our liquor cabinet when you were teenagers." He shook his head in bemusement.

"Daddy, we never did that," Blair lied, taking a large swig of champagne.

"Ha!" Harold laughed. "I wasn't as out of touch as you may have thought."

Yes, he was.

"Well, you girls had to learn how to socialize somehow. And it all turned out for the best. You hosted your first benefit when you were only sixteen," Harold recalled with pride.

"Oh my God, the Kiss on the Lips party," Blair remembered. They'd organized a party to benefit the Central Park falcons or pigeons or sparrows or whatever those endangered birds were. After too much champagne, she'd nearly thrown up on one of the foundation representatives. Nate had rescued her, making an excuse to the representative and steering Blair discreetly toward the bathroom. She looked at him gratefully now, wondering if he was thinking about the same thing. Nate smiled back, and then, as if remembering something, tore his eyes away.

"I did the invitations for that party!" Jenny piped up from the corner of the table. As a young, ambitious freshman, she'd wanted to be invited to the party so badly that she'd offered to use her calligraphy skills to address the invites.

Dan stared down at his plate. He had nothing to contribute to this trip down memory lane, except that he had rescued Jenny from the bathroom, where she'd been cornered by a date-raping Chuck at the same party. But that wasn't exactly appropriate for the dinner table.

You think?

He couldn't believe it had snowed all day and they were stuck in Newport for *another* night. All he wanted was to be back in his apartment with Serena, a cup of coffee, and a good book.

"Oh my God, Blair, remember when we were Jenny's peer counselors?" Serena laughed. The guidance department had chosen her and Blair to act as role models for some of the younger Constance girls. They'd been assigned a group of freshman with whom they met once a week to discuss topics like peer pressure, teen sex, and drinking. Instead, they'd spent most of their time talking about boys and sample sales. Serena shot a sidelong glance at Jenny. She seemed to have turned out okay anyway.

"We were great role models. Unlike Nate's role model, L'Wren." Blair smirked, naming a supremely slutty University of Virginia freshman who'd almost deflowered Nate when he was fifteen.

"Oh my God, L'Wren! I'd almost forgotten about her!" Serena cried, clapping her hands.

Nate shook his head ruefully. In truth, he still had a soft spot in his heart for L'Wren, the girl who'd taught him how to smoke a bong.

Ah, memories.

Dan shifted uncomfortably in his seat, wishing he had more to offer to the conversation. What would he say? *Hey Chuck, remember when you locked me out of a party? Nate, remember when you invited yourself on my and Serena's college visiting tour senior year?* "Hey beautiful," he whispered to Serena, trying to pull her out of this lame remember-when conversation about people he'd never met and parties he'd never been invited to.

"Hey," Serena said distractedly, putting her hand on his arm as if to shush him. She leaned forward over the table, looking from Nate to Blair. "What I really want to know is: How did none of us get arrested?"

"I went to rehab." Nate shrugged.

"I followed you there," Blair said in disbelief. Had she ever really been that crazy?

Does she want the long answer or the short answer? Oh wait, there is no long answer.

"And I rescued you!" Serena piped up. The three of them collapsed into a fit of giggles.

"Okay, this officially enters 'I don't want to know' territory. Giles and I will excuse ourselves," Harold said bemusedly, pushing his chair back and beginning to clear the table.

Dan sighed, bored. Jenny was hanging on to every word, giggling like a maniac even though she hadn't really been a part of any of this either.

"Serena, remember the first time we met?" Dan whispered in Serena's ear. He hoped that would be enough to get her to start paying attention to him.

"Yeah." Serena smiled, but she didn't elaborate. "Oh my God, remember when we lived in the *Breakfast at Tiffany's* apartment, Blair?"

"Remember the Raves?" Jenny asked, butting into the conversation. She wasn't sure if it was because she was older or because they were all out of high school, but suddenly, all the things that had seemed die-of-embarrassment awful when she was fourteen—like the time a semipornographic video of her and Nate rolling around in the snow together was leaked on the Internet or the time she appeared in just a bra in a photo spread for a national magazine—seemed almost funny. Jenny felt vaguely proud of herself for surviving all that and ending up here.

"Of course! And our awesome photo shoot for *W* right before graduation? I still get compliments on that."

Jenny beamed. Soon she'd be telling Serena she once stole her jog bra from her locker.

Dan stood up from the table, needing a break. He picked up the empty casserole dish and headed toward the kitchen after Harold and Giles. He paused when he saw Harold's hand on the back of Giles's neck, and made his way back to the table. He plunked down next to Serena and drained the rest of his wine. Maybe he could at least get some good poetic inspiration from his misery.

*The grown-up beauty queens, Lipstick traces of glory faded*
*In ghost hallways, empty yearbooks. Angry. Jaded.*

Or not.

Serena's cheeks ached from laughing so hard and she knew she was going to be more than a little hungover tomorrow, but she didn't want to get up and leave the party yet. Dinner had been over for almost an hour, but everyone was still sitting around the table, drinking wine and happily swapping stories.

Almost everyone.

"Okay, so what do you miss the most about high school?" Serena waved her empty wineglass around like a Madison Avenue divorcée at a ladies-only luncheon and glanced around the table. Dan had been silent the entire time. Serena knew he felt out of place. Even though he'd come to a lot of the parties they were remembering, he'd never really been part of their group of friends back in high school. Still, that didn't mean he had to *sulk.*

Jenny shrank lower in her seat, waiting for someone else to

answer. Of course, she was still *in* high school, but she didn't want to call attention to that fact.

"I miss stealing homework from the smart kids," Chuck offered with a wry smile at Dan.

"Thanks," Dan said stiffly. He had supplied Chuck with most of his English assignments for a year.

"Just kidding," Chuck laughed. "Didn't I give you an autographed picture one time in exchange? God, I was a douche." Chuck shook his head.

Blair shifted back in her chair. All this talk about their high school escapades had made her feel restless and antsy. There were now half a dozen empty champagne and wine bottles on the table. Outside, an almost-full moon reflected on the still falling snow, making the whole world look magical. She didn't want to sit across from Nate anymore or watch Jenny gaze at him with puppylike adoration or remember any of the reasons why Chuck was a freak in high school. She needed to get outside and do something.

Or someone?

"Let's go sledding," Blair announced, already scraping her chair across the cherrywood floors.

"Yay!" Serena yelled, clambering to her feet.

Dan cringed. He *hated* snow in his socks or in the wrists of his jacket and the feel of icy snow on his skin. He hated trudging through the cold only to ride a piece of plastic down a hill. Why walk up just to slide down? But more than anything, he was scared. When he was ten, he'd gone sledding with Zeke, his former best friend with unfortunate wide hips, and they'd crashed into a three-hundred-pound man, who toppled on top of them. Dan had lain there on his back with the wind knocked out of him, thinking he was destined to die under the fat man's girth. He hadn't gotten on a sled since.

"Let's go!" Serena needled, grabbing Dan's hand and trying to drag him to his feet. Blair, Chuck, Nate, and Jenny were already in the mudroom, searching through old mittens and hats for things to wear.

Dan shook his head. "I can't."

"Why not?" Serena's eyes narrowed. What was Dan's problem? He'd been moody ever since they'd left Providence. Serena had tried as hard as she could to include him in the conversation tonight, but he wouldn't even *try*. Giles had talked more than Dan tonight, and not only did Giles not know who anyone was, English wasn't even his first language.

"I think I might be getting sick," Dan lied. "Besides, I thought we could curl up in front of the fire. You know, just do something quiet. I think that would make me feel better." Lying on a rug next to a roaring fire with Serena was exactly what he needed to just chill out from the last twenty-four hours.

"If you're feeling sick, I don't want to catch it," she told him coldly. Then she half ran to keep up with the rest of the group. "Don't leave without me," she called after them.

Dan sighed heavily as he trudged toward the small library off the main living room. The fireplace was stacked with wood, but Dan had no idea how to make a fire. The shelves were neatly organized by color—deep greens, blues, and burgundy, and Dan quickly realized they'd been purchased at the Strand through their books-by-the-yard program, where you could buy books based on your house's color scheme rather than their literary merit.

Dan gazed unhopefully at the musty maroon volumes in front

of him. He stopped at one thin volume with gold script on the spine. It was *The Sorrows of Young Werther,* by Goethe, about a guy's unrequited love for a beautiful woman. It had been Dan's favorite book in high school.

Wonder why.

He settled into a stiff red leather wingback chair under a cathedral-like window and flipped open to a random page. It was where the hero, Werther, realizes he either has to kill his love, her husband, or himself. Dan frowned. This probably *wasn't* the best choice for tonight.

Instead, he pulled his cell phone out of the pocket of his old tan cords. No missed calls. Of course.

He idly scrolled through his phone book. He didn't have many numbers stored—just some other creative writing majors from college, his dad, Jenny, and Serena. As he reached the end of the list, he paused at the lone *V.* Every other entry had a first and last name, but he'd just put a *V* for *Vanessa* the first time he'd programmed her into his phone and never bothered to change it. He'd always sort of loved the simplicity of it. Why would he ever need to say more than that?

Dan gazed at her number. He hadn't spoken to Vanessa in almost two years. He'd thought that, living in the same, geographically small city, they might run into each other. But then again, he lived way uptown and rarely left the neighborhood, while she probably spent all her time in Brooklyn. He'd heard she was still dating that famous indie film director. She probably never even thought about Dan anymore. But maybe she did.

WOULD YOU RATHER EAT MY DAD'S FONDUE FOR A MONTH OR GO SLEDDING EVERY DAY FOR A YEAR? he wrote quickly, then, without thinking, hit send. Jenny tortured him with the would-you-rather game, coming up with absurd scenarios like would he rather have uncontrollable back hair or uncontrollable nose hair. But he knew Vanessa liked absurd questions. Besides, it was just a little innocent blast from the past.

And since when are blasts from the past ever innocent?

# *love don't live here anymore*

"You want to go out?" Vanessa asked Norma. The little chow-poodle mix cocked her head and emitted a low-pitched whine. Vanessa understood what she was trying to say: that she was bored and antsy and didn't know what to do with herself. Vanessa felt the same way. It was nine o'clock, but Hollis was still in a meeting with Streetscape execs over distribution for *Rowing to Reykjavík*. She'd called him a few times, but the phone had gone straight to voice mail.

Vanessa had hoped they could spend some quality time alone, now that he was finally home, but he had such a crammed schedule of meetings and mandatory studio holiday parties and conference calls that they'd barely spent any time together. In fact, they hadn't even exchanged Christmas presents yet—unless you counted the several pairs of ugly wool socks he'd presented to her his first night back. He said that they were the only thing that kept him warm in Iceland. Vanessa was planning on giving him a framed photo of the dilapidated picnic table on his old roof. She'd begged his old roommates for access, and had spent one chilly afternoon shooting it, recalling their first kiss. But she hadn't even had the chance to give it to him. It felt like he'd only come into the apartment to dump his stuff and then leave again. A collection of gray wool socks were balled up under the glass coffee table like nesting chinchillas, and a collection of coffee mugs were in a Stonehenge-like formation around the sink. Huge stills from *Rowing to Reykjavík* were lined up along the hallway, blocking the way as they waited to be hung.

The elevator door finally slid open. "Hey babe!" Hollis yelled happily.

"Hey!" she called out. She tried not to let her annoyance show when she noticed the two skinny, goateed guys trailing behind Hollis.

"These are two Streetscape interns. Josh, Randy, this is Vanessa." The two guys trailed Hollis into the kitchen and stood there, not taking off their shoes or coats. Instead of handshakes, they each offered Vanessa a limp wave before leaning against the wall, turning to Hollis to play ambassador.

"We're going to this party in Red Hook," Hollis announced, traipsing gray slush on the freshly cleaned pine floors. It had been snowing, sleeting, and slushy for three days all across the northeast. Brooklyn was blanketed in a thin layer of white, barely concealing the dingy gray slush beneath it.

"Okay." Vanessa resisted the urge to trail after Hollis with the WetJet. She'd much rather order in and have sex, but she didn't want to be a bitch. Besides, there'd be plenty of time for that later. "I'll just get ready." Vanessa smiled, trying to figure out what she should wear. It had been a long time since she'd been to a party.

"Oh, you want to come?" Hollis asked in surprise. "Okay, that's cool. Guys, want some beers? You picked some up, right, babe?" Hollis asked Vanessa, already midway to the Sub-Zero refrigerator. He hadn't even taken off his jacket.

Vanessa shook her head in disbelief. Um, no she hadn't, and since when was her job to go on beer runs for the guys she didn't know were coming over?

"That's fine. We have a bottle of wine." Hollis grabbed the bottle of white Ruby had brought over the other night.

*That's mine!* Vanessa wanted to yell. But that was ridiculous. It was Hollis's apartment. "You know, I think I'm actually going to stay in for the night. Have fun, guys." Vanessa shrugged.

"You sure?" Hollis asked. "I won't be home too late. So good to be back!" Hollis said, kissing the top of Vanessa's head.

Vanessa collapsed back on the leather couch and pulled her phone from the crevice behind the cushions. One new text. She smiled. It was probably Hollis, texting from a cab, sweetly saying that he'd miss her and that he'd be back soon.

Instead, it was from *Dan.* Asking if she'd rather sled or eat his dad's fondue. She immediately thought of Rufus, his crazy outfits and his crazier culinary creations, and then of Dan's traumatizing story about being mowed over by a large man on a sled when he was a kid. She laughed out loud, the tension of the last half hour slowly seeping from her limbs.

She looked down at the keypad and quickly typed in I HATE SLEDDING. BRING ON THE FONDUE!

Immediately, her phone lit up again: WOULD YOU RATHER BE LOCKED OUT OF A PARTY IN TRIBECA OR LOCKED ON THE ROOF OF YOUR OLD APT IN WILLIAMSBURG?

Vanessa smiled. Dan was alluding to the first time they'd met, when they'd both found themselves locked out of a party back in high school. Vanessa had come out onto the fire escape to get some air, and Dan had come out for a cigarette, closing the fire door behind him and locking them both out. Together, they'd climbed down the side of the massive brick building, and wound up at a nearby bar, talking late into the night and quickly becoming friends. That felt so long ago now.

Vanessa pulled her legs underneath her and spread a blanket over her legs. It was nice to hear from Dan, and especially nice that he didn't seem to hate her anymore. Outside, she could hear people from the bar across the street talking and laughing. She smiled to herself, then texted back: DEPENDS WHO I'D BE LOCKED OUT WITH.

Now who says texting is impersonal?

## *tangled up in s . . .*

Serena scampered up the snowy hill, pulling a handmade toboggan behind her. "Natie, let's race!" she called, her breath coming out in small white puffs. The floodlights outside the house were on, casting the property in an eerie glow. Chuck and Blair were already halfway down the hill. Jenny was still struggling up with her toboggan. It kept slipping from her mittened hands and sliding back down.

"Okay." Nate ran after Serena. It struck him that they were twenty—actual adults—and yet all they wanted to do was act like little kids. It was like that dumb cliché: The more you change, the more you stay the same. Maybe growing up was just about becoming closer to the person you always were.

And he came up with that without any herbal aid. Impressive.

"Hey!" Nate easily caught up with Serena, wrapping his arms around her willowy, athletic frame.

Serena whirled around to face him, her blond hair whipping his face. She playfully pushed Nate so he took a lurching step backward into a snowbank.

"No mercy!" Nate yelled, pulling her down with him and wrestling her into the snow.

Serena squealed in protest as she wriggled free, making an impromptu snow angel. Clumps of snow clung to her long eyelashes.

For a second, Nate was transported back to their sophomore year, to an afternoon when they'd been goofing off in the piles of snow in his courtyard. It was the first time he'd seen Serena not as plain old Serena, his best friend since kindergarten, but as a beautiful *girl*. A girl he loved.

He hastily stood up, brushing the wet snow off the back of his khakis.

"Here," he offered, holding his hand out to help Serena up.

"Thanks." Serena got to her feet, still holding Nate's hand. She held his gaze. The air felt thick and the world around them seemed muted.

"Nate, can you help me?" Jenny called from the bottom of the hill. They both looked up to where she was sitting on top of a toboggan, her cheeks rosy from the cold.

"Sure," Nate said, reluctantly turning away from Serena.

"Watch out, he's brutal!" Serena called after them, trying not to feel disappointed. When Dan had refused to come sledding, it was almost a relief. Playing in the snow had always been something she and Nate shared.

Nate grabbed the sled and tossed it halfway up the hill. He caught it and ran the last of the way, Jenny laughing and trudging behind. They both climbed on and he wrapped his arms around her small frame. "Let's go!" he cried, pushing them toward the edge of the slope.

As they hurtled down the hill across the crisp fresh snow,

Jenny felt the sting of the wind against her face. This was nothing like traying at Waverly, where everyone used the dining hall trays to slide down the teeny-tiny hill behind Dumbarton, one of the girls' dorms. Toboggans were so much more authentic and quaint. She felt like one of the sisters in *Little Women*. They were always going sledding with their neighbor Laurie, who was too cute for his own good.

Sort of like a certain green-eyed Adonis we all know and love?

The sled coasted to a stop at the foot of the hill. Jenny breathed out in wonderment. Fat snowflakes circled furiously around them, and the majestic pine trees were coated in white. She felt like she was trapped in a snow globe.

"Was that too fast for you?" Nate turned around, his brow furrowed in concern. His arms were still circled tightly around her waist. She shook her head.

She knew what she wanted to do when they got back to the house tonight. She was a virgin, and had been waiting for the right person and the right time. Waverly was such a small school and everyone knew everyone's business. Soon after she got there, she realized that when she did lose her virginity, she wanted it to be with someone special, someone she trusted. Someone like Nate.

"Hey hornyheads!" Serena called cheerfully as she coasted down the hill by herself on a red toboggan. Jenny broke away guiltily and waved.

"Want to race?" Nate called to Serena, a devilish gleam in his eye as he grabbed the toboggan rope and began pulling it back up the hill.

"I want to race," Blair called from the other side of the

hill, where she and Chuck were setting up their own sled. She couldn't believe little Jenny Humphrey was getting all cozy with Nate in front of everyone. Who the fuck did she think she was?

"You want to steer, or should I?" Chuck asked, gesturing to the sled.

"I don't care." Blair plunked down on the toboggan. She crossed her arms, then uncrossed them, remembering she wasn't supposed to care about Nate anymore. Chuck sat down behind her, stretching out his long legs and crossing them over hers.

"Actually, I've had enough." Blair stood up abruptly. "I'm wet and freezing and I'm going inside," she huffed, stomping toward the garage. What twenty-year-olds sledded for fun? Serena's lame boyfriend had the right idea to drink wine in the library instead of coming sledding. Maybe she'd go join him.

Jealousy loves company.

# when the lights go out

Blair stormed into the sunken living room and flicked on the Tiffany lamp on the end table. Nothing happened. "Don't tell me the fucking power is out."

"Do you know where the fuse box is?" Chuck asked, coming up behind her.

"Hey." Dan emerged from the library. "Do you know where the fuse box is?" he asked.

Blair shook her head. Why did boys care so much about fuse boxes?

"I'm going to bed," she announced haughtily.

Dan nodded, squinting past Blair into the darkness. He could hear Serena, Jenny, and Nate taking off their boots in the kitchen. Dan suddenly felt guilty for abandoning them. He and Vanessa had been texting for the past few hours, volleying remember-whens and would-you-rathers back and forth. He hadn't even *noticed* that the power had gone off until Blair stomped in. It made him worried that there might have been other things he hadn't noticed.

Like that his little sister's all grown up?

"I think we should *all* go to bed," Blair added, stamping out the memory of Nate's hands around Jenny's waist on the hill. It was the last thing she wanted to think about right now.

Upstairs, Blair took a long hot shower by candlelight, trying to let the water wash away her nagging frustrations. Nate had looked so happy tonight, so different from the tormented Nate of last winter. When she closed her eyes she saw him laughing, tugging a toboggan up a hill. She saw him lobbing snowballs at Serena. Hugging Jenny. She saw him smiling, his green eyes glittering. She stepped out of the shower and toweled off, pulling on a Cosabella tank top and shorts set before heading into the bedroom. Chuck was already asleep, his breathing deep and even.

She climbed into bed and lay next to Chuck, turning over so she was lying on her side. She couldn't get comfortable. Lying next to Chuck didn't feel right. Instead, she found herself thinking about a certain attic bedroom.

Maybe she and Nate needed to talk. Or kiss. One more time. One *last* time. Just to say goodbye, so she could get rid of all the confusing feelings swirling around her brain. So that she could *finally* enter her grown-up life, without any worries about her past coming back to haunt her. She swung her legs out of bed, grabbed a candle from the antique oak dresser, and headed for the door.

Next door, Serena lay awake in bed. Dan was sleeping with his cell phone clutched to his chest like a tiny electronic life preserver. She felt alone with her jumbled thoughts.

Being outside with Nate had been so fun, so natural. She wasn't playful when she was with Dan. She always hesitated for a half second before she said anything, worried she'd disappoint him by not sounding smart. She hated worrying.

She wondered what Nate was doing upstairs. He'd seemed disappointed when Blair wanted to go inside, like he wished he could stay outside and play forever. And that was what Serena loved most about him.

She swung her feet onto the cold floor.

There was no way in hell Jenny was even going to try to sleep. The whole evening—playing in the snow as if she were a heroine in a nineteenth-century novel, coming back to a power outage, feeling Nate's warm breath on her cold skin—had been so romantic. And there was no reason the evening had to come to an end. She pulled on a camisole and the leggings she'd worn on her RISD tour. It wasn't ideal, but there was no way she would go upstairs to *lose her virginity* in one of Blair's discarded T-shirts. The makeshift jammies would have to do.

*Okay,* Jenny whispered to herself. She felt excited and nervous all at the same time. She creaked the door open and stepped into the dark hallway.

Blair climbed up the rickety attic stairs, a Tocca candle in one hand. It was fig scented and perfect for the bedside, but not very helpful in casting light on her path. She looked up when she heard a sound coming from the door at the bottom of the stairs.

*Serena.* She wore one of her ancient C&C California T-shirts from high school, without a bra underneath. The candlelight flickered over her pale hair and perfect features, making her look more beautiful than ever.

"What are you doing?" Blair whispered, balancing precariously on the stair.

Serena sucked in her breath. What was Blair doing here? "I was going to the bathroom. Dan was taking a shower in ours and I remembered there was a bathroom up here," she lied, shrugging nonchalantly. "What are you doing?" she asked, even though she had a feeling she knew the answer to that question.

"I was making sure the window upstairs was closed," Blair shot back. At least that made more sense than Serena's ridiculous lie. It was so fucking obvious Serena was trying to sneak into Nate's room.

"Do you need help? With the window?" Serena asked, arching an eyebrow.

"I'll just text Nate to get it. No use waking everyone up. And there's a bathroom downstairs. I can show you," Blair challenged.

Serena paused. Finally, she nodded.

Blair escorted Serena down the hallway like a policewoman with a petty criminal, standing sentry at the door. She heard Serena turn on the faucet before emerging a few seconds later.

"Good night," the two girls said, daring each other to be the first to turn back and climb the attic stairs.

Blair didn't budge. It was her goddamn house. She was going to stay up all night if that was what it took. "Good night," Blair said again, more pointedly.

"See you tomorrow morning," Serena said before heading reluctantly down the hallway. Would Blair go back to Nate's bedroom after she left?

Or would someone else get there first?

# *things that go bump in the night*

Nate had fallen asleep quickly. He was having a dream about chasing Blair and Serena all over Central Park but never being able to catch them when the door to his room creaked open.

"It's me." A girl's voice pulled him out of his soupy, half-conscious state. Nate blinked to adjust his eyes to the light. The girl held a candle that cast a glow on the ecru walls, making it impossible to see her clearly. The figure was too short to be Serena's, but the voice was too breathy to be Blair's.

Nate sat up and ran his hand through his hair. "I can't really see you," he said. Jenny held the candle closer to her face, casting her skin with a warmish golden glow. She wore a pair of tight black leggings and a lacy black tank top. "Here, you'll get cold," he said, holding up the flannel covers and patting a spot on the mattress next to him.

Jenny placed the candle on the nightstand and tried to smile seductively. Her heart was hammering in her chest and she wanted to scream with excitement. It was happening. It was finally happening!

Easy there, tiger.

She climbed into the bed next to Nate and pulled the flannel comforter over their legs. Their hips were touching, and she could smell the scent of fabric softener and shave gel. His hair was still damp from the snow outside.

She turned and kissed him, enjoying the feel of his stubbly cheek against her smooth one. Outside, the storm was still raging, but in the attic, next to Nate, she felt cozy and warm and safe.

Nate kissed her back hungrily. Her tiny, curvy body felt so good in his arms. He edged down one strap of her lacy camisole and kissed her milky white shoulder. It felt so nice, so familiar to be with Jenny, even though the last time they'd hooked up was three years ago. But that was the thing about Jenny. She was comfortable, soft, sweet, easy.

Watch it—no girl likes being called *easy*. Especially in a bed.

"Wait." Jenny pushed his hand away and held it. Her hands were tiny, like little kid hands. She led his hand to rest on the center of her chest, on top of the little rosette on her bra. "I'm a virgin." Jenny smiled shyly. "I want you to be my first. I'm just letting you know in case . . . you know," she finished.

"Oh," Nate said. It made him feel protective of her. He didn't want to hurt her. "Are you sure?" he asked, intertwining his fingers in hers. He hadn't been with anyone for a year. At Deep Springs, the nearest women were tens of miles away, and until recently, they were even further from his mind.

"Yes, I'm sure." Jenny smiled at him softly, invitingly. She eased her camisole straps all the way down her shoulders. "I just wanted you to know."

Nate nodded and blew the candle out. Then he took Jenny—sweet, uncomplicated, sexy Jenny—in his strong, capable arms.

That's one way to end a year.

*Disclaimer: All the real names of places, people, and events have been altered or abbreviated to protect the innocent. Namely, me.*

# hey people!

**when the lights go out**

You know how in Jane Austen novels, the most scandalous things always happened in the country, never in town? Well, we may be more than a century away and an ocean apart, but the same thing happens here. Say what you will about city living, but something about the one-with-the-elements, outdoorsy lifestyle seems to bring out the frisky in everyone. Is there anything more romantic than cuddling by the fireside and kisses by candlelight?

Statistics say the average woman kisses twenty-nine men before she gets married. But my friends and I have never been average, and we're a loooong way from getting married. Whether you keep track with scratches on the bedpost or notches on your lipstick case, every girl has her list of conquests. According to my sources, one girl is about to begin her way-more-than-kissed list with none other than **N**. Godspeed, sweetie. We are all dying little deaths back in town.

**your e-mail**

**Q:** Dear Gossip Girl,
I'm at my family's boring vacation house in Newport, which is even more boring than usual because the power went out. I was

stargazing with my telescope and my view landed on this couple getting totally hot and heavy in the attic across the bay. The shadows are ridiculous. Do you know who they are?

—voyeur

**a:** Dear V,

If it's the couple I'm thinking of, they already have a history of overexposure on the Internet. I'll spare them any more. And, by the way, it's more than creepy that you're watching.

—GG

## houseguest hints

As you've learned by now, *home for the holidays* may be a catchy phrase, but it's hardly where you want to spend your entire break. You should always have an emergency crash pad lined up, devoid of annoying relatives or whiny younger siblings. What to do when the Tribeca Star, W Union Square, and the Hudson are all full? Here's the need-to-know for holiday house-crashing.

Give freely. They thought they were done opening their presents, so please your hosts-to-be by bringing a bottle of wine and a tray of Citarella holiday cookies. You're practically guaranteed the guest bedroom.

Show up during the witching hour. You know that time around four o'clock when it's already dark, even though it feels like you've only been up for a few hours? It's too late to do anything productive, but too early to go out. Show up when boredom's at its peak, and your hosts will be thrilled to see you.

Play the poor-me card. I don't usually advocate whining, but desperate times call for desperate measures. If you truly have nowhere to go, let your hosts know exactly why. Honesty can go a long way in finding you a place to stay.

Finally, once you're settled, remember the three rules of being a great guest: Don't hook up on the host's bed unless it's with the host, don't puke in their planters, and, whatever you do, don't overstay your welcome.

You know you love me,

gossip girl

# the ghosts of christmas past

Blair woke up with a start and impatiently pushed Chuck's arm off her. She used to think it was cute that he threw his arms over her in his sleep, as if trapping her in a hug, but right now it felt suffocating. The bedside lamp was on, meaning the electricity must have come back in the middle of the night. Outside, the snow had tapered into flurries. That meant there was nothing keeping Serena and Nate here anymore.

She rose from the grand four-poster bed and threw on an old pair of Habitual jeans and a Cacharel black cardigan, not bothering to shower. She pulled her hair back in a ponytail and stomped toward the door. She needed coffee and carbs, and to make sure nothing looked amiss in Nate's attic bedroom.

"Morning, gorgeous." Chuck sat up, looking sleepy and satisfied. "Happy New Year's Eve Day!" He climbed out of bed, wearing Calvin Klein boxers that hung low on his hips. "I have a present for you," he murmured, rifling through his Tumi leather suitcase.

"But why? Christmas is over," Blair pointed out. Chuck had already given her a pair of sapphire earrings, and they'd made plans to go skiing in Switzerland in January.

"I know, but I wanted to give you something else. More like an anniversary present. I remember how sad you were around this time last year. This year, I want you to be happy." Chuck smiled, and Blair couldn't help but soften. "Here you go." He handed her an orange box with an Hermès ribbon around it.

Blair pulled the ribbon open. Inside were two enamel bangle bracelets, each one printed with hieroglyphic designs.

"It's to remind you of our first real date," Chuck said softly. He'd taken her to London, to the British Museum, where they'd wandered through the Egyptian Wing, then headed out to a cute little wine bar, where they'd talked for hours. After missing the last bus back to Oxford, they'd checked into a Bloomsbury boutique hotel. Chuck had given her the bed, insisting it was better if he slept on the floor.

"Thanks." Blair shoved the bracelets onto her wrist and gave Chuck a peck on the cheek. But how could she be happy this New Year's when everyone she'd been *trying* to get away from had decided to follow her here? She glanced out the window, where snowflakes were picking up in speed and intensity. *Fan-fucking-tastic.*

"What's wrong?" Chuck gently rested his hand on her arm.

"Nothing!" Blair snapped. "I need some coffee."

And a personality makeover?

Serena combed her long blond hair back and pulled on a black Marc Jacobs sweater that had been Blair's in high school. She gently closed the door to the guest room, where Dan was still sleeping, and headed toward the stairs. She'd tossed and turned all night, sure she could hear giggles coming from Nate's bedroom.

"Giles and I slept right through the storm! We didn't realize the power had gone out until we woke up to find all the lights in the house on. I hope you slept okay. You look a little tired, Bear." Serena stiffened when she heard Harold Waldorf's pleasant, lawyerly voice drift up the stairs.

"I didn't sleep very well," Blair grumbled.

"I can always change room arrangements when your friends leave, so you can get your beauty sleep," Harold offered.

"They're not my friends," Blair muttered. "I don't know why they're here. I thought it would be a relaxing holiday with just the family, and I have to read *Ulysses*, and I can't do anything when I'm so stressed out. Look, Daddy, do you think I'm breaking out?"

"Morning!" Serena said loudly as she clattered down the stairs.

"Serena," Harold boomed jovially. "Coffee?"

"Yes please." A bowl of fresh pumpkin spelt scones, courtesy of Giles, sat on the counter. Serena took one, plunging her thumb into the flaky pastry.

"Hi," Blair said icily.

"Hi," Serena responded, taking a buttery bite. "I like your bracelets."

"Thanks. My boyfriend gave them to me," Blair said pointedly. "Speaking of, where's yours?" *And when are you all leaving?* she wanted to add.

"He's still sleeping." An awkward silence fell over the kitchen as Serena tried to search for clues about whether or not Blair and Nate had been together last night. It was hard to tell. Blair seemed edgy and bad-tempered, but that didn't mean anything. She was often edgy and bad-tempered.

"How are your parents?" Harold asked politely, breaking the silence as he settled on a chair opposite Serena.

"They're great. Right now, they're in St. Barts for New Year's. My brother, Erik, is getting married next year, so they've been really busy with plans." Serena nodded happily. Erik had met his fiancée when he went to Australia for his junior year abroad, and they'd been inseparable since. The only downside to the wedding was the floor-length lilac taffeta dress she'd be obligated to wear as a bridesmaid.

Blair resisted the urge to roll her eyes. Who cared? And why was Serena up so early? Had she sneaked back into Nate's room?

"What time are you leaving?" Blair asked rudely.

Serena felt like she'd been slapped. Apparently, their truce had ended.

And the cold war is back on.

"Blair!" Harold chided. "The snow is still coming down. It's New Year's Eve Day. You kids are free to stay as long as you like," he said, glancing out the window.

Serena followed his gaze. The flurries from earlier this morning were now large, swirling flakes. She and Dan were supposed to be back in New York this evening for Rufus's infamous New Year's Eve flambé party, but now it looked like they would be forced to stay another night. She was as trapped as the animals at the Central Park Zoo.

And about to fall prey to a lioness.

# heartbreak hotel

Vanessa woke up with a start on New Year's Eve Day. She turned over and stretched, realizing that she was alone in bed. Since he'd gotten back, her and Hollis's sleep schedules had been so off, it felt as though they were roommates rather than a couple sharing a bed.

She got out of bed and sleepily padded down the winding staircase into the living room. She sniffed the air, surprised not to smell any muffins baking or eggs frying. Hollis loved cooking breakfast, and Vanessa had gotten used to waking up to a feast. She smiled happily at Hollis, sitting shirtless at the counter in a pair of flannel pajama pants and the same type of thick, woolly socks he'd given to Vanessa.

"Happy New Year! *Glidilegt Nytt Ar.* Isn't that how you say it in Icelandic?" She'd looked up the pronunciation on the Internet, sure that the phone was the only way they'd communicate on the holiday. She skipped down the stairs and plunked down on the chair opposite him. But Hollis was busy squinting down at his iPhone.

Finally, he looked up, his gaze icy. "How's Dan?"

A shiver of fear ran up her spine. Hollis was reading the texts on *her* phone. "Dan and I were texting last night. While you were out," she said coldly. She wasn't going to be made to feel guilty when she hadn't *done* anything.

"Just texting? *'Depends who I'm meeting on the roof?'*" he said in a mocking tone. "No wonder you didn't come out with my friends. You wanted to go meet up with Dan."

"What? No!" Vanessa screeched, her voice echoing in her ears. This was ridiculous. Nothing could be further from the truth. Last night she'd eaten half a tub of Ciao Bella on the couch with her feet under Norma. Which was pretty much how she spent all her time these days. For the last year, she'd been stupidly devoted to Hollis. She'd put her whole life on hold for him.

"What else am I supposed to think?" Hollis asked in exasperation. Norma emitted a low-pitched whine from the floor, as if to say she didn't want any part of this. "You didn't want to go out last night, you didn't even try to be friendly with the Streetscape people—it's like you don't even care. . . ." Hollis shook his head ruefully. "Long distance sucks, I know that. But it wasn't like I was in Iceland for fun. I was *working*. You of all people should appreciate that."

Vanessa blinked back angry tears. Outside, the city was blanketed in snow, quiet and cold. "You've been with the film people all the time; then you just come home and expect me to be your personal assistant," she retorted. "I didn't want to go out because I was fucking *exhausted* from picking up after you."

"Really? Really, Vanessa?" Hollis snorted. "Guess you weren't too tired to text Dan all night. How come you never texted me like that?" The hurt was evident in his voice.

Vanessa shook her head. At one point in her life, Dan had meant more to her than anyone ever had. He'd been her best friend, her confidant, the only person in the world who knew her better than she knew herself. Even though they hadn't spoken for two years, she knew he still understood her.

But it seemed too impossible to try to explain her relationship with Dan. To explain any part of what she was feeling right now. It was as if she and Hollis had lost their ability to communicate a long time ago but were only just now realizing it.

She gazed at his balled-up socks under the coffee table, which he never put in the hamper. Hurt and anger and confusion bubbled up inside of her. Suddenly, she felt exhausted. "Look, this isn't working," Vanessa found herself saying, her voice breaking. "But I want you to know I wasn't cheating."

"I'm going to go," Hollis said. He stood and headed up the spiral stairs to their sleeping loft. "Spend a few days away. Clear my head."

"No, it's *your* apartment. Don't be ridiculous. I just need a few minutes to pack."

Upstairs, she threw her things into a huge army green duffel. She had nowhere to go. Ruby and Piotr's extended family were having a New Year's Eve goat roast that she didn't want to crash. There was too much snow on the ground to get a bus to Vermont to her parents'. She suddenly found herself thinking of the Upper West Side and Rufus's flambé.

Maybe there was someplace she could go, after all.

# a lot can go wrong in the cold light of day

Jenny felt like she was about to explode from the secret of what had happened last night. She didn't want to sit too close to Nate, in case anyone might suspect anything, so she'd watched *Two for the Road* and *My Fair Lady* sitting on an uncomfortable leather ottoman. Now, the sun was beginning to set, Blair was about to put in *Breakfast at Tiffany's*, and Jenny wasn't sure if she could stand watching another romantic movie in the dark.

"Want to play a game?" she asked, kneeling down before the glass-fronted cabinet of games in the corner of the den. The snow had let up, and she wondered if they'd all head back to New York. She hoped they'd stay just one more night, even if it *was* New Year's Eve and she was supposed to go to a party in the city with Tinsley, one of her friends from Waverly. But she didn't want to go to a party. All she wanted to do was sneak back up to Nate's attic bedroom again.

"Let me see." Serena stood behind Jenny, peering at the games. "Oooh, Clue! Remember how your nanny taught us to play this and you were terrified Colonel Mustard was coming to get you?" she called over to Nate. He smiled slightly.

Serena set up the board. "Can I be Miss Scarlet?" she asked.

"I don't see why not. You always get what you want," Blair said under her breath from the corner. She was *so* over this snowbound adventure. All she wanted was a quiet New Year's Eve with her boyfriend, where they toasted their calm, peaceful lives, and planned their Gstaad skiing vacation. Was that too much to ask?

"Who do you want to be?" Jenny asked Blair as she took the Mrs. Peacock piece.

"I don't care," Blair said tersely. Everyone was acting strangely today. Serena and Dan were barely talking, Jenny seemed jumpier than usual, Nate was spacey and quiet, and Chuck was trying to make everyone get along. Harold and Giles had wisely spent most of the day playing outside with the twins, as if they sensed drama on the horizon and wanted no part of it. "I'll be Mrs. White," she said finally, sneaking a glance at her white gold Rolex. Four o'clock. Too early to lie and say she was going to bed, even if it was practically dark outside. They began halfheartedly playing.

Serena rolled the dice. "Six. Right behind Blair," she noted as she moved her game piece. Maybe she and Dan could get on the road after this game, and take their chances with the snow.

"Of course you're following me," Blair muttered. Just like Serena had followed her to Yale. Just like Serena had followed her to Newport. She imagined them in their fifties, Blair having to move from home to home to keep away from Serena.

"A little self-centered, Mrs. White?" Serena asked. Her tone was light, but she was deadly serious. What was Blair's problem?

Blair glared at Serena. "I suspect Miss van der Woodsen, outside Nate's room, with a really slutty candlestick," Blair hissed.

Serena gasped. "You were there too. Don't try to act all innocent."

"What?" Jenny chirped, backing away from the game board. What did they mean, outside Nate's room?

"Sorry, Dan, but you should know Serena was trying to sneak into Nate's room last night." Blair stood up abruptly.

Serena felt anger slice through her stomach. It was so *typical* of Blair to blame everything on her. "Let's go, Dan." Serena pulled at his arm. "I need to talk to you."

Dan climbed to his feet uneasily. He felt like he was about to throw up. So Serena had tried to hook up with Nate last night. She hadn't even denied it.

"Blair?" Chuck asked from the corner. "Are you okay?"

"I'll be fine once Serena gets out of here," Blair snapped.

"Christ, not again." Nate angrily kicked the table leg. Why did this always happen? Every time he came into contact with Serena and Blair there was a giant blowout. He suddenly remembered learning about catalyst reactions in his high school chemistry class. One random chemical could change everything between two otherwise normal chemicals. It all made sense. He was a fucking catalyst.

Um, you think?

He walked out of the living room, leaving everyone staring after him. He couldn't stay in the house with Blair. He couldn't drive back to New York with Serena. But he had an idea. His dad kept the *Charlotte* docked in Newport, and it wasn't snowing that hard.

Nate ran up to the attic, grabbed his black Lacroix wallet

from the oak dresser, and shoved it in the back pocket of his khakis. He picked up what few things he had with him, shrugged on his coat, and made for the door.

When he opened it, he found Jenny standing there.

"It's not a good time," he mumbled, trying to sidestep her. "I'm leaving."

Jenny stayed where she was, blocking his path. "I want to go with you, Nate," she said, her large brown eyes wide and pleading. "Please?"

"I'm not going back to New York. I'm taking my dad's boat and heading up to Maine," Nate invented. He wasn't sure where to go, but he knew he needed to get far away from here.

"I've never been to Maine." Jenny offered a small smile. "I know you didn't hook up with Blair or Serena. I know you're different. And . . ." She paused and looked shyly at the ground. She was wearing her red coat and hunter green galoshes, and looked adorably Christmasy. "I really want to be with you."

Jenny bit her pink bottom lip as she waited for his answer. Her sophomore year at Waverly, she'd been in a love triangle of her own, locked in a vicious battle with her roommate over Easy Walsh, a sweet boy from Tennessee. True, Nate and Blair and Serena had known each other for a long time, and the emotions ran deep. But she knew Nate, and she knew he had good intentions. She glanced up again and met his eyes.

Nate paused, taking in Jenny's sweet, hopeful expression. He could still hear Blair and Serena's shrieks from downstairs. But Jenny . . . Jenny didn't look like she'd yell at anyone.

"Are you sure?" he asked finally.

Jenny nodded. "There are stairs over there." She pointed

to the service entrance she'd found this morning when trying to sneak back down to her room.

Nate nodded slowly. They were only about a mile from the harbor. They could walk. "Let's go."

They do say that every ending is a beginning of sorts.

# the end of innocence

Blair threw herself facedown on her dad's bed and let out a wail.

"Bear?" Harold emerged from the bathroom, tying a robe around his waist. He perched on the side of the bed and rubbed Blair's back. "Giles and I heard you while we were in the hot tub. Are you okay?"

"My whole fucking life sucks," Blair said, her voice muffled by the thick goose-down comforter.

"Talk to me," Harold said, sinking down beside her on the bed.

Blair sat up. "It's Nate," she said between choking sobs. She caught a glimpse of her reflection in the mirrors her dad had creepily installed all around the bed. Her face was splotchy and her eyelashes were clumped together, wet with tears. She looked like a scared little girl. "Whenever he comes into my life, I do stupid things. Now Chuck hates me, I hate Serena, and everything's all fucked up," she said as she burst into a fresh sob.

"Bear," Harold said seriously, "right now there's a man in this house who is still here, who loves you, who gives you New

Year's Eve presents." Harold smiled and placed his hand on the enamel bracelet around Blair's wrist. "It's a great time for a fresh start. Go tell him that you're confused. Everyone makes mistakes," he added tenderly.

Blair looked skeptically at her father. She'd never gotten love advice from him before. But he made a good point. Chuck knew better than anyone that people changed. Even her. "Thanks, Daddy," Blair said, rising.

She wiped her tears with the back of her hand and headed down to the kitchen. Chuck was sitting at the island, looking at the financial section of the *The Wall Street Journal*. It was obvious he wasn't reading anything.

"Hi," Blair said in a small voice.

"Hi." Chuck stood up. He kept his arms at his sides.

Blair took a deep breath. "I'm so sorry. I wasn't going up there to sleep with Nate. I mean, I just . . . I don't know what I was doing. It's like, whenever he and Serena are around I act like this person who I don't even like," Blair confessed in a rush of words. It felt good to say it out loud. "But I'm in love with you. I know that." Blair sucked in her breath and her nose made a loud snot-sucking sound.

Chuck pulled Blair into his arms and tenderly pushed her hair off her face. "I love you too," he said simply. "And I know you."

Blair resisted the urge to look away from Chuck's brown eyes. It was true. He'd known her in high school, when she used to lock herself in bathrooms to throw up, when she and Serena would put fake tattoos on their butt cheeks and go out underwearless in too-short dresses, when she would get ridiculously drunk on pink drinks at the Tribeca Star. And he knew her now.

He knew how she took her coffee, where she liked to study, what she looked like when she woke up in the morning. He knew what she needed on a rainy day and on a sunny one.

"Can we start the day over again?" Blair asked. Chuck pulled her close to him.

"Yes," he breathed into her hair. "We can. And tomorrow, it'll be a new year."

Blair nestled into his broad, strong chest. Maybe if she stayed here, close and safe with Chuck, everything would be okay. Maybe she'd never have to think about Nate and Serena again.

Or maybe avoidance can't solve all your problems.

## *where do you go when you're lonely?*

Dan opened the door of the Buick Skylark, not bothering to brush off the inches of snow that clung to the roof. Serena slid silently into the passenger seat, staring straight ahead. She was trembling ever so slightly, but Dan didn't place his hand on her knee. He didn't know how he felt yet.

Dan began to drive, slowly following the signs to I-95. The car felt oddly empty without Jenny. He still couldn't believe she'd gone off with Nate. She'd texted Dan to let him know that she was safe and taken care of, and that she'd be home in a few days. The fact that his girlfriend *and* his little sister had both fallen for that guy's charms was seriously fucked up.

"Why were you going to Nate's room?" Dan asked once they were on the highway. It was the first sentence he'd spoken since they left.

"I don't know," Serena said, staring straight ahead. Something about her matter-of-fact tone made Dan know she was telling the truth. "I think I mainly just wanted to talk to him. To see him. We'd been talking about the old days and it just brought up a lot." Serena took a napkin from the cup holder and began ripping it into smaller and smaller pieces.

Dan nodded. That sort of made sense. It was how he felt when he was texting Vanessa. Like sliding back into something familiar.

"Would you have slept with him?" Dan asked.

Serena bit her lip. Over the years, whenever she and Nate were alone together, things happened beyond their control. But that was in the past. "No," Serena decided.

"I don't get it," Dan said tightly. "Are you in love with him?"

Serena sighed, searching for the words, for a way to explain the whole messy situation so it would make sense to Dan. She rubbed her hands in front of the heater to warm them. How could she answer that? "No. But he was my first love. And that's hard to get over."

Dan nodded, staring straight ahead at the dark road, thinking of Vanessa. The snow had finally stopped and the roads were plowed, but they were completely empty. It was like the whole world was drinking eggnog and counting down to midnight somewhere. "I get it." It had taken him two years to get over her. And then, with one text message, suddenly it felt like she was back in his life.

"I love you," Serena said, her voice catching in her throat.

All of a sudden, Dan started laughing. "If we got through this weekend, we can get through anything."

Serena smiled. Soon they'd be back in New York, back to their real lives, and this would all feel like a dream.

Doesn't she mean nightmare?

"Vanessa, I need you to really flambé the soufflé. Humphrey tradition," Rufus roared. A plastic top hat that read NEW YEAR'S

EVE in silver foil letters was perched on his grizzly salt-and-pepper hair, and he wore a T-shirt with a cartoon of reindeer sitting on a couch drinking beers.

Vanessa used a match to set the chocolate soufflé on fire. It felt good to be surrounded by noise and people after so many weeks of silently hanging around the loft. Rufus's friends were sitting on the couch, drinking vodka and grumbling about Communism versus Marxism. None of them had even asked who she was or why she was here. Rufus had opened the door as if he'd been expecting her. He'd told her that Dan, Serena, and Jenny were snowbound in Rhode Island, and that he was glad to have some young blood in the house. That was hours ago, and since then she'd perfected Rufus's recipe.

Suddenly, the door opened and Dan and Serena tumbled in, holding hands, snowflakes dusting their hair.

"Look who's here!" Rufus cried proudly, gesturing to Vanessa as if he'd made her appear by magic.

Dan's gaze shifted from Serena to Vanessa. "I'm so sorry, I didn't mean to intrude," Vanessa said hastily. She was still holding her wooden soufflé spoon, and set it down on the counter. "It's just . . . Hollis and I broke up and Ruby has, like, seventeen houseguests." Vanessa wiped her hands on her apron. "But I can leave," she added helplessly. Why did she think it was a good idea to barge back into Dan's life? Why had she thought the texts from last night meant anything at all?

Dan dropped Serena's hand. It was so strange, and yet so familiar, to see Vanessa here, in his kitchen. Her dark hair was shoulder length and choppy, and she wore a pair of tight jeans and a white tank top underneath his dad's dorky Kiss the Cook apron. Her milky white skin contrasted with her jet-black hair. He'd forgotten how beautiful she was.

"Sorry to hear that," Serena said, an edge to her voice. It was too bad that Vanessa had broken up with her boyfriend, but why was she so comfortable crashing at Dan's?

Asks the girl who breaks and enters Newport summer homes.

"Thanks. At least I'm earning my keep," Vanessa cracked, pointing to the charred soufflé.

Dan smiled. Vanessa had always been a good sport about his dad's experimental cooking. It was nice to have her here again, back at their apartment. It felt like home.

"So . . ." Vanessa trailed off. "Is it okay if I stay?"

Dan looked straight at Vanessa as if he hadn't heard. "You can always stay," he said softly. Vanessa smiled back, nodding her head, a slight blush creeping over her cheeks.

"Right, sure. Of course," Serena said sulkily, sitting down at the kitchen counter. Above her, the cuckoo clock struck midnight, its lilting, carefree chirp seeming to mock her. It might be a new year, but she felt like she'd experienced this all before.

Two girls, one guy, and New Year's Eve . . . Talk about déjà vu.

# IV

Disclaimer: All the real names of places, people, and events have been altered or abbreviated to protect the innocent. Namely, me.

| topics | sightings | your e-mail | post a question |

# hey people!

Only six more months until we're out in the real world, and the signs are everywhere. Theory suits and Prada pumps scream "signing bonuses." The student center is packed with seniors writing Fulbright grant proposals to study contemporary indigenous literature in Canada, applying to grad school, or creating a backpacking-through-Latin-America itinerary. And then there are those undecideds, who head to any and all on-campus career fairs, just to guarantee they'll have *something* to do once May rolls around.

Even though our mailing addresses will stay the same for the next few months, our minds are already a million miles away. **D** found out he'll be leaving the Big Apple and heading to the land of corn at the famed Iowa Writers' Workshop come September. So what will come of his relationship with the lovely **S**? Rumor has it she'll be graduating from Yale this spring, despite the small technicality that she's only a *sophomore*. How does she do these things? And should we even be surprised by now? **V** may have an address on the Upper West Side, but judging from the pile of mail outside her door and her frequent sightings at Lit, Boxcar Lounge, and Barcade, she's rarely there. After spending a semester apart—she at Yale, he at Oxford—**B** and **C** spent a romantic summer in the south of France, which seemed to ease the pain of separation. Then there are couples like **N** and **J**, who can't even seem to be apart for a few *hours*. They're often seen kissing outside the library . . . and Brown dining hall the Ratty . . . and in the middle of the green. Get a room!

**your e-mail**

q:  Dear Gossip Girl,
I'm the owner of a collection of blogs. Come work with me and I'll make you a star.
—Nick

a:  Dear Nick,
While I don't know what my future holds, I intend to remain an independent operation.
—GG

q:  Dear Gossip Girl,
Okay, here it is: I have loved you since your first post. I'm graduating, I guess you're graduating, and all I want for Christmas is you. I just received my fat signing bonus with a certain hedge fund, and I want to fly you down to St. Barts for the holidays. Come with me and let's toast the rest of our lives.
—Rich

a:  Dear Rich,
While I'm flattered to hear you're a longtime devotee, there's no way I'm spending this holiday anywhere other than the Upper East Side. And while the affections of some ordinary girls may be for sale, I'm no ordinary girl.
—GG

**stress case**

As we all bustle about trying to figure out our futures, I'm experiencing déjà vu. Didn't we do this once already? It's senior year stress all over again—except this time, we're not applying to college, we're applying to *life*. My advice is the same as I gave four years ago: Sometimes, you just need to pour the pinot, turn on some tunes, and chill out. After all, don't we have the rest of our lives to worry?

You know you love me,

gossip girl

# old rivalries, new real estate

Blair stood on the terrace of her mother and stepfather's new Central Park West penthouse and took a drag of her Merit Ultra Light. In the past year, she'd almost given up smoking, but something about her mother's dinner parties always made her want to break the rules.

The new penthouse was on the top floor of a sprawling French Renaissance and German Gothic sandstone building that, on Seventy-second and Central Park West, lay almost exactly across the park from the Fifth Avenue building Blair had grown up in. It may as well have been in a whole other country. They were here because Cyrus was creating a huge development on the west side, but Blair had a feeling that Eleanor had also pushed for the move because she missed her old stomping grounds. Blair didn't blame her. The few times she'd been out to LA, she'd hated it. The clothes were gaudy, the hair and boobs fake, and you had to drive everywhere. Even the sun felt too accosting and bright.

Blair had finally gotten used to Eleanor and Cyrus living in LA, though, and now that she was planning to move to New

York after graduation, she wasn't sure she wanted them in the same time zone, much less the same city. The only *good* thing about the move was that she could see her sister, Yale, more often. Yale might even grow up relatively normal if they spent enough time together.

Or not. Normal is highly overrated.

Blair shivered and hugged her arms around her chest. It was surprisingly warm for December, but she was only wearing a silky black and tan Chloé halter sheath. She wasn't quite ready to go back inside, where Eleanor and Cyrus were hosting a holiday party for all the Upper East Side couples they'd been friends with for years, including the van der Woodsens, the Coateses, and the Basses. Chuck was still in England, due back on Christmas, so Blair had to fend for herself. It was times like these a long-distance relationship was hard. At Yale, she kept busy with classes and the college friends she'd made, but in New York she hated being all alone.

Blair gazed down at streetlight-lined paths that zigzagged through the dark expanse of Central Park greenery. It just felt so *wrong* to be looking at the park from this angle.

The terrace door slid open and her stepbrother, Aaron Rose, stepped outside, carrying Yale on his hip and a glass of champagne in one hand. Aaron was a senior at Harvard, insisted on wearing his hair in little brown dreadlocks, and had spent all of last year on a study-abroad program in Burkina Faso. Now, starry-eyed at the notion of making a difference in third-world countries, he was in the process of applying to the Peace Corps to an even *more* remote third-world country.

"Hey sis!" Aaron said cheerfully, taking a large swig of champagne as he set Yale down. Yale had large blue eyes, dark brown hair tied back with a dark red ribbon, and wore a green velvet Bonpoint party dress. Blair grinned. She was fucking adorable.

The second coming of Blair Waldorf?

"Let's go inside—it's cold!" she said, holding her hand out to her baby sister. Blair wasn't exactly the maternal type, but the almost-four-year-old was impossible to resist.

"No!" Yale stomped her foot indignantly. "I don't *like* anyone in there," she whined as she intertwined her sticky fingers in Blair's manicured ones. Aaron burst out laughing.

Blair picked up Yale, inhaling the scent of her baby shampoo. "Don't worry, Yaley, I don't like anyone either."

Together, Blair and Yale swept through the sliding door of the terrace and into the expansive living room. Eleanor hadn't begun decorating yet, so the entire room was empty save for a large Douglas fir that skimmed the vaulted cathedral ceiling. In a way, the room looked more impressive *without* furniture. The white moldings of the ceiling contrasted with the dark oak of the window ledges, and the art deco chandelier cast a romantic glow against the cherrywood floors.

"Blair, darling!" Misty Bass caught Blair's elbow. She was an imperious-looking woman with a crisp blond bob who never left the house without first putting on a large amount of jewelry.

"You know, darling, seeing you with your adorable baby sister makes me imagine you as a mother," Misty said, leaning in close. Blair practically recoiled from the scent of her spicy perfume. "I know both your mom and I would love grandchildren! After the wedding, of course," she added sternly.

Blair smiled tightly. Who said anything about *marriage*? She and Chuck had been dating for over a year, and they'd spent the entire summer at her dad's South of France vineyard, but they'd been separated by the Atlantic Ocean for the past three months. Besides, what was this, 1952? She was going to get a *job* after graduation, not an entryway ring.

"Blair!" Yale whispered urgently, tugging on Blair's hand. "I have to pee."

"Looks like you need to attend to the little one!" Misty reached out to ruffle Yale's hair.

"Ow!" Yale yelped loudly.

"Oh." Misty drew her hand back and pursed her lips as if she'd sucked on a lemon. "I'm sorry, little dear."

"Nice to see you!" Blair called over her shoulder as she ran Yale toward the nursery. "Good job," she whispered in Yale's ear as she brushed past guests. "I owe you a pony."

Sounds like she'll make a fine mother.

Once Yale was safely deposited in the arms of her nanny, Bridget, Blair reentered the party, determined to avoid Misty for the rest of the night. She scanned the room to see if any of her old friends had tagged along with their parents. Last she'd heard, Nate was attending Brown and shacking up with Jenny Humphrey. She saw Serena on campus often enough, usually talking on her cell or walking quickly across the quad, latte in hand. She'd never said hello. She'd almost gotten to the point where Serena could be anyone on campus—like Emily, an annoying red-haired girl in Blair's Shakespeare class who read each line as if she were a member of the Royal National Theater. Serena was just a vaguely familiar, vaguely annoying face who had nothing to do with Blair's real life.

"Blair, darling! Over here!" Her mother's unmistakable voice floated over the string quartet playing holiday music in the corner. At the entryway, Eleanor Waldorf waved frantically, her Cartier tennis bracelets jangling on her wrist. She wore a silver, cleavage-baring dress that might have been acceptable for a party at a producer's house in the Hollywood Hills but was completely inappropriate for New York, even if it *was* on the Upper West Side. "Look who's here," Eleanor crowed. Blair's eyes flicked to her mother's side and landed on Serena.

Serena, wearing a tight red Catherine Malandrino dress, squeezed Eleanor around the waist as if they were long-lost bosom buddies. Her hair was impossibly long and shiny, her skin glowing and tanned, as if she'd just returned from a sun-drenched Maldives vacation.

Blair set her mouth in a firm line and marched over to them.

"My two favorite girls!" Eleanor said fondly, pathetically unaware anything was amiss between them. "I was just telling Serena how terrific it is that you two have had each other all these years. I felt good moving to California knowing Serena was in New York for you to come home to." Eleanor rested her hand on Blair's shoulder.

Blair hadn't told her mom she and Serena hadn't even spoken this past year, how every time they saw each other they managed to have an enormous fight, how Serena was like some bloodsucking leech, desperate to take everything of Blair's and literally ruin her life.

"I feel the same way, Eleanor," Serena said sweetly, knowing it was what Blair's mom wanted to hear. "I like knowing Blair's at Yale, even though I hardly see her. She's so busy with pre-law and everything." In truth, she didn't know if Blair even was a political science major with a concentration in pre-law anymore.

She sometimes saw Blair around campus, striding across the lawn with a group of girls or her advisor. Blair always looked so confident and capable and in control, like a picture torn out of a Yale catalog.

Meanwhile, Yale still felt like a holding place for Serena. While she knew a lot of people, she hadn't made any real friends, especially since she spent every weekend with Dan in the city. It felt like she spent Monday through Thursday waiting for the weekends and her real life to begin.

"What are you majoring in, dear?' Eleanor asked, plucking a mini quiche off a passing tray. "Do you have any idea what you'll be doing after college?"

"I don't know. I thought I had a few more semesters of undergrad, but it turns out I don't." Serena shook her head. There was a silver lining to missing Dan and having no social life: It had forced Serena to keep herself busy, signing up for back-to-back lectures and seminars. Her advisor had called her in for a meeting on the last day of finals. Serena had been nervous, sure she'd failed a philosophy exam or accidentally forgotten to turn in a French paper. Instead, she found out that because she'd amassed so many credits from her regular classes and classes at the New School while she was in New York, she'd be able to graduate in spring without having majored in anything. Serena bit her lip and shrugged. "I'm graduating in May, so I have to figure it out."

*What?* Blair wanted to throw her champagne glass on the floor. "How?" she spat. Serena had started college a full *two years* after Blair, and hadn't even taken as many AP classes as she had back in high school. In fact—Blair racked her brain— had Serena even taken *any*?

Who needs APs when you've got charm?

"I took a bunch of New School classes the year before I started, and I've been taking a lot of credits. I didn't know, though." Serena shrugged blithely. "Dan got into grad school for poetry at Iowa, so I might go there." She hadn't mentioned it to Dan, but really, it didn't seem like such a bad option. Wasn't Iowa City supposed to be really quaint? And what else would she do?

Um, get a life?

*Good riddance*, Blair wanted to scream. Serena could go off to Iowa and live on a farm and milk cows, or whatever people did there.

"That sounds amazing. You should *definitely* go there," Blair said, so sweetly that no one but her nearest, dearest, and greatest enemies would hear the threatening subtext.

"How marvelous to be dating an artist. That's how Cyrus is. Always seeing the world a different way," Eleanor mused, gazing adoringly at her tubby, bald, red-faced, gold cuff bracelet–wearing husband. He'd gotten fatter in the four years since they'd been married, something that hardly seemed possible.

What Cyrus and art had to do with each other Blair didn't know. "I'm starting at McMahon Cannon," she announced to no one in particular. Or she would be once she got the official offer. McMahon Cannon was one of the premiere litigation firms in the city and would look great on her résumé when she applied to law school. Her interview had gone well . . . she hadn't tried to kiss the interviewer, thank God, and they'd had a nice conversation about Yale. She was confident that she would be accepted.

"That's great, Blair," Serena said, sounding so genuinely

happy for her that Blair wanted to tear her pretty blond hair out of her head one bloody clump at a time. She reminded herself that while Serena was going to be reading poetry to cornstalks, *she* was going to be wearing power suits and Louboutin pumps and doing things that *mattered*.

"You girls were always so ambitious!" Eleanor trilled, then headed off to the kitchen to ensure that Myrtle, the cook, was handling the dinner preparations exactly according to her no-carb specifications and hadn't drunk herself into a frenzy.

"Well, glad everything's going well with you," Blair said flatly, making her way toward the dining room table.

Serena nodded and sank down into her assigned seat next to Blair. The two girls stared quietly down at their empty plates. They were inches apart, but it felt like miles.

There, there. A reconciliation might be closer than you think.

# love is blind . . . and embarrassing

Jenny felt like a movie star as she slid out of the leather seat of the Lincoln Town Car and onto Seventy-second and Central Park West. She teetered slightly on her four-inch heels.

"You okay?" Nate asked, catching her by the crook of her elbow. Jenny nodded gratefully and leaned against him for support. He smelled like Ralph Lauren Romance. Jenny had always wanted a boyfriend who used that cologne.

Which was exactly why she'd given him a bottle for his birthday.

Nate squeezed her shoulder. "You sure, Meow?" he asked, using his pet name for her. They'd called each other Meow Meow ever since an orange and white tabby kitten appeared on their Providence porch. She'd begged Nate to let her bring it inside the house, just once. But Nate refused. He hadn't wanted to be an asshole about it; he just really hated cats. They were so creepy, the way they climbed on top of you when you least suspected it, the way they couldn't play fetch, the way they stared at you while you were naked.

Sort of like girlfriends.

But instead of sulking, Jenny made a joke out of it. She began acting like a cat at the most random times, crawling toward him on her hands and knees in bed and making pleading little meows that made him laugh. That was the thing about Jenny. She was sunny and sweet and uncomplicated. It made him feel not so fucked up, not so confused. And he needed that in his life, especially tonight. He was pretty sure they were going to see Blair and Serena for the first time since their disastrous Christmas in Newport last year.

"We're here for the Rose party," Nate told the doorman.

The doorman nodded and waved them through to the elevator bank on the other side of the palatial marble lobby. A large Christmas tree was set up in the corner and the air smelled like pine and nutmeg.

Jenny caught her breath, trying to hold in her excitement. She and Nate lived in a ramshackle two-story house in Providence. He was at Brown, she was at RISD, and everything almost seemed too good to be true, beyond her wildest high school daydreams. But going to a fancy pre-Christmas dinner thrown by a New York society hostess proved that their relationship existed beyond Providence, that they were really and truly *together*.

After leaving Newport last Christmas, they'd sailed to Mt. Desert Island and camped out in Nate's family's gorgeous unwinterized summer home. They toasted the New Year on a blanket in front of the fire. It was impossibly romantic. Then, her last semester at Waverly they'd talked every night on the phone. They spent the summer sailing and house hunting in Providence. So far, living together had been amazing. She loved waking up to Nate. She loved brewing an extra-large pot of coffee and pouring a travel mug for him so he could drink it during his 9 a.m. poli-sci class.

She loved texting him in between portraiture and her Art in New Media class, and she loved attempting to make dinner for them, even though most of the time they wound up just ordering in and eating in bed.

The elevator glided up to the top floor, and they followed the merry voices and jazzy sound of Miles Davis to the door at the end of the hall. Nate pushed it open and Jenny breathed in again. In a New York in History and Literature class she'd taken last year at Waverly, they'd discussed the importance of the Four Hundred—the prominent New Yorkers who could comfortably fit into Mrs. Astor's grand ballroom circa 1880. Walking into the large living room of Eleanor Waldorf's Central Park West penthouse made her feel like she was part of the *new* Four Hundred—the New Yorkers who really mattered.

"Nathaniel!" A woman with gold highlights approached them. "Blair will be so thrilled to see you. Everyone is just getting seated. I put you in between Blair and Serena."

Mothers.

"Oh." A shadow of a frown crossed the woman's face as she noticed Jenny standing by Nate's side.

Jenny blushed. Had she done something wrong? "Hello," she said.

"I'm Eleanor Waldorf," Blair's mother replied, looking at Jenny's thrust-out hand without shaking it. Jenny let her hand fall slack against her side.

"Jenny's my girlfriend. We're both in Providence for school," Nate explained. Behind Eleanor's shoulder, he glimpsed Blair and Serena making their way to the table. He could only see their backs, but Serena's hair was blonder than ever while Blair's chestnut hair was loose and long, hanging down to her shoulder blades.

"Lovely. Well, I'll set up another seat." Eleanor gestured toward the large dining room.

"Natie!" Serena grinned when she spotted her old friend making his way toward them, Jenny Humphrey clinging to his hand. Nate looked the same as ever, clad in a Brooks Brothers jacket, neat dress pants, and a kelly green Hermès tie. "And Jenny."

"Nate," Blair said, nodding. She turned to the beak-nosed man seated next to her, as if they were engaged in a very important conversation she just had to continue.

"Hey," Nate mumbled, unsure of whether or not he should sit. There was only one seat available, right in between them. Of course, he'd known Blair and Serena would be here, but it still took his breath away to see them. They both looked so grown-up. Blair wore a sexy black-and-tan halter dress, Serena a tight red dress that hugged her body. Seeing them, so secure and confident and beautiful, momentarily made him flustered. It would've been nice to have smoked a large bowl before coming here. He rarely smoked pot anymore, but he often missed it. Especially when he was stressed out. And this was the most stressed out he'd been since . . .

Last Christmas?

Jenny tugged his arm. "I'll sit on your lap for now!" she announced, giggling. Against his better judgment, Nate sat on the chair and Jenny slid onto his knees, wiggling back and forth until she found a comfortable perch.

Serena rolled her eyes good-naturedly as she took a swig of her wine. "I would have brought Dan, but I didn't know he was invited."

"Oops," Jenny squeaked nervously. Her curly dark hair was

right underneath Nate's chin, and Nate could smell her lilac-scented shampoo. It reminded him of taking showers together. But instead of picturing Jenny in the shower, an image of Blair popped into his head. Nate squeezed his eyes shut to block out *those* memories, concentrating only on the feel of Jenny resting on his lap.

"Wine?" a white-shirted server asked behind Nate's shoulder, proffering a bottle of vintage 1981 L'Evangeline Bordeaux.

"Meow Meow?" Nate asked before picking up Jenny's glass. Jenny nodded her consent. As the waiter poured, Nate nuzzled Jenny's dark curls with his nose.

Serena shot Blair a horrified glance, surprised to find Blair's face contorted into an equally horrified grimace. *Meow Meow?*

Just then, Jenny felt a tap on her shoulder.

"Jennifer?" She whirled around and found Eleanor Waldorf frowning at her in annoyance. For a second, she felt like an awkward ninth grader, caught by Mrs. McLean for gossiping in the hallway when she was supposed to be in class. "If you don't mind, I'm going to move you over to the other end of the table. There's a bit more space for you down there," Eleanor said. Even after three years in LA, which had a looser social code than New York, it was clear Eleanor Waldorf was uncomfortable with public displays of affection at the table.

Can you blame her?

Jenny meekly slid off Nate's lap and followed Eleanor to a seat next to a shaggy-haired guy about her age. She glanced down the length of the table, where Nate was staring into his glass of wine, looking lonely. She sighed unhappily. Now they were *separated*.

Calm down, Juliet. It's just dinner.

"Hey. You're Jenny, right?" the boy next to her asked.

Jenny nodded, even though she had no idea who he was.

"Didn't you go to some boarding school?" he continued, brushing his shaggy bangs out of his large brown eyes.

"Yeah, I went to Waverly, but now I'm at RISD," Jenny said distractedly, watching Nate awkwardly make conversation across the table with Blair's chubby, red-faced stepfather.

"I'm Tyler," he told her. "Blair's brother."

"Nice to meet you." Jenny nodded. "Are you in school?" she asked to be polite.

"Nah." He shook his head. "I graduated a year early back in LA. I'm just DJ'ing around town for the next couple of months." He shrugged.

"Oh," Jenny murmured. She was dimly aware that before meeting Nate, she would have been ridiculously attracted to Tyler. Delaying college to DJ sounded so cool and downtown. But at the end of the table was Nate scraping his chair back and heading toward her. Her heart skipped a beat. The only good thing about being separated, even if it was only for five minutes, was how *amazing* it felt when they saw each other again.

"You holding up, Meow?" Nate asked sweetly before turning to Tyler. "How are you, man?" he asked, clapping him on the back.

Jenny smiled up at Nate. "Meow!" she purred goofily, not caring who heard her. After all, they were in love. People as in love as they were spoke a language all their own. So what if no one else could understand.

M-*ew*, m-*ew*.

# *great minds think alike*

Blair poked at the gelatinous duck confit on her plate. She couldn't wait until Chuck got back to New York tomorrow. It was torture being at her mom's dinner party without a date—especially now that she had to witness Nate and Jenny together. Not like she was *jealous*, it was just . . . nauseating.

"Meow?" Blair felt someone's breath tickle her ear. She turned to see Serena, her fingers curved toward Blair like claws.

"Hey, Meow Meow," Blair reciprocated, giggling. At least she had someone else to talk to besides Dick Cashman, the cowboy hat–wearing associate of her stepfather's seated on her right. Blair watched as Nate, hovering over Jenny, took a forkful of asparagus from her plate and popped it in her mouth, making little choo-choo noises as if she were a baby. "Are they for real?" Blair shook her head in disbelief.

Serena wrinkled her nose. "What would you do if Chuck started feeding you in public?"

"Stab him with a fork?" Blair guessed. She was all for being pampered by her boyfriend, but that meant him opening doors or massaging her shoulders, not treating her like an infant or demented prisoner who couldn't be trusted with utensils.

Serena giggled as Nate fed Jenny another bite. "Well, she's young."

"She's not *that* young," Blair scoffed. After all, Jenny Humphrey was a freshman in college. When Blair had been a freshman, she'd practically turned down a marriage proposal.

"Well, whatever, she has time," Serena said loyally, draining her glass of wine. She put her knife and fork to the side of her plate. It was nice that she and Blair were talking like normal people. In fact, it was just nice to be talking to someone who wasn't Dan. Every Thursday after her Madness and Literature class, she'd take the train into the city and she and Dan would stay holed up in his tiny bedroom until Sunday evening, venturing out only to Lincoln Plaza to see a movie or to the diner on the corner for breakfast. She loved Dan and loved spending time with him, but she sometimes felt they were missing out on something.

Um, like, *life?*

"Actually, it is kind of weird," Serena decided, watching the way Jenny was gazing adoringly up at Nate. She wasn't annoyed to see Nate with Jenny—in a weird way, it made sense. But she *did* care that Jenny was getting so caught up with playing house when she still had all of college in front of her, and that Nate didn't seem interested in anything besides taking care of Jenny.

Blair gazed at her little brother, Tyler, across the room. He was sixteen, and had grown up from being a weirdo little Cameron Crowe–obsessed kid to kind of a cool guy. A smile played on her lips.

"What are you thinking?" Serena nervously chewed her bottom lip. With Blair, you never knew.

Behind them, the servers cleared their plates away, making room for the dessert course. "Tyler doesn't have a girlfriend," Blair began.

Tyler *was* cute. He was skinny, with shaggy hair, and looked like the downtown DJ he was, Serena thought. And he was a really good kid.

"I'll have Tyler e-mail her and invite her to one of his events," Blair announced. "He needs a girlfriend. He sometimes turns his dirty socks inside out and then wears them, because he thinks that means they're clean."

Serena burst into laughter. "Dan used to do that, too!" she squealed.

Dick Cashman peered over at the two girls. "Can you little ladies let me in on the joke? Sounds like a good one!"

"Meow meow," Blair responded, choking on her wine.

Serena spat her wine onto her plate. It was exactly like those times when they used to ride the Madison Avenue bus, speaking to each other in fake foreign languages and annoying everyone on the bus.

"We have to be excused," she gasped between snorts, dragging Blair out onto the terrace.

"Oh my God, I haven't had this much fun in *months*!" Serena yelled. She tried to remember why she'd been so angry at Blair last year. Why had Nate been so important to both of them? Why had they dropped the most important relationship of their lives: them?

"To us!" Blair said, holding out her wine glass, as if reading Serena's mind. The two girls clinked glasses in the crisp night air.

We'll see how long this peace treaty lasts. . . .

## *good things come in small packages*

Vanessa pulled on her leather bomber jacket, bracing herself to leave the house. The idea of staying in was incredibly tempting, especially since she had the Humphreys' apartment all to herself: Dan was at some fancy Welcome to Iowa reception at the Metropolitan Club, Jenny was out with her boyfriend, and Rufus was celebrating an early Christmas with his anarchist group at the KGB Bar downtown.

Although she'd been living in the Humphrey apartment for almost a year, she rarely spent the night, especially on the weekends when Dan and Serena were cozied up in his bedroom. Instead, she'd crash with film school friends in their overcrowded Crown Heights or Greenpoint apartments, or offer babysitting for Moxie in exchange for couch space at Ruby and Piotr's apartment in Prospect Heights.

Vanessa grabbed her purse from the couch and headed for the door. She was going to see Hollis's film, *Rowing to Reykjavik*. She and Hollis hadn't really talked since last year, although they'd seen each other at parties and always said hello. She felt like she owed it to him—and to herself—to at least see the movie. She was curious to see how the story, which had started out as *her* life story and quickly became the furthest thing from it, would end.

She flung open the apartment door and came face-to-face with a man wearing a brown uniform, an envelope in his hand. "Looking for a Vanessa Abrams? You're my last delivery. Glad you're here," he said. Vanessa nodded in confusion.

"Here you go." He thrust a thin envelope at her. Vanessa took it with trembling hands. Suddenly, she realized exactly what she was holding. Back in November, she'd applied for a two-year film fellowship in Indonesia. She hadn't realized they'd be mailing decisions so soon.

"Thanks." She wasn't sure if she should open it right away or wait. But what was she waiting for? And would they really UPS a rejection?

"Can you sign?" the deliveryman asked impatiently, oblivious to Vanessa's internal turmoil.

"Oh, sure." Vanessa hastily scrawled a signature and yanked the envelope open.

"Happy holidays," the delivery guy said as he turned away. But Vanessa wasn't listening. She pulled a packet of papers from the envelope. A single sheet fell out and fluttered to the hardwood floor. Vanessa grabbed it, noting the purple *Filmmakers for Change* crest at the top of the page and read the first sentence: *Dear Ms. Abrams, We are pleased to offer you a Filmmaker for Change grant for your proposed project in Indonesia. . . .*

The rest of the sentences swam together on the page as Vanessa shrieked in excitement. A Filmmaker for Change grant was notoriously hard to get, which was why she'd practically forgotten about sending in the application. She hadn't wanted to get her hopes up. But now, her future spread out before her like a promising sunrise. Instead of drifting from one production assistant job to another, she was going to be working on her own project *in* the place where film originated. Which was way better than Iceland.

"Yes!" she yelled, her voice echoing down the stairwell. She was so busy jumping up and down on the landing in glee, she didn't even notice the sound of footsteps on the stairs.

"Are you working out or something?" Dan asked nervously as he reached the landing. Although he and Vanessa were perfectly cordial toward each other, being roommates had its awkward moments, like the one time last spring Vanessa had burst into Dan's bedroom to look for her old camera equipment, only to find Serena and Dan entwined on his bed.

Vanessa spontaneously threw her arms around Dan's skinny waist. "I got the fellowship! I'm going to Indonesia! I'm a fucking *filmmaker for change*!" she screamed into his ear, her voice echoing in the stairwell. She felt Dan's body stiffen and she immediately let go. "Sorry," she said sheepishly.

"No, congratulations!" Dan said, a smile crawling across his face. "I've never seen you jump up and down like this. What is it for?"

"Oh my God, I'm freaking out!" Vanessa exhaled and tried to compose herself. She gripped the iron railing for support. In her excitement, she'd forgotten that Dan would have no clue what she was talking about. She hadn't told anyone she'd applied. And she and Dan hadn't really talked much in the last year.

"I need some fresh air! Come outside with me?" Vanessa asked, practically running down the winding staircase. She threw open the front door and took big gulps of cold air. "Woo-hoo!" she yelled into the night sky.

"Wait, so you're going to Indonesia?" Dan asked, slightly out of breath from running after her.

"Yeah! I applied for a grant to make my own film in Indonesia. It's where film was born."

"Wow," Dan said, impressed. "That's fucking huge! Congrats."

"Thanks." Vanessa smiled shyly. "I can't believe I'm going to be moving to *Indonesia* in less than six months."

Dan believed it though. Vanessa was so smart and motivated. It was really *nice* to see her get something she obviously wanted so badly.

"Let's go somewhere to celebrate," Dan decided. Vanessa deserved it.

Vanessa smiled giddily. For a second, she imagined what Hollis would say if he heard about the grant, but then she pushed the thought out of her mind. She didn't need him anymore. "Can we go to that hummus place? I'm starving!"

"Sure." Dan turned on his heel, heading toward the hole-in-the-wall on the corner that had a different name every month. He loved that Vanessa considered hummus celebratory. "I'm hungry too. They just had those teeny-tiny chicken skewers and pigs in a blanket at the Iowa thing."

Vanessa wrinkled her nose. "Besides that, how was it?" She asked as she fell into step with Dan. She'd forgotten he wouldn't be in New York next year, either.

"It was amazing," he told her eagerly. "A couple of the professors were there, and it's really intense. These are all guys who've won Pushcarts and been short-listed for the National Book Award." He shrugged and opened the door. The restaurant was empty except for one lone employee behind the counter. "I just can't wait to really work with them, you know? Just immerse myself in writing," he said as he sat at one of the rickety tables in the corner.

"I'll order. I know what you always get." Vanessa headed to the counter and returned with a tray laden with pita bread and bowls of hummus, and falafel balls. Dan took a bite of falafel, then passed the rest to Vanessa. Vanessa smiled. They always used to share food.

"Sorry," Dan pulled his hand back, as if he saw Vanessa's hesitation as rejection.

"No, I want it," she said, accepting the half-eaten falafel.

"So, are you really ready to leave New York?" Dan asked. It was weird to think about Vanessa leaving. Even though he hadn't really spent any time with her in the past year, it had been comforting to see her camera on the counter, her army green messenger bag by the door, her boxes of Sleepytime tea in the cabinets.

"I won't know until I'm gone," Vanessa replied. "How 'bout you?"

Dan shrugged his reply. A comfortable silence fell between them as they ate. They were always able to talk, or not talk. Sometimes Serena would assume that he was angry if he didn't say something all the time.

It was nice, just sitting at a hole-in-the-wall restaurant on Broadway, splitting a late-night snack. It reminded him of a time when everything was easy and safe. He randomly thought of a Proust quote he'd read in one of his lit classes: *The true paradises are ones we have lost.*

Does that mean there's trouble in his current paradise?

# *time to party . . .*

**From:** Tyler@DJTyRo.com
**To:** jenniferthumphrey@risd.edu
**Subject:** party

Hey Jenny,
It was cool to meet you at my mom's place last
night. Wanted to let you know that I'm spinning at
the Plastic Party People Party on Saturday. It's
at Filter, on Fourteenth and Tenth, starting at
midnight. Bring friends, you're on the list.
—Ty

From: jenniferthumphrey@risd.edu
To: Tyler@DJTyRo.com
Subject: Re: party

Dear Tyler,
It was great meeting you too! Your party sounds like
a ton of fun, but my boyfriend already got us tickets
to see *The Nutcracker* that night. Break a leg or a
disc or whatever the DJ term for good luck is!
—Jenny

## the best presents are surprises

"Thanks, Mom," Serena said as she pulled a pair of strappy silver and blue Jimmy Choos from out of a brightly wrapped box. It was ten o'clock on Christmas morning, and the family had already had a formal Christmas breakfast in the dining room. She tried to conceal a yawn. She hadn't slept at all last night.

"I thought that color would look great with your eyes. And I'm sure you'll have so many events to go to next year." Lily van der Woodsen looked fondly at her daughter from a club chair in the corner of the living room. Now that Serena and Erik were grown up, they no longer opened presents at dawn beside the towering tree in the living room. Instead, they opened a few small expensive trinkets, after breakfast.

Serena took a swig of coffee. In truth, she probably wouldn't have *any* events to go to next year in Iowa. Except maybe poetry readings.

Last night, after her parents had gone to bed, she, Erik, and his fiancée, Fiona, had had a long conversation about long-distance love while drinking homemade cocktails from her parents' extensive liquor cabinet. Fiona was a six-foot-tall blond Australian surfer whom Erik met on a beach in Melbourne during his junior year abroad. She was clearly head over heels for Erik, she was funny as hell, and Serena was glad they were going to be sisters so soon. After a few drinks, Serena had worked up the courage to ask them if they thought long-distance could ever really work. Ever since Dan had found out he was going to Iowa, she'd been nervous about how they'd deal with the separation. Of course, that was when she still thought she had a few years of college left. But now that she was graduating, she could do anything she wanted. And all she could think to do was follow Dan, even though they'd never officially talked about it.

What Fiona had said when it came to her and Erik's relationship sealed the decision for Serena. "I told him I'd follow him wherever he went," Fiona had said proudly, without apology. "And if he was with another girl when he got there, I'd cut his balls off."

"Who could say no to that?" Erik had teased, kissing her.

That was all the reassurance Serena needed. If Dan was going to Iowa, then so would she. She'd even found a place for them. The house was a fantastic two-bedroom bungalow designed by Frank Lloyd Wright, next to a river and surrounded by trees. The grainy picture on the website made it almost look like a sailboat with all these wonderful built-in cabinets and furniture. It was forty-five minutes away from Iowa City, but that wasn't too bad. Besides, they'd both have cars, and after living in the middle of the biggest city in the world for their whole lives, Serena couldn't think of anything more romantic than settling down with her boyfriend so far away from the rest of humanity. After all, all they needed was each other.

No Barneys, no Elizabeth Arden, no City Bakery cookies . . . Is she crazy?

According to the Web site, the house was available for rent, but Serena wanted to work out all the details before she told Dan. She was fine waiting a day to tell him in person, even if it did feel like torture right now.

"This is from me," Fiona said, smiling as she held a thin, silver-wrapped present toward Serena. Serena slid her finger under the tape and eagerly ripped off the wrapping paper. Inside was a photo album. On the inside cover was inscribed:

To Serena—
   "The world is a book and those who do not travel read only one page." —St. Augustine.
   Enjoy!
   Love, Fiona

"Oh my God, so cool!" Serena grinned as she flipped through the pages. Fiona had traveled the world for two years before she started college, a fact that always made Serena envious. Serena had always wanted to do that, but the closest she'd come was a few weeks in the south of France when she was a senior in high school. Inside were pages of photographs, hand-drawn maps, contact lists, and need-to-know information about different countries and cities around the world. "Did you really make this?" Serena asked.

"I know you like adventure, but you'd be well off to avoid making my travel mistakes." Fiona winked.

"Not like you'll have too much time to travel. Once you find a job, you'll really need to buckle down for those first few years,"

Mr. van der Woodsen remarked as he peered over Serena's shoulder.

Serena smiled tightly. She'd tell her parents about the Iowa plan after she told Dan.

"This is great, Fiona," she said, continuing to flip through the pages. As she came across a photo of Carnivale in Spain, it dawned on her that a life spent with Dan in Iowa wouldn't leave her much opportunity to travel. They wouldn't have any money, and he'd be too busy writing all the time. Serena felt unexpected tears spring to her eyes.

She rubbed her eye with her index finger, as if she were just readjusting a contact lens.

Fiona winked at her. "Now what do you say we set up a Bloody Mary bar in the kitchen?"

Serena nodded and trailed behind Fiona toward the kitchen, feeling deflated. Fiona saw her as an adventurous, gutsy girl who needed practical travel tips for Belize and Thailand. Instead, her grand adventure was booking a one-way ticket to a flat state few New Yorkers could point to on a map.

Well, maybe if she moves there, people will start to visit.


"Essa!" Moxie blurted happily from Ruby's hip as Ruby opened the paint-caked door to her Prospect Heights walk-up on Christmas Day. Moxie was dressed in a T-shirt with a pigeon wearing oversize headphones and black leggings, her thin brown hair tied in two sloppy braids. She looked like a very short Williamsburg hipster.

"Merry Christmas, little sis!" Ruby hugged Vanessa warmly. Ruby wore a pair of gray pajama pants and a black SugarDaddy tank top with no bra. Behind her, Piotr had on red Santa-print flannel pants and a felt Santa hat. As children, Ruby and Vanessa had never celebrated Christmas. Their dad was Jewish and their mom thought the holiday was too commercial. Ruby was obviously determined to let Moxie have her fun with Santa.

"Merry Christmas, guys!" Vanessa exclaimed, breezing into their cheerful one-bedroom apartment. It looked so domestic, with a silver garland wrapped along the molding of the ceiling, a pile of presents in the corner, and a small tree in the center of the room. The only relic from their artistic past was the large painting of a nude figure astride a bull mastiff dog wedged behind the couch.

"Watch this." Ruby grinned as she picked up Moxie and put her next to the pile of presents. Moxie curiously pulled on a silver bow and then tossed the present back under the tree.

"She doesn't really get it yet." Ruby shrugged. Vanessa grinned absently, her mind a million miles away. What would Christmas be like in Indonesia? What if she didn't make any friends and her movie sucked? What if while she was gone, Dan and Serena got engaged?

Which apocalyptic scenario does not belong with the others?

"Hello?" Ruby snapped her fingers in front of Vanessa's face, breaking her out of her reverie.

"I got that Filmmakers for Change grant to go to Indonesia for two years. Everything paid for." Vanessa grinned shyly. Saying it made her feel better, more sure of herself. The grant was an honor most young filmmakers only dreamed of.

"Oh my God!" Ruby squealed, hugging her.

"God!" Moxie yelled happily from the floor, the silver bow

clutched in her chubby hands. Ruby rolled her eyes. "Piotr, Vanessa's going to Indonesia!"

"Well, I mean, I got it, but—"

"But you are going," Piotr said in his slow, careful English from the couch.

"There goes our free babysitting," Ruby said mournfully. "Just kidding," she added quickly.

Vanessa smiled wanly. Could she really do this? The fellowship was for two years, and while theoretically she could visit home, she couldn't imagine a trip back to the U.S. would be cheap. And two years was sort of a long time. Moxie would be talking in full sentences by then. What if she didn't even remember Vanessa?

"Should I go?" she asked in a small voice she didn't quite recognize as her own.

Ruby pursed her lips together as she sat down next to Piotr. "Well, I met Piotr when I left for that SugarDaddy foreign tour. I was scared too, but it all worked out so totally well."

"Same for me," Piotr said in his still heavily accented English. "I came to the U.S. because I fell in love."

"Like that's the only reason? You also said you couldn't wait to try New York City pizza." Ruby shot Piotr a skeptical look. "Vanessa, you're twenty-one. You need to get out and see the world!" Ruby said in her big-sister voice.

Vanessa nodded slowly. She'd lived in New York for the past seven years of her life. A change would be good. But all she could think about was how far Indonesia was from Iowa. . . .

Here we go again.

## on the street where **b** lives

Blair surveyed the brightly colored wooden block tower she'd built in the center of Yale's nursery and nodded in satisfaction. The Waldorf-Rose family had always opened presents first thing in the morning, and right now Tyler was in his room, setting up a bunch of DJ equipment he'd gotten, Aaron had taken the train to Scarsdale to visit his mom and friends from high school, Cyrus and Eleanor were grossly feeding each other eggs at the breakfast table, and Blair was happy to be hanging out with Yale.

"Yale, over here!" she cajoled. Her sister sat in the corner, setting up her stuffed animals in an elaborate pile. She had determined that none of the other stuffed toys liked the giraffe, so she'd relegated it to the far corner of the room.

It starts early.

Blair's cell buzzed, skittering on the hardwood floor. She glanced down at the display. Chuck. His flight had probably just landed, and Blair couldn't wait to see him.

"Hello?" she asked.

"I want to talk!" Yale demanded, reaching for the phone.

"No," Blair snapped, yanking the phone from Yale's little hand. "Hey," she said sweetly as she settled into the pink glider by the dormer window in the corner.

"Merry Christmas, gorgeous," Chuck said.

"Are you back?" Blair asked eagerly. After so much time apart, she was looking forward to an uninterrupted month together.

"I'm at the Village apartment," Chuck said, referring to the Cornelia Street one-bedroom his parents had bought him for his twenty-first birthday. He'd barely lived in it at all, since he was at Oxford all year and they'd spent most of last summer in the south of France. "Can you come over? There's something I want you to see," he added mysteriously.

"Yale, go find Tyler," Blair commanded, leaving the nursery and heading next door to the guest room where she'd been staying. "See you soon," she said into the phone before hanging up.

Once Blair emerged showered, shaved, and wearing a black silk Theory high-necked silk dress that was just the right combination of nice and naughty, she took the elevator to the lobby and had the doorman catch one of the many empty cabs that was sailing down Central Park West.

The city looked beautiful, like the front of a holiday card. Snow was beginning to fall, but the sun was shining brightly and reflecting the light off all of the Midtown skyscrapers. Blair sighed happily. She loved New York in the winter. Anyone could love the city in the summer, when cafés set up tables outside and you could spend hours sitting on the steps of the Met drinking iced coffees. But in the winter, you had to seek out the things that made New York magical: steak frites at Le Refuge, cuddling into a warm Searle peacoat, your hand intertwined with an adorable boy's.

"Thanks," Blair said when the cab turned off Sixth Avenue

and onto Cornelia Street. Cornelia was Blair's middle name. It felt like destiny.

She stood in front of the five-story brick building and pressed buzzer number two, stamping her feet against the cold. Chuck buzzed her in and she quickly ran up the steps, surprised to see him standing in front of the black apartment door.

"Hi!" Blair threw her arms around his broad shoulders. He wore a pair of khakis and a dark blue button-down, and his hair was a little longer than it had been at Thanksgiving.

"Merry Christmas," Chuck breathed. He kissed her and Blair eagerly kissed him back. "Your present's inside. It's a surprise," he breathed into her ear. It was then that she realized Chuck was tying a blindfold over her eyes.

*Now that's what I call a Christmas present.*

Blair readjusted the blindfold so it wouldn't flatten her hair. Chuck placed his hands on her shoulders and directed her inside. Blair heard the pop of a champagne cork. Was *that* the surprise?

"You can take it off."

Blair reached up and swept the blindfold, which was actually one of Chuck's flamingo pink ties, off her forehead. She blinked in surprise. Before, the one-bedroom apartment had been decorated in blacks and grays, with leather couches and ottomans and chrome tables and silver lighting fixtures. Now, it was decorated in shades of pewter and lavender, the walls painted a soft dove color. An antique silver mirror hung over the fireplace, and there were fresh-cut flowers on the long walnut dining room table.

"To us," Chuck said simply, handing Blair a glass of champagne. "Welcome home, Blair-Bear." Besides her dad, Chuck was the only person who ever called her Blair-Bear.

"Why . . . what . . ." Blair trailed off. The apartment was beautiful, but what did it mean? Did he mean he wanted her to move in with him? She'd never really thought about where she'd live when she moved to the city after college, but she'd always assumed it would be on the Upper East Side.

"Since we'll both be back in the city for good once we graduate, our apartment should feel more like our home. If there's anything you don't like, the decorator will work with you. This is just the beginning. I can't wait for us to live together." Chuck cupped her chin and kissed her.

Blair pulled away. "It's very nice," she said faintly, glancing around the living room. She tried to imagine sitting at the head of the table, hosting dinner parties. Setting up Fresh Direct deliveries and carefully placing perishables in the Sub-Zero refrigerator in the sunny south-facing kitchen. Taking showers together in the morning and then picking out clothes in the side-by-side closets in the bedroom.

It was the life Blair had always wanted . . . but did she really want it so soon? It was one thing to live together for a few months in Oxford, but another to live together for the foreseeable future. Did this mean they were engaged? Suddenly, her mind flashed back to the conversation with Chuck's mom. Everything was moving too quickly. "I think I need to sit down," Blair choked, settling on a lavender-upholstered wingback chair.

Chuck held out a champagne flute and perched on the chair arm. "Here you go. Merry Christmas," he said, brushing his lips against her cheek.

"Merry Christmas!" Blair parroted, clinking her champagne flute a little too forcefully against Chuck's.

Would she have rather he kept on the blindfold?

# the trouble with fairy tales is that they always end

On the day after Christmas, Jenny stood outside her apartment building, stamping her tiny feet on the sidewalk to keep warm. She wore knee-high boots and her favorite red wool coat. Her dark brown hair was loose around her shoulders, and even though her ears were freezing, there was no way in hell she'd risk hat-head.

Nate was going to pick her up any second to see *The Nutcracker*, and she didn't want to bring him upstairs and subject him to her dad. Rufus meant well, but he could be overprotective, and didn't entirely approve of Nate. Rufus remembered all too well how hysterical Jenny had been when they'd broken up her freshman year of high school, and no amount of explaining would convince him that Nate was different now.

A town car glided down the street and came to a stop in front of her building. Nate rolled down the back window, and Jenny's heart thudded against her chest. Most of the time Nate was just Nate, the boyfriend whom she woke up to every morning and who became grumpy if he didn't eat breakfast. But at times like these, Jenny was reminded of the dreamy, gorgeous, almost unapproachable boy she'd first fallen in love with when she was only fifteen.

"Hi." Nate smiled his adorable, lopsided grin as the chauffeur rushed around the door to let Jenny in. She scooted onto the leather seat beside Nate.

"Meow!" Jenny nuzzled her nose into his neck and breathed in his delicious boy scent.

The town car turned down Broadway, where the sidewalks were crowded with people ducking in and out of the stores still decorated for Christmas.

"I'm excited!" Jenny said, intertwining her fingers with his. She and Nate had seen *The Nutcracker* four years ago when she was a freshman, and she'd loved it. Back then she'd been too amazed by the fact that Nate was sitting next to her and holding her hand to pay any attention to the performance. Then they'd made out in Central Park and then . . . well, she wasn't going to think about what happened next: Vanessa Abrams had unwittingly filmed them goofing around in the snow, including Nate playfully pulling down Jenny's pants. The footage of Jenny's bare butt wound up on the Internet. Jenny smoothed her DVF dress down on her lap, as if to remind herself to keep her clothing in place.

For now, anyway.

"Me too," Nate said as the car lurched between stoplights. He'd seen *The Nutcracker* every year since he was born—usually with Blair—so he was kind of over it by now, but Jenny's enthusiasm was contagious.

The car pulled up in front of the sprawling Lincoln Center complex of glass-and-iron-wrapped concrete buildings. Jenny smiled happily. "'Bye!" she yelled to the driver.

Nate held her hand as he led her to the New York State Theater building. Jenny felt like she was in a fairy tale. She imagined them in ten years: Jenny would be a freelance graphic artist and Nate would be a high-powered lawyer. Every year, the day after Christmas, they'd bring their two kids to *The Nutcracker*.

Nate led them to orchestra seats. A set of blond toddler triplets sat next to Jenny on one side, and on Nate's other side were four elderly ladies with grayish-blond bouffants lacquered two inches above their Botoxed foreheads. They were practically screaming as they bragged to each other about their grandkids. Jenny frowned. This wasn't what she'd imagined. Maybe it would get better once the show began?

The lights dimmed and one of the toddlers next to her started shrieking. Jenny tried not to be frustrated, but this was supposed to be their big night out in New York, and suddenly it didn't feel romantic or magical at all. It felt like a field trip gone wrong.

Nate leaned back in the plush velvet chair. He'd been baked every other time he saw *The Nutcracker*. Maybe it would be really cool sober.

Or maybe not.

Nate smiled as the giant tree grew out of the slick black stage of the New York State Theatre. That used to be Blair's favorite scene. After that, she'd get antsy and they'd usually skip the second act to drink cappuccinos in the lobby and spy on the couples walking around the promenade below.

Nate closed his eyes, imagining what it would be like if Blair was here. She'd looked terrific at her mom's dinner party. And so had Serena. It had been unnerving, the way they'd kept giggling whenever they glanced toward him and Jenny. And then they'd excused themselves to the terrace and when they finally reentered, they smiled sneakily at him. He knew them too well and was pretty sure they'd been talking about him. And no matter how much he loved Jenny, he wanted to know what they'd been saying.

Nate realized everyone around him was clapping. Was the first act over already? He clapped politely. "Want a cappuccino?" he asked Jenny. Suddenly, he didn't really feel like being there.

"Sure." Jenny shrugged, looking so innocent and sweet that Nate felt a weird lump in his throat like he was going to cry.

Imagine if he *was* stoned. . . .

"So, what did you think of the show?" Jenny asked later. They were in the library of Nate's town house, sitting side by side on the tan calfskin couch, drinking merlot out of Riedel glasses. A sailboat documentary played on the flat screen in front of them. Nate had been quiet for the rest of the show, even during the romantic end when Clara and the prince are finally together, happily ever after.

"Nate?" Jenny asked again, realizing he was sound asleep, his head flopped against his shoulder. Jenny sighed in frustration. This was *not* how she'd expected the evening to play out. She'd been hoping they would come back and sit in front of the fire, not the flat screen, and that they'd be drinking wine and whispering sweet nothings to each other, not asking each other questions like they were strangers.

Jenny bounced up and down on the couch, hoping he'd wake up. It wasn't even eleven yet, and she was still all dressed up. If she wasn't going to get *undressed* by her boyfriend, she didn't want the outfit to go to waste. Suddenly she realized that tonight was Tyler's party, the one he'd e-mailed her about. It would be fun to just go out and dance and not feel like she was part of an old married couple.

Jenny debated waking Nate up, but he looked so cute and peaceful lying there that she felt it was better to just leave him be. She grabbed a tartan Asprey throw from a corner club chair and carefully tucked it around him, then took her purse and tiptoed into the living room, thankful that Nate's parents were on vacation and she had the town house to herself.

She pulled out her phone from her knockoff Louis Vuitton purse, perched on a white love seat by the window, and called her old friend Elise Wells. They'd kept in touch a bit while Jenny was at Waverly and Elise was at Constance, and Jenny knew she'd be home on break from Stanford.

"Jenny?" Elise squealed, answering the phone on the second ring. "Are you in New York?"

"Yes, I am!" Jenny said brightly, then cut to the chase. "Want to go to a party?"

On the other end of the line, Jenny could sense Elise hesitating. "Is your boyfriend coming?" she asked finally.

"Nope, just me. Sorry it's short notice. Remember Blair Waldorf? Her brother, Tyler, invited me to a club where he's DJ'ing tonight. It's somewhere downtown," Jenny said, trying to remember the name of the club. Something that reminded her of coffee. "At Filter?" That sounded right.

"Wait, Tyler Rose, as in the DJ TyRo?" Elise sounded excited.

"Yeah!" Jenny said in surprise. Elise had heard of him?

"Pick me up in ten minutes," Elise commanded.

Outside, Jenny looked at the rows of green-awninged buildings on Fifth Avenue. Most of the lights in the windows were out, and she felt a shiver of excitement course through her body. She hadn't had a wild and crazy night in forever. She hadn't realized until now how much she missed the feeling of an anything-can-happen adventure. She hailed a cab and directed it to Elise's building several blocks away.

A figure brushed out of a door. It was Elise, looking taller, blonder, and skinnier than Jenny remembered. She wore a cleavage-baring Alice+Olivia purple tank top and a tight black Marc by Marc Jacobs skirt without a coat.

"Hey!" Elise exclaimed, bursting into the cab and hugging Jenny.

"Hi!" Jenny grinned excitedly. She'd missed her old friend. "Um, we're going to Filter? On Fourteenth and Tenth," Jenny told the cabbie through the Plexiglas partition.

"I brought some stuff to get the party started." Elise grinned mischievously as she passed her a bottle of Diet Coke. Jenny took a swig, coughing when she realized it was saturated with vodka.

"Thanks!" she grinned, taking another, more careful, sip.

Some things never change.

The cab pulled up to a one-story black building. A red velvet rope held back a line that snaked its way down the block, and a beefy bouncer stood with his arms crossed, blocking the ominous-looking steel door entrance.

Jenny boldly marched up to the bouncer, ready to tell him she was on the list. But she didn't have to. He just grinned, showing his gold-capped teeth, and waved them in, clearly finding the two overeager girls to be a welcome change from the bored-looking hipsters who made up the rest of the line.

"Nice, Humphrey!" Elise said, clearly impressed. She made

her way to the bar while Jenny picked through the crowded club. It was dark and dingy, and girls with asymmetrical haircuts and short mod dresses were dancing with guys wearing skinny ties and vests. Tyler—it was hard to think of him as TyRo—was playing a weird but cool mix of Ladytron and the Cure and the Clash. It was the type of music her friend Brett loved, but Jenny never really understood. She always preferred cheesy Top 40 music. Still, there was something decidedly cool about the scene.

Elise tapped her on the shoulder. "I got you a drink." She held a vodka soda out to Jenny. "I should tell you, I have a boyfriend back at Stanford, so I have to behave tonight."

"How good is good?" Jenny arched an eyebrow.

"Dancing is okay, cheek-kissing is fine, number exchange is fine because who knows, but no lip-kissing," Elise said, rattling off the rules as if they were officially sanctioned.

Rules *are* made to be broken.

"Deal!" Jenny grinned, then goofily tapped her glass against Elise's.

"Jennifer!" Tyler greeted her. His black T-shirt was soaked with sweat, but Jenny didn't mind. "I'm glad you came. I have a break right now. Drink?" he asked. Without waiting for an answer, he led her through the crowd and toward the bar. "Two double Red Bull and vodkas," he ordered.

The bartender was a superskinny girl with jet-black hair and tattoos of stars on her arms. "Whatever you want, TyRo," she said with a wink as she passed the drinks to Tyler. Condensation dripped down the sides of the highball glasses.

"I need energy," he explained, nodding toward the Red Bulls.

"Totally." Jenny nodded. Now that she was here, she wanted to dance all night.

"So, do you like the music? I'm trying to do this Brit pop indie rock thing, but I'm trying to give it this sort of post-post-punk New Wave shoegazer edge."

"It's so cool," Jenny said honestly. When she'd listened to this kind of music in her dorm room at Waverly, she'd never really gotten into it, but here in the club, with the bass thumping and so many bodies moving to the beat, she could feel it humming through her bones.

"So do you go out a lot?" Tyler asked companionably, placing his elbows next to her.

Jenny shook her head. She rarely left her Providence apartment, much less went out to parties. If they polled this club, she'd probably be the most boring person here. She'd probably be the most boring student in the entire RISD student population—*including* the girl who made elaborate wire sculptures of unicorns. "I want to go out more," she said finally.

Since when?

"I have parties every night this week. You should come. But first . . ." Tyler possessively grabbed her hand and led her toward the dance floor. "Let's dance."

Jenny grinned and nodded eagerly. As Tyler gripped her warm hand in his, she felt a rush of electricity shoot through her that she hadn't in a while.

Let's just hope she remembers the rules!

# two girls in the bed usually means trouble

"Shh! Be quiet!" Blair whispered sharply to Serena. She didn't want it to be obvious to every Upper East Side Peeping Tom that they were about to break into the Archibalds' ivy-covered town house.

Earlier tonight she and Chuck had been at home, drinking muscadet and discussing couches when Serena called, asking if Blair wanted to grab a drink. The phone ringing was like an alarm.

Alert: You're officially middle-aged!

One glass of wine with Serena had become two bottles, and the conversation had quickly evolved into an *isn't it weird we're all grown up* discussion. Which had turned into a *let's go back to the old days* scheming session. Which was why Blair was now standing outside Nate's town house, freezing her ass off in her Antik Batik brown leather jacket and high-waisted Tahari sailor pants.

"What if they're here?" Blair asked, watching as Serena twisted the key in the lock. In all the years they'd both had an extra set of keys to Nate's apartment, they'd never sneaked in together. "Ew. What if they're, like, doing it?"

"Gross. Nate's parents always go to St. Barts the day after Christmas and stay until New Year's," Serena said over her shoulder. "So they probably are. But who cares? That will just make it more fun. You were the one who said Jenny and Nate needed shaking up," Serena pointed out as she pushed the door open. Serena cocked her head like a cocker spaniel. "Shhh," she whispered, as if Blair had been the one talking.

She exaggeratedly tiptoed up the mahogany staircase. "I hear the TV upstairs," she explained.

"You guys *better* be decent!" Blair called as she pushed the door open to the second-floor study, where they'd spent hours watching old movies when they were younger.

They found Nate, asleep by himself, his mouth open and a trail of drool heading down his angular chin. A tartan throw was pulled over his body and his dark blond hair was all tangled. He looked adorable.

A smile played on Serena's lips. "What do we do now?" From her tone, it sounded as if she knew *exactly* what she wanted to do.

"The usual?" Blair arched an eyebrow.

"I'll get the supplies," Serena said, heading into the Archibald master suite as Blair raced up to Nate's bedroom. It was a lot cleaner than the last time she'd seen it. The king-size bed was perfectly made, and there were no piles of DVDs or notebooks on the floor. It reminded Blair of a hotel.

And we all know what good luck she has in hotels.

She climbed into the bed, pulling the green flannel sheets around her. She'd always hated flannel, because the material felt so scratchy compared to her own Frette sheets, but Nate had refused to sleep on anything else. Tonight, though, the sheets felt cozy and warm against her body. She leaned back against the pillows contemplatively. It was weird that the last time she'd really spent time here was four years ago. In four years, she'd be twenty-six. What would that be like?

Serena burst in, holding a bottle of Grey Goose in one hand, two highball glasses in the other, and two DVDs between her laser white front teeth. She scattered them on the duvet cover and grinned.

"*Breakfast at Tiffany's* or *Some Like It Hot*?" Serena asked, setting up a makeshift bar on Nate's dresser and splashing vodka in the two glasses.

"Do you even have to ask?" Blair asked, wiggling out of her pants and throwing them out from under the covers. She sighed happily. It was like old times.

Old times without underpants?

Serena grinned and took a large sip of her drink. "Obviously," Serena said, popping *Breakfast at Tiffany's* into the DVD player. "Here you go." Serena offered a glass to Blair. Then, she unbuttoned her own knee-length black Dries van Noten dress and pulled her black Wolford stockings off.

"So much better!" she said, crawling into bed next to Blair in her beige Cosabella boy shorts and pink Calvin Klein camisole and cuddling up next to Blair like an overgrown puppy. Blair lay back against the pillow and gulped her highball, feeling giddier and more at home than she had in ages.

Nate woke up with a start. He'd been dreaming that he was sailing by himself in the middle of a calm, blue, endless sea, until all of a sudden his boat had been attacked by sharks. He glanced at the flat screen, currently playing Shark Week reruns, before flicking it off. He rubbed his bleary eyes. Where was Jenny? And what time was it? He heard muffled voices coming from upstairs. "Jenny?" he called, his voice echoing in the town house.

"I'm coming to find you," Nate called, taking the stairs to his bedroom two at a time. But there, lying in a tangled heap as if they belonged there, were Serena and Blair.

He blinked in amazement. They were singing along to the black-and-white movie on his TV. *Breakfast at Tiffany's*. Of course. It was a scene he'd walked in on a million times back in high school. But this wasn't high school. What were they doing here? Was he still dreaming?

"'Moon River and'—Natie!" Serena squealed, bounding off the bed and rushing toward him. She was wearing only a pair of underpants and a tank top that didn't match. Nate blushed.

"Where's Jenny?" Nate asked suspiciously, glancing between the two of them.

"We didn't kill her." Blair snorted. "My brother invited her to a party downtown. She's probably there."

He glanced from Serena to Blair, not knowing what to do. They looked like they'd been there for a while. Wrinkles from the pillowcase were indented into Blair's cheek, making her look adorably rumpled and reminding him of all the sleepovers they'd had over the years. Serena's tank top strap had fallen off her shoulder, revealing her glittery skin, surprisingly tan for December.

Nate gingerly perched on the edge of the bed, watching as Holly and her boyfriend wandered around Tiffany. He must have watched this movie a hundred times. What was one more?

"I'm getting ice cream," Blair announced, stepping out of bed. Nate gazed at her as she padded toward the door. She was wearing her bra and underwear and every inch of her looked amazing. And Serena was so long and lean and leggy and . . .

Down boy!

Blair came back with a two-gallon tub of Rocky Road that she'd unearthed from the back of the freezer and three spoons. "Natie, you've got to have a talk with Regina about her ice cream selections. What happened to the mint chocolate chip?" Blair settled back into bed, loving how she could say whatever she wanted—*be* whoever she wanted—in front of her two oldest friends. She hoped no matter what happened, it could always be that way.

"Let's make a promise!" Serena said spontaneously, as if reading Blair's mind. She took a gigantic scoop from the carton, licked her spoon, and held it up. "No matter who we marry or how many kids we have, we'll always have slumber parties."

Blair clinked her spoon against Serena's. She took another large scoop of ice cream and bit into it, not caring about the calories or the fact that she was dripping all over herself or that they were acting like a bunch of seventh graders.

"I'm in, but only if I can hold the carton." Nate grabbed the ice cream and scooped out a large spoonful. He felt happier than he had in a long time.

Next up: creative use of whipped cream?

## *a kiss is never just a kiss*

Vanessa lay on her bed in the Humphreys' apartment, Marx by her side and Norma snoring contentedly on the floor. Norma loved living at the Humphreys', so at least Vanessa wouldn't have to worry about finding a home for her while she was in Indonesia. The dog actually *begged* for Rufus's soufflés and other kitchen experiments gone wrong.

Unlike everyone else with a sense of smell.

The only sound in the apartment was the annoying-yet-comforting hum of the fluorescent light in the hallway that Rufus always meant to replace but never got around to. Vanessa typed *Indonesia* into Google's search box and pressed enter. Immediately, maps, travel reviews, and NYTimes.com articles sprung onto the screen. Nothing helpful. Nothing that told her whether or not she should go. She heard the key scrape in the lock. Rufus was spending time with his anarchist friends, and Jenny was probably with Nate, so it had to be Dan coming home. Vanessa was surprised by how eager she felt to see him. She slid off the bed and headed toward the living room to investigate.

"Hey," Dan said as he unwrapped a Burberry scarf from his

neck and flung it on the couch. Serena had given him the scarf as a Thanksgiving present.

Usually, the fact that he and Serena had grown up in such different worlds didn't matter to him. But there were times—like when he received a Thanksgiving present that cost more than a month of working at the circulation desk in Butler Library, or when she invited him to stay at her parents' sprawling Connecticut house—that it became apparent how fundamentally different their backgrounds were.

Dan had been thinking about this more than ever recently. He hadn't seen Serena since before Christmas, four days ago. He'd called her tonight to invite her to a movie, but she was meeting Blair. Dan had gone to Film Forum alone, and surprised himself by buying a ticket to the new Hollis Lyons film.

He'd thought about Vanessa the whole time, which made sense, since it was her ex's movie. But it was more than that. He was thinking about Vanessa and her film grant, and how excited she was for her future. Serena wasn't like that. Serena was smart, but she was never especially ambitious.

Vanessa sauntered into the kitchen. "Hey," she said casually. She didn't want Dan to think she'd specifically come out of her bedroom to see *him*. She opened the refrigerator and made an elaborate show of pawing through its contents.

"I don't think there's anything there. I haven't eaten yet, either. Want a pizza?" Dan asked.

"Sure." Vanessa shrugged.

Dan moved over to the counter and ordered a large double cheese, onion, and pepper. He turned to Vanessa after he hung up. "Serena had plans with Blair, so I saw your ex's movie tonight. The one about the Maoris in Iceland?"

"And?" Vanessa asked curiously. She still hadn't seen it, though the movie posters were on subway cars and bus shelters everywhere. She really didn't know if she wanted Dan to love or hate the film.

"You could have done it better," Dan added. "I can't wait to see what you make in Indonesia."

Vanessa smiled, her heart melting a little bit. *That* was exactly what she wanted to hear.

Dan grinned. "Did you ever think this is who you'd become?" he asked, settling onto the counter.

"What do you mean?"

"I mean—going to Indonesia. Being a real filmmaker. Like, back when you were eighteen, wouldn't you be so excited if you knew this was who you'd be four years later?" Dan asked, stirring his Folgers coffee crystals into his favorite chipped white mug.

"Yes, I'd be excited. But I always thought . . ." She trailed off. She'd meant to say that back then, whenever she imagined her future life, she imagined herself and Dan together. "I don't know." She shrugged, not finishing the sentence. "What about you?"

Dan closed his eyes. He'd thought he'd be more in control of his life, be more sure of what he was doing. Of course, everything *seemed* perfect. Outside of his two poems in *The New Yorker,* he'd been published in some of the most prestigious literary journals in the country. He was dating a movie star. He was heading to the best grad program for writing in the world. But somehow, something seemed . . . incomplete. "Yeah, things worked out." Dan shrugged.

"You and Serena seem good together," Vanessa offered after

a pause. She'd never really talked about Dan's relationship with Serena before.

"Yeah, she's great," Dan said distantly. Serena *was* great. But no matter what, they didn't have as strong a connection as he described in the poems he wrote about their relationship. It *wasn't* the marriage of two minds, not really. It was more like falling in love with an illusion of perfection.

Sounds like we've got the beginnings of another poem.

Just then, the buzzer rang.

"Saved by the bell." Vanessa grinned as she stood up and pulled a twenty from the back pocket of her tight black jeans. After paying the delivery boy, she set the steaming box of pizza on the coffee table in the living room.

She grabbed a slice of pizza and sat cross-legged on the scuffed hardwood floor. This was what she was going to miss: the Humphreys' comfortably ramshackle apartment, Marx, Norma, and the overarching feeling of pride that somehow, despite all odds, she'd transformed from the scrappy, friendless daughter of hippie parents from Vermont into an inspiring young film-maker who mattered.

Dan grabbed a slice and sat down next to her. A glob of sauce landed on the front of his brown sweater.

Vanessa cracked a grin. "I'd have thought you'd have better manners four years later, that's for sure," she said as he dabbed the sauce away with a paper napkin.

"That's for sure," Dan said sheepishly as he leaned against the couch and took a large bite of pizza. Vanessa smiled fondly at him. It was cute the way he'd spilled all over himself. It was nice to know that some things would always stay the same.

Another small glob of sauce dripped from Dan's chin, threatening to spill onto his sweater. "You're a mess." She shook her head bemusedly as she leaned in to catch it. But Dan leaned in too, and suddenly, their lips were connecting. Dan tasted like pizza and coffee and something else—a Dan-ness she'd forgotten she missed.

Dan leaned closer to Vanessa, running his fingers through her thick, shoulder-length hair and tracing the back of her neck with his hand.

As if they were following the steps to a dance only they knew, they stood without breaking their kiss. Vanessa took Dan's hand, and led him to her bedroom.

So *this* is what their younger selves imagined.

*Disclaimer: All the real names of places, people, and events have been altered or abbreviated to protect the innocent. Namely, me.*

| topics | sightings | your e-mail | post a question |

# hey people!

### bad behavior

Just when I think we're all too old for the over-the-top antics of our youth, several of our favorite people have proven they still know how to bend the rules: **B** and **S** were spotted sneaking into a certain Eighty-second Street town house. **J** was spotted rediscovering her rock star self and dancing all night at Filter. That's just as well, since **N** was in bed with **B** . . . and **S**. And **D** didn't seem to miss **S** because he was awfully busy with . . . dinner.

So what's up with the recent spate of bad behavior? It could be a result of senior year stress. It could be a flirtation with the past. Or it could be us coming to terms with the yin and the yang, the bad and the good existing in all of us. The realization that even though we might be older, we might wear better clothes, we might be able to spout off Proust and Plato with aplomb, we're still just figuring out our place in the world, one mistake at a time. We're old enough to stop pretending to be perfect, to stop pretending the past never happened, to realize that drama keeps life interesting. And, that said . . .

## hangover help

I don't know about you, but now that I'm legally allowed to drink, my hangovers have been ten times worse. Talk about youth being wasted on the young. If this season you find yourself with a pounding headache the likes of which you haven't felt since freshman year, I can sympathize. My advice? Go back to sleep and have your significant other brave the cold for bagels. Indulge in a carb- and snuggle-fest in bed, and stay there until the sun dips low into the sky. After all, it's vacation and you deserve the break.

## your e-mail

 Dear Gossip Girl,
My best friend has a boyfriend but loves to go out and dance. And boys—especially one boy in particular—loves to dance with her. Should I stage an intervention or something or just realize she can make her own decisions?
—caligirl

Dear Cali,
Last I heard, dancing isn't cheating. I say, just dance—but be ready to cut in if things look like they're getting a little too down and dirty.
—GG

Dear Gossip Girl,
So, where's the New Year's party?
—partylikearockstar

Dear Party,
Ordinarily, a query like this would force me to break the sad news that you just may not have been invited to the fete of the season, but this year, it seems our favorite reformed bad boy has yet to send out invites. Shall we add sloth to our list of sins as well?
—GG

**sightings**

**N** ordering a dozen bagels at daybreak at **Pick-a-Bagel**. Impromptu brunch plans? . . . **B** and **S** stumbling down **Fifth Avenue**, also at day-break, heading toward **S**'s house. Haven't seen that in a while! **J** and her friend **E** ordering eggs at **Three Guys** at 6 a.m., looking sweaty and disheveled in that *I've been dancing my ass off all night* way. Good for them! **V** making a coffee run to the deli on the corner, looking blissful for early in the morning. Why so happy?

**one more theory**

Maybe all of our bad behavior is just gearing up for the final countdown: I'm talking New Year's Eve in just a few days. Will our favorite party pad be up and running this year, or will we need to find an alternate venue? Will we kiss the same people, different people, or ring in the new year with only our cat for company? And what will this year bring? I'll be the first to know and you'll be the first to find out.

You know you love me,

gossip girl

## out with the old, in with the new?

"A large latte, please," Serena said to the surly-looking server behind the counter of the Hungarian Pastry Shop on 112th and Amsterdam. Her head was pounding and her mouth felt dry. Last night, after drinking a few of her extra-strong vodka gimlets, she and Nate and Blair had fallen asleep in a tangled pile midway through *Breakfast at Tiffany's* and had woken up to a river of melted ice cream in the bed with them.

People have woken up to worse. . . .

Despite the shaky start, Serena had actually managed to have a productive morning. She'd called the real estate agent for the Frank Lloyd Wright house and had already made all the arrangements for an August move-in. She couldn't wait. And she *really* couldn't wait to tell Dan. That was why she'd chosen the pastry shop to meet. Serena hated it, but it was Dan's favorite place.

"Thanks," Serena said to the barista as she grabbed her latte. The barista snorted in response. Serena sat down at one of the tables in the corner, which had only three legs and shook whenever she placed her cup on its surface.

The bell above the door dinged as a new customer entered. Dan. He was red-faced from the wind and holding his place in *The Tropic of Cancer* with his index finger.

"Hey," he said, sinking down into the seat across from her.

"Hi." Serena smiled at her rumpled, absentminded poet boyfriend. She pulled out the photos she'd printed of the house and spread them across the table, silently beaming in satisfaction.

"Wow." Dan picked up the papers to look more closely. The house looked familiar, like someplace he'd studied in school or seen in a coffee-table book about architecture.

"It's a Frank Lloyd Wright house, one of his early, Prairie-style ones. It's one of the first ones he created," Serena said proudly, as if she'd built the house herself. "And it's ours. Just outside Iowa City!"

Dan looked around so he wouldn't have to gaze into Serena's eyes. The coffee shop was almost empty, except for two couples cozily leaning over their lattes. The events of last night came rushing back to him in a flash of jet-black hair strewn over his bare chest. *Vanessa.*

He combed his hand through his messy hair. "Um, I've been thinking . . ."

"Do you like it?" Serena asked, biting her bottom lip.

*Large concrete-pool empty eyes.*
*Dive in. . . .*

Dan realized just then that he'd never imagined Serena joining him in Iowa. He'd imagined himself, alone, scribbling poems. Driving past endless cornfields. Mingling with other students at poetry readings while drinking warm white wine in paper cups. In all of his visions, he was by himself.

"But what would you do in Iowa?" The words were out of Dan's mouth before he could stop them.

"You don't want me there?" Serena asked in a small voice. She began chewing on her thumbnail. It was one of her worst habits, one the makeup artist at *Breakfast at Fred's* had desperately tried to stop, but Serena couldn't help it. She couldn't believe Dan didn't want her. It was so unexpected that she didn't know *what* to think.

"No. I mean . . ." Dan trailed off. "I need to just write, and you need to . . ." What *did* Serena need to do? For the past couple years, it had felt as though her whole life revolved around him. And it had been kind of nice, to be such a central part of her world, to be her world *completely*. But Serena deserved to have her own thing. "I mean, I think I need to do this by myself."

Serena nodded slowly, looking at the photos of the house, a dot against a flat green landscape. She'd never live there now.

"I guess—I guess I need to find my own Iowa," Serena said slowly. Around them, couples were gazing adoringly at each other over their lattes, their tabletops scattered with interchangeable notebooks and books. Serena glanced down at their own table, which held her cranberry pink Miu Miu bag and Dan's tattered, stained paperback. Even their drinks didn't match: Hers was a large latte in a paper cup, his a tiny, chipped espresso mug. No matter what they did together or how they spent their time or how much she loved him, they were just completely different people. She'd always known that, but she didn't want to admit it.

"You can still keep the house. I paid the first few months. It was your Christmas present," she said, offering a small smile.

Dan shook his head. The house was beautiful. It just wasn't right for him. Just like Serena. "I'm sorry," he said simply. He hadn't said they were over. He didn't have to. Serena already seemed to know.

"I don't want to do that goodbye stuff here." A small smile formed on her lovely face as she glanced around the coffee shop.

She settled her gaze on Dan. "I've always hated it here," she confided.

And now she never has to go back!

# it's called a breakup because it's broken

"To the smartest, sexiest lawyer I know! This is just the beginning, Bear." Chuck held out a glass of champagne, waiting for Blair to clink her glass against his. They were squeezed into a corner table at Blue Ribbon Bakery, nearby Chuck's apartment on Thursday morning, and the bright sun streaming through the windows was only aiding Blair's pounding headache. She couldn't even think about what she was planning to order for brunch, let alone toast to her future.

Since when does Blair not want to toast something?

"*Future* lawyer." Blair rolled her eyes. "I have to go to law school before I can actually practice law."

She knew she should be more excited that she'd been officially offered a job at McMahon Cannon, but she'd received the call right in the middle of eating a bagel in Nate's kitchen. The offer was an unwelcome reminder that she really *was* a grownup, that the fun and giggly and totally innocent night in Nate's bed was probably her last, that, whether she liked it or not, she'd chosen a path for her life.

Which is a heavy realization pre-brunch.

Blair cautiously sipped her champagne. She hadn't told Chuck where she'd spent last night. It was just easier if he assumed she and Serena had one glass too many of wine before they'd both headed back to the Upper East Side.

"What are you thinking?"

Blair tried to suppress a sigh. She'd always *hated* that question. "What am I thinking?" she parroted. "That there should be some fucking service here. We've been sitting here for twenty minutes," she snapped in annoyance. She hated waiting.

"Are you okay?" Chuck asked, placing his hand protectively on top of hers.

Blair resisted the urge to pull away. For some reason, Chuck was so *annoying* today.

"I'm just tired. Maybe it's a cold or something," Blair lied, pulling on the sleeve of her black Vince cashmere sweater. She hadn't even gone home to change after the impromptu sleepover. Maybe *that* was her problem. A nap, a shower, and a change of clothes and she'd be fine.

If only it were that simple. . . .

Chuck nodded. "I thought we could plan our summer, now that your job is all set. You know, for something to look forward to. Maybe we could do Capri or the Maldives, and then a place in Water Mill. I don't know if I'm ready to buy yet, though," he mused.

Blair's stomach lurched. Where the *fuck* was the waiter? She felt like she was going to throw up. And why was Chuck talking about *buying* a house in the Hamptons? She'd only just turned twenty-one. Couldn't they act like normal college students? She wouldn't mind a little more fun and a little less real estate.

She took a deep breath. She felt like the cream walls of the restaurant were closing in on her. Around her, patrons were chatting and clinking their silverware. But suddenly, the noise was intolerable. "I can't do this," she blurted, the words out before she could stop them. She glanced up at Chuck. His face was impossible to read. "I can't," she said more firmly. Her voice trembled, but she was more sure of herself than she'd been in a long time.

Chuck's face fell. "Do you mean the apartment? You can redo it if you want. . . ."

Blair shook her head. The apartment was beautiful. But it wasn't right. For one, she'd never wanted to live in the Village. Ever since she was little, whenever she'd imagined her life as an adult, she pictured an apartment off Fifth Avenue within walking distance of Barneys and the park. But it wasn't just location. It was the fact that deep down, she wasn't sure if she wanted to be in a relationship. At least not right now. Not with someone who was so ready to settle down. Weren't your twenties supposed to be wild and crazy and full of adventures?

Let's hope so.

"Sorry." Blair absentmindedly pulled the ugly red carnation out of its vase on the table and began ripping it apart. The dark red petals fell to the oak table like little drops of blood. "I'm just—I think I need a break," she said just as a black-shirted waiter approached the table, order pad in hand.

"I'll come back," the waiter squeaked in a high falsetto, turning terrifiedly on his newly shined heel.

"I mean, the apartment is great, but what if I get into Harvard Law? Then what? What if I decide to take a year off before law school and live in Paris?" Blair said in a rush of words, surprising herself as she heard them.

"I understand," Chuck said thickly. His dark eyes clouded over and he glanced out the steamy restaurant window at the pedestrians passing, as if to compose himself.

Even though it was what she wanted to hear, tears sprang to her eyes. Chuck knew that she liked dirty martinis with extra olive juice at the Campbell Apartment bar in Grand Central, surprised her with lilacs on the days she had exams, and had redecorated his apartment in her favorite colors. Maybe they *could* be together at some point in the future. But not right now.

"Thank you," she whispered. It was funny. For once in her life, the movie in her mind wasn't playing. She had no idea what her next line was or how she should exit. She had no idea if any man was waiting in the wings.

Blair scraped her chair back and stood up. She didn't want to make a scene, but she was worried if she didn't stand up and get out, she never would. The last thing she wanted was to find herself in ten years having the same conversation about Hamptons homes with Chuck.

She felt tears beginning to well in her eyes. "'Bye," she said finally, running out before the deluge.

# notes from around the world

Serena sat on the center of her bed in her childhood bedroom, hugging her knees to her chest. She hadn't moved since coming home from her coffee date turned breakup with Dan. It was too exhausting to figure out what to do with herself. She wanted to cry, to release all the confused feelings inside her, but she couldn't.

She glanced from the white molding on the ceiling to the framed *Breakfast at Fred's* poster over her antique bureau to the tiny silver Tiffany box on her night table. The box housed all her baby teeth. In high school, Nate loved shaking them out onto her white eyelet pillowcase, counting the teeth, and marveling at how tiny they were.

Serena sighed. Dan had noticed the tiny box, but only to note that it was pretty. He'd never asked what was in it. It was sort of like their relationship—on the surface it seemed perfect, but they were both too afraid to really look at what was inside.

In a way, their breakup had felt inevitable. When she was at Yale and he was at Columbia, they'd make plans for the next weekend or next break, but they'd never talked about the future.

And Serena never *really* wanted to move to Iowa. It was just that she had no idea what she wanted to do.

Her eyes fell on the travel scrapbook Fiona had given her, sitting on her bureau. She crossed the room and picked it up, flopping back down on her bed. A familiar hum began to course through her body.

Wanderlust?

Serena stared out the window. A snow flurry had begun, swirling feathery white flakes down Fifth Avenue and onto the treeless expanse of park across from her bedroom. It was such a wonderfully familiar old view, one that she'd cherish forever. But she could leave and it would still be there when she got back. Serena's heart beat excitedly. A small smile formed on her lips. For the first time in a long time, she knew exactly what she wanted to do.

And who she wants to do it with?

# miss independent

Jenny ran up the steps of Nate's stately, ivy-covered town house on Monday night, ready for their date. She and Elise had gone out the past few nights, following Tyler to all of his DJ gigs around the city. It was just so much *fun* to dress up and be ushered into a whole other world where music ruled, to dance until 4 a.m., to shake her long hair until it got sweaty and tangled.

In the past, Jenny had never been one for clubbing—she'd been too young when she was living in the city, Waverly was out in the middle of nowhere, and in Providence she and Nate were often in bed by ten o'clock. It wasn't like there was anything else to do. Sure, she had acquaintances from her classes with whom she attended student art shows, and Nate had a few sailing buddies, but neither of them had any real *friends*. Reconnecting with Elise had reminded Jenny how important it was to have people around you who could make you snort Diet Coke out your nose, who could spend hours debating whether or not a Proenza Schouler dress for Target looked like the real thing, who could physically restrain you from making out with a cute young DJ.

Wait, what?

Jenny pressed the doorbell with a pink-polished finger. She shifted her weight from one Frye boot to the other, wondering if Nate would be able to sense that she'd almost kissed Tyler. Who knows if it actually would have happened. But last night while they were dancing, he just looked so *cute*, with his hair flopping over his hazel eyes, his T-shirt just tight enough to show off his toned arms, lip-synching the lyrics of the song that was playing because he was so into it. Just as Jenny had leaned in, Elise had grabbed her by the crook of the arm and yanked her out of the club and into a cab.

Jenny had felt relieved, but ever since, she'd found it impossible to get Tyler out of her head. What would've happened if they *had* kissed? And if it was just an innocent lean-in, then why did she feel so guilty?

"Come up!" Nate yelled into the intercom, interrupting Jenny's reverie.

Jenny climbed the winding staircase toward Nate's top-floor bedroom. The town house always seemed spookily quiet whenever she walked in.

"Hi." Jenny pushed open the heavy oak door.

"Hey!" Nate said from his corner desk, not looking up from his Mac Air. He wore a pair of red flannel Ralph Lauren boxers and no shirt. Jenny paused at the doorway. Of course she didn't mind seeing his abs, which looked as taut and tan in December as they did in July, but he wasn't exactly dressed for dinner.

"Are you going to get ready soon?" She tugged at the frayed hem on the cute flapper-style dress she'd bought senior year at What Goes Around Comes Around, the vintage store in Rhinecliff.

Nate shrugged. "I thought we'd just stay here and order in," he said easily. One of the things he loved most about Jenny was how easy she was to be around. Back when he'd dated Blair, he'd sometimes felt like a cruise ship director, always having to come up with an activity to entertain her. But Jenny was fine lying around in bed and eating Chinese food.

How romantic.

"Oh," Jenny said, disappointed. She sat on his bed, crossing her tiny legs. The clock on his nightstand read eight twenty-one. Suddenly, the evening seemed to loom endlessly in front of them. "Are you sure?" Jenny asked, already knowing the answer. Of course Nate wanted to stay in. Just like always. But Jenny was itching to go out, to *do* something.

"Yeah." Nate sat down next to her and slipped her coat off her shoulders. His fingers brushed underneath the skinny strap of her dress. "All I need is you." He leaned over to kiss her.

Jenny pulled away. She didn't want to just eat takeout in bed, like they did every night in Providence. She wanted romance and intrigue and maybe a little bit of drama. She wanted to yell over music until her voice hurt.

"I think . . ." Jenny trailed off and looked down at her tiny hands.

"What's wrong, Meow?" Nate asked, his hand at the midthigh hem of her dress.

"I don't think this is working," Jenny said, gaining her voice as she went. This wasn't just about Tyler—not really, anyway. There was a huge world out there, and Jenny needed to do more than eat spareribs in bed.

"What?" Nate blinked. Was Jenny dumping him? "But I love you, Jen," he said, fumbling for words.

"I'll always love you," Jenny said softly. It was true. He'd always be the boy of her dreams, her Upper East Side prince. She leaned in to give him a final kiss. His lips felt warm and dry, but almost too comfortable. And right now, she needed a challenge.

Jenny felt tears prick her eyes but brushed them away before Nate could see. She pulled her coat around her small frame.

"'Bye," she whispered before she ran down the stairs. Once she got outside, she hailed a cab, her heart hammering in her chest. She wasn't sure what the future held, but she couldn't wait to find out.

And we're sure it will have an awesome sound track.

# the final countdown . . .

From: cbass@oxford.edu
To: undisclosed recipients
Subject: NYE party

Tonight: Same time, same place, same libations, new
year. The soiree's last-minute, but you can't allow a
tradition to die without giving it a proper send-off.
Bring friends, family, mistresses, strangers, and
anyone you covet. Hot tub will be running.

Who knows where we'll be next year? Let's make this
party count.
CB

# back to the scene of the crime

"Are we *really* doing this?" Serena giggled tipsily as she clinked her highball glass against Blair's martini. They were sitting in the Tribeca Star Lounge, filling up on liquid courage before heading upstairs to the Bass suite. Chuck had e-mailed Blair directly to say he hoped she'd come, and after reading his mass e-mail and remembering all the wild times they'd had at Chuck's suite, she realized she wanted to.

"It's tradition." Blair took a long sip of her dirty martini and let the liquid swirl around in her mouth. That was one nice thing about being single. She could drink as many martinis as she wanted and not worry about kissing someone with olive breath.

Around them, the lounge was filling up. Next to them sat a giggling group of shiny-haired girls wearing four-inch heels and glittery eye makeup. They looked like they were in high school. Blair gaped at them in amazement. How had she and Serena ever been that young?

Well, according to their fake IDs, they've always been twenty-two.

"Look, there's Kati and Isabel! Hey!" Serena called, standing up and waving. She was oblivious to all the people who turned to stare at her sequined Marni shift dress riding up dangerously high on her thigh.

"Hey!" Isabel yelled, clomping into the bar in a pair of five-inch Miu Miu Mary Janes. She wore an all-purple jumpsuit and looked like a psychedelic plumber. Her hand was intertwined with Kati's: Kati wore a simple black dress and a huge grin on her heart-shaped face.

"Hey." Blair's eyes flicked down to their hands. They were both wearing matching silver rings on their ring fingers.

"You guys are friends again!" Serena clapped her hands in glee.

Isabel shrugged shyly. "Yeah. I don't know what took us so long."

"We're just heading up. Are you guys ready? It'll be just like old times, right?" Kati asked, still holding Isabel's hand.

*Almost* like old times.

In the dim amber light of the bar, Blair's former classmates looked almost sweet together. "Sure," she said. She drained the rest of her drink and stood up, wavering slightly in the snakeskin thigh-high Christian Louboutin boots her father had sent her for Christmas. It was comforting that no matter how much things changed, Blair always had the best shoes in the room.

They do say it's the little things that give life meaning.

"Are you sure it'll be okay for you to see Chuck?" Serena whispered to Blair as they followed Isabel and Kati toward the elevator bank.

"What if you see Dan?" Blair countered.

Serena paused. She hadn't thought about that. But she doubted Dan would be there; everyone had been invited, but parties were never his thing.

As they reached the elevator, Serena spontaneously threw her arms around Blair's shoulders. "I have you, who else do I need?" she exclaimed.

"You guys are meant for each other," Kati said, shaking her head knowingly at Isabel.

The elevator opened and the four girls headed down the plush gray–carpeted hall toward the suite. Inside, Blair spotted her brother setting up his DJ equipment in the corner. Jenny Humphrey was sitting on one of Tyler's synthesizer cases, wearing a cleavage-baring black tank top, her curls piled messily on top of her head and held in place by an oversize butterfly-shaped barrette.

Blair arched an eyebrow. She'd almost forgotten her matchmaking plan. But it looked like it had worked. Hopefully she wouldn't regret it.

"Wait, do you think that means Jenny and Nate are broken up?" Serena asked, following Blair's gaze toward Jenny and Tyler.

"I'll find out," Blair announced, marching toward her brother.

In the corner, Rain Hoffstetter and Laura Salmon were mixing elaborate pastel-colored shots. Kati and Isabel clutched hands and looked fearfully toward Blair.

"What do you think she's going to do to Jenny?" Kati asked.

"She can't do anything. She has this anger management issue and she's on probation. That's why her mom moved back to New York. She wanted to keep an eye on her," Rain said, downing the pink shot Laura had concocted. She wore a high-necked purple wool dress that hid her unfortunate infinity symbol tattoo.

"That's why she's applying to law school," Laura offered, slurring her words drunkenly.

Blair picked her way through the crowd to Jenny and Tyler. Tyler's arm was slung possessively around Jenny's tiny shoulders as he worked the turntables. She tapped Jenny on the arm. "Come with me," she demanded, turning on her heel without waiting for an answer.

She led Jenny to the opposite end of the bar and pulled out one of the modern black stools. "Sit," she ordered. Jenny meekly perched on the edge of the stool, her legs dangling like a little kid's.

Blair perched on a stool next to her. "Are you cheating on Nate?" she asked, getting straight to the point.

Jenny shook her head, her curls grazing her milky white shoulders. "No. We broke up. It was just moving so fast, and I still have all of college ahead of me, and I . . ." Jenny babbled, glancing up at Blair's foxlike face. Blair's features suddenly relaxed and flashed the briefest of smiles, so small it could easily have been Jenny's imagination. She'd been expecting Blair to scream at her, to blame her, to tell her it was ridiculous that *she* be the one to break up with Nate. But instead, Blair shrugged, as if to say, *Do whatever you want.*

Blair arched an eyebrow at the younger girl. Well, wasn't Jenny full of surprises? She slid off the stool. "Don't break my brother's heart," she called over her shoulder. The fact that Meow Meow was over meant Nate was single. And probably heartbroken. Interesting . . .

"Thanks," Jenny said, mystified. She smiled slowly at Tyler.

She didn't think anything would happen with them tonight—but it was nice to get Blair's blessing.

Well, not quite, but that's as close as she's going to get.

Vanessa walked into the swanky lobby of the Tribeca Star, still trying to get used to the loud clicking noise her black pumps made with every step across the marble lobby. She wore a dark blue dress from one of her favorite Williamsburg boutiques, her hair pulled into a messy bun at the back of her head. By the check-in desk, a guy in khakis and a button-down nodded appreciatively at her. Vanessa smiled. She *knew* she looked good. She didn't have to prove to the world she was an artsy independent filmmaker by wearing all black and a surly expression. Maybe it was because she'd been single for a year and had finally really gotten to know herself. Maybe it was because she finally realized how much people liked her for her.

And maybe it was because she sort of wanted to impress a certain boy?

Vanessa rode the elevator upstairs. She'd never been to one of Chuck's parties before, but now that she knew she was leaving New York, there seemed no reason to avoid it. Besides, she needed to talk to Dan, and she had a feeling he'd be here with Serena. After spending the night together, Vanessa had felt horribly guilty. She'd been camped out at Ruby and Piotr's since, but she couldn't stay there forever. She wanted to apologize for what had happened and tell Dan that while she'd always love him, it was for the best that he and Serena were together. She hadn't meant to come between them.

The elevator doors slid open, and several teenage girls tumbled out a door down the hall.

"Let's find boys to make out with!" one of them squealed, racing to the elevator. Vanessa walked through the open door, shaking her head with bemusement. There was so much *material* in the world, so much fodder for film.

Especially when it comes to subjects wearing far too *little* material . . .

The suite was crowded, and Vanessa elbowed her way through packs of people toward the open terrace, where a lone figure was facing uptown toward the Empire State Building, smoking a cigarette. Dan. Without Serena. Vanessa shivered in the night air and pulled her leather bomber jacket closer around her body.

She tapped him on the shoulder. "Don't you know those things will kill you?"

Dan whirled around. Vanessa looked beautiful. Her hair was pulled back to expose her collarbones and she was wearing a sexy, formfitting dress underneath a leather jacket. She looked nothing like his Doc Marten muse. And yet . . .

She looked even better.

"Where's Serena?" Vanessa asked, hoping she sounded more curious than confrontational.

"Serena and I broke up. . . . I'm going to Iowa by myself," he finished. He wasn't sure what he wanted Vanessa to say, but she needed to know.

Vanessa sucked in her breath. Dan was single. Now, when it was no use. "I'm going to Indonesia for two years."

"I'm glad," Dan said earnestly. Vanessa's face immediately fell. "I mean, I'm glad you're doing it. But I'll miss you," he said. He missed her already, and she was standing just inches from his touch.

"I will too," Vanessa said shyly. "Iowa's two years, right?"

She rested her elbows on the concrete balcony ledge and looked down at the street below, which was surprisingly quiet for New Year's Eve. Besides one town car idling outside the Star, there was no other traffic. The boulevard stretched wide and free in the inky night.

"Yeah," Dan said.

Vanessa nodded. The more she thought about it, two years didn't seem very long at all. After all, she and Dan had spent two years of college practically ignoring each other.

When you put it that way . . .

"Well . . . if you need a roommate in two years, I'm really good at making your gross coffee."

"And I'm good at helping you eat your heart-attack-special pizza," Dan countered. It was crazy how they'd lived in the same orbit for so long, had dated and broken up and hooked up for years, how they'd shared an apartment when they were both together and apart. How she could still make him smile more than anyone else in the world.

"Deal!" Vanessa said.

She'd meant to just shake his hand, but she found herself leaning in. Her lips connected to his, slowly at first, then more insistently.

As the shouts and music blared from inside the party, the icy wind slicing through her dress, Vanessa was suddenly reminded of another party she'd missed, another night spent out in the cold night air—the night she and Dan met. She couldn't have scripted it better herself.

Parting is such sweet sorrow. . . .

# breaking the cycle . . . finally

"So, do you have any New Year's resolutions?" Serena asked, slipping down in the hot tub and letting her long blond hair fan out behind her. She'd seen Dan at one point, smoking Camels on the balcony like the angsty poet he was. She'd say hi to him later. For now, she just wanted to have fun.

"Fuck no," Blair murmured, taking a drag of her Merit Ultra Light and letting the ashes fall into the steaming water of the hot tub. Fuck resolutions. All she really wanted to do was have fun. For so long, her resolutions had been more like an endless list of to-dos: date Nate Archibald, get into Yale, get into law school. For once, she just wanted to go with the wind, do what she felt like.

Sounds like someone else we know . . .

Out of the corner of her eye, Blair spotted Chuck wearing a dark red smoking jacket. She was about to get out of the hot tub to say hi, but then she saw Rain Hoffstetter sidle up to him. Blair sighed and eased back into the water.

Just then, Serena's phone buzzed, skittering across the marble edge of the hot tub. She grabbed it with her wet hand.

Serena grinned as she pulled her hair up into a high wet pony-tail at the nape of her neck. She searched around the edge of the hot tub for her dress. It seemed like fate. After all, why travel the world alone when she could ask Nate to come with her?

"Who was that?" Blair asked, glancing up at Serena.

"I have to go," Serena said, sliding one slippery foot into a strappy Christian Louboutin sandal. "I'll be right back," she fibbed, climbing out of the hot tub, slipping on her dress, and disappearing into the crowd.

Blair stared at her friend's retreating back. Her phone buzzed.

WAITING OUTSIDE. YOU HERE?—NATE

Blair blinked at the message. What the fuck? Had Serena gotten the exact same message? She pulled herself out of the hot tub, threw on her dress, even though it was silk and would stain, and raced out of the party.

And who says all the drama happens *at* midnight?

Nate glanced up at the towering Tribeca Star Hotel, his hands jammed in his pockets, unsure whether or not to go in. Part of him wanted to find Anthony or Charlie or any of the old St. Jude's guys, fire up a gigantic bong, and flirt with as many hot girls as he could, just to prove that he still had it in him. The other part of him wanted to go back to his parents' town house and sit in the living room and eat Jell-O pudding cups. How was it that he'd sailed the world, learned how to milk cows, debated the arguments of all the Greek philosophers, and majored in American studies at an Ivy League university—but was still as confused as ever?

He'd texted Serena and Blair, but neither of them had responded. Maybe he'd missed his chance with them. He glanced up at the sky. There were no stars, at least none that could be seen through the New York smog. He just wished he had something to follow, some kind of sign.

Just then, one of the gold revolving doors whooshed open, and Serena burst out. Her long blond hair was wet and pulled into a ponytail that stuck to the back of her leather coat. She still looked gorgeous.

"Serena!" Nate exclaimed. Was *that* his sign?

She smiled broadly. "I got your text." She threw her arms around him and pulled back. Her teeth were chattering.

"Are you okay?" Nate asked.

"Just cold," Serena said, and Nate pulled her closer toward him. Maybe Serena *was* whom he was looking for the whole time, and he was just too much of an idiot to realize it.

"So, I was thinking . . ." Serena gazed into Nate's glittering green eyes and took a deep breath. "I wanted to ask you . . ." She pictured setting sail, seeing ancient temples and forgotten ruins and eating food she had never tasted before. But when she pictured the person across from her, it wasn't Nate. "I wanted to ask you to come inside," she finished.

Serena felt a rough tap on her shoulder. She whirled around and saw Blair, hands on her hips, not wearing a coat, her silk dress clinging to her bikini-clad body. Serena pulled away from Nate.

"Blair!" Nate glanced between the two girls.

"What are you doing?" Blair asked them coldly. She glanced from Serena to Nate. Serena looked amused, while Nate looked incredibly confused, his mouth hanging open slightly and his eyes flicking between the two of them as if he were watching a tennis match.

"I was thinking we need to go on an adventure," Serena began. "We could take one of those sleeper trains that you've always wanted to go on. We could start with Europe," she said, coming up with a trip itinerary on the spot. She and Blair had the biggest fights, sure, but they also had the best times together.

Blair narrowed her eyes in anger. She couldn't *believe* Serena was planning a romantic adventure with Nate. "Have a great time," she spat, turning on her heel.

Serena burst into laughter.

"What the hell?" Blair whirled around, ready to launch into an angry tirade. "You run out, and then—"

"Would you just shut up for one second?" Serena cut her off, still giggling. "I meant an adventure with *you*, Blair. I want to travel with *you*. You're my best friend."

Blair started laughing too. Was Serena serious? "I knew that," she lied. "I'm starting at the firm this summer. . . ." Blair trailed off. There really wasn't anything to think about. "I'm in!"

"This summer?" Nate asked. Way back in sophomore year of high school, they'd had a plan to go to Europe, the three of them, together. Now, six years later, it was finally coming true. Maybe he needed a summer with both of them to finally make a decision. "I can come," he decided.

"Sorry," Serena replied softly, chewing her bottom lip. "The invitation was for Blair."

"No boys!" Blair shrugged. "You ready, Serena?" Not waiting for an answer, she opened the door to one of the yellow cabs idling in front of the hotel. "Good luck, Nate," she said as she slid in.

"We love you," Serena called before hopping in after her.

"Wait!" Nate called. "When will I see you again?"

Serena pulled the door shut and rolled down the window. "Same time, next year!" she yelled, giggling as the cab pulled away.

Nate stared, slack-jawed, as the cab merged with the traffic and became impossible to spot. That was it.

They chose each other.

Just then, the dark sky lit up with fireworks. A cab sailing up the street honked in celebration. In the night air, Nate thought he could hear Serena and Blair's laughter, though of course he knew that was impossible; they were too far away by now.

But as we know, in this city, *anything* is possible.

Disclaimer: All the real names of places, people, and events have been altered or abbreviated to protect the innocent. Namely, me.

# hey people!

No matter what may happen, some things always stay constant. New Year's Day wouldn't be the same without a no-foam cappuccino, an extra-large bottle of water, a chocolate-chip scone with extra butter (everyone knows resolutions don't *really* kick in until the second), and a whole list of curious and curiouser questions.

Where will **S** and **B** end up—both geographically and in their love-hate relationship? Is **C** really as reformed as he seems? Will **N** ever find the right girl for him, or is he a tragic hero who's looking for love in all the wrong places? Will **J** revert to her boy-crazy ways now that she's single and, after a semester of playing house, more than ready to mingle? Will **V** become an international filmmaking sensation, and will **D** become the next poet laureate? Will the stars ever align for them to be the creative power couple they once were? Will **K** and **I** move to Massachusetts and get married? Who am I and will I ever reveal myself? That's a question I could answer—but I'm not going to. As for all the others, the answers will reveal themselves in due time.

**one final word**

Even if college didn't leave much time for book learning, one knowledge-by-experience lesson should have stuck: We're more alike than we think. We've all had to deal with broken hearts, crazy roommates, messed-up parents, disappointing grades, and all those other less-than-ideal details that make life complicated, infuriating, and, admit it, interesting. So, in the spirit of growing up, hug that girl who made your high school career a living hell. Forgive that boy who dumped you without warning, only to date your best friend. Not only will you keep your enemies close, you may even make a new friend. Let's all make nice for now, and who knows what tomorrow will bring? One thing's for sure: I'll be there when it happens. Here's to a wild and wicked future.

You know you love me,

gossip girl

# Spotted: **B, S, N, D** and **Little J** on Limited Collector's Editions of the #1 bestselling Gossip Girl novels that inspired the CW's hit show.

Each edition includes an exclusive poster on the reverse side of the jacket featuring a gorgeous, frame-worthy image from the show.

Add style and scandal to your library.
*Collect all twelve!*

poppy

**www.pickapoppy.com**

© 2009 Alloy Entertainment